THE EMISSARY

A FIRST CONTACT NOVEL

MICHAEL J EDWARDS

ELLIDA PUBLISHING

Cover by Ariana Bove (arianasstudio@gmail.com), based on an anonymous modification of a photograph by photographer Heine Mann, who graciously gave me permission to use it.

For inquiries regarding this book, please email:
michael@michaeljedwards.com

Ellida Publishing, Bellingham, WA, USA

ISBN: 979-8-9853879-0-2 (kindle)

ISBN: 979-8-9853879-1-9 (paperback)

Library of Congress Control Number: 2021924725

❀ Created with Vellum

For Joshua, as promised.

1

The aliens arrived on a Tuesday morning during rush hour. A fireball came hurtling meteor-like out of the heavens toward the city, eventually revealing itself to be a stubby-winged spaceplane drawing great, swooping arcs in the sky to throw off speed. It soared low over the Great Sea Wall and the Marina Bay Golf Course, and lower still over the bay bridges before finally plunging into Marina Bay in the middle of Singapore's downtown district, where it disappeared in an eruption of steam and water. A few minutes later, a white ellipsoid object bobbed to the surface and casually made its way to the dock at Singapore's National Stadium Square.

All of this, Holly witnessed from the balcony of the hotel suite she and her dad were staying in. A window-rattling boom had brought her to her feet, and she had gripped the railing with both hands as the fireball fell toward her. Even when it became obvious that it was a spaceship or a space-plane, it still looked like it was going to plow right into the hotel. Then it plunged into the bay a couple of kilometers away. It was a miracle it had come down in the bay. A couple hundred meters in any direction would have caused a lot of damage. Not to mention lives.

Satellites sometimes fell out of orbit, but this didn't look like a satellite. It looked like a spaceplane. Only a few nations had spaceplanes, so whose was it? She went inside and said, "Room: Play SNN."

The wall screen lit up with an image of the bay littered with swamped water craft. Inner Marina Bay was a popular boating place. The view zoomed in on the teardrop-shaped object floating in the water next to the National Stadium. The chyron scrolling across the bottom of the screen read: *SNN breaking news: Unidentified spacecraft lands in downtown Singapore.* Had she not seen it for herself, Holly would have thought it was a joke or that somebody had hacked the SNN feed. But she *had* seen it for herself.

The familiar voice of SNN's senior presenter John Hong said, "The unidentified craft plunged into Singapore's Marina Bay just minutes ago, causing a mini-tsunami that swamped water craft and inundated streets and parks around the bay. As you can see, it is now floating alongside the dock at National Stadium Square. We are getting eyewitness reports claiming it had stubby wings when it came down, though I don't see any. We are also hearing that the two box-like objects and what looks like an antenna appeared after it came to a rest at the dock."

Holly rummaged through a suitcase until she found her dad's binoculars and returned to the balcony. It took a moment to find the craft and bring it into focus. Then it sprang large into view. Goose bumps climbed up her arms.

It was the size of one of those mega-yachts you could see docked at the New Auckland Yacht Club; the ones that never seemed to go anywhere. Its smooth, white surface showed no signs of a fiery ride through the atmosphere. Black crenelated ridges ran along its sides at the waterline.

"Holly Margaret Burton!" Her dad's voice broke into the moment. "Do not lean over the railing. You know better than that." He had come out of the bathroom with a towel wrapped around his waist, drying his hair with another.

"There's a spaceship in the bay," she said.

"What?"

He looked at the vidscreen.

"We are getting reports that the Americans and the Chinese both picked up the unidentified craft on radar shortly after it entered the atmosphere. According to—"

A female voice broke in. "John, we have just learned that the Russians and the Australians also tracked it. Nobody seems to know where it came from, but a consensus is forming that it may be from another world. My God, this is really happening."

"It does seem that way. Gentlepersons, we may be looking at a visitor from another world. I . . . I don't know what to say."

Her dad joined her on the balcony. She handed him the binoculars, and he brought them to his eyes. A minute later, he handed them back and returned to the room, where he sank onto the couch and stared at the image on the vidscreen.

John Hong said, "We have confirmation from several sources that government authorities are viewing this as a possible alien spacecraft."

Holly followed him in and said, "Can we go down and see it?"

His head snapped up. "No! I mean . . . they will be blocking off access to the bay."

He walked out onto the deck again and stood there, not looking at anything as far as she could tell. When he turned toward her, his face bore a somber expression.

"Do you know what this means?" he said.

"Uh, first contact? And us at ground zero to see it?" She giggled, which was embarrassing. She sounded like an over-excited fifteen-year-old kid, which, of course, she was, and being the youngest student at the University of New Auckland didn't change that.

He took a moment to respond. "If it *is* in fact an alien visitor—which we don't know for sure—then yes, we are witnessing first contact with an alien species. And if that is true, it means the fate of the human race will probably be decided in the next few days; maybe the next few hours."

She frowned. Whatever she might have expected him to say, that wasn't it. Other than the occasional sci-fi vid, she hadn't thought much about alien visitations. She knew about SETI, of course, and she knew that astronomers had found thousands of exoplanets, some of which were the right size and at the right distance from their sun to support life, and she had always assumed there must be other intelligent life out there. But she had never stopped to ask herself what it would mean for them to actually show up. Now, suddenly, they were here.

"Is this the beginning of an invasion?" she asked.

"What? No, of course not." He came back into the room and began pacing back and forth. "At least not in the sense you're thinking. I mean, I suppose it could be an invasion. Any species that can travel between the stars is going to be more than capable of conquering us or destroying us or putting us in zoos, or anything else they want to do. But that's not what I mean."

He pursed his lips, which meant he was about to launch into teaching mode.

He said, "Let's assume, for the sake of discussion, that these really are visitors from another world and that they are benevolent. I say benevolent because if they are *not* benevolent, there isn't much to talk about. We would just have to wait and see what they decide to do about us."

"Okaaay. I'll go with benevolent aliens."

"Now, in our own history, what happens when a more

4

advanced civilization encountered a less advanced civilization?"

Yup. Teaching mode. He often engaged her in discussions about . . . well, just about anything. He was a knowledge omnivore and was determined to make her one, too.

"Uh . . . bad things happen to the less advanced one?"

"Exactly. New Zealand's Maoris are a good example. As are the indigenous peoples of pretty much every place Europeans went. But in this case *we* are the less advanced civilization. See the problem?"

She did now that he had pointed it out. Even if the aliens were benevolent, their appearance would inevitably change everything, and not necessarily in a good way.

"If this is a first contact scenario," he said, "I am encouraged by the unthreatening nature of the spaceship they sent for first contact. It's small and innocuous looking, probably unmanned. Much less alarming than, say, a fleet of warships appearing in the skies overhead."

He grabbed two bottles of water from the mini-fridge and tossed one to her. Then he sat down again, his elbows resting on his knees so he could stare at an invisible spot on the carpet. Holly waited.

"The biggest question is not their reaction to us, but our reaction to them. Humans do not deal well with the unknown. Especially if they perceive it as a threat, and the arrival of an alien spaceship is, by its very nature, threatening. It will frighten people. And frightened people are unpredictable people."

As if on cue, the balcony slider door rattled as jets thundered overhead. She and her dad returned to the balcony and watched three military jets in formation make a wide sweep around the bay. Missiles hung from their wings. Two military helicopters held position over the bay. They had rocket launchers.

Her dad was right. It was not the aliens they had to worry about. It was the humans.

———

The aliens took control of three communication satellites and, over the next two days, broadcast a message every hour in Chinese, Spanish, and English. It was brief:

An invitation is extended to the following leaders to come to Singapore for a meeting between our two species:

- Nashwan Bedew of the African Federation
- Daniel Fitzgerald of the Christian Republic of America
- Gunther Holstrom of the European Federation
- Archie Smythe-Robson of Great Britain
- Xi Xiadong of China
- Druve Batra of India
- Edward Smith of Australia
- Jonathan Wilson of New Zealand,
- Dmitri Blavatsky of the Russian Federation
- Gabriel Firea Rocha of the South American Federation
- Nayla Gao of the Southeast Asia Confederation
- Barak Ben David of Israel
- Mario Alvarez of the Republic of Pacifica

At least they were familiar enough with Earth's geopolitics to know there was no single government to talk to. It would have been awkward if they had shown up and said, "Take us to your leader."

The invited leaders were the current rulers of the thirteen alliances that had emerged after the Great Collapse—that catastrophic event that occurred when global warming reached a tipping point and plunged the world into an ecological collapse that brought civilization to its knees. Six-and-a-half billion people died in the next decade from famine, disease, and war. Fifty-four enclaves of civilization survived; fifty-four city states; fifty-four islands of order in a sea of chaos, poverty, and violence. They eventually formed the thirteen alliances.

Every one of the alliances was a *de facto* dictatorship and every one of the named leaders was a ruthless dictator who remained in power by serving the interests of the elites and the military. There were no democracies, though most of the alliances maintained the trappings of democracy in one form or another. Democratic forms of government had proven singularly inadequate for the challenge of salvaging civilization from the wreckage of the Great Collapse.

And there would be no one at the table to speak for the two-thirds of the world's population that lived outside the heavily defended enclaves. They were scattered across vast, inhospitable, unforgiving landscapes. They lived in a post-apocalyptic nightmare ruled by an ever-changing cast of warlords who fought among themselves for territory and resources in a world ruined by the disaster humankind had brought upon itself. Even if the aliens wanted to include them in the conversation, who would they invite? Warlords? There were hundreds of them.

Holly was incredibly lucky to have been born in an Enclave. She ate well. She lived well. She was getting an education. She could choose her own future. None of these things were available to the Outsiders. Sometimes she felt guilty about that, but mostly she didn't think about it. After all, what could she do?

By the morning of the third day, the news feeds were reporting that all the invitees were in Singapore. It wasn't like they could decline the invitation. None of them was going to miss the most important meeting in the world's history. According to SNN, they had agreed among themselves to gather at the National Stadium at noon. That was five hours away when Holly walked into the living room. SNN was on without volume. Her dad was reading something on his tablet.

He put the tablet down and said, "I'm going down to get something from the breakfast buffet. Want to come?"

When they stepped off the elevator and into the lobby, the ground was shaking and the floor-to-ceiling windows facing the street were oscillating with a whump-whump sound. The chandeliers hanging from the high ceiling like glass stalactites swayed back and forth. At first, she thought it was an earthquake, but a rumbling sound drew her attention to the street, where a column of tanks and heavy trucks clanked past the hotel. The tanks were huge, taking up nearly the entire width of the street.

The police had cleared the streets of civilian vehicles the day the alien craft arrived, but a crush of pedestrians stood on either side of the street watching the convoy make its way down the hill toward the bay. The markings on the vehicles identified them as belonging to the Johor Enclave on the other side of the channel that separated Singapore from the southern tip of Malaysia. Singapore must have asked for backup from the other Enclaves in the Southeast Asia Confederation. Hopefully nobody would get trigger-happy and start an interstellar war.

Her dad, having decided it wasn't an earthquake, loaded up a plate from the breakfast buffet and headed down the hall toward the conference room where the quantum topology working group had been meeting. That's why they were in Singapore. He was a presenter at the mathematics conference and had brought her along for the life experience. He was a big fan of life experience.

Holly said, "I'm gonna hang out here and read for a while."

He waved his hand without looking back. Despite his occasional attempts at being The Parent, he had given up trying to manage her life. In part, this was because she was in her second year at the University of New Auckland and pretty much ran her own life. But mostly it was because of the dark years after her mom died and her dad fell into a deep depression. Her brother Robert had moved—fled, really—to Christchurch, leaving Holly to take care of their dad. Since then, she and her dad had developed something of a peer relationship.

She snagged a bagel, a packet of jam, and a carton of chocolate milk. Breakfast of prodigies.

The lobby was long and narrow, extending the length of a city block. The shaking had stopped, but the chandeliers still swayed. She avoided walking under them. Opposite the wall of windows stood a massive marble check-in counter a third as long as the lobby. The impeccably dressed staff at the counter were attentive and unfailingly polite. Singapore was a polite city.

The staccato of shoes on the shiny tile floor provided a counterpoint to the murmur of voices as people streamed through the lobby; people with places to go and things to do; people going about their business as though there wasn't a foreign military convoy making its way through the business district; as though one of the most momentous events in history wasn't unfolding just a few kilometers away.

She settled into an over-sized, stuffed chair at one end of the lobby, pushed her shoes off, and let them fall to the floor with a satisfying thud. The chair's floral-patterned fabric smelled faintly of pipe tobacco, which was odd since smoking was prohibited in the hotel lobby and probably had been for decades. It brought back memories of warm summer nights on the back porch of their bach overlooking Awahou Bay, her dad's feet propped up on the railing while he puffed cherry scented clouds into the still night air. That was before her mom died. Before her dad's depression. Before Robert abandoned them.

She pulled her tablet out of her tote bag and brought up *The Iliad*. No matter what was happening down at the bay, Professor Orson would expect to see an analysis of Homer's epic poem next week. She soon lost herself in the story.

After a while, she realized something was wrong. She looked up. The lobby had become quiet and people were standing or sitting, watching the big screens hanging from the ceiling. The clock above the check-in desk said it was quarter to twelve. She had lost track of time.

The screens showed a closeup of a tall man getting out of a limousine. He wore a suit and tie, and his full head of white hair identified him as the President of the Christian Republic of America. A tight circle of men in black surrounded him; his Secret Service detail. They were easy to identify because they were the only ones not looking at the president.

The view zoomed out to show other vehicles disgorging their occupants and security details. There was enough firepower there to give the Singaporean army a run for its money. The image blurred for a moment as the SNN drone zoomed in on the spaceship. The surrounding water was churning, and the antenna and cubes had disappeared. Wings were extending from the sides near the backend of the craft.

"Holly?" Her dad strolled across the lobby toward her. "Do you want to join us in the conference room? We have a big screen there."

An intense flash of blue-white light filled the lobby, its brightness forcing her to close her eyes. The tiled floor heaved under her, accompanied by a long, low moan that made her skin crawl. She opened her eyes. The floor was undulating like waves on the ocean. Her dad fell backward onto a low, glass-topped table, which collapsed under him in an explosion of glass.

Then the wall of windows shattered, and a blast of hot wind roared into the lobby, sounding like an old diesel locomotive. Someone behind her screamed, and she turned to look. A middle-aged woman was lifted off her feet by the wind and propelled across the lobby where she collided with a pillar and slid to the floor, leaving behind a smear of blood. Chairs and tables were being swept up in a whirlwind, along with potted plants, lamps, books, anything that wasn't tied down. The air was full of glass. People were shouting, crying, screaming. An ominous rumbling sound came from somewhere, getting louder, like some monstrous machine rolling inexorably toward her.

It occurred to her she should get under a table or something, but her body wouldn't move. She just sat there, frozen in the moment, her eyes staring without seeing, her mouth open, her mind unable to come up with anything resembling a coherent thought.

Her dad staggered toward her, scooped her unceremoniously out of the chair, and ran toward a stairwell leading to the parking garage below. The howling whirlwind chased them, caught them, flung them into the stairwell. Holly tumbled down the stairs and landed hard on her back with the wind knocked out of her.

A screeching came from above and made her look up just as the stairwell turned to dust and blew away. The ground bounced up and down, tossing her about like a rag doll. The awful moaning she had heard before was closer now and louder, reaching a crescendo as pieces of broken concrete rained down on her.

It was quiet when she regained consciousness. Deathly quiet. A shaft of dusty light drifted in from somewhere, revealing that she was in a small space under a pile of broken concrete and twisted rebar. The air was hot and heavy with white dust, accompanied by the smell of smoke and something like burned electrical equipment. She looked around and found her dad pinned under a steel girder. His eyes were closed. He wasn't moving.

"Dad?"

He didn't answer.

"Dad? Wake up, daddy."

She crawled over to him and shook his shoulder. He didn't respond, and her hand came away sticky, and the coppery smell of blood joined the other smells. An urge to scream welled up inside her, but she clenched her teeth and put two trembling fingers on the carotid artery along his neck. After a moment, she moved them a bit. She couldn't find a pulse. She put her ear to his chest. He wasn't breathing. She knew CPR, but the unnatural angle of his neck told her it was broken.

She sat up as best she could in the cramped space and yelled: "Help me! Somebody help me!" She sobbed as she attacked the mountain of concrete above her, pushing and pulling at ragged-edged pieces, tears streaming down her face. Pieces of concrete gave way and broken shards showered down on her. She kept digging and digging and digging. Her fingers were bleeding, but she couldn't stop. She had to get out.

An opening appeared, and with more digging and pushing and pulling, she was able to climb out onto the side of a mountain of smoking rubble. She looked around. The gleaming glass towers of Singapore were gone. In their place lay a wasteland of rubble and fire and smoke and wreckage; nothing over one or two stories left standing as far as she could see in every direction. The air was hot and thick with dust and ash and smoke. A ghostly grayness blanketed the world, and a mournful wail floated across the barren landscape, rising and falling like the cries of ten thousand souls snatched away and hurled down to Homer's House of Death.

Something dragged her unwilling eyes upward toward a mass of angry, black, roiling clouds that had swallowed up the sun and sky. A sickening dread settled in the pit of her stomach when she realized what she was looking at. It was a mushroom cloud; the kind that marks the aftermath of a nuclear detonation. In the distance, where the alien spaceship had been, a dark, spindly stalk rose from the center of the devastated city and climbed high into the ash-gray sky where it merged with the expanding maelstrom. Somebody had nuked the alien ship and took out most of Singapore with it.

She didn't see any people, and no one answered when she shouted for help. She wished the wailing would stop. It had gotten inside her head and was eating away at her. Maybe this was what it felt like to lose your mind. She crawled back into the hole, pulled down into the waiting darkness by a painful knot in her chest. She lay beside her dad and draped an arm over him. She stayed there until someone came and took her away.

2

Twelve years later

A kiss brushed Holly's cheek, followed by a pleasant-sounding male voice: "Good morning, beautiful."

It was a familiar voice, but she couldn't put a name to it, or a face. She had picked him up at New Amsterdam's Café Thijs, though she let him think he had picked her up, men having such fragile egos and all.

A familiar headache asserted itself and her stomach did a slow flip-flop, warning her it was thinking about throwing up. She tried to picture the layout of his apartment so she could map out the quickest route to the bathroom, but that part of the previous night seemed to be missing.

The man with no name moved closer and spooned her. His morning stubble pressed rough against her bare shoulder; his morning wood pushed insistent against her bare ass. It was not difficult to figure out where this was going.

"Last night was fun," he said. "Want to go one more time?"

Her memory of the previous night was as vague as her memory of the man she found herself in bed with, so she was unable to form an opinion about how much fun it had been. In any case, she did not want to go one more time. Fortunately, she was an old hand at extricating herself from situations like this.

"Gotta pee." She rolled out of bed and landed on all fours with a thud.

"You okay?"

"Yeah."

She took a moment to talk her stomach out of doing something rash, and wobbled toward his bathroom, wondering not for the first time what she found appealing about this.

She closed the door and leaned against it for a while with her eyes closed, then filled his tooth brush cup with cold water and sipped at it while she peed. In one end, out the other. There was a kind of elegant symmetry to it. Well, maybe not elegant. The water calmed her stomach enough for her to swallow four acetaminophen capsules she found in his medicine cabinet.

The bathroom was surprisingly clean for a single guy's. At least she assumed he was single. The bathroom betrayed no hints of female occupancy. She climbed into his shower and let hot water flow over her for a while. Amazing how much grime a hot shower could wash away.

The unidentified man in the other room would be disappointed to hear the shower running because it meant he would have to deal with his problem by himself. She tried to feel guilty about that, but came up empty. Face it: he was a one-night stand. She was glad he enjoyed it. She assumed she did, too.

Rain greeted her when she got off the bus near the university. A brisk walk through the law school building and the arboretum brought her to the social sciences building, where she stopped at a restroom for a visual once-over before her first class. She was wearing the same clothes she had worn the day before, and it showed. Her hair was especially disappointing. It was one of her better features: wavy, longish, dark blonde; nicely framing her roundish face. This morning it had a wild, feral look. She tied it back in a ponytail. There was nothing to be done about the shadows under her eyes; nor the blood-shot look.

Her first class was an undergraduate course in first contact scenarios. After the Singapore Incident, universities had rushed to add alien contact studies to their curriculum, usually tucked into the Department of Astrobiology if they had one. The Free University of Amsterdam took a different approach and put it under their Department of Social and Cultural Anthropology, which made a lot more sense to Holly because she believed that any interaction between humans and aliens would have more to do with language and culture than with biology.

"Amundson. Chapter four. Friend or Foe?" she said as she walked into the classroom. A few students were still finding their seats, and two more followed her in. She had a reputation for being a demanding and unforgiving instructor, which she was. That was fine with her graduate students; not so much with the undergrads.

"Any takers?"

A young man with a tattoo of a dragon winding around one arm raised his hand. "With all due respect, Dr. Burton, you look like you partied hard last night."

This produced a stunned silence, followed by a smattering of laughter. Holly's face warmed. She took in a deep breath and let it out with an audible sigh. Most days she would have responded with some witty remark and let it go, but this day found her in the grip of a massive hangover that did not lend itself to charitable feelings toward smart-ass undergrads.

"Mr. Munzer, thank you for that insightful observation," she said. "You are an anthropology major?"

He nodded, still grinning.

"You graduate at the end of this term, I believe."

The grin disappeared.

"And since this class is required for your major, it would be something of a setback if you had to take it over next year, wouldn't it?"

Pin-dropping quiet filled the room.

"One cannot help but wonder about the wisdom of publicly embarrassing the only instructor at this university who teaches the course."

The silence that followed must have seemed like an eternity to the young man. He stood and said, "I apologize, Dr. Burton. I was trying to be clever and obviously failed badly. It won't happen again."

Well, give him credit for that. "Thank you, Mr. Munzer. Apology accepted."

He sat. Her eyes wandered across the faces of the other students.

"For the record," she said, "I did indeed party hard last night. We zenoanthropologists have a reputation for being a hard-partying bunch, you know."

This produced some smiles, at least from those who knew she was the entire zenoanthropology department. The class proceeded without further incident.

Afterward, she headed to The Green Basket and made herself eat some granola and yogurt. Then to the gym for her twice-weekly ass kicking from Camille, a petite Belgian woman who was a much better kick-boxer than Holly, which was why she sparred with her. You learned the most when up against someone better than you.

After a strenuous workout and a second shower, she engaged in mortal combat with the ancient vending machine down the hall from the closet that passed for her office. It surrendered an egg salad sandwich, which she took to her office where she dropped into her chair, unwrapped the sandwich, and brought up her vidmail.

A priority message was waiting for her from the dean of the Faculty of Social Sciences, which included Social and Cultural Anthropology. He was, in essence, her boss, and he wanted to see her in his office at 4:00. The egg salad sandwich suddenly looked less appealing than it had before; not that it had looked all that appealing to begin with.

A one-on-one meeting with the dean was rarely a good thing. If it was good news, he would have put it in the vidmail and skipped the meeting. Bad news, on the other hand, always seemed to require a personal touch. She spent the rest of the day doing research for a paper she was writing for the *European Journal of Astrobiology*. A little before 4:00 she walked into the dean's office.

Howard Gerstentveer was a tall, thin man, somewhat frail looking. His gray, thinning hair always looked unkempt. She suspected he intentionally cultivated the look. He had a proper office, with a real wood desk, and bookcases overflowing with actual books and *objets d'art* collected over a lifetime in academia. There was even a nice carpet on the floor and real paintings on the wall. Someday she would have an office like this, though she didn't know whether that would be a good thing or a bad thing.

"Dr. Burton," he began. "Holly," he amended it. Not a good sign. "Thank you for meeting with me on such short notice."

As if she had a choice. She couldn't think of anything to say to that, so she said nothing. She was tired and felt like crap and anyway it was his meeting, so let him carry the water.

"Another meeting just came up," he said, "so let me come right to the point. Your application to renew your post-doctoral position for next year has been declined."

She tried not to look too disappointed. Post-docs rarely

stayed at one university for more than a couple of years. This was her third year at the Free University, and she liked it here. She had built a comfortable niche for herself. She had hoped they would offer her an assistant professorship. Now she would have to start over at another university.

She gave Gerstentveer a polite smile. "I admit I am disappointed, but not surprised. I knew it was a long-shot."

And that was where the conversation should have ended. But it didn't. Instead, he leaned back in his expensive leather chair and gave her what was probably meant to be a fatherly look.

"I want to be honest with you, Dr. Burton. I feel we owe you that."

She dropped the smile. He was under no obligation to offer further explanation. That and the first person plural 'we' told her a second shoe was about to drop.

"No one questions your academic qualifications," he said, "or your innovative research. If that was all there was to it, the committee might have offered you an assistant professorship. It was discussed. But to be frank, some on the committee expressed concerns about whether you are a good fit for the university."

The room had gotten uncomfortably warm. "What concerns are we talking about exactly?" she said, though she already knew the answer.

He let out a breath and sat forward. "To put it bluntly, you have a certain . . . reputation; a reputation that some on the committee feel is not compatible with the reputation the university seeks to maintain; aspirationally if not always in practice. I only mention this because it represents an impediment to your career; not just here, but other places as well. My hope is that you will find a way to deal with it before a brilliant career comes to a crashing end."

She could not deny that she had a reputation; a reputation for being outspoken, for being short-tempered, for being promiscuous, for being a hard drinker, for being, not to put too fine a point on it, a bitch. A familiar voice that lived in some dark corner of her mind asked the question it always asked at times like this: "What do you want, Holly?" She had a number of less-than-satisfying answers to that question: she wanted her mom not to have died; she wanted her dad not to have died; she wanted the aliens not to have come.

No, that last part wasn't right. She did want the aliens to have come. She just wished they hadn't gotten nuked for their trouble, because what she really wanted, more than anything in the world, was to meet them.

She realized Dr. Gerstentveer was waiting for a response.

"I appreciate your forthrightness," she said. "I'm sure this isn't your favorite part of the job. I suppose I have some decisions to make now."

He looked relieved and stood. She accepted his hand and left.

———

It was getting dark when she got off the train one stop short of her usual stop in Amstelveen. There was a market here. She picked up some items and walked the rest of the way home. The clouds had moved off, and it was turning into a pleasant evening; not quite dark enough to see the stars yet, but dark enough to see Jupiter sitting high above the horizon, surveying his domain. Of all the planets, only Venus shined brighter in the sky, but the goddess wouldn't put in an appearance until dawn. Even then, she would lie too low on the horizon to be seen unless you were up high enough to see beyond the forest of high rises. For now, Jupiter reigned unchallenged in the darkening sky.

The aliens were there. They hadn't been heard from since Singapore, but images from telescopes showed structures of some kind on Europa and Ganymede, two of Jupiter's moons, so apparently they had settled in. Attempts to make radio contact with them, offering apologies for Singapore, went unanswered. Probes sent out to take a closer look went mysteriously silent before they could gather any useful information. The aliens were watching and waiting, but for what?

They were the reason her father was dead. Not that they had done anything except drop in to say hello. That had gotten them nuked, along with her dad. Nobody had ever claimed responsibility for it, but the most popular theory was that someone had used the opportunity to get rid of a dictator so another could take his place. Certainly it had launched power struggles in several of the alliances. In any case, Holly did not blame the aliens for her father's death.

Still, if they had chosen a different place for first contact, maybe a less populated place . . . she stopped herself. She had been down that crazy-making "what-if" path before, and it never led to a solution to the Gordian Knot that tied her anger about her father's death to her dream of meeting the aliens. Anger and awe, curiosity and fear; they swirled around in her head in a dance of contradictions whenever she let herself dwell on it. If she could just *talk* to them . . .

The elevator was out of order again, so she climbed the six flights of stairs to her apartment. She lived in a thicket of low-rent apartment buildings crowded against the eastern section of the wall that kept the Outsiders out of the Amsterdam-Rotterdam Enclave. From her apartment, she could see two of the guard towers placed at thousand-meter intervals along the wall, as well as the minefield on the other side. Every once in a while, the dull boom of a mine exploding would break through the walls she had constructed in her mind to keep thoughts of the Outsiders out. She could think of no moral justification for the walls; neither the ones outside, nor the ones inside. Yet here she was, surrounded by walls that kept her safe and walls that kept her sane. This was not the way it was supposed to be.

She put away the items she had gotten at the shop, sat down at the table, and allowed herself a good cry. When she was done with that, she made stir fry for dinner, which she ate at the only table in the space that doubled as dining room and living room, separated from the tiny kitchen by a counter-top. Add a bedroom and a bathroom and you had the place she called home. She lived alone and rarely had company, so she was fine with the size. Besides, it was all she could afford on her meager salary. Now she was going to have to find another job, which would probably require her to move to another enclave. Just thinking about it was exhausting.

She had missed a call from her brother. She played the vid. His hair was beginning to gray around the edges, which made him look like the successful attorney he was.

"Hey, sis. Just checking in to see how you've been lately. Call me when you get a chance."

After her dad's death, Robert had moved back to Auckland and became her legal guardian. It took a while for her to get over being mad at him for abandoning their dad and her, but they worked through it. He was married now, with three children.

The house AI announced: "You have an incoming call from Theo Dreyfus Peeters."

Theo? She hadn't heard from him in a long time. "House, accept call. Audio only." He didn't need to see she had been crying.

"Hello Theo," she said, aware of the wariness in her voice.

"And hullo to you, Dr. Burton." Somehow, he always managed to sound cheery. "Having trouble facing the world today, are we?"

Hearing Theo's voice set off a cascade of memories and emotions; some good, some not so good. He had been her only long-term relationship; nine months being long term for her. It might have lasted longer if he hadn't suggested she move in with him. That was a bridge too far. She couldn't let him—or anyone—past the emotional walls she had so carefully constructed around herself. She had broken off the relationship. She knew then, and she knew now that it was the worst decision she had ever made, which was saying a lot because she had made a lot of bad decisions in her twenty-seven years.

She activated the video. His receding hairline encroached a little more on his silvery gray hair than she remembered, but other than that he had not changed: wire-frame glasses, blue eyes, square jaw, graying reddish-blond mustache and stubble beard, immaculate black suit, white shirt, and tie. And that perpetual hint of laughter in his eyes and the slight quirk of the mouth, as though he had just thought of something hilarious. Her breathing picked up, and she realized she was smiling. Damn him. Even after all this time, he could still make her heart sing.

"Why are you calling, Theo?"

A ripple of disappointment flowed across his face. He took a deep breath and let it out with a sigh.

"Do you know Cinta Alejandre?"

Everybody knew who Cinta Alejandre was: the most well-known talk show host in Europe. Her late night show pulled two hundred million viewers from around the world. A spot on her show was guaranteed to skyrocket you to fame.

"I know who she is."

"She will be in New Amsterdam tomorrow morning to interview you."

The wheels in her mind lost traction for a moment. If she had made a hundred guesses about what he was going to say about Cinta Alejandre, this would not have been on the list. She waited for the punch line.

"I'm sorry I did not check with you first," he said, "but I knew what you would say, so I went ahead and scheduled it. You know, easier to seek forgiveness than get permission."

Apparently, he was serious. It did not surprise her that he could arrange an interview with Cinta Alejandre. He had been with Belgium's diplomatic corps for most of his adult life and was currently Belgium's Senator to the European Federation's Governing Council. He had made a lot of contacts and collected a lot of favors over the years, so pulling strings to get an interview with Alejandre was not as far-fetched as it might seem. But why?

She took a deep breath and let it out slowly. "You set me up for an interview with Cinta Alejandre."

He nodded.

"Without asking me."

He nodded again.

"What the hell, Theo. What makes you think I want to be interviewed by Cinta Alejandre? For that matter, why would she want to interview *me*? And what gives you the right to do that, anyway? Call her back. Tell her I'm not interested."

"It's about the aliens."

The aliens. It had been a while since anyone had asked her about the aliens. Mainly because she always dismissed them with a curt "No comment." She had nothing to say about them that she hadn't already said a thousand times. Apart from having had a front-row seat at the destruction of the alien spaceship in Singapore, and despite having made herself the world's foremost expert on alien first contact protocols, she didn't know any more about the aliens than anybody else did.

"You know I don't talk about that anymore."

"In a few days you will have no choice."

"Why? What's happening in a few days?"

"You just published your second book, didn't you? What's it called again?"

He was being disingenuous. He knew very well what it was called. She said nothing.

"Another best seller, I'll bet."

Now he was just being mean. She was an academic

writing for other academics. She didn't *expect* to make money off her books, though *Protocols for First Contact* had made a minor splash when it came out and was used at a lot of universities. It brought in a small royalty check each quarter.

"You haven't given me a reason for doing the interview yet."

"An interview with Cinta might net some free advertising for both books. If nothing else, it would raise your professional profile, which can never hurt."

She snorted. "The Venn diagram of Cinta Alejandre's audience and my audience is two circles that don't intersect."

"It will at least make you known to a larger audience. And who knows? It might open up opportunities not currently on your radar."

She tilted her head to one side and gave him an expression intended to ask, What are you smoking and can I have some of it?

"Just trust me on this, okay? The interview will get you on the right side of a big story that is about to blow wide open. A story that might change the trajectory of your life, which God knows needs changing."

"It's my life, Theo. Butt out."

The hint of a smile disappeared. "Holly, you are one of the most intelligent people I have ever met, but you are also one of the most underachieving. Isn't it time you crawled out of your shell and took charge of your life? You are incredibly gifted, but you have to *do* something with it or it's just a waste. You need to figure out who you are supposed to be and be that person."

His vehemence surprised her. There had been a time when she dreamed of changing the world. Then the aliens came and her dad died and it all went sideways. Changing the world wasn't on her bucket list anymore. Hell, she didn't even have a bucket list anymore.

"Just do the interview," he said. "What harm can it do?"

She sighed. "When and where?"

That night, in the twilight zone between being awake and being asleep, she heard her dad's voice again: "What are you doing, Holly?"

She still didn't have an answer to that question.

3

Hotel Twenty-one was one of New Amsterdam's more expensive hotels, and Cinta Alejandre's suite was almost decadently luxurious. Not that Holly blamed her. If she made the kind of money Alejandre made, she would probably stay in the best hotels too when she traveled. So no judgment; only a little envy.

There were two people in the suite's living area when she got there, neither of them Cinta Alejandre. The woman sat Holly on a tall, low-back chair, shined two bright lights at her, and studied her face for several seconds.

"I am Lucia," she said as she tied an apron around Holly's neck. "I make you beautiful for the camera." She had a Spanish accent.

"Is that necessary?"

"The camera does not forgive. It finds all wrinkles and blemishes and shows them to the world. I hide them for you."

She worked fast, with quick little strokes, switching brushes several times. After a few minutes, she held up a hand mirror so Holly could see the result, and said, "You are now beautiful for the camera."

Holly was astonished by what she saw. The makeup had

been applied sparingly but made her face light up in a way she hadn't realized was possible. She had probably never looked so good.

"That's . . . well, it's . . . amazing," she said.

The woman directed her to a padded chair on one side of a scallop-edged, rectangular coffee table. An identical chair waited on the other side of the table, presumably for Alejandre.

While Lucia had been working her magic, the man had been setting up a camera so that it would peer over Alejandre's shoulder and into Holly's face. He added a light and a reflector. Having a camera staring at her that close was intimidating. He moved to her side of the table and set up another camera that would peer over her shoulder at Alejandre. It was obvious he had done this before.

Cinta Alejandre swept into the room like the force of nature she was renowned to be. Her makeup had already been done, and it made her look years younger. If Holly had not known the woman was nearly forty, she would have guessed late twenties or early thirties. She wore a low-cut, full-length red dress, which nicely set off her long, flowing black hair. Holly felt underdressed.

"Dr. Burton," she said. "I am so pleased that you agreed to do this interview."

Holly accepted the extended hand and said, "Theo can be persuasive."

"He can, can't he? I tell you what, you call me Cinta and I will call you Holly. Okay?"

"Okay." Tension drained from Holly's body. She was getting the famous Alejandra treatment, though she wasn't sure how the woman did it.

"So, this is how it will go," she said as she settled into her chair. "You and I, we are having a pleasant chat in which I ask you some questions and you answer them."

She was one of those people who wave their hands around when they talk.

"If you do not like a question, just say so. It will be edited out later. Also, if you dislike how you answered a question and want to do it over, we can do that. Everything will be edited from the cameras to make a single vid that moves seamlessly back and forth between us, and any minor hiccups will magically be gone."

Holly occasionally watched Cinta's show and had seen what Cinta was describing: a live show with pre-recorded reports or interviews woven in seamlessly.

"When will this air?"

"Tonight." Holly must have looked puzzled because she added, "I fly back to Madrid right after this."

"Do you do that a lot?"

"You mean fly around doing interviews during the day and then back to Madrid for that night's program? Not usually, no. The novelty of jetting around the world and living out of hotels gets old quickly. But Theo told me I would be lucky to get you for an interview at all, let alone persuade you to come to Madrid." She shrugged. "So I am here."

"Did you fly here just for this interview?"

Cinta hesitated. "Yes."

"And we're going to be talking about the aliens."

She hesitated again. "Among other things."

Between Cinta's hesitations and Theo's evasions, it was obvious that more was going on than met the eye.

"Theo told me we would be talking about the aliens," she said with more force than she had intended. "He also said I would have a chance to plug my books which, to be perfectly honest, is the only reason I agreed to do this. But obviously there is something more to it. So . . . what *didn't* he tell me?"

Cinta grinned and said, "He warned me that you can be quite forthright."

"How well do you know him?"

"Well enough to let him twist my arm to give you this interview."

"You flew here from Madrid to get an interview that will occupy maybe ten minutes of air time. That's a lot of arm twisting."

"Let's just say he called in some IOUs."

"Why?"

Cinta looked at her for what seemed like a long time; long enough to start feeling awkward. She said, "There are some things happening that have to do with the aliens. I will break the story tonight. Theo somehow caught wind of it and suggested I bring in the world's foremost expert on the subject. That would be you."

Holly replayed this in her mind to be sure she had heard it right. Cinta was about to break a big story about the aliens. Theo had persuaded her to bring Holly in as an expert on all things alien. Theo had also said it was something that might change her life.

Cinta continued. "I am curious, though. How does one become an expert on aliens when nobody has ever seen one? Aside from the people who claim they were abducted by them."

"You're right," Holly said. "Apart from the Singapore Incident, we don't know anything about aliens. But if we assume that the same laws of physics and molecular chemistry that govern our world also govern other worlds, we can make some reasonable guesses about what is likely and what is not likely for alien life forms."

"Can you give me an example?"

"Sure. Any alien species that visits our world will almost certainly come from a planet not too dissimilar from ours."

Cinta looked surprised. "Why is that?"

"There are several reasons. First, they will almost certainly be a carbon-based species like us, simply because carbon is by far the easiest element to build life around. Silicon is the next best element in the periodic table to base life on, but it would be very difficult for complex life to develop around silicon because it lacks many of the properties that make carbon an excellent foundation for biological life. Beyond that, there really aren't any other options."

"So it will be a carbon—"

"Second." Holly held up a hand to stop her. "They will almost certainly come from a planet with a nitrogen-oxygen atmosphere similar to ours. While it is theoretically possible for life to emerge on a planet with, say, a chlorine-based atmosphere, it would be almost impossible for a technological species to evolve there. The reason is that you can't have fire in a chlorine atmosphere, and that puts almost all technology out of reach; metallurgy, for example. So you might get life on a chlorine world, maybe even intelligent life, but it would be a technological dead end, locked forever in the stone age. Nobody from that world is going to show up on our doorstep in a spaceship. The same is true for other hypothetical atmospheres, like ammonia or sulfur. Life is theoretically possible on such worlds, but they will never produce a race capable of interstellar flight.

"Third, they will—"

Cinta threw her hands up in mock surrender. "You convinced me. Any aliens out there probably come from a world more or less like ours. But I still do not understand how we can know anything about them without having met them?"

"Well, we can't *know* anything about them; not with certainty. But if we assume the laws of physics are the same everywhere, we can again make some educated guess about what they *might* be like. Tall, spindly creatures from a low-gravity world, for example. Or short, thick creatures from a high-gravity world. We can be pretty sure they won't be insectoid, because exoskeletons limit how big a creature can get, which limits how big its brain can get, which limits how intelligent it can be. Space-faring insects is a highly unlikely scenario."

"So no giant insects."

"Or giant amoebas, or dolphins."

"Why not dolphins? They're pretty smart, aren't they?"

"A species that lives underwater and never migrated to land probably lives there because it's a water world with little or no land. For much the same reasons we should not expect to run into someone from a world with a chlorine atmosphere, we should not expect to meet fish in space. Though dolphins in our oceans show that intelligent life on such a planet is possible, it will never produce the technology required for space flight.

Cinta seemed to think about that for a few moments, then said, "In your book, *Understanding Alien Cultures,* you claim that any aliens we meet will be psychologically and sociologically similar to us. But I'm wondering—"

"That's not quite right," Holly said. "I offer a number of educated guesses about how an alien species *might* be organized psychologically and socially, and then extrapolate from there. But that doesn't mean I have thought of all the possibilities. Nor that an alien visitor will match any of the possibilities I have thought of. In my book *Protocols for First Contact*, I point out that we have to set aside our preconceived notions about what an alien species might or might not be like, because they may well be unlike anything we have ever imagined. I know that sounds odd coming from someone who claims to know a lot about aliens, but it really is true that the best we can do is extrapolate from what we know and hope we aren't too far off base."

"Let's change gears," Cinta said. "What do you know about a secret collaborative effort between the European, Chinese, and Indian space agencies to build a spaceship to carry a team of astronauts to Jupiter to establish contact with the aliens?"

"What? You can't be serious."

"Why not?"

"I'm sorry, but I hope you haven't bought into somebody's wild-eyed conspiracy theory. I've not heard that one before, but I can tell you right away that it doesn't even pass the initial sniff test. No one would take it seriously . . . "

She realized she was about to insult the woman's intelligence. "Sorry. I don't mean to offend."

"No worries. I have been insulted by some world class insulters in my time. You will have to work harder than that if you want to offend me. But humor me for a moment and tell me what makes it unbelievable?"

"I don't even know where to start." She stared at the ceiling for a few moments while she sorted through a mental inventory of objections.

"To begin with, it is beyond our current technological capabilities."

"We are already in space."

"Sure. But it is one thing to put a few space stations in orbit and a mining base on the moon. It is an entirely different matter to send a manned mission to Jupiter and bring them back alive. Jupiter is a very long way away. Even with the most favorable alignment of planets, which is right about now and won't happen again for at least ten years, the journey would take upwards of five years. That's one way, so ten years for a round trip."

"So it's a long trip."

"Exactly, and that's the problem. Apart from the social and psychological challenges that would arise from living together in the cramped quarters of a space capsule for ten years, the cost of carrying fuel and supplies for a journey that long would be prohibitive. Then there's the radiation their bodies would absorb from the sun and from cosmic radiation. Even if they somehow made it back alive, they would battle cancerous tumors for the rest of their lives. Then there's muscle atrophy and loss of bone density from extended time in microgravity. That's just the most obvious problems off the top of my head. I haven't even touched on the technical requirements for building a spaceship that can make the journey."

"Okay," Cinta said. "It's dangerous, and it's hard to do. But it could be done, couldn't it?"

"No. From what I know about our space programs, we aren't anywhere near being able to send humans to Jupiter and back. I'm sure we will go to Jupiter someday, if the aliens let us, but this is not that day."

Cinta looked at her for several long moments and said, "According to my sources, just such a program has been underway for the last two years and the spaceship is expected to leave Earth sometime in the next few months."

Holly would have laughed outright if Cinta's expression had not been dead serious. Then something clicked in the back of her mind. Theo had said that something big was coming down the road, and that he thought Cinta Alejandre knew about it. Theo was nobody's fool. Neither was Cinta. He had also said that it might change the trajectory of Holly's life. A mission to Jupiter would certainly do that if she was on it, but that was such an unlikely scenario that she couldn't bring herself to take it seriously. She couldn't even get her head wrapped around the idea that such an improbable mission was being considered.

"Holly?"

"I'm sorry. What was the question?"

"I am wondering . . . what would bring three space agencies and their funding governments together for such a project, and why would they keep it a closely guarded secret?"

"Well." She paused for a moment. This was not something she had thought about before, but it was a fair enough question, even if the premise was improbable to the point of absurdity.

"It would have to be something big. Game changing big. Like the aliens suddenly started talking to us. Or some activity on their part forced a high-priority push in our space programs. Or an impending mega-disaster that we can't deal with on our own. I'm just casting around in the dark here."

"Would a rogue planet headed for Earth qualify?"

Two things happened at this point. First, Holly's jaw dropped open as she realized that a rogue planet headed for Earth was the big story, not a secret space program. Second, she noticed the green light on the camera peering over Cinta's shoulder. She didn't know how long it had been on.

Cinta noticed she had spotted the light. "Yes, we are doing the interview. Please don't be offended. I wanted to get authentic reactions from you, and that required an element of surprise. You are doing great. Better than I hoped. What if I change the line of questioning to something more in your area of expertise?"

"Like what?"

"The aliens hanging out around Jupiter."

Holly wasn't buying it. Clearly, she was being used as the foil for Cinta's revelations; to lend scientific credibility to some crackpot rumors or conspiracy theories. Theo had some explaining to do, assuming she deigned ever to talk to him again. Right now, she needed to extricate herself from this interview as quickly as she could.

Her two books lay on the coffee table between them. She had brought copies of her own, but they were still in her tote bag, so Cinta evidently planned to bring them up. Maybe she could salvage something from this debacle before she bailed. She pursed her lips and nodded for Cinta to continue.

"Speaking hypothetically," Cinta said carefully. "*If* there was a rogue planet coming our way"—she paused—"what *is* a rogue planet, anyway? Is it like an asteroid?"

"No, not an asteroid. Asteroids are relatively small, though a few are large enough to do considerable damage if they actually hit us; like the one that probably wiped out the dinosaurs 66 million years ago, along with 90% of all life on the planet.

"Something the size of a planet would completely destroy the Earth if it hit us. If it's a big planet, even a near miss might wipe out all life and leave our world uninhabitable for millions of years. And there would be no way to stop it. We don't have the technology to destroy or deflect something that massive."

"Why is it called a *rogue* planet?" Cinta asked.

Holly sighed. She was not happy with the direction the interview had taken.

"Planets form as a normal part of a star's birth," she said. "Some of them get kicked out of their solar system for various reasons and end up roaming the vast spaces between the stars. There are probably more rogue planets than planets orbiting stars. They are difficult to detect, which is why astronomers have discovered only a handful of them. But we know they are out there."

"So," Cinta said, "*if* a rogue planet was coming our way, and *if* the leaders of the world's governments believed it was going to destroy our world, and *if* they could not find a way to stop it or deflect it, and *if* they exhausted every other option they could think of, like underground bunkers or colonies on the Moon or on Mars . . . *if* all these things were true—and I admit it is a lot of ifs—wouldn't a rush project to reach out to the aliens for help be a reasonable course of action? And might not that explain why they would keep the endeavor secret, since they might not be ready to announce the end of the world?"

Holly took a moment to unpack the run-on sentence. "Assuming all those ifs are true, then yes: trying to reestablish contact with the aliens would be a reasonable thing to do. And yes, knowing a rogue planet was coming our way would be something they would want to keep quiet for as long as possible because people are apt to panic if they think the end of the world is nigh."

Cinta's eyes sparkled as she opened her mouth to say something.

"But," Holly said, stopping her with a raised hand. "Keeping two enormous secrets like that under wraps for two years is a real stretch. There are thousands of astronomers around the world, professional and amateur, studying the skies all the time. Some of them would have noticed a rogue planet on a collision course with Earth.

"And then there is the difficulty of keeping a space program secret when thousands of people would have to be involved in it. It's nearly impossible to keep *anything* secret for very long if more than a handful of people know about it. Something this big? Someone would leak it."

"To the media."

"Sure."

"To someone like me."

"Yes, to someone like you."

"Let's talk about something more in line with your expertise," Cinta said. "What sort of reception could the crew of this hypothetical spaceship expect when they reached Jupiter? After all, our last contact with them did not go well."

Holly snorted. "No kidding. We nuked 'em. A great way to introduce ourselves to a space-faring civilization about which we know almost nothing and which is almost certainly far more advanced than we are in every way that matters."

"Yet they haven't retaliated," Cinta said.

"No, they haven't. And I find that encouraging. Maybe they are not as aggressive a species as we are. Maybe they recognize we are a young, immature race given to doing foolish things without considering or even being aware of the consequences."

Cinta said, "Or maybe they *have* retaliated."

It took Holly a moment to see what she was getting at. "You mean the rogue planet."

"Yes."

"Well, let's think about that." She took another sip of water. "Capturing a rogue planet that happens to already be headed more or less in our direction, which would be a requirement, and then nudging its trajectory so it will be caught in our sun's gravity well and pass close enough to Earth to wreak havoc or even destroy our world . . . a sufficiently advanced race might be able to pull that off, but I don't know why they would. Any civilization that can throw planets at us could surely find any number of easier ways to kill us. I don't think the aliens have anything to do with this hypothetical rogue planet."

"A different question then. Assuming the aliens don't want to destroy us, why would they want to help us?"

The answer to that came right out of her first book. "The same thing that motivated them to come to our solar system in the first place. The same thing that motivated them to initiate first contact. The same thing that has motivated them to leave us alone for the last twelve years. In a word, curiosity."

"Curiosity?"

"Yes. I believe we are going to find that they are every bit as curious about us as we are about them. After all, they came a long way to meet us. That is a commonality we can build on."

Cinta picked up one of her books and looked into the camera behind Holly.

"If you want to explore this further, I recommend Dr. Burton's book *Understanding Alien Cultures*." She held the book up so the cover would be clearly visible. "Dr. Burton is the world's leading expert in this field, having devoted her entire adult life to it. This is an academic work written for use at the university level, but I read it and I think I understood most of it, so it can't be that hard." She flashed her thousand-watt smile at the camera and held up the other book.

"*Protocols for First Contact* is *the* definitive text about first contact with alien civilizations. Dr. Burton was in Singapore twelve years ago when our first contact with the aliens went bad, so she has a personal as well as professional interest in the subject. I tried to read it, but frankly it was too technical for me, especially the deep dives into linguistic theory. I think it is a book best left for people with a scholarly inclination or at least an acquaintance with the field."

And just like that, Holly had gotten the recommendation of a lifetime, not only for her books but also for herself as a scholar and expert. Once this story broke, which apparently would happen that very night, she was going to be in demand on the news feed circuit, with everyone and his grandmother trying to book her for interviews. It might even change her circumstances at the university.

Cinta was smiling at her. "One more question, Dr. Burton. If you were asked to be on this hypothetical mission to Jupiter, would you go?"

She didn't have to think about that. "In a heartbeat," she said.

4

Twenty-seven years before the end of the world

The next morning, Holly woke to a world in crisis. The image of Gerard Blumenthal appeared when she brought up the Euro One feed.

"For those of you who have just dropped in, the big story for the day is: 'In a Heartbeat.' That's right. As incredible as it sounds, this headline has gone globally viral, beating out the other two major stories: 'End of the World' and 'Mission to Jupiter.'"

The screen behind him showed a collage of shifting images from various feeds, all carrying the 'In a Heartbeat' headline, most with a picture of Holly staring into the camera with an intensity she had not been aware of at the time.

Gerard's co-anchor Viera Petra said, "Euro One has verified that the two blockbuster stories Cinta Alejandre broke on her show last night are true. Astronomers have detected a rogue planet headed for Earth. It is twenty-seven years away, but when it gets here, it will destroy all life on the planet. In response, the world's three largest space agencies are constructing a spaceship to carry a crew of six to Jupiter to contact the aliens and seek their help. The European Space Agency, the Chinese Space Agency, and the Indian Space Agency will make coordinated public statements later today.

"But the story that has gone viral is the answer given by Dr. Holly Burton when Cinta Alejandre asked her if she would join the Jupiter Mission if asked. Her answer, 'In a heartbeat,' rather than either of the other headlines, is the one that has grabbed the world's attention. How do you explain that, Gerard?"

"Well, Viera, Ms. Alejandra's revelation gave the world two conflicting messages: doom and hope. People around the world have latched onto the second message: hope. It was the absolute certainty and enthusiasm in Dr. Burton's embrace of the Jupiter Mission that did it. I can't imagine anyone else who could have had that impact with those words. She was, you may remember, present at the Singapore Incident and is the world's leading expert on alien first contact."

Viera said, "So the world now knows it is facing an extinction level event, but it also knows there is hope, thanks to an obscure academic at the Free University of Amsterdam. I think this is—"

Holly's house AI interrupted: "You have an incoming call from Theo Dreyfus Peters."

Holly switched the vidscreen to the caller, and Theo's face appeared. "Congratulations, Dr. Burton. You are an international phenomenon."

As if to confirm this, the house AI said: "You have thirty-seven unseen vid messages and one hundred four unheard voice messages."

What? How could she have a hundred and four voice messages and thirty-seven vid messages? She didn't even know that many people; at least not well enough to take a call from them. Then she realized the obvious: she probably didn't know *any* of them. They were media people trying to get an interview.

She told Theo to hold while she got a cup of tea steeping and some toast toasting. She plopped herself in her one easy chair and tried to wrap her mind around what had happened. Cinta had framed her twin revelations as a thought experiment, a hypothetical, which had somehow kept Holly from fully embracing them. She had gone to bed thinking the whole thing would be debunked the next day. Well, the next day had arrived, and far from being debunked, the stories had been confirmed. An extinction level event really was heading their way, and a manned mission to Jupiter really was in the works. It was like a story right off one of the tabloid feeds, or the storyline for a sci-fi vid, except it was true.

"Earth to Holly," Theo said. She had forgotten about him. "I have to drop off now, but a word of advice: Sign nothing until you have talked with my attorney."

———

Holly's in-a-heartbeat line may have been the story everyone latched onto at first, but it was the rogue planet story the world reacted to over the next few weeks. Astronomers gave the planet a technical designation, but the rest of the world took to calling it the Death Bringer.

Global financial markets crashed. There were runs on the banks and riots in the streets. Governments fell and then fell again. Both crime and religious attendance skyrocketed. Many countries declared martial law, which wasn't that big a step since they were all *de facto* dictatorships, anyway. World-wide chaos ensued for two-and-a-half months, and then something strange happened: everything calmed down. It was as though the whole world took a collective step back and asked, "Now what?"

Yes, a rogue planet was coming to wipe out the human race. But that was twenty-seven years away, and humans weren't made to live in permanent crisis mode; it was just too exhausting. So people responded to the coming apocalypse with a kind of pragmatic denial. Life went on. People married, had children, buried their dead. As one man in a person-on-the-street interview said: "What else can we do?"

The financial markets made a recovery of sorts, as did the consumer and manufacturing sectors. Economies found new ways of doing business. Black markets filled the gaps in the system, and governments mostly left them alone because they served an essential role in keeping their economies going.

About three months into the new normal, Holly received a call from Otto Jurgen, general director of the European Space Agency. She had met him once at a conference.

"Dr. Jurgen," she said. "This is an unexpected surprise. How are you?"

"I am well, thank you. I hope you are, too."

"I am. It turns out both my books have become best sellers, so I'm keeping busy doing talks and interviews and so on. Who would have thought?"

"I am pleased to hear that. Let me come directly to the point, if I may. Four days ago, two members of our Jupiter Mission team died in an automobile accident."

"Oh, I am so sorry. I didn't see anything on the feeds."

"We haven't announced it yet. One of them was Kako Haidoshi, the team's first contact specialist."

"I know Kako . . . I mean, I knew Kako. She was an excellent choice for the mission. My condolences to you and the team."

"Thank you," he said. "We would like you to take her place."

Holly's mind stopped working for a few seconds.

"Don't you have a backup?"

"Burak Yildiz is Kako's backup, but he contracted a particularly virulent coronavirus and is in the hospital. With the launch seventeen days away, we cannot count on him. We need a replacement."

"And I happened to be number three on your list," she said. It came out sounding snarky, which she hadn't intended. "I'm sorry, that didn't come out right. I meant I am surprised to be on your list at all. I have no astronaut training and I doubt I'm going to pick it up in seventeen days."

He said, "When the decision was made to attempt the Jupiter Mission, your name was at the top of the list for first contact specialist. However, you have a reputation for being a difficult person to work with, and there are reports of a drinking problem and—how to put this—a somewhat promiscuous lifestyle, which presents a public relations problem for us. These factors eliminated you from consideration. I am sure you can understand why."

Her face grew warm. She wanted to object to his characterization and tell him to take his precious Jupiter Mission and shove it. But she really did want to go on that mission. Besides, he wasn't wrong. She was a difficult person, and she had an alcohol dependency, and she slept around. She settled for nodding, not trusting herself to say anything.

"Obviously, things have changed now," he said. "Call it whatever you want, but we need you on this mission, Dr. Burton. The world needs you on this mission."

It took more than a heartbeat for her to answer. But only a little more.

5

_____

Twenty-two years before the end of the world

Holly dreamed she was floating on a still, mist-shrouded sea, at peace with herself and the world. After a while, a question emerged from the tendrils of mist and forced itself to the fore-front: *Where am I?* She batted it away, but it came back, insistent. *Where am I?*

Space . . . yes, she was in space. Adrift in space without a care . . . No, that wasn't right. She was on a spaceship. The *Asimov*. Why? Oh . . . the aliens. She was on her way to Jupiter to find the aliens. A frisson of excitement bloomed in her chest, and she opened her eyes. The lid of the stasis pod slid quietly into the wall, leaving her staring at the metal-gray ceiling of the hibernation room.

"Welcome back, Doctor Burton," the AI said in its usual baritone voice. "How are you feeling?"

It took her a moment to remember that she had to move her lips to speak. "You tell me . . . Albert." She congratulated herself on pulling the AI's name from her still-foggy mind.

"Your physiological metrics are nominal. You have suffered minor physical damage related to radiation and microgravity; all within acceptable parameters."

Within acceptable parameters. Such an innocuous-sounding euphemism. Despite *Asimov's* state-of-the-art shielding, their bodies would, over the course of their journey, receive a cumulative dose of radiation that would be considered deadly back home. Earth had an ozone layer to protect it from most of the radiation found in space; *Asimov* did not. Also, the inevitable loss of bone density from time spent in microgravity would require years of physical therapy to recover from; though that would be a good thing because it would mean they had gotten back, something not to be taken for granted. None of them thought for a moment that this was anything other than a high-risk venture.

Notwithstanding Albert's upbeat appraisal, she felt like crap. Her head felt like a balloon pumped full of air to the bursting point. Her mouth felt like she had been sucking on a dirty sock for the last five years. And she was thirsty, really thirsty. On the other hand, it was not as bad as some hang-overs she had known.

Holly did not like deep sleep. Nobody did. The sleeping part wasn't the problem. That was a dreamless state. And as bad as waking up was, it wasn't nearly as bad as the going to sleep part. The pod sedated her first, of course, but the fire still burned through her veins as a chemical cocktail replaced her blood to hold her in a state of stasis, hovering between life and death. But even that wasn't the worst part.

The worst part had nothing to do with the physiological and everything to do with the psychological. Surrendering herself into the hands of an artificial intelligence for five long years—*that* terrified her. She did not trust AIs; never had. You just never knew when one might arrive at a perfectly logical and completely wrong conclusion, with potentially disastrous results. Life was an analog affair; AIs were digital, and notoriously poor at solving analog problems.

Most of the time, an AI's misunderstandings of human situations were just a nuisance, maybe an inconvenience, sometimes downright hilarious. Like the time she told the house AI she didn't want to listen to the current playlist anymore, so the AI deleted it from her music archive. It had taken her an hour to reconstruct it. An inconvenience, to be sure, but hardly the end of the world. However, an AI's misunderstanding while she was in stasis was an entirely different matter. That could get her killed.

But she was alive. Albert hadn't managed to inadvertently kill her. Not this time, anyway. Stasis was a new field and far from perfect. It had a five-year outer limit for its reliability, and each of them had a 92% chance of waking up with no major problems. That meant an 8% chance of waking up with major problems, or not waking up at all. And that was just the outbound trip. They got to roll the dice again for the return trip. Assuming there was a return trip.

When she pulled herself into a sitting position, a stench came swirling up around her. "Holy crap," she said. "I stink." She had been told to expect excessive body odor when she woke up, but that had not prepared her for this gag-inducing olfactory assault.

Kari was sitting up in the pod next to hers, staring at nothing in particular. Gina was disappearing down the well to the deck below. Wang Li emerged from one of the two showers and followed her. Tolya and Benny would already be on the command deck. Albert had a specific order for waking the crew. Kari and Holly were last in the queue because they were considered the least essential personnel in the event of an emergency. It was always good to know where you stood in the pecking order.

"Hey," Kari said.

"Hey yourself."

Kari rubbed her eyes with the heels of her hands. "You'd think . . . after five years of sleep, I'd . . . be up feelin' . . . um . . . bright and . . . uh . . . I feel like shit."

She looked like it too, but Holly kept that observation to herself. She probably looked just as bad.

Kari got her eyes focused on Holly. "Albert says I'm fine . . . But what does he know?"

"Same here." Holly stretched her arms over her head and yawned. "Applare . . . apparently my internal organs are still functioning, none of my limbs have fallen off, and I have not become a mental vegetable." She pulled the IVs out of her hands and unzipped the stim suit. "Let's get showered and dressed. We'll both feel better."

"You go ahead. I need a few minutes."

"Are you sure?"

"Yeah."

If there was anyone on the *Asimov* Holly could call a friend, it would be Karishma Patil. She'd had two weeks to integrate into a team that had been training together for more than a year. Except Benny. He joined the team at the same time she did because the Asimov's pilot died in the same crash that killed Kako, and Benny was his backup. Since he had been on the backup team to begin with, he'd had at least some interactions with the rest of the crew, but it wasn't the same. Both of them—she and Benny—were outsiders trying to break into a closed group. Everybody understood the psychology of it, of course, and worked to overcome it, but understanding human nature and controlling it were two different things.

She wriggled out of the stim suit, which remained attached to the pod, grabbed the hand holds above her head, and pulled herself free. A gentle push with her feet against the wall sent her gliding toward the showers.

A shower was a necessity after deep sleep, to wash away the layers of dead skin that collected on the body, not to mention the unpleasant odor. She had not gotten to use the shower in training or on the ship, but had been told it would be an adventure. And it was.

First came the wash cycle, which consisted of being slimed from head to foot with green goop that claimed to be soap. It smelled like iodine. The rinse cycle followed, which got rid of the green goop by pummeling her body with high-pressure jets of water coming from several directions at once. Finally, the drying cycle: a severe buffeting with warm air that she imagined must be what it was like inside a tornado.

She had been told that the only way to survive the experience without bruises and a possible concussion was to grab the handholds on either side and hang on for dear life, which she did. Despite the assault and battery aspect, it wasn't as bad as she had been led to believe, and when the shower was done with her, she felt tingly, alive, wide awake. Kari had found her way into the other shower by the time Holly pulled herself out.

She glided to the pole in the middle of the room and pulled herself down through the well to the crew deck below. Not that there was any up or down in zero-gee, but with the hibernation deck being furthest forward and engineering furthest aft, everyone thought of moving from hibernation toward engineering as down, which would be true if the nuclear thermal thrusters were firing.

The crew deck was composed of a walkway around the well and a circle of seven sliding doors. Six of them were private crew quarters, and the seventh was the head. She placed her palm on the door with 'Burton' on its nameplate, and it slid open.

A narrow bed took up most of the space, the rest being taken up by a small desk and two upright lockers. There was no chair because the phrase 'sit down and take a load off your feet' made no sense in the absence of gravity. The desk did, however, have a foot bar that she could hook her feet under to keep from drifting. Everything drifted in space; at least every-thing that wasn't secured. If you left something just sitting around, it would not be there when you came back, and there was no telling where it would turn up: in your shoe, under your bed, on the ceiling, in someone else's cabin.

From a locker, she selected a utilitarian jumper from a collection of identical utilitarian jumpers—no fashion state-ments on this trip—and went through the contortions required to get into it in zero-gee. A look in the mirror on the locker door revealed that her hair looked like it had been through a tornado, which, in a manner of speaking, it had. She brushed it out as best she could and tied it back in a ponytail.

Attached to the wall next to the desk were two holo-graphs; one of Robert, Janet, and their three children; the other of Theo. She touched each image to watch its 15-second vid loop.

She caught up with Wang Li on the common deck. He held a water bottle in one hand and an energy bar in the other, alternating between the two. From her perspective, he was hanging upside down with one foot jammed into a hand-hold. He had that faraway stare people got when in a virtual reality. VR implants were still experimental, and only Li had one.

It was difficult to be fully present in virtual reality and physical reality at the same time. The human mind objected to interpreting two overlapping worlds and insisted on choosing one or the other. The solution was to focus on one and let the other fade into the background. People who spent a lot of time in virtual realities claimed they could do both at the same time, but really they had just gotten good at switching back and forth.

She gave Wang Li a wave and said, "Hey." He did not acknowledge her, though she was sure he knew she was there. Early in her mission training, such as it was, she thought he was just socially inept. That was true enough, but she eventually decided he really just didn't like people very much. She didn't either, so she could live with that.

She got herself a bottle of water from the dispenser and drained it in several large gulps. The sleep pods kept their bodies hydrated and provided essential nutrients, but now that she was awake, her body wanted a lot more of both. She was reaching for an energy bar when Tolya's baritone, Russian-accented voice sounded over the speaker.

"All crew, report to the command deck."

Wang Li came back to reality; physical reality, that is. He finished his water bottle in one long swig, grabbed another one, and said, "Let's go, princess. Sounds like something interesting has come up." He grinned and disappeared down the well.

Everyone was there except Kari. Holly floated to her station at the left end of the semi-circle that allowed all of them to see the main viewer and each other. She strapped herself in, both because it was standard procedure and because it was the best way to ensure she didn't float away at some inconvenient moment. A control panel and two small viewers slid out of the armrests and dropped into place over her lap.

On the main viewer, Europa occupied the bottom third of the view, with Jupiter rising above the horizon. The gas giant looked about three times larger than Earth's moon seen from Earth. The apparent rising of the gas giant was an illusion. Europa was gravitationally locked with Jupiter, so the same side always faced the planet, just as Earth's moon always presented the same face to Earth. It was *Asimov* that was moving as it orbited Europa. Were she standing on the surface of Europa, Jupiter would appear stationary in the sky.

"As you can see," Tolya said, "we are not in orbit around Europa."

6

Holly turned her gaze away from the banded gas giant and back to the surface of the moon. Tolya was right. It wasn't Europa. It had way too many craters; craters within craters. Europa's dynamic geology ensured a slow but continuous resurfacing, so you just didn't get craters like that.

Kari chose that moment to drift in. "Wow," she said, looking at the image on the main viewer. "That's an incredible view. But I don't think that's Europa."

"We noticed," Gina said.

"Albert, where are we?" Tolya said.

"We are in a more-or-less stable geostationary orbit around Ganymede, the seventh of the eight regular moons of the planet Jupiter. It is the largest moon in the solar system by size, but is not—"

"Albert, why are we orbiting Ganymede instead of Europa?"

"A course correction was entered into the navigational computer altering our trajectory to bring us into orbit around Ganymede."

"Albert, who made the course change?"

"That information is not in my logs."

A shocked silence followed. That couldn't be right. Everything that happened on the *Asimov* was recorded in Albert's logs. Supposedly they couldn't be altered; not even by Albert.

"Explain," Tolya said.

"I have no explanation, Commander. I am performing diagnostic tests on the navigational and event logging subsystems, and will inform you when those tests are complete."

"Albert, *when* was the course change made?"

"Approximately 31 months, 16 days, 4 hours, 12 minutes ago."

Two and a half years ago, at the midpoint of their journey. They were somewhere in the Asteroid Belt when the course change was made.

"Sabotage," Benny said.

"That's a big leap," Gina said. "Let's not jump to conclusions without evidence."

"What other explanation is there?"

Li said, "The hypothesis that one of us changed *Asimov's* course is a possibility. There are others. For example, it is possible there is a trojan buried in Albert's code."

"It would have to have been inserted before we left Earth," Kari said.

"Why is that?" Gina said.

"Because they encrypted and locked down the code base before we launched. It is a security provision in case the *Asimov* fell into alien hands."

Holly laughed. "Like the aliens would have any trouble getting through our best encryption."

"Quantum encryption. They would have to be very good to defeat it."

"Albert," Tolya said. "Were any of us revived from deep sleep prior to reaching the Jovian system?"

"No, commander."

"At least, not according to the logs," Benny said.

"But whoever did it would still have to overcome the encryption," Kari said. "None of us has the key."

Gina said, "So someone back home put a trojan into the system before the code base was encrypted."

"Still jumping to conclusions," Li said. "We don't know it was a trojan. That's just one hypothesis."

"You have a better one?"

"The aliens," Holly said. Everyone looked at her. "Occam's razor. The simplest explanation is often the best explanation. Entering a course change into our navigation system and leaving no trace behind would be child's play for the aliens."

No one spoke for several seconds.

Albert broke the silence. "Commander, I have detected an object in geostationary orbit a little higher than ours. We will pass beneath it in 47 minutes."

"Albert, show us."

A yellow arrow appeared near the horizon, pointing to a bright star. The viewer zoomed in on it, and a fat disk came into view. Above it was an asteroid attached to the disk by several supporting structures. Holly brought it up on one of her screens and magnified it further. Something was hanging beneath it as well.

"Albert, how big is it?" Tolya asked.

"It has a diameter of 250 meters, Commander."

"Two football stadiums end-to-end," Li said.

"A hell of a big spaceship," said Gina.

"I don't think it's a spaceship," said Kari.

"Kari's right," Holly said. "It's a space station. And not just a space station. It's the upper terminus of a space elevator. You can see the tether emerging from its underside."

There was more silence.

"I believe you are correct," Li said. "The asteroid sitting on top is the counterweight for the tether, which weighs a lot because it has to reach all the way to moon's surface. For a geostationary orbit, that would be . . . let's see . . . around

46,000 kilometers; further out than on Earth because Ganymede rotates so slowly. I don't know what material the tether is made of, but that much of anything must weigh tens of thousands of tons. It's an amazing feat of engineering. We're nowhere near being able to—"

Bright lights suddenly lit up a section on the edge of the disk, revealing a familiar structure. Holly started laughing.

"What's so funny?" Benny asked.

"It's a docking ring," she said. "They turned on the lights for us."

Benny zoomed the main viewer in on it. "It looks like the docking ring at *Tiangong Station.*"

"Can you dock with it?" Tolya asked.

"Sure. If it's the same as at *Tiangong.* Even if it's only close."

"Any trouble matching orbit with it?"

Benny did some calculations. "You guys aren't going to believe this. Or maybe you will after what we've seen so far. All I have to do is move us up into the space station's orbit and our velocity will exactly match its velocity."

This provoked another silence.

Holly said, "I think we now know who altered the *Asimov's* course. Back in the Asteroid Belt, the aliens changed our trajectory to one that would put us right here."

"Benny, take us in," Tolya said.

"With all due respect, commander," Gina said. "I'm not sure we should do that."

"Why not?"

"If it is the aliens who rerouted us to Ganymede, it's still an act of sabotage. We're supposed to be at Europa. The mission has been compromised."

"I'm with Gina," Benny said. "By overriding our systems, they have committed a hostile act."

"What do you propose we do?" Li asked.

"Go to Europa."

"Do we have enough fuel for that?"

Benny did some calculations. "Yes, but we won't have enough fuel left to escape Jupiter's gravity well." He did some more calculations. "On the other hand, by rerouting us to Ganymede, the aliens have ensured we don't have enough fuel to get home, anyway."

A few moments passed. Gina said, "They've killed us."

"It doesn't matter," Holly said.

Gina gave her an incredulous look.

"It doesn't matter because investigating Europa was never our mission. Our mission is to establish contact with the aliens and find out if they will help us deal with the Death Bringer. The original mission brief assumed Europa was the most likely place for a meeting with them because we knew they had a substantial presence there. But the aliens brought us to Ganymede instead. We should accept their choice of meeting site. If that means we never get home, so be it. It was never about us, anyway."

That convinced Tolya. "Take us in, Benny."

"Yes, sir."

Nobody said a word while Benny used the maneuvering thrusters to bring the *Asimov* alongside the space station. He inched them toward the docking ring until two huge mechanical arms reached out, grabbed the ship and pulled it in, leaving the ship rocking back and forth until Benny shut down the maneuvering thrusters. A few moments later they felt a bump as the station's docking bridge attached itself to the *Asimov's* hull at its airlock.

Holly could hardly believe this was happening; that she was on a spaceship docked at an alien space station three quarters of a billion kilometers from Earth; that she was about to meet an alien species face-to-face. She swallowed hard to keep the lump in her throat from bursting out.

Apart from the quiet hum of the air conditioning system and the random beeps from various other systems, the command deck was still. Tolya broke the silence. "I think that qualifies as a first for humankind."

He turned to Holly. "Dr. Burton, you are our resident expert on alien first contact. I would like to hear your assessment of the aliens' actions up to this point and your recommendations for how we proceed from here."

Well crap. She was so excited about the prospect of meeting the aliens that she had forgotten that this was where she was supposed to step up and offer words of wisdom. An assessment. Did she have an assessment? They hadn't even met any aliens yet, so she had nothing to go on. Or maybe she did.

"Well, um, I think there are a few obvious things to begin with." Her voice sounded tentative, even shaky. She took a deep breath and tried to sound more confident. "First, there was the Bracewell Probe." They looked puzzled.

"Back in the mid-Twentieth Century, an Australian astronomer named Ronald Bracewell proposed the use of autonomous space probes to explore our interstellar neighborhood and potentially make contact with other intelligent species. The idea didn't get much traction because of the time spans involved. Space is really, really big. It would take tens of millennia for the probe to reach our nearest neighbor, Alpha Centauri, hundreds of millennia to explore the immediate neighborhood. It's hard to get excited about a project with that kind of timeline.

"But the underlying concept of an autonomous probe with a smart AI caught on as a way to make first contact if we ever did encounter an intelligent alien species. Say we one day developed faster-than-light propulsion and find a planet with intelligent life. The thinking is that a Bracewell Probe would be a good way to make first contact with them because it would put physical and psychological distance between our two species, reducing the possibility of miscommunication and misunderstanding until we got to know each other better. Nobody knew if an alien species might do the same thing when initiating first contact with us until one showed up in Singapore seventeen years ago. Unfortunately, we nuked it and that was the end of that.

"The good news is that it suggests a spacefaring civilization that wants to make contact with us and wants to do it cautiously, giving us time and space to get used to the idea that we are not alone in the universe. In that sense, you could say their Bracewell Probe was a success. We've had twelve years to get used to their presence in our solar system before we decided to reciprocate.

"We also know they do not want us at Europa. But that doesn't mean they don't want us here at all. They could have sent us spinning off into deep space with no chance of getting back. Instead, they redirected us to Ganymede. They went out of their way to put us on a course that would bring us right to this space station. And they provided a docking ring that's compatible with ours. They even turned the lights on for us. All of which leads me to the conclusion that they want to meet us every bit as much as we want to meet them, and Ganymede is where they want it to happen."

She paused and looked around.

Gina said, "You have interpreted everything in the most optimistic light possible. But that's not the only interpretation. This supposed Bracewell Probe, for example, might not have been a friendly introduction at all. It might have been a warning that they are in our system and are not to be messed with. I know the official conclusion was that we nuked the probe. But there are people who don't buy that theory. After all, it killed thirteen world leaders and destroyed the Singapore Enclave. There's nothing friendly about that."

She started to object, but Gina stopped her with a raised hand. "It is also significant that we have heard nothing from them since then. If they are so eager to make contact with us, why have they not tried again?

"Finally, they knew our destination was Europa, but they hijacked our computer system to put us in orbit around Ganymede instead, demonstrating that they are the ones in control, not us. That was not what I would call a friendly gesture."

Holly said, "We don't know that they would see—"

Tolya interrupted. "I am not looking for a debate here. I asked for Doctor Burton's professional assessment of the aliens' actions to-date, and she has given that to us. We are all familiar with this argument, which has been bouncing around ever since the Singapore Incident. We don't need to rehash it here. We simply need to decide what to do next.

"Taking a page from Dr. Burton's book *Protocols for First Contact*, the assumption of peaceful intent on the part of the aliens is the only assumption that holds out any hope of a good outcome. The opposite assumption—that they are hostile—leaves us with a doomed mission from the start, and we might as well not have come."

Holly was surprised he had read her book.

"From this point forward," he said, "we will operate on the assumption that the aliens were extending a hand of friendship in Singapore and are extending it again now. I need to know that each of you can move forward with that assumption whether you fully agree with it or not."

He looked at each crew member and waited until they nodded their assent. His gaze returned to Holly. "How should we proceed?"

She had been holding her breath and now let it out with a puff of her cheeks. "There are so many unknowns, and we have to take it one step at a time. But, taking another page from my book, there are some guidelines we can follow.

"First, we present as non-threatening a profile as possible. I recommend three of us debark to the space station while the others remain on *Asimov*.

"Second, we are on their turf, so we let them call the shots.

However they want this to unfold is how we want it to unfold.

"Third, there will be opportunities for linguistic and cultural misunderstandings. Under no circumstances do we become defensive or belligerent, no matter what the seeming provocation.

"Finally, let's remember that we are not what's important here. What's important is that this goes well for Earth. Everything else is secondary, including our survival."

Tolya waited until he was sure she was finished, then looked around the room and grinned. "All right then, let's go find us some aliens to talk to."

7

Holly, Tolya, and Gina made their way to the engineering deck and into the airlock changing room, where they stripped down to their underwear and helped each other with the laborious process of getting into the skin-tight inner suit and then into the bulky environment suit. This had been a relatively straightforward exercise back on Earth where they had gravity to work with. It was ridiculously difficult without gravity. They checked each other's suits to make sure everything was properly sealed.

"Albert, open the inner airlock hatch," Tolya said. It swung open, and they pulled themselves in.

"Albert, close inner airlock hatch."

Holly examined a readout that showed atmospheric conditions in the docking tunnel on the other side of the outer hatch. "14.7 psi," she said. "Just like home."

"Just be sure it's something we can breathe without dying a hideous and painful death." Gina said it in a lighthearted way, but there was an undertone of worry there.

"Nitrogen 78%, Oxygen 21%, traces of argon, carbon dioxide, water vapor. We may not be in Kansas, but the air is the same."

"Albert, open the outer airlock hatch," Tolya said. The hatch swung open into the docking tunnel connecting the *Asimov's* airlock with the space station's airlock. The tunnel was about ten meters long with a smooth, off-white surface that glowed enough to illuminate the tunnel.

He examined the interface between the tunnel and the *Asimov*. Earth's space programs had long ago settled on a standard mechanical structure that allowed anybody's docking tunnel to attach to anybody else's. The aliens' docking tunnel matched that standard.

"These guys don't miss much," Gina said, peering around.

Tolya used the frame around the hatch to propel himself through the tunnel to the other side. Holly was next. A wave of panic passed through her as she realized that whatever the tunnel was made of, it was the only thing between them and the emptiness of space.

Life was a precarious thing. One minute you were alive; the next you could be dead from some random event you didn't even see coming. Life in outer space was especially precarious because you were always surrounded by opportunities to die. Space was a hostile environment; an unforgiving place; an alien place; a place humans did not belong.

She launched herself down the tunnel, grabbing a handhold to bring herself to a stop next to Tolya. Gina closed *Asimov's* airlock behind them and followed. The space station's airlock hatch was the same size and shape as *Asimov's*, but was round. Gina pointed to a small panel next to it. Tolya touched it and it popped open to reveal what looked like a common light switch. It was in the down position.

Wang Li's voice came through their helmet speakers: "Gosh, I wonder what that does?" Kari, Benny, and he were watching through cameras attached to the left shoulder of each of the environment suits. "You know, if there is a vacuum on the other side of that hatch, it's going to suck you right out of the tunnel and into space."

"And your suggestion is . . . ?" Tolya asked.

"Open the hatch," he said cheerfully. "I'm just pointing out yet another way the aliens could kill us if they wanted to."

"Thanks for that." He flipped the switch to the up position.

A tiny aperture appeared in the center of the hatch and spiraled open, revealing an airlock about twice the size of the *Asimov's*. There was an identical hatch on the other side. Holly let out the breath she had been holding. She had half expected to find a delegation of aliens waiting for them in the airlock, but of course it was more likely they would find the aliens on the other side of the inner airlock hatch.

They pulled themselves in and closed the outer hatch.

"Benny, audio okay?" Tolya asked.

"Affirmative, Commander."

"Visual?"

"Affirmative."

"Okay then, here goes nothing." He flipped the switch for the inner hatch and it spiraled open.

Holly was disappointed to find no alien delegation behind that door, either. They stepped out onto a catwalk overlooking the cavernous interior of the space station, which was easily big enough to hold two football stadiums. The catwalk followed the curve of the station in both directions and looked like it went all the way around.

Metal beams crisscrossed the vast open space, forming a seemingly random three-dimensional web. A few monorail-like vehicles were parked here and there, but none were in motion. In the middle, a large sphere sat atop a stanchion some ten meters wide. That would be the terminus of the space elevator. Materials mined from deep within the moon below would be brought up the space elevator to the station and then transferred to cargo ships that would carry them to other locations in the Jovian system or elsewhere.

"I don't see anything happening," Tolya said.

"Maybe it's automated," Holly said, "though that doesn't explain why nothing is moving."

Tolya reached out and touched a transparent wall separating them from the interior. This was just as well, since it was a long drop to the bottom. Not that they could fall in zero-gee, but knowing that didn't keep a feeling of vertigo from sweeping over Holly as she looked down.

"Solid," he said, rapping his knuckle against it. "It looks like glass, but I'll bet it's some material we've never heard of and couldn't replicate if our lives depended on it."

Gina chuckled. "And *I'll* bet we're going to see a lot of that before we leave this place."

"If it's any consolation," Holly said, "the air is still from Kansas."

She unsealed her helmet's faceplate and pushed it up and back over her head. The air was room temperature. She took a deep breath and exhaled. There was a scent in the air, like the smell just before a thunderstorm.

"Definitely breathable," she said. Tolya flipped his faceplate back as well.

Gina said, "Maybe we should keep our suits sealed. Just in case the next door leads to a vacuum or something toxic."

Tolya and Holly stared at her.

"Or not." She flipped her faceplate back.

Benny's voice sounded in Holly's ear. "Commander."

"Go ahead, Benny."

"Something's happening out here."

"Talk to me."

"Li was using the external cameras to examine the outside of the station when another space ship arrived and docked a ways down from us."

Li's voice took over. "It's about a third as long as *Asimov*. Narrower. Uniformly gray, rounded ends; like a giant cigar. I don't see any openings or markings. There is a single rocket thruster at the other end. Wait . . . yes . . . it has maneuvering thrusters as well, fore and aft."

"How far from you?"

"Forty, maybe fifty meters."

"What a coincidence," Gina said, pointing down the catwalk.

A diaphragm had opened onto the catwalk about fifty meters from where they were standing. A silver sphere the size of a soccer ball emerged and hurtled toward them at an alarming speed, stopping with a whoosh of air in front of Holly, who happened to be standing closest.

"Ack!" She threw her hands out in front of herself in an instinctive defensive gesture.

"It appears I have startled you," it said. "My apologies." The voice was male with a New Zealand accent.

Holly gaped at it for several seconds, unable to formulate anything resembling coherent speech. Whatever she had expected the aliens' first words to be, that was not it. Of course, she had not expected them to look like silver spheres, either.

"It has an Australian accent," Gina whispered.

"Kiwi," Holly said automatically, which seemed to get her brain and mouth reconnected. Without taking her eyes off the sphere, she said, "Commander?"

Tolya calmly said, "I believe this is why we brought you along, Dr. Burton."

"Thanks a lot."

She addressed the sphere. "Um . . . yes . . . you startled us." She couldn't quite suppress a nervous laugh. "Scared me half to death, actually."

"Oh, I think not," the sphere said. "Your vital signs are well within normal parameters for your species, with slight increases that are adequately explained as a fight-or-flight response or simply a reaction to a novel situation. There is no need to be alarmed. I intend no harm."

Holly dug around in her memory for an appropriate approach to the situation. After all, this was the event she had spent her entire adult life preparing for. She glanced back at Tolya and Gina, who looked like they were more than happy to let her show off her expertise.

"My name is Doctor Holly Burton," she said to the sphere. "Doctor is a status identifier that in this case refers to my level of education. Holly is the name my parents—"

The sphere interrupted her. "Perhaps I can save us all some awkwardness and time by assuring you that I already know who you are, including the three crew members who remained on your spaceship. According to your book *Protocols for First Contact*, self-designations may provide information helpful in furthering understanding between two species that have not met before. Logically, you will next ask for my name."

It had read her book? This must be what Alice felt like when she stepped through the looking glass and found herself in a world where the old rules no longer applied and she had no idea what the new rules were.

"Um . . . Okay . . . How *would* you like us to address you?"

"Sphere will do. I wonder if we might postpone further questions. Jupiter's radiation is harmful to your species, and this station is not as well shielded as your spaceship. If you don't mind, I would like you to accompany me to a base beneath the surface of Ganymede."

"On the space elevator?" Gina said.

"The space elevator would be an inappropriate mode of transportation for beings such as yourselves. The time required for transit would leave you exposed to radiation for many hours. Also, it would not be compatible with your psychological experience of time. I have provided a transport vehicle—what you might call a shuttle." With that, the sphere floated off at a leisurely pace in the direction from which it had come.

They stared after it. Gina said, "I think it just told us we can't use the elevator because if the radiation didn't kill us, the boredom would."

"That's my take on it," said Tolya. "Benny, are you getting all this?"

"We are, Commander."

"We're going to take the aliens up on their invitation."

"If it takes you very far beneath the surface, we might lose radio contact."

"A chance we will take."

"Yes, sir."

They followed the sphere along the catwalk and through the open hatch, which opened onto a docking tunnel. There was no airlock on either end. They passed through it and found themselves at the rear of a passenger cabin with six seats, three on one side of the aisle and three on the other. The sphere floated to the front of the transport and settled into an indentation in an alcove.

"Please sit and secure yourselves with the safety harnesses," it said. "You may put your helmets back on if you wish, but it is unnecessary."

Holly grappled with the six-point harness that could have been lifted straight out of Earth's space programs. A few minutes later, she felt a jolt, followed by a thumping sound, followed by silence.

"I think we just left the station," Tolya said.

An image appeared on a vidscreen at the front of the shuttle, showing the massive hull of the space station on their right and *Asimov* docked in front of them. Stars dominated the rest of the view. *Asimov* and the station drifted out of sight as the shuttle adjusted its angle of departure. Then they accelerated away from the station.

The view was now mostly stars leaping out from the black of space with astonishing clarity. At the bottom of the view, the gentle arc of Ganymede came into view. The moon had an atmosphere, but it was too thin to be visible. They were in a steeply descending orbit, which she guessed would take them to the surface in a single circumnavigation of the moon. Jupiter abruptly rose over the moon's horizon, dominating the view. At the same time, Ganymede expanded to occupy more of the view. Just as abruptly as it had appeared, Jupiter rolled out of sight, and their view was dominated by the heavily cratered surface of the moon toward which they were plummeting. Details of the pock marked ice that covered its surface flashed by.

A mountain range abruptly rose up and rushed toward them. Holly gripped the armrests and stifled an urge to scream. Gina gasped. Tolya grunted. Then the viewer went dark. They had flown into the mouth of a cave and were hurtling through a pitch-black tunnel at a frightening speed. The shuttle rapidly decelerated and after a while, came to a stop. Everything was quiet. Holly became aware of gravity.

8

The hatch at the rear of the shuttle spiraled open, allowing bright light to stream into the dimly lit cabin. Several seconds passed before Gina asked the obvious question: "Now what?" She and Tolya looked at Holly as though she should know.

"Sphere," she said. "Should we disembark?"

"Please do."

It showed no sign of moving from its place in the alcove at the forward end of the shuttle. Tolya took the opportunity to call the ship. "*Asimov*, this is Fedorov. Are you still receiving us?"

Benny's voice fought through static. "We are . . . der but it's stati . . . vid . . ."

Tolya frowned. "*Asimov*, we are deep underground. That may be why the signal is breaking up. See if Albert can clean it up. We're going to look around."

They exited the shuttle and found themselves in a room about ten meters long and five meters across. It reminded her of an underground train platform. Diffused white light from the ceiling illuminated beige walls that lacked any features except a door at one end of the room. There was something off about the door, and she had to stare at it for several seconds before she figured out what it was. She laughed, which drew the attention of Tolya and Gina.

"You know what's odd about that door?" She didn't wait for an answer. "Nothing. Absolutely nothing. It looks like a perfectly normal door you would find on Earth. If that's not odd, I don't know what is."

"Damn," Tolya said. "You're right."

He walked up to the door and ran his fingers over the smooth surface. "It looks like wood. Mahogany, I'd say." He put his face close and sniffed. "Yep, definitely mahogany. And it has a brass door knob. These guys are sticklers for—"

He jumped back as the door opened and a man stepped into the room. A human man.

"Holy shit," Gina said.

A tall man, he had a narrow face, brown eyes, dark hair cut short with a part down the left side, and light brown eyebrows turned slightly up on each side. He wore blue jeans, a pale blue shirt, and sneakers, and could have strolled down the streets of New Auckland without drawing a second look from anyone. But what was someone from Earth doing here?

"Welcome to Ganymede," he said, offering his hand to Tolya. "Commander Tolya Fedorov, I believe."

Tolya hesitated and shook the offered hand.

He released Tolya's hand and turned to Gina. "Doctor Virginia Walker. It is a pleasure to meet you."

"Uh, yes." Gina started to accept his hand but then pulled it back. She looked like she might bolt.

He seemed to take this in stride and turned to Holly. "Doctor Holly Burton. I am pleased to meet you again."

His eyes were a deep, liquid brown that seemed to pull her into them. She accepted his hand. It was warm; his grip was firm. Then she realized what he had said.

"We . . . have we met before?"

"In a manner of speaking. You were in Singapore when I

first attempted to make contact with your species. You were fifteen at the time. I am sorry for the loss of your father."

"How . . . " She stopped. The alien knew she was in Singapore when the aliens first came. He knew she was fifteen at the time. He knew her father had died there. All of this was public information. There was nothing mysterious about it. He had simply done his homework.

"You look human. Are you?"

"No, I am not. This physical manifestation is an avatar; what you, Dr. Burton, describe in your books as an alien-human interface. But please, all of you, come with me. I will try to answer all your questions."

As he disappeared through the doorway, he said, "Can I interest anyone in a cuppa?"

They looked at each other. Tolya seemed to have trouble getting his mouth working, but finally blurted, "Did he just offer us tea?"

"Come into my parlor, my dearies," quipped Gina.

They followed him through a short entry hall into a circular room at least fifteen meters across. A burgundy carpet with random blue swirls covered the floor, and in the middle sat a low-set, round table surrounded by seven cushioned chairs. The scent of wood smoke hung in the air. A brick fireplace occupied one side of the room, complete with a crackling fire. On another side of the room hung a large wall screen displaying a spectacular image of the planet Jupiter as it might appear from the surface of one of its many moons, like Ganymede.

Four open arches were placed equidistant around the room, one of them being the entry hall they had just come through. It wasn't clear where the others led.

"Please sit," their host said. "I will make tea." He disappeared through an arch.

"I wonder if that's a real-time image?" Tolya said, standing in front of the image of Jupiter.

Gina ran her hand over the brickwork of the fireplace. "This can't be real brick, but it's a damn good imitation. The fire puts out heat and looks like it's burning real wood. There's even smoke, and it smells like a wood fire."

The avatar returned carrying a tray, which he placed on the table. "English Breakfast," he said, "with milk and sugar on the side. I hope this is acceptable?"

There was a slight upward emphasis at the end of some of his sentences, a not uncommon Kiwi trait. Tolya and Gina looked at her, waiting for guidance from their resident expert on alien etiquette. Neither of her books mentioned tea parties.

"When in Rome . . . " She settled into a chair, which startled her by molding itself to her body.

"That's creepy."

"Would you prefer that it not do that?" The avatar asked. "I can disable the feature."

"No, that's all right. It surprised me is all."

She took one of the teacups. It looked and felt like real china, cream colored with a red floral pattern. The contents looked and smelled like tea, and when she took a sip, she was pleasantly surprised to discover it tasted like tea. She added a little milk and sugar and stirred it with a small silver spoon. She didn't believe for a second that the sugar and milk—or the teacup and the silver spoon—were the real thing, but they sure seemed like it. This whole setup was the most elaborate and convincing simulacrum she had ever imagined. Even knowing this, her second sip of tea put a smile on her face.

She shrugged at Tolya and Gina. "It looks like tea, smells like tea, tastes like tea. I think we might as well accept it as tea." They helped themselves.

"An excellent cup of tea," she said to their host. "Thank you."

"I am pleased you find it acceptable."

"The automaton we met on the space station told us to call it sphere. What should we call you?"

"No doubt this seems like a simple question, one that ought to have a simple answer. Unfortunately, it presupposes a conception of being that is not applicable to me; which is to say, it is the wrong question to ask. As I am sure you know, if you ask a wrong question you will probably get a wrong answer. Your question is literally nonsense. No offense intended."

Okay. That was interesting. Apparently, the aliens had no use for names because . . . well, she didn't know why.

"However," he continued, "I understand your predicament. I have no use for a name, but perhaps 'Fragment' would be as useful a designation as any, though it obscures as much as it reveals."

Thank God. She got a name out of it. Even if it did obscure as much as it revealed, whatever that meant.

"Thank you, Fragment. Please bear with . . . uh . . . be patient with our limited understanding of your species. We want to understand." She needed to avoid figures of speech, which were notoriously culture specific. There was no way to know how an alien might interpret them. That was in her book, too.

She took a moment to reflect on what she had learned from this little exercise in introductions. Apparently, they did not use self-designations to differentiate themselves from others of their kind. But what did that mean? Were they some kind of hive species, in which individual members defined themselves only in relation to the collective? That was a chilling thought, though she immediately realized that her reaction was colloquial at best and probably downright xenophobic.

She had also learned it was willing to accommodate their limited understanding of its species, shown by the fact that it offered her a name even though it had no use for one itself.

He waved his hand expansively. "I created this environment to be as familiar to you as possible."

He pointed to the arch he had brought the tea from. "Through there is a kitchen; more an automated kitchenette, really. You will find a variety of foods and beverages that I assure you are nutritious and safe. I have attempted to imitate the flavors and scents of human foods, though I cannot guarantee I have gotten all of it right. You will have to be the judge of that."

He pointed to another arch. "Through there you will find private sleeping quarters; one for each of you, each with its own bathroom, which includes a shower."

The three of them exchanged glances. It seemed their host expected them to stay for an extended period of time. He continued without seeming to notice, though Holly doubted he missed anything.

"I have also made clothing for you. I did not know what your stylistic preferences would be, so I provided a variety, using—"

"Wait a minute," Gina said. "You made clothes for us? How long do you expect us to stay?"

Holly stared hard at her, willing her to shut up. The last thing they wanted to do was offend their host. Gina either didn't notice or chose to ignore her.

Their host turned his head toward her. "Do you wish to leave already?"

"No," Tolya said quickly, giving Gina a glare of his own. "We have come a long way to meet you, and it is my hope that we have a great deal to talk about." He looked at Holly and then back at their host. "But perhaps this is a good time to ensure that we have the same expectations for this visit. For example, if we *did* wish to leave now, would that pose any difficulties?"

"I understand your concern," he said. "Please be assured that you are not prisoners in any sense of the word and are free to leave whenever you wish. I can instruct the shuttle to return you to the space station, where you will be free to board your ship and depart. I will even refuel your ship, since you do not have enough fuel to get back home."

Gina relaxed visibly, as did Holly. The aliens really were going out of their way to establish a cordial relationship.

Tolya said, "You have an impressive operation here. A space station, a space elevator, presumably a mining operation."

"You are correct, Commander," their host said. "This is a mining base, though it has not been used in a long time. Materials from deep inside the moon were used to build a base on Europa to support the study of some interesting life forms that live in its oceans."

Holy crap. There was life on Europa? Planetary scientists had speculated about the possibility of life in oceans beneath its surface, but the only way to find out was to go there, and the Great Collapse had put a serious crimp in Earth's space programs.

"Why an avatar?" Gina said. "Why not show yourself as you are?"

"An excellent question, Dr. Walker. I would if I could, but I can't. I am a trans-dimensional being. Your mental constructs are anchored in your four dimensional space-time continuum. As a result, you literally cannot see most of me, and if you could, you would likely find the experience disorienting and possibly frightening."

"Are there more of you?" Holly said. "Or are you alone here?"

"It's just me, I'm afraid. There are more of my kind, but none of them are currently in this galaxy. We are solitary explorers. I have, however, reported your existence to them, and they are curious about you. Advanced biological entities such as yourselves are rare. Your discovery has stirred up considerable interest."

"Wait a minute," Gina said. "If none of them are in our galaxy, how do you communicate with them?"

MICHAEL J EDWARDS

"Ah yes, the problem of communication over large distances. Another excellent question, Dr. Walker, but one not easily answered because—again—you humans lack the mental framework necessary to understand it. Perhaps there will be an opportunity later to pursue it."

Holly wanted to pursue it right then, but Tolya waved his arm to take in the entire room. "Is this real?"

"By real I assume you mean physical as opposed to, say, a hologram or an illusion. Yes, it is real. I constructed it specifically for you and your crew from materials mined here on Ganymede."

"Obviously you knew we were coming."

"I have followed your space programs with great interest."

"Uh, Fragment," Gina said. "Your command of English is quite good. Excellent, really. And not just English, but a specific variant of English; New Zealand, I believe."

"I am fluent in most of your world's languages."

"Really?"

He tilted his head again and offered an apologetic smile. "What can I say? I am a highly intelligent being."

My God, Holly thought, he has a sense of humor. Or at least he understands human humor well enough to emulate it convincingly.

She faced something of a conundrum now. The field of first contact studies had mainly to do with developing a common basis for communication. Hopefully, one that avoided anthropomorphic false equivalents which could lead to dangerous misunderstandings. In the literature, this was called, as the Fragment had pointed out, an interface. She had always assumed it would be the first and most important hurdle to overcome in any first contact scenario, which why she was on this mission. But if she took the Fragment at its word, this was an impossible task because their limited little brains were incapable of forming a meaningful concept of the alien. Their host, however, had solved the problem by providing his own interface in the form of the avatar. What they could not do, he had done for them.

All her studies, all her research, all her ideas, all her books and articles . . . none of it mattered. None of it was of any use. All she had to do was show up, and the alien took care of the rest. She was overtaken by a feeling of humility, of unworthiness, almost as though she was in the presence of a god. How arrogant of her to think she could bring anything of value to an encounter with an advanced alien species.

She said, "What do you—"

He interrupted her with a raised hand and said to Tolya, "Commander, two of your crew are leaving your ship."

He pointed toward the wall screen, which now showed the inside of the docking bridge seen from the space station side. The *Asimov's* outer airlock hatch was open, and Kari and Li were pulling themselves through. Or rather, Kari was pulling Li through. It looked like he was unconscious. When she kicked off to carry them both across the gap between *Asimov* and the space station, globules of blood trailed behind them. Neither of them wore an environment suit.

The color drained from Tolya's face. He stood. "*Asimov*, this is Fedorov. Come in, please."

He waited a few moments.

"*Asimov*, this is Fedorov. Please respond."

Again, nothing. He looked at the Fragment. "Is our signal reaching them?"

"I have tuned a repeater to your frequency to boost the signal. The space station is receiving it clearly, and I can think of no reason your spaceship would not be receiving it as well."

"Albert," Tolya said. "Ship status."

Nothing. Not even static.

"The ship is attempting to leave the station," the Fragment said calmly. "I have opened the space station's airlock for Dr.

Patil and Dr. Wang, but I do not believe they will reach it in time."

"In time for what?" Gina said.

"In time to avoid being sucked out of the docking tunnel into space."

9

Kari's breath caught in her throat as Wang Li's body flew across the room and crumpled into the food dispenser. It tried to bounce back toward the middle of the room, but his left hand had gotten trapped in a handhold, so his body jerked into the dispenser again. Blood from his left nostril formed a darkening blob in front of him, and a cloud of red mist collected around him from a gash on the back of his head where he had hit the corner of a cabinet.

"Li, you fuckin' cretin," Benny screamed. Kari turned toward him. He was floating upside down from her point of view, his left arm sticking out at an odd angle. He had made the mistake of threatening Li with a knife. Li was a practitioner of Aikido, which included extensive use of joint locks. He had used one to disarm Benny and another to break his upper arm with a horrible cracking sound as the bone snapped. Benny howled in pain, but used his position against the wall to kick Li in the face, which sent him tumbling across the room and into the dispenser where he hung unconscious from the collision.

Benny retrieved the knife and kicked off from the wall,

sailing across the room to Li, where the knife sank deep into his abdomen. Kari started crying.

"Shut up," Benny said, "or I'll cut you too."

He oriented his body toward hers, his face contorted in pain or rage or both. The knife in his hand was red with Li's blood, and Benny's own blood was seeping through his shirt, which meant the bone had broken through the skin. His eyes were wild, and she knew with panicked certainty that he was going to kill her.

But he didn't. Instead, he freed Li's hand and gave him a shove in Kari's direction. She caught his body and let his momentum carry them both into a wall so she could take as much of the impact as possible. Pain exploded in her right shoulder when she connected with a handhold.

"Benny," she cried. "Stop. Please. Why are you doing this?"

Benny's voice was low and dangerous now. "Get out. Both of you."

Kari heard the words but couldn't make any sense of them. Her heart thudded against her chest and she gasped for air. Her vision narrowed down to a space in front of her. Benny was in that space, drifting toward her, knife in hand. His mouth was moving, but she didn't know what he was saying. She started crying again.

"Stop that," he shouted. He slapped her hard across the face, which pushed her against the wall and set him flying backward. He got himself stopped on the opposite wall and shrieked in pain.

"Into the airlock," he gasped. "And take the great Wang Li with you."

"What?"

"You have five minutes to get off this ship and onto the space station. Otherwise, I'm going to disengage *Asimov* from the station and toss you both out the airlock."

Kari was suddenly alert, her head clear. He was giving them a chance. All she had to do was get Li and herself to the alien space station. She grabbed Li's body and pulled him down three levels to the engineering deck. Benny followed. She reached for a space suit.

"You won't be needing that," he said.

Her hands were shaking, and she thought she might throw up. She had never been so frightened in her life.

It seemed to take forever, but she got Li and herself into the airlock. Benny slammed the hatch shut behind her and secured it. The outer hatch swung open. Blood floated around the airlock in thick, dark blobs. She dragged Li into the docking tunnel, moving as fast as she could. She was pretty sure Benny was going to disengage the *Asimov* from the station, and if they were still in the tunnel when he did, they would be blown out into space. She had read somewhere that as ways to die went, it was one of the better ones, but she had no desire to find out for herself. She kicked against the airlock door, propelling the two of them down the tunnel toward the space station. Miraculously, its hatch spiraled open. She hit the side of the opening, and Li's body hit hers. He groaned.

"Sorry," she said automatically, but she was relieved to know he was still alive.

The docking bridge lurched, and she heard the high-pitched screeching sound of air escaping through a tear somewhere. She sobbed as she pushed Li into the airlock. The screeching gave way to a whooshing sound. *Asimov* was leaving, and the tunnel was coming apart. She grabbed both sides of the airlock and pulled herself in, only to be pulled back out as the air in the tunnel exploded out into space.

———

Benny took his seat on the command deck and buckled himself in. He punched in the vector he wanted and ordered Albert to execute it.

The AI balked. "This course will cause the ship to crash

into the surface of the moon below. I cannot comply."

Benny issued a command override, and Albert complied. The ship pulled away from the station, taking part of the docking bridge with it. Had Kari and Li made it to the station in time? It didn't matter. They would die either way. They were collateral damage. An unfortunate but unavoidable loss necessitated by his mission; a mission he had committed to eight years ago.

Rain skittered across the water as Ben walked along the path that wandered around the lake. From here, the lodge on the opposite side presented a postcard perfect picture of an old two-story log building set against a misty green background of Douglas Fir and Western Red Cedar. He stopped and inhaled. He loved the smell of the rain forest. The fir needles, the cedar bark, the decomposing detritus that made the ground spongy to walk on. Even the rain had a smell all its own.

Having set the *Asimov* on its course, he removed the detonator from his pocket. He didn't know how the organization he worked for had gotten a nuclear device on board; nor how it had remained undiscovered. Apparently, they had people placed in key positions throughout both the European Space Agency and the Asia Pacific Space Agency. The deaths of Burak Yildiz and Kako Haidoshi were no accident. It had been necessary to open up a spot on the Jupiter Mission for him. A lot of planning had gone into his mission.

The lodge had recently been renovated and was not nearly as rustic on the inside as it appeared from the outside. There were five other people in the dining room when he sat down for dinner: a young couple with a child who was not pleased about being made to sit in a booster seat, and an older couple who ate their meal quietly, apparently not requiring any conversation.

He ordered the grilled salmon with asparagus and baked potato. The asparagus was overcooked, as it usually was at restaurants, but the salmon and potato were excellent. A glass of Cabernet Sauvignon capped it off. Supposedly white wine went best with fish, but

Ben didn't care for most white wines; too bitter for his tastes. He had read somewhere that the only rule with wine is that you enjoy what you are drinking.

A tall man in a suit and no tie walked up to his table and sat across from him. He took his hat off and set it on the table. His hair was short, and he was clean shaven. There were no laugh lines on the man's face.

"My name is Darren Flocker," he said.

The trajectory Benny had programmed into the AI would take the ship once around Ganymede, losing altitude as it went, until it reached the space elevator again a few hundred meters above the alien base. He would detonate the device then, obliterating the base and killing any aliens who happened to be there. It would vaporize the bottom part of the space elevator's tether, which would shift the tether's center of balance and, he hoped, send the station careening off into space.

"We are looking for patriots, Mr. Clark. Patriots not just of a country, but of the world. Patriots like you. The survival of the human race is at stake."

The mission was to sabotage the effort to make peaceful contact with the aliens, and to strike a mortal blow against them instead, and Benny was the linchpin of the plan. It was up to him to detonate the device at a time and place that would cause maximum damage. He had almost panicked when he realized they were not in orbit around Europa, but he knew that even the best laid plans often went astray when they collided with reality. He would take out the base and station at Ganymede instead.

He keyed the activation code into the detonator and eyed the red button. Why red? It was such a cliché. His arm throbbed, and he was having trouble concentrating. He was going into shock. But it didn't matter. Only the mission mattered. He was going to be a hero. He was going to die a true patriot.

10

James Braxton Cartwright, Secretary of the Department of Homeland Security of the Christian Republic of America, held a match to the nondescript pipe clenched between his teeth. The pipe was an affectation he had made part of his public persona many years ago. It was also one of the few truly enjoyable vices he insisted on keeping, despite his doctor's orders and his wife's gentle harangues. Getting old sometimes seemed like a long, slow process of ejecting from his life all things pleasurable. He was determined to hang on to a few of them to the bitter end. Scotch was one of those; his pipe another. A curl of smoke emerged from the bowl of the pipe, followed by two energetic puffs, suffusing the room with the scent of cherry tobacco that mingled with the scent of the fire in the fireplace and the scent of ancient cedar, of which the private hunting lodge was built a century and a half ago.

Six people were present for the meeting: five members of the Mansfield administration and one Supreme Court Justice. They were there to watch a few seconds of vid.

"Show us what you've got, Mr. Franklyn," Cartwright said.

Lee Franklyn had ascended to the position of interim

National Security Advisor after his boss was forced to resign in the face of allegations of insider trading. The young man was obviously in way over his head, but with proper grooming, he might prove useful. Franklyn started the vid, and a star field appeared on a vidscreen set up for the meeting. He used a pointer to draw their attention to a particularly bright star; one that almost resolved into a disk.

"This is the planet Jupiter, as seen from a satellite in Earth orbit. You can see three of its moons here, here and here." He brought the pointer back to the first moon. "This is Ganymede, the last known location of the *Asimov*."

Several seconds passed and then Ganymede flared almost as bright as Jupiter, and just as quickly dimmed again. The vid ended. Franklyn got up to turn on the lights, but Cartwright stopped him.

"I'd like to see it again."

They watched the vid again, and Franklyn turned on the lights.

Cartwright puffed thoughtfully on his pipe. "That was a nuclear detonation?"

Franklyn cleared his throat. "That's what the techs say. Nuclear detonations have a distinctive energy signature that—"

"I didn't ask you for a technical report. I asked you if you are sure it's a nuclear detonation. It's a yes-no question, son. If you are going to be of any use to this President, you'll have to learn to give him the answers he needs, clearly and succinctly. He assumes you did your homework, so don't waste everybody's time explaining how you got to your conclusions."

The room was silent. Franklyn cleared his throat again and sat down. His face and neck were red.

"It was a nuclear detonation."

There was another pause, broken by the gravelly voice of Janice Ferguson, the Secretary of State. "It would appear the aliens have initiated hostilities by attacking our peace envoy."

"That is one interpretation," Franklyn said.

She pursed her lips. "What other interpretation is there?"

"The *Asimov* might have detonated it."

She snorted. "The *Asimov* carried no weapons; certainly not nuclear weapons. It was on a mission of peace, a hail-Mary pass hoping to secure the aliens' help."

John Burner, Mansfield's Chief of Staff, walked over to a window and pulled the curtains back, letting the light of the setting sun paint the room with an orange glow. He stood there for a few moments and then turned to face the others.

"I believe a de facto state of war now exists between the aliens and humans. There were two CRA citizens on the *Asimov*. I am going to recommend to the President that he ask —no, that he *demand* that Congress declare war on the aliens. Does anyone disagree?"

Cartwright watched Franklyn's face as it dawned on the young man that this had all been a foregone conclusion, and that he was merely a pawn in a game he didn't fully understand. For a moment it looked like he might object, but then he settled back in his chair, his body language signaling surrender. Cartwright smiled to himself. Yes, Lee Franklyn had potential.

———

Later, after everyone had left except Janice, he poured two fingers of scotch into a whiskey glass and handed it to her. He poured one for himself and returned to his seat.

She took a drink from her glass and allowed herself to savor the burn as it went down. "So, Jimmy, what is the next move?"

He relit his pipe and puffed it to life. "The press will spin it as an unprovoked attack on an unarmed ship on a mission of peace. There will be a public outcry. Congress will have no choice but to line up behind the President. Most of the world will fall into line. Except maybe the Europeans or the Chinese. Some arm twisting may be required."

He watched a passable smoke ring float upward, gradually losing its form until it faded into the ceiling.

"On a related note, the CRA launched four armed spaceships a few months after the *Asimov* left Earth. They will reach Europa in two weeks. Their original mission was to look for alien tech in the aftermath of the nuclear detonation there. When the *Asimov* ended up at Ganymede instead, the task force rerouted one of its ships there to survey the aftermath of the nuclear detonation. The main force is continuing on to Europa, where it will attack the space station and base there. Hopefully, they will come away with some alien technology we can use against them in the future."

Ferguson stared at him. Her glass made a loud clunk when she set it down. "Shit, Jimmy, that's a huge gamble you're taking. Nuking them with the *Asimov* was risky enough, but you're talking about an all-out offensive. Are you *trying* to start a war?"

"War is inevitable. Sooner or later they will come for us, anyway. It's only a matter of time. By striking hard and fast, we might set them back, disrupt their plans, give us more time to prepare."

He allowed his large, gray eyes to settle on her. "This is an existential war. Either we destroy them or they destroy us. I have spent most of my adult life defending my country against all threats, foreign and domestic: terrorists, illegal immigrants, economic chicanery, corporate over-reach, Republicans . . ." They both smiled at the small joke.

"The Death Bringer is a whole other level of threat, an existential one. But my people tell me it is survivable. It won't actually hit us. It will pass near enough to wreak havoc with the planet, but we can survive that without help from an alien race. That fact of the matter is that the aliens are the real threat. I saw that when they first arrived seventeen years ago." He puffed furiously on his cigar, creating a cloud of smoke around his head.

"And you didn't mind taking out all the alliance leaders, including Fitzgerald? Not to mention Singapore?"

"Unfortunate. But acceptable losses when you consider what was at stake. It was important to stop any dialogue with the aliens. And it did. We haven't heard from them since. It was just as important to stop the Jupiter Mission. Janice, the aliens are not our friends and never can be. They are the real threat to our existence. So I repurposed the Jupiter Mission to be a declaration of war."

"What happens next?"

"I hope a one-two strike will buy us enough time to do two things: build an international space force using their own technology, and construct underground cities that can survive the Death Bringer."

"Isn't it possible that they have come in peace?"

"It makes no difference." He stood and began pacing back and forth. "I drove through the Rappahana Indian Reservation a few weeks ago. The poverty, the hopelessness . . . it struck me that this is what happens when a superior civilization encounters an inferior one. In our case, we invaded, wiping out most of the native Americans who were here before us. That's just the way of the world. But as I drove through that reservation, I realized that those who survived the coming of the Europeans were in some ways worse off than those who died. They were once a proud people, a warrior people. Look at them now. They have lost their land, their independence, their culture . . . everything. The only emotion I could conjure up for them was pity."

He puffed on his cigar again, replenishing the cloud of smoke following him around the room. "Whether these aliens are hostile or not is beside the point. The outcome is the same either way: our civilization dies. I intend to do everything in my power to make sure that doesn't happen."

He sat, and they were quiet for a while. She said, "What do you need from me?"

"Madam Secretary, I need you to manage the Council of Enclaves, which is going to have a hissy fit when they figure out what we are doing."

———

After she had gone, he wandered out to the dock on the pond behind the lodge. A wobbly reflection of the moon floated on the pond's surface. The evening's symphony of frog songs had mostly died down, leaving only the occasional forlorn call of a lone male still hoping to get lucky. Cartwright sat on a wood slat chair on the dock, holding an empty whiskey glass in one hand and a forgotten pipe in the other. He was tired. Tired of the fight. Tired the politics. Tired of the games. Marie wanted him to retire; spend more time with the kids and the grandkids. He was more than ready to do that, but his country still needed him.

Presidents came and went, as did party control of Congress. He, on the other hand, had held his position as Secretary of Homeland Security for nearly three decades and had become the most powerful man in America; maybe in the world. Most people attributed this to knowing where the bodies were buried, which was true enough, but his political longevity also owed a great deal to his ability to rise to the challenges and opportunities presented by the Great Collapse. As economic, political and social chaos spread across the globe, national security became the country's over-riding priority, and it fell to him to transform America into a "Fortress of Freedom" as he liked to call it; a fortress that could survive the socio-economic tsunami and come out the other side ready to re-assert its preeminence on the world stage.

Now he faced the two greatest challenges of his life: the

Death Bringer and the aliens. It was no longer just America he had to save; it was the entire human race. He didn't know if he could pull it off, but he had to try. He would rise to the challenge one more time because there was no one else who could. He would stand in the gap between his people and annihilation. The rest was in God's hands.

The grandchildren would have to wait.

11

Captain John Hirram Grant sat impassively on the bridge of the destroyer *Robert E. Lee,* his eyes fixed on the three monitors in front of him, particularly the one that displayed the changing status of the ships that comprised his tiny fleet as they came alive after five long years. Not that it had seemed that long to him. Or to any of the people under his command. They had all slept through it, unaware of the passage of time. Now they were waking up and preparing for war.

The *Robert E. Lee* showed full battle readiness. Its crew had been the first to be awakened as they approached their targets. The frigate *Carolina* also showed full battle readiness status, though it wasn't expected to engage in hostilities. It was a reconnoissance ship whose mission was to verify that the alien base on Ganymede had been destroyed. If they found any sign of alien activity, they had half a dozen nuclear missiles.

The crew of his other destroyer, the *Thomas J. Jackson,* was awake but not yet battle ready. Between the two destroyers, Grant had at his disposal enough nuclear firepower to lay waste to any nation on Earth, and he was prepared to use that firepower against any aliens who got in his way. Grant was confident, but he was not given to hubris, nor was he inclined to underestimate an enemy. Any race that could travel between the stars would be more advanced than humans. How much more advanced? They were about to find out.

The remaining ship at his disposal was the *Lewis B. Puller*, a troop carrier named for the American general who led a successful marine assault against larger, entrenched Japanese forces at Guadalcanal. It was the largest of his ships and held a contingent of forty marines, led by Lieutenant Sam Puller, who happened to be a direct descendent of the famous general. The marines were still waking up and would not be battle ready for at least an hour, but that was all right because the battle plan called for the troop carrier to stand off until the destroyers neutralized the enemy's defenses. Then they would go in, secure the enemy base, and begin the search for alien technology. That, of course, was the number one objective of their mission: alien technology.

One factor that weighed heavily on his mind was the fact that the enemy knew exactly where his fleet was and exactly where it was going, and there was nothing he could do about it. The laws of inertia and gravity saw to that. His fleet was like a billiard ball that had been put in motion years before and was now on a predetermined trajectory that was, for all practical purposes, impossible to change this late in the game. The *Carolina* was locked into a course to achieve orbit around Ganymede. Grant's destroyers and troop carrier were locked into a course to achieve orbit around Europa.

The science fiction trope of space battles with ships buzzing around this way and that like airplanes in aerial combat was simply not possible in space. No, the aliens knew where he was and where he was going, and there was nothing he could do about it. The only saving grace was that he also knew where their space station and base were at Europa, and there was nothing *they* could do about *that*. There would be no sneak attacks or surprise maneuvers. The ball had been put in motion years ago; everything else was down to Newton's Laws of Motion.

"Incoming message from the *Carolina*," his communications officer said.

"Let's hear it."

A moment later, he heard the voice of the commander of the *Carolina*: "*Robert E. Lee,* this is *Carolina*. We have established orbit around Ganymede and passed over the alien base. There is no sign of activity. Nothing is left but a crater of slagged ice. It looks like a good deal of the space elevator tether was destroyed as well. The space station is nowhere to be seen and there is no sign of debris. We are assuming it was thrown into space."

"Any sign of life underground?"

Even at the speed of light, there was a small but noticeable lag as their signals traversed the distance between them. Grant waited patiently. This was not his first rodeo. Though it was his first rodeo in space.

The expected lag came and went, and the silence stretched out with no answer to his question. He looked at the communications officer, who said, "We've lost the signal, sir."

"What do you mean, we've lost the signal? Get it back."

"The problem is not on our end. As near as I can tell, they stopped transmitting."

The first officer looked up from his station. "We have lost telemetry as well. Something has happened to them."

Grant rubbed a scar above his right eye.

"Keep trying," he said. "They can't have—"

"Sir," the navigator said. "The alien space station is coming into view."

"Let's see it."

A graphical visualization appeared on the main screen. It showed the two destroyers approaching Europa. A bright dot sat on the horizon of the moon.

"Give me a visual," he said.

The large screen split into two windows, one showing the graphical visualization and the other showing a live image. He didn't see the space station. Then the view zoomed in, and the space station appeared. It was shaped like a fat disk, with several towers poking up from its top and bottom surfaces. An especially large tower rose from its center; a docking tower perhaps, though there was no evidence that it was being used at the moment. A tether stretched down toward the surface of the moon. They had a space elevator.

Two panels slid open on the edge of the station, and two small spheres emerged from each. Four more came around from behind the station, and the eight spheres assumed a defensive position between the station and Grant's fleet.

"Sir, activity on the moon's surface."

"Show me."

A visual of the surface of the moon replaced the space station and zoomed in on an area that was deep in shadow.

"It's hard to see because it's in a shadow," the navigator said. "I'll enhance it."

The shadow became grayish-yellow and several structures became visible. Now Grant could make out tractor-like rigs leaving one of the structures that made up the above-ground part of the alien base.

"Mobile missile batteries?" Grant asked.

"That would be my guess," his first officer said. "The spheres surrounding the spaces station are probably an anti-missile defense system."

"Open a link to the *Jackson*."

One of the screens in front of him lit up with an image of the commander of the *Thomas J. Jackson*.

"Looks like they are ready for us," Zachary Vance said. "So far it looks like a defensive posture."

"I agree," Grant said. "But I wouldn't discount offensive measures as well."

"No," Vance chuckled. "We're in for a fight for sure."

"We lost contact with the *Carolina*."

"We did?"

"Lost telemetry too. Right after they reported the destruction of the alien base on Ganymede."

Vance rubbed his chin with his thumb and index finger. "Several possible explanations: jamming, equipment failure, out of line-of-sight."

"Sure. But it doesn't make any difference as far as our mission is concerned. The *Carolina* has no role to play in this battle." He hated how callous he sounded.

"What are your orders, John?"

"I see nothing that would dictate a change from the original battle plan, so for now, we'll stick with that. Sound battle stations and we'll get this show on the road."

He tried to sound confident, but he had no illusions that they would escape this battle without casualties. Truth be told, he doubted any of them would live to tell the story. He looked toward his first officer and gave him a nod.

"Battle stations! Battle Stations!" the first officer said into the ship-wide com. "All hands to your stations. Prepare for combat."

Grant could hear the same orders from the bridge of the *Jackson*. The two destroyers were about to unleash the fury of hell itself on the alien interlopers.

"Target the space station. Conventional missiles. Launch on my command." He rolled his shoulders to release some tension, took a deep breath, let it out, and said, "Fire missile one."

"Fire missile one," the XO said.

"Firing missile one," the weapons officer said. The ship vibrated as an angel of death left it and accelerated toward its target. "Missile one away."

"Time to target?"

"Six minutes," the weapons officer said.

"Fire missile two," Grant said.

"Firing missile two." Again, the ship vibrated as the missile blasted out of its launch tube. "Missile two away."

"The *Jackson* has launched its first missile," the XO said. "And its second."

Now they waited. Though they had nuclear-armed missiles, they were using conventional missiles. They did not want to destroy the station. They wanted to disable so they could board and look for the tech. The enemy would have a missile defense capability, but only one of his missiles needed to get through.

The graphical representation showed the locations of his ships, the space station, and the four missiles. He glanced around the bridge. Everybody was watching the missiles creep toward the space station. In war—any war—the waiting was the hard part. Either their attack would be successful or their attack would fail. He had no control over the outcome now, but with each minute that passed, he felt a little more confident. The missiles had been accelerating all the way, and the difference was visible on the display. The closer they got, the faster they moved, and the more difficult they would be to intercept.

After what seemed like an eternity, the weapons officer said, "Thirty seconds."

More time passed. The aliens' window of opportunity was closing fast.

"Ten seconds."

The first missile disappeared from the graphical display. Then the second, and the third, and the fourth.

"What happened?"

The weapons officer was busy at his station. "I don't know," he said. Then, "Holy shit."

"Talk to me."

"Lasers. They took them out with lasers."

"Show me."

"This is the last twenty seconds," he said. The image on the visual side of the main monitor adjusted, giving them a close-up view of a missile racing toward the space station, which was getting larger by the second.

"This is the first missile as seen from the second missile," he said.

The missile flared in a burst of white light and vanished. He replayed it in slow motion, and Grant could see the moment the missile was struck. Its midsection vanished in a cloud of vapor, followed by an explosion that obliterated the missile.

"A laser, you say?"

"Only thing I can think of that would vaporize the missile's superstructure like that. The explosion that followed was the missile's fuel tank exploding."

A long silence filled the bridge. Grant glanced toward the screen showing the bridge of the *Jackson*. He imagined the astonished expression on Vance's face was a mirror image of his own.

He heard the *Jackson's* weapons officer say, "It came from one of the spheres. It fired four times in three and a half seconds . . . one, two, three, four . . . and the missiles were gone. Very fast targeting. Very accurate. Very impressive."

Her last words struck Grant as singularly inappropriate given the situation, but he had to admit that he too was impressed. They knew the aliens had advanced technology. They just didn't know what form it would take. Now they knew.

Vance said, "We might be able to overwhelm them with sheer numbers of missiles. Only one has to get through to do the job."

Grant looked at his own weapons officer who shook his head and said, "Even if we could fire all our missiles at once, which we can't, I doubt any would get through. Their fire control computers are too fast and too accurate. They only used one sphere. They have eight of them. We should assume they are interlinked so they don't all go after the same targets."

Grant said, "Coms, send a message to Earth notifying them that attack plan Alpha One failed, and we are executing Alpha Two."

He looked at Vance on his monitor. "Rail gun status?"

Vance looked to one side and then back. "Charged and ready to fire."

He looked at his own weapons officer. "Charged and ready," the officer said.

"Initiate attack plan Alpha 2 on my command."

Each destroyer carried two rail guns. Each rail gun used a massive electromagnetic pulse to launch a projectile at high velocity and depended on its kinetic energy to destroy whatever it hit. Unlike a missile, which had to accelerate a relatively heavy payload to its maximum velocity, which wasn't particularly high, a rail gun got its enormous velocity from the initial launch and, in the absence of friction in space, would not lose any of that velocity as it traveled. In theory, it would continue in a straight line at its original velocity until it ran into something. The projectile also had the advantage of being small, making it a difficult target to hit. And unlike the six minutes it took the missiles to cover the distance between them and the space station, a rail gun projectile would reach its target in under a minute. He had never heard of one being intercepted.

"Let's see them shoot down one of these puppies," he said. "Weapons, fire."

An audible thump accompanied the simultaneous firing of the two rail guns. The *Jackson* fired a second or two later.

Then they waited.

"Forty seconds," the weapons officer said.

On the graphical display, the projectiles were closing on their target fast.

"Thirty seconds . . . Twenty seconds."

A brilliant flash of light appeared on the real-time display. All four projectiles vanished from the graphical display.

Grant's chest tightened. "Talk to me."

The weapons officer looked up. "They're gone."

"What's gone?"

"The projectiles, sir. They're gone."

"How?"

"That flash? As near as I can tell, instead of targeting each projectile, they fired a single widespread laser. It would be like running into an invisible wall of energy. It vaporized the projectiles when they ran into it."

"Missile launch detected," the tactical officer said. "From the surface."

Grant saw it on the graphical display. "It's moving fast," he said.

There was a pause before the tactical officer replied. "*Very* fast, sir. Even climbing out of Europa's gravity well, its velocity is at least five times that of our missiles."

"Target?"

"Coming right at us."

"Just the one missile?"

"Just the one missile, sir."

That was when Captain John Hirram Grant knew they had lost. Maybe if they had a dozen ships like the *Robert E. Lee,* they could overwhelm the aliens' defenses with sheer numbers. But somehow he doubted they would prevail even then. They were simply outclassed by the aliens' superior technology.

He turned to Vance's image on his monitor. "Commander Vance, break off and make a run for it. I'll try to provide cover."

He held up a hand before Vance could voice an objection. "That's an order, Zack."

Vance's face fell, but he nodded and turned to his bridge crew to give the order.

There was little room for maneuvering in orbit. The forces of gravity and the laws of orbital mechanics made anything other than minor course corrections impractical in terms of fuel consumption. But that didn't mean there was nothing they could do.

Grant turned to his XO. "Set a collision course for the space station and execute a hard burn."

His XO gave him a questioning look and then spoke into the ship's intercom. "All crew prepare for emergency hard burn. I repeat, prepare for immediate emergency hard burn." He turned to the helm officer. "Helm, set collision course. Maximum thrust."

The roar of the *Robert E. Lee's* powerful main thrusters kicked in, reverberating through the ship. The acceleration slammed Grant into his chair as the ship began moving. He hoped that would raise his threat value and cause the aliens to focus on his ship instead of the *Jackson*, which was moving into a higher orbit.

"Open a channel to the *Lewis B. Puller*."

A moment later, the captain of the *Puller* appeared on one of his monitors. "Looks like we're outgunned," he said. "What are your orders, sir?"

"I have ordered the *Jackson* to run. I'm ordering you to do the same, Sam. Good luck."

He watched the lieutenant give the order and then turned his attention back to the battle. There was nothing more he could do for the other two ships.

"Thirty seconds to missile impact," the tactical officer said calmly.

"Activate PDCs," the XO said.

They felt more than heard the point defense cannons' rapid fire as they tried to shoot down the incoming missile. The *Jackson* was doing the same. Despite firing a thousand rounds between them, they failed to hit the missile as it passed between them in the blink of an eye. It was just too fast.

"Missed us," said the XO.

"No sir," said tactical. "We weren't the target. It's going for the troop carrier."

Grant watched in horror as the blip representing the missile on the graphical display board closed with the blip representing the *Lewis B. Puller*, which was trailing them at a considerable distance. The two blips converged and disappeared from the screen.

"Another launch, sir," the tactical officer said. "Two missiles."

Grant didn't have to ask what they were targeting. This was what must have happened to the *Carolina* at Ganymede. It galled him that they had inflicted no damage whatsoever on the enemy. They were being swatted away like flies. They had rolled the dice and lost.

Zachary Vance's voice interrupted his thoughts. "It has been an honor to serve with you, sir."

Grant gazed at his friend for a moment, then straightened and saluted. "The honor has been mine, Commander."

12

Twenty years before the end of the world

Holly woke with a start. Memories were waiting for her: the earthquake; the floor jerking one way, then another; the ear-piercing screech of metal on metal; the low, mournful wail. The ceiling had collapsed, raining rocks and ice down on her, crushing her legs, crushing her arms, crushing her chest, crushing her head. She *heard* her bones breaking, *felt* them breaking. Then came the pain, like fire rushing through her body, consuming everything. Something had rammed into her chest, and she couldn't catch her breath. She choked on the blood filling her mouth. Then, in a moment of perfect clar-ity, she knew she was dying. A sadness swept over her like a wave and carried her into the waiting darkness.

But she wasn't dead. Her heart was thumping in her ears. Her chest rose and fell as she breathed. In and out. In and out. Such a wonderful thing, the simple act of breathing.

She opened her eyes. The ceiling above her glowed with

soft bluish-white light that seemed to emanate from everywhere and nowhere, providing just enough illumination to
see by. She wiggled her toes. They were under something;
something lightweight, like a sheet. Her gaze followed the
ceiling to a wall and a low dresser at the foot of the bed. A
yellowish-green sheet covered her; an ugly vomit yellow, but
she could live with that as long as it meant she was alive. She
shifted her body a little and discovered that the bed was both
firm and soft. She wiggled her toes again. The sheet felt like
satin but didn't try to slide off onto the floor like every satin
sheet she had ever owned. Well, she had never owned satin
sheets, but Theo had.

The light from the ceiling brightened when she sat up. She
looked around the room. A door on her left stood ajar,
revealing a bathroom; then a closet with a mirrored sliding
door; and in the corner, another door, this one closed. Then
the dresser and a corner desk with a tall, narrow vase
displaying a single white rose. The room could have been any
mid-range hotel room in New Amsterdam. Except for the
large painting that dominated the wall to her right.

Two meters long and a meter high, it was a seascape; the
most bizarre seascape she had ever seen. In the foreground
was a rocky shoreline curving out and away on both sides,
forming a bay with gentle waves rolling in. No plants or
seaweed or any other signs of life were in evidence. Rugged
hills rose in the red-hazed distance in both directions, equally
devoid of life. The sea stretched toward a too-near horizon
under a red sky streaked with scudding reddish-brown
clouds caught in mid-flight by the artist's brush. A moon with
an achingly beautiful set of rings hung just above the horizon.
The waves rolled lazily up the rocky beach and just as lazily
back out, oddly sluggish.

Whoa! The waves really were moving! So were the clouds.
It wasn't a painting. It was a vid of some place that shouldn't

exist. She slipped out of bed and took a step toward the vidscreen, then had to put her hand on it to keep from falling because the gravity was lower than she had expected. Was she still on Ganymede?

She looked at the vid again. The air was denser than she had at first thought, like rust-colored fog. Standing closer had brought more of the rocky beach into view. She took a step back and sat on the bed, staring at the scene, her mind balking at the inescapable conclusion: The vid wasn't a vid. It was a window. A window looking out on an unearthly seascape. The ringed moon in the sky wasn't a moon at all. It was the planet Saturn, which meant she was on one of Saturn's moons, and there was only one moon in the solar system with an appreciable atmosphere.

She was on Titan.

It was . . . she couldn't find the words. A tiny disk in the red sky peered through a break in the clouds; another of Saturn's moons, though she did not know which one. Saturn had a lot of them. Searching the sky, she found two more. She was seeing with her own eyes something no human had ever seen before. Tears pooled in her eyes.

The Fragment had brought her here—of that she had no doubt—and had repaired her broken body and built this room for her. An unexpected giggle burbled up. He had built a house on Titan for her. It was wonderful; fairy tale wonderful; wonderful in the truest sense of the word, full of wonder.

She walked around the bed to the mirror on the closet door and examined herself. She ran her hands over her breasts, across her tummy, down her hips and thighs. There were no scars. Not even the scar on her arm from an altercation with an electric carving knife one Thanksgiving with her brother's family. No moles, none of those odd little bumps and tags you inevitably picked up with age. Even the birthmark on her left thigh was gone.

In the top dresser drawer, she found a supply of panties,

bras, and socks. She ignored the lacy black panties and the racy red thong, which the Fragment must have thought she would like, and chose a practical light blue pair. They fit perfectly. As did the matching bra. In fact, the bra might have been the most comfortable one she had ever worn. Bra makers on Earth, who she suspected were all men, could learn a thing or two from the Fragment. On the dresser sat a small box containing a variety of makeup items, which she ignored. Who was she going to impress on Titan?

In the other drawer, she found two pairs of jeans, and a pair of nice looking slacks. She went for the slacks which, of course, fit perfectly. In the closet hung a full-length dress, two skirts, several blouses, two T-shirts, and, on the floor, several pairs of shoes. She selected a light blue blouse and black pumps with one inch heels.

She stood in front of the mirror and liked what she saw. "Not bad for a thirty-two-year-old woman whose last memory was of being crushed to death deep beneath the surface of one of Jupiter's moons."

How long had she been asleep? Long enough to travel from Ganymede to Titan, which was a long way, Saturn's orbit being twice as far out as Jupiter's. She had no idea what kind of propulsion technology the Fragment had, but the *Asimov* would have taken another five years to travel that far, ten if Saturn and Jupiter were on opposite sides of the sun from each other.

Was she the only survivor? The closed door in the corner presented another one of those extraordinarily ordinary looking door knobs. She stepped out into a nondescript corridor curving away in both directions.

The door clicked shut behind her, making her jump. She opened it and peeked in, just to reassure herself that the room was still there. It was silly, but it made her feel better. Turning to the left, she immediately came to an archway opening into a circular room. It was smaller than the room on Ganymede, but otherwise looked the same: the same burgundy carpet with blue swirls; the same brick fireplace; the same coffee table, though smaller and with only two chairs. A hollowness formed in her chest as she considered the implications of that.

The Fragment—or rather his avatar—sat in one of the chairs with one leg casually crossed over the other. He was reading a book. It looked like a real book, which it couldn't be. Or maybe it could. Who knew? In any case, the Fragment could probably access any information he wanted in an instant without resorting to anything so primitive as dead tree technology. It was an archaic affectation for her benefit, part of the human-alien interface he had created for her.

He placed the book on the table and stood. "Holly, you look well. Can I interest you in a cup of tea?"

"Yes, please."

He disappeared into the kitchen and returned a few minutes later with a tray holding two cups of tea, a sugar bowl, and a small pitcher of milk. They settled into their chairs with their cups of tea.

"Am I the only survivor?" she asked.

"I could not save the others," he said. "I am sorry."

A tear formed in one eye and rolled down her cheek. She hadn't known them all that well; only a few weeks before the long sleep and a single day after. But they had shared the greatest adventure humans had ever embarked on, and that was enough to make them family. Now they were gone, and she was alone.

"What happened?"

"The *Asimov* was carrying a small thermonuclear device. Major Clark took control of—"

"A what?"

"A thermonuclear device. A bomb."

"That's not possible. How could someone smuggle a nuclear bomb onto the *Asimov* with no one noticing?"

"It appears not everyone on your world is pleased with

the presence of aliens in your solar system and they took advantage of your mission to express their displeasure."

She set her cup down. It did not surprise her that there were people who might want to do something like this, but it would require people on the inside, people high up in the space programs. They had to have gotten a nuclear bomb from somewhere, and somehow gotten it onboard the *Asimov* undetected. Neither of those was trivial.

And Benny was part of it? She pictured him at the training center's food court, laughing at something Gina said. He was like a kid who never grew up, a trait both endearing and irritating. But a suicide bomber? She couldn't find a place for that in her mental image of him.

"You're sure it was Benny."

"You saw Dr. Patil and Dr. Wang trying to escape the *Asimov*. That left only Major Clark on the ship when it pulled away from the station, resulting in their deaths."

She shuddered. Her mind replayed the image of Kari trying desperately to get Li into the space station airlock, the docking bridge tearing away, Kari being sucked out of the airlock, her face frozen in terror, Wang Li's body tumbling head-over-heals after her. Those images would follow her around for the rest of her life.

The Fragment must have sensed she was struggling to process this and waited a few moments before continuing.

"When I realized Major Clark had put the *Asimov* in a descending orbit that would put it a hundred meters above the surface when it was over the mining base again, I ordered the three of you into an elevator that carried us deeper into the planet. Do you remember that part?"

Her memory of it was fragmentary, like a partially assembled jigsaw puzzle, but it was there. She nodded.

He continued. "When the nuclear device detonated, it vaporized a section of the space elevator's tether, and sent the space station flying off into space. The force of the blast traveled down the main shaft into the moon's interior and obliterated my mining operation. Drones recovered the space station and towed it to another moon until I decided what to do with it. Had Major Clark waited half a minute longer, I could have rescued Dr. Patil and Dr. Wang from the station."

Half a minute, just thirty seconds, and Kari and Li would still be alive. But Benny hadn't waited.

"The section of the base we were in collapsed. Dr. Walker was decapitated and died instantly. Colonel Fedorov's injuries, though not as dramatic as Dr. Walker's, were beyond my ability to repair in that setting. You suffered extensive damage too, but I was able to stabilize you and induce a temporary state of stasis until I could bring in a ship capable of making the journey to Titan. I already had—"

Holly held up a hand to stop him. She remembered most of what he described. At least the conscious parts. She closed her eyes and tried to bring the last few minutes of it into focus.

"You threw yourself over me," she said. "To protect me."

"Though not indestructible, this body is quite durable."

"Why not Tolya?"

He paused, as though he was thinking about how to respond. "I realized I could try to save one of you, but not both. I chose you."

He had not really answered the question, and she had the impression he was holding something back. Maybe he employed some kind of algorithm that determined she had a higher likelihood of surviving than Tolya. Or maybe he flipped a coin, and it was her lucky day.

"How long have I been asleep?"

"Five hundred ninety-six of your days."

"A year and a half."

"A little more than that, but yes."

If he was to be believed, he possessed propulsion technology capable of traveling from Jupiter to Saturn in a year-

and-a-half. Or less, depending on how long she was asleep after they reached Titan. That was astonishing, but she had experienced so many astonishing things in the last twenty-four hours—at least from her point of view—that she had run out of astonishment and had to make do with merely being amazed. She finished her tea and walked over to the fireplace. It burned brightly and smelled wonderful; just another perfectly ordinary piece of amazing alien technology. She turned to face him.

"You went to considerable trouble to rescue me from an attack aimed at you by others of my race. Why?"

"What you call the Death Bringer. Is that not why you sought me out?"

"Our mission was to establish contact with you," she said, "in hopes you can help us survive the Death Bringer. Can you?"

"Please sit and let me tell you a story," he said. He refilled both their cups and stirred in her usual amount of milk and sugar for her.

"I discovered your species 11,734 years ago," he began. "That was near—"

"Wait," she said, holding up a hand. "You discovered us 11,734 years ago?"

"Yes."

"Earth years?"

"I am older than I look."

He maintained a straight face for a moment and then smiled. Holly couldn't help but smile back. His humor might be a simulacrum, but it was an awfully good one.

"That was near the end of your world's last ice age. Your ancestors were well on their way toward establishing themselves as the dominant species on the planet, having outcompeted most other hominids. It was obvious you had the potential to become an advanced species. You intrigued me, and I have been observing you ever since."

He paused, which was a good thing because she was still trying to wrap her mind around this revelation. Up to this point, she had thought of him as an alien who happened upon the human race and decided to introduce himself. This was true enough, but it turns out he had allowed twelve thousand years to pass before revealing himself. What was she supposed to make of that?

"How old *are* you?"

"The question is not as easy to answer as you might think. I am what one of your speculative writers once called an 'outside context problem,' by which he meant something that exists in a context entirely outside your own, leaving few if any common points of reference by which to orient yourself to it. As a result, it defies any rational explanation."

She paraphrased something he had said earlier: "I lack the conceptional framework with which to understand something like you."

"As to my age, let's just say I was alive when your planet was forming out of the accretion disk of a recently born star. My initial—"

"Wait," she said, holding up her hand again. He was claiming to be at least four and a half billion years old. On that scale, the entire history of her species was barely the blink of an eye.

"Are you immortal?"

"No, just long lived."

So not immortal, but maybe close enough to be a distinction without a difference. His life span was on the scale of the life spans of stars. How could a being live that long? What would it be like to live that long? How did he avoid being bored out of his gourd? The whole thing was preposterous, although she herself had once written: Set aside your preconceived notions about what an alien might or might not be like. It won't be like anything you can imagine. Ha! *That* Holly Burton had no idea.

"Okay," she said. "I do not know whether to believe you, but please continue."

He smiled apologetically; at least, she would interpret it as apologetic if it appeared on another human being's face, which was presumably what he intended, since the avatar was a human/alien interface. Whether he experienced anything remotely resembling human emotions was a different question, one to which she suspected she would never have a satisfactory answer.

He continued. "My initial assessment of your species proved correct. You have dominated your planet and now stand at the edge of space travel. You have avoided destroying yourselves with thermonuclear weapons, though that possibility still exists among the many possible but as yet undetermined futures that lie ahead of you. You are in the grip of a global environmental catastrophe brought on by the damage you have done to your world, which might or might not prove survivable. Now you face a planet killer, which is not survivable. You are familiar with the Fermi Paradox?"

The abrupt change in direction threw her. He was certainly taking a roundabout way to tell her whether he could save them from the Death Bringer.

"I am familiar with it," she said. "Given the magnitude of the known universe in both space and time, it seems unlikely that ours is the only technologically advanced species. In fact, there should be lots of them out there. The Fermi Paradox asks: Where are they? Why haven't we detected them?"

"They are indeed out there," he said. "The nearest one is only 237 light-years away; a hop, skip, and a jump on a galactic scale. Unfortunately, their civilization died out some 65 million years ago, around the time the age of the dinosaurs on your world came to an end, making room for the explosion of mammalian life that followed. That civilization called itself the Lormna. At a spatial distance of 237 light-years and a temporal distance of 60 million years, you and they are practically next-door neighbors, though you will never meet. In my journeys, I have discovered the remnants of 157 advanced civilizations, three of which survived long enough to achieve space flight."

That was interesting. One hundred and fifty-seven alien races, only three of which developed the technology to leave their home world and venture into space, and even they eventually perished. Why was that? Were all sentient species doomed to extinction by one means or other?

He continued his story. "Many civilizations have come before you; many will come after; some are emerging as we speak. When set against the backdrop of the entire history of your space-time continuum, your civilization has been here barely any time at all, and will disappear just as soon.

"This, then, is the answer to your Fermi Paradox: intelligent life is rare, and when it does appear, it is fragile. There are many ways for it to perish. The longest-surviving civilization I have found lasted some 17,000 years. Internecine warfare brought them down, and they never recovered. Another civilization created a particularly virulent bioweapon that got out of control and wiped them out. Another polluted their planet so badly it turned into a green-house world not unlike your neighbor Venus. External catastrophes cut others short: brief but deadly flares in their sun's output, planet killing asteroids, things like that. Which brings us to the Death Bringer."

Finally. This was the only question that mattered as far as the *Asimov's* mission was concerned: Could he save her world? And if he could, would he?

"The Death Bringer," he said, "is not an asteroid, as some of your astronomers think, or even a rogue planet, as others think. It is a failed star, a brown dwarf that wasn't big enough to ignite its core and become a full-fledged star like your sun. It is about the size of Jupiter, but sixty-five times more massive, and happened to pass close enough to your sun to be pulled into its gravity well, though it is moving too fast for your sun to capture it, so it will pass through your solar system in an arcing orbit, swing around your sun, and leave on a new vector. As it passes, it will throw Mars out of the solar system, obliterate Venus, toss Earth into the Sun, and take Mercury with it when it leaves."

Her mind slipped mental gears as she tried to grasp this revelation. The inner planets gone? All of them? That just couldn't be true. But, of course, it *could* be true, and according to the Fragment, it *was* true. It took her several seconds to formulate the obvious question.

"Can't you stop it? Destroy it or deflect it or something?"

"I cannot. Your world is doomed, and there is nothing anybody can do about it."

Despite the preparation he had laid down leading up to this, it hit her with an almost physical force. Their mission had been for nothing. Humanity was doomed to disappear from the stage of history; a breath, a sigh, a brief cry in the night, 'We were here.' Then nothing.

She wanted to weep; to weep for Earth; to weep for all that might have been; to weep for all the unborn generations that would never be. But all she found inside herself was an emptiness, a numbness, a hopelessness that could not even bring forth tears. The room was silent, except for the crackling of the fire in the fireplace.

She finally asked, "Why am I here? Why did you bother saving me? If my people are going to die, take me back to Earth so I can die with them."

He brought his hands together so that the fingertips of one touched the fingertips of the other, as if in prayer.

"I cannot save your world. But it might be possible to save a remnant of your people; enough to rebuild human civilization somewhere else. I would like very much to see your species survive, if only to see what it becomes."

He paused.

"So, Holly Burton, do you want to save the human species?"

Her heart caught in her throat. "Y-yes."

"It will require you to become a very different person than you are now."

"I don't care. Whatever it takes, I'll do it."

13

Eighteen years before the end of the world

Cheung Tung glared at the offending vidscreen and swiped a hand over the virtual control board to clear yet another lost game of Min Tsa. It was one of those solitaire games that was easy to learn but infuriatingly difficult to master. The clock told him that two hours had passed since the *Irtuks* had departed with two scientists for the *Roatunga Science Station* at the Earth-Moon L4 point. There were no other ships in or out of *Tiangong Station* on this shift. Another slow night on the Earth's busiest space station. But regulations required two operators on duty at all times. At least they had gravity now that the command center had been moved from the hub to the rings.

He looked over at Song Guan-yin. "What are you watching?"

She looked up from her tablet. "*Hong Kong World.*"

"Really?"

"Unlike you, I try to keep up on national and foreign

affairs." She was ribbing him. She was as likely to pass the time playing Min Tsa as he was. There had been a time when traffic passing through *Tiangong Station* was heavy enough that they didn't have time for games.

"Anything interesting?"

"Another piece by Zhou Jinjing demanding that the Lunar mining base be shut down."

"Well, it is an expensive endeavor and nobody will ever make any money off it."

"Think they'll shut down *Tiangong*?"

"Eventually."

She raised her hands over her head and stretched. "Some people think getting off the planet is our best chance for survival as a species."

Tung snorted. "The Great Collapse put an end to that kind of thinking. Nobody can afford space programs anymore. Except maybe the CRA, and their space program focuses on military and scientific interests."

"What's that on your board?" She asked.

He looked at the blinking blue light. "Huh. When is the last time we had an unscheduled arrival?"

"Uh . . . like never? Want me to take it."

"Nah, I've got it." He brought the hailing channel up, looked at Guan-yin, and put it on the main viewer.

The image of a woman appeared, seated in a dark green, wing-backed chair that could have come from his grandmother's house. She looked to be around thirty, probably of northern European extraction, with dark blonde hair cascading over her shoulders. She wore a white blouse and white skirt.

But what stood out most about her was the web of glowing fiber-optic cables radiating away from her in all directions. That, and the neural cap perched on her head. She was directly linked with her ship. He had heard of such technology but as far as he knew, it was still theoretical.

"Spaceship *Gabriel's Fire* calling *Tiangong Station*," she said. "Repeat, spaceship *Gabriel's Fire* calling *Tiangong Station*." She spoke Mandarin better than a lot of native speakers he knew.

"I'll check the registry," Guan-yin said.

Tung waited a moment, activated his mic, and said in English, "*Gabriel's Fire*, this is *Tiangong Station*."

He glanced toward Guan-yin, who shook her head.

"We do not have a record of a ship by that name. Could you provide a registry number, please?"

The woman on the screen smiled and said in English, "I'm afraid I do not have a registry number for you. *Gabriel's Fire* is not from Earth."

Tung looked at Guan-yin, who stared back with a 'what the hell?' expression. Guan-yin recovered her composure first. "I'll wake the commander."

"*Gabriel's Fire*," Tung said. "Please stand by."

"Of course," the woman said. "I imagine you need to wake someone up about now."

———

Colonel Zhang Feng examined himself in the mirror and tugged at one of the several medals on his uniform to get it lined up with the rest. He was a veteran of six wars and had seen more than his share of death and ruin, mostly to no good end, as far as he could tell. Politicians declared wars, people died, things went back to the way they were, and little changed. He had frown lines and gray hairs to show for his service; and the medals, of course, which he planned to put in a box and never look at again. *Tiangong Station* would be his last posting, after which he would retire and spend time with his children, grandchildren and, if fortune smiled on him, great-grandchildren.

He replayed in his mind the message from General Hu. He was to prepare for the arrival of a VIP. The message did not say who the VIP might be or when he might arrive, but Hu's message suggested it would be soon and made it clear that this person was to be received with utmost honor and respect, and assisted in every way possible. "The honor of the People's Republic is at stake," Hu said.

Feng closed his eyes and let out a sigh. When he was a younger man, he would have seen this as an opportunity, but at sixty-three years of age, he could only view it as a danger; an opportunity to mess something up. Danger and opportunity: always two sides of the same coin. Such was life.

The comm unit on his wrist vibrated. He tapped it.

"Colonel, this is Second Lieutenant Song Guan-yin in the command center. We have been hailed by an unscheduled vessel calling itself *Gabriel's Fire*. We have no record of a ship by that name. The pilot claims she has no registry number because the spaceship is not from Earth."

"A spaceship, Lieutenant? Or a spaceplane?"

"She claims it is a spaceship, sir."

"I will be there shortly. In the meantime, you are to treat this visitor with utmost honor and respect."

So this was the VIP General Hu had referred to. But in a spaceship not from Earth? As far as he knew, there were no space docks anywhere else in the solar system. But that was someone else's problem. His job was to welcome this VIP with honor and respect, lend whatever help he could, and hope nothing went wrong.

Ten minutes later, he strode into the command center. First Lieutenant Cheung Tung and Second Lieutenant Song Guan-yin were on station. The image of the pilot of the mystery spaceship was still on the big viewer. He took in the woman and the neural network she was plugged into.

"I have command," he said.

"You have command, sir," Tung replied.

"Show me the ship."

"We are still trying to locate it, sir," Chueng said. "It is coming up behind us to match orbit, but we can't get an exact fix on it. Wait ... got it. The radar return is so faint I would not have noticed it if I wasn't looking for it."

"Put it on the vidscreen."

Feng stared at the image of a spaceship unlike any he had ever seen. It was basically a spindle-and-wheel design, the same design used for *Tiangong*. The wheel, located near the forward end of the ship, had a diameter somewhat less than half the length of the spindle. It was not rotating, which meant no gravity.

Fore and aft of the wheel were wide hexagonal sections wrapped like collars around the spindle, with the forward sections extending only a short distance in front of the ring and the aft sections extending half the distance to the end of the ship, where the main thrusters were located. At the point where the hexagonal sections aft of the wheel ended, a half dozen silvery arches emerged from the spindle, curving out and then back toward the thruster cones. It reminded him of a squid's tentacles trailing behind it, though these were rigid. If he had to guess, he would say they had something to do with the ship's propulsion system, but he couldn't imagine what.

The ship filled most of the view but was nearly invisible against the background of space; more an absence than a presence.

"Reduce magnification to normal." He wanted to get a sense of its actual size.

"This *is* normal magnification, sir."

That meant it was alarmingly close to the station, or alarmingly large, or both.

"Are you sure?"

"Yes, sir."

"Range?"

"Two thousand meters. It appears to be holding position relative to us."

It was two kilometers away and still filled most of the screen.

"How big *is* it?"

Chueng hesitated. "According to my instruments, it is five hundred meters long, and the ring is two hundred meters across."

Half a kilometer long. Feng's heart rate picked up. The behemoth was bigger than his space station.

"How did it get so close without setting off proximity alarms?"

"I can answer that," Lieutenant Song said. "Apart from presenting an extraordinarily small radar profile, it is using some kind of signal-absorbing technology. I have been pinging it across a range of frequencies and nothing is coming back. I think the only reason we can detect it at all is because they want us to."

"Stop scanning immediately," he said. "Your orders were to treat our visitor with respect."

"Yes, sir." Her face darkened.

He brought the image of the ship's pilot back up and studied her face. She was definitely of northern European extraction. She was in her late twenties or early thirties, with shoulder-length dark blonde hair. He activated video from his side so she could see him as well.

"*Gabriel's Fire*, I am Colonel Xhang Feng, commander of *Tiangong Station*. With whom do I have the honor of speaking?"

A pleasant-sounding alto voice came back. "Colonel Xhang, I am Doctor Holly Burton, formerly of the spaceship *Asimov*."

Cheung and Song exchanged looks. Feng stared at the viewer, at a loss for words. Lieutenant Song brought up an image on a secondary viewer. It was the crew of the *Asimov* before they left Earth. She zoomed in on Holly Burton. He looked back and forth between the two. It was the same woman. He rubbed his chin with his thumb and index finger. So this was General Hu's VIP. He cleared his throat.

"Doctor Burton. On behalf of the People's Republic of China, it is my honor to welcome you to *Tiangong Station*. My orders are to provide any assistance you require. How may I be of service?"

Chueng and Song exchanged another look.

"Thank you for your welcome and your hospitality, Colonel. I require no assistance at this time. I merely wanted to inform you I am going to park *Gabriel's Fire* two kilometers away from *Tiangong Station* while I am on Earth. I assure you it poses no threat to your station."

He was not happy with the colossal ship parked so close to his station, but his orders were clear.

"Certainly. And thank you for the notification." He paused. "I wonder if you can make your ship more visible so incoming and outgoing ships can avoid it?"

"Oh. Of course."

The spaceship abruptly lit up as though someone had turned on all the lights in a city skyscraper at once. One of their monitors began pinging its location.

"Will that be sufficient?" she asked.

"Indeed. Thank you."

"One other thing," the woman said. "*Gabriel's Fire* is a warship. It is under the control of an advanced AI when I am not on board and will defend itself if the AI believes it is being threatened. I advise you to warn approaching ships to keep their distance."

A warship. The biggest spaceship he had ever seen was parked two kilometers from his station, and it was a warship. Doctor Burton's assurances notwithstanding, he was definitely not happy with the arrangement. But there was nothing he could do about it.

"Understood. Do you require the use of a spaceplane for your journey to Earth's surface?"

"A kind offer, Colonel, but *Gabriel's Fire* carries its own spaceplane."

"Would you care to visit the station? It would be my honor to share a meal with you."

"Ah . . . well, no. I am on something of a tight schedule. But thank you for the offer. Perhaps another time?"

"Of course," he said. "If there is any way I can be of assistance in the future, do not hesitate to call on me. I believe I speak for the People's Republic of China in this matter."

"Thank you, Colonel Xhang. Until next time." She ended the call.

Cheung and Song were both grinning at him. He couldn't help but grin back. This would be one hell of a story to tell his grandchildren.

14

Holly took in a deep breath and let it out again. Her heart was pounding and her hands were trembling. She had somehow managed to look and sound like she knew what she was doing, and as much as she would have liked a proper meal made by human hands, she wasn't sure she could maintain the illusion of self-confidence all the way through a dinner with Colonel Xhang. Besides, she really was on a tight schedule.

"An auspicious beginning," the ship's AI said.

She said, "The PRC does seem to be taking a positive position toward our arrival, but I doubt we will meet with the same response from all the alliances."

"Nonetheless, you acquitted yourself well."

"You mean I faked it pretty well."

She understood impostor syndrome; had lived with it most of her adult life. But this Emissary thing took it to a whole new level. She really *was* an impostor; pretending to be someone she was not and never could be. He should have sent an avatar instead. Maybe even one that looked like her.

A lethargy settled over her as the adrenaline rush wore off.

"Would you like me to adjust your body chemistry?" The ship asked.

She sighed. "I suppose so."

She could do it herself. She had some control over her nanites. Or she could do some deep breathing exercises and eventually get the same result. But it was easier to let the ship do it. A few moments later, the trembling stopped, the lethargy abated, and she felt energized, ready to take on the world.

"Disengage neural net," she said.

The flowing lines disappeared, and the neural cap lifted off her head. There was always a momentary feeling of emptiness when she disconnected from the ship, as though she had lost one of her senses.

She released the harness that secured her in the chair, and launched herself across the common area, which was modeled after the main room of the habitat on Titan.

"Prep *Eos* for departure," she said.

"I wish you would take a few guardians with you," the ship said. "There are people on Earth who perceive you as a threat and will go to any lengths to stop you."

She reached her private quarters. "We've been over this," she said while she changed her clothes. "The whole point of an Emissary is to provide a non-threatening intermediary between the Fragment and the human race. An alien warship in orbit will already have frightened them. What are they going to think if I show up with a cohort of alien killing machines?"

"I *can* make them look and act human, you know."

"Yeah, like that would be easier to explain."

She hung an amulet around her neck. It enabled her to communicate with *Gabriel's Fire* from anywhere and was one of the many places in the universe where the Fragment maintained a presence; albeit a small one. Satisfied with the look, she headed toward the hangar bay.

"Holly," the ship said. "Three spaceships have come over the horizon. Their current trajectory will intercept ours in twenty-two minutes."

She returned to the command chair and plugged back into the neural net. A virtual three-dimensional image of the ships appeared in front of her.

"Zoom in."

Details came into view. Their markings identified them as British. They were definitely spaceships, not spaceplanes. Two had point defense cannons, missile launchers, and rail guns. The third had PDCs, but no offensive weapons that she could see.

"Analysis?"

"Two are attack ships; high speed, high damage. Each is equipped with two PDCs, four missile launchers, two rail guns. The third ship is a troop carrier equipped with PDCs and breaching pods."

The Fragment had told her that some Earth alliances were building space-based military forces, including warships, so it didn't surprise her to see them. But what did they hope to accomplish? Had they learned nothing from Europa?

"Nukes?"

"I detect no signs of thermonuclear devices. We are being hailed."

"All right, then. Let's see what they want. Voice only."

A male voice came over the speaker. "Alien vessel, this is Major Mike Reed commanding the British warships HMS *Churchill*, *Warnock*, and *Sheffield*. You have entered Earth's space and are considered a hostile presence. Stand down and prepare to be boarded."

He had to be kidding. Did they really expect her to let them board her ship? On the other hand, the British were close allies of the CRA, which had shown itself more than willing to initiate hostilities against the aliens.

"Can you rebroadcast this channel worldwide?" she asked the ship.

"What a delightfully devious idea. Give me a moment . . . there, I have taken control of four communications satellites. On your command, I will broadcast this channel live to most of Earth's population in several languages."

"Do it." She unmuted the mic. "Major Reed, this is Dr. Holly Burton, the only survivor of the Jupiter Mission and the Commander of *Gabriel's Fire*. The Council of Enclaves is expecting me, and has been informed that this is a peaceful mission to establish a dialog between the people of Earth and the aliens. It would be foolish in the extreme for you to engage me with hostile intent. I advise you stand down before you do something that might prove disastrous for the people of Earth."

There was no hesitation on the Major's part. "Negative, *Gabriel's Fire*. My orders are to quarantine your vessel until we can ensure it is not carrying anything that would be harmful to the inhabitants of this world. Prepare to be boarded. Do not attempt to leave the—"

Another voice cut in. "HMS *Churchill*, this is Colonel Zhang Feng, commander of *Tiangong Station*. Major, your hostile intentions present a clear and present danger to this station. Beyond that, Dr. Burton is a guest of the People's Republic of China. I strongly advise you to stand down before you commit an act of war against the PRC."

This time there was a pause before the Major replied. "Colonel Zhang, with all due respect, my business is with Dr. Burton and the aliens we believe are on her ship. You would do well to stay out of it."

Holly drew in a deep breath and let it out in a whoosh. The British were in bed with the Americans, and the Americans had some kind of irrational animosity toward aliens; even aliens offering to help avert an extinction level event. But enough to risk war with an alien race *and* the PRC?

"Gabriel, can the station defend itself?" She sometimes referred to the ship as Gabriel. It didn't seem to mind.

The ship replied, "I have accessed the station's security and military systems. Its defensive capabilities are limited to three point defense cannons designed to destroy meteors and man-made junk floating around the planet. They would be minimally effective against missiles, which may have their own countermeasures. The station has no offensive capabilities."

"Recommendations?"

"Try to dissuade them from attacking us. If that fails, and they persist in this hostile course of action, I recommend neutralizing the destroyers' offensive capabilities. There is a small risk that one or both destroyers will be inadvertently destroyed in the process. The troop transport can be ignored until it gets close enough to launch breaching pods; even then, it is unlikely they can breach the ship's hull. However, it may become necessary to destroy the pods at some point."

She waved her hand over the panel in front of her to activate the mic. "Colonel Zhang, do whatever you think necessary to protect your station, but do not concern yourself with my well being. *Gabriel's Fire* is more than capable of defending itself."

She muted the mic and said, "Put some distance between us and the station. Let's try to keep them out of the line of fire."

She unmuted. "Major Reed, I want to be as clear as I can, so let me repeat myself. I am Dr. Holly Burton, formerly of the Jupiter Six. I am here as the aliens' emissary to establish diplomatic relations between Earth and the aliens to support the transfer of advanced technologies that may enable humanity to survive the coming of the Death Bringer.

"In light of your aggressive stance and your threat to board my ship, I must inform you that hostile actions against *Gabriel's Fire* or *Tiangong Station* will be answered with whatever force is required to repel the attack. Do not test me on this."

She muted the mic. "Are we clear of the station?"

"I am moving us into a lower orbit so the station will not be in anybody's line of fire."

"What are the British ships doing?"

"The *Churchill* and *Warnock* are matching our new orbit. They are one hundred twenty kilometers away and closing. The *Sheffield* is moving toward our previous location. I suspect it intends to approach from above and launch breaching pods."

She stared at the viewer for a few seconds. "Go to battle mode."

She imagined what Major Reed was seeing as *Gabriel's Fire* prepared for war. A dozen dish antennae emerged from blisters located here and there on the hull. He wouldn't know what they were, but would guess they had to do with the ship's defenses. Four heavy-looking tubes emerged from the bow, which he would likely identify as rail guns, especially when *Gabriel's Fire* slowly turned to bring them to bear on the approaching ships. Two mean-looking guns emerged from the hull, one on each side, and pivoted toward his ships. Four missile launchers rose from blocks on the hull and pivoted toward his ships as well. A large, stubby gun with a short barrel appeared and turned toward his ships; he would have no idea what to make of it, and she hoped she wouldn't have to show him.

There would be no doubt in the Major's mind that *Gabriel's Fire* was a warship preparing to engage his task force. What would he do?

Nothing happened for several minutes; the destroyers had stopped a hundred kilometers out. The troop carrier had moved to within ten kilometers.

"What are they doing?"

"Exchanging encrypted communications with each other.

They are preparing a coordinated attack. The *Churchill* and *Warnock* will launch a full barrage of missiles and then rail guns, hoping to surprise us and overwhelm our defenses. The *Sheffield* will launch breaching pods."

"You would think it would have occurred to them that deciphering encrypted messages would be trivial for an advanced alien AI."

"One would think. Do I have your permission to respond to their assault per my earlier recommendations?"

"Yes."

Several more uneventful minutes passed. Then the ship said, "They have launched missiles and are preparing to fire rail guns." The image on the main screen showed eight red dots closing fast on her ship.

"The *Churchill* has fired its rail guns. The *Warnock* is preparing to do the same."

She felt the rail guns' projectiles hit the hull.

"Two hits, no significant damage," the AI said.

Gabriel's Fire's tactical lasers flashed and *Churchill's* two rail guns turned into slag. A moment later, the *Warnock's* rail guns suffered the same fate. Then the *Warnock* blew apart, leaving behind an expanding sphere of debris. Holly had hoped to avoid loss of life, but it was not to be. A moment later, *Gabriel* destroyed the *Churchill's* four missile launchers, leaving it with no offensive capabilities.

Four of the incoming missiles vanished from the graphical display, followed shortly by the remaining four. They were no match for *Gabriel's Fire's* point defense lasers. She imagined Major Reed demanding that someone tell him what happened to his missiles and why his rail guns were offline.

The *Sheffield* chose that moment to launch its breaching pods.

Holly unmuted her mic. "Major Reed, I had hoped to avoid loss of life by targeting only your weapons. I regret the loss of the *Warnock*, but such is the way of war. You attacked me, and I responded. I appeal to you to order the *Sheffield* to recall its breaching pods. Otherwise I will have to destroy them."

The ship said, "I am picking up increased communication traffic between the *Sheffield*, the *Churchill,* and a ground station in the Manchester Enclave. The London Enclave is being inundated with calls from other alliances, the general tenor of which is a demand that they cease hostilities."

"Well, I guess we have everybody's attention now."

"The People's Republic of China has put their military forces on high alert and moved their nuclear launch status to the highest level short of actually launching. The European Federation and the Russian Federation appear to be doing the same."

"I hope we haven't started a war. What are the British doing?"

"They have not heightened their military posture, which under the circumstances could be construed as a de-escalation. The same is true of the CRA."

The Christian Republic of America and Britain were probably having a little tête-à-tête about what to do next. She waited. After a while, the *Sheffield* recalled its breaching pods and began moving off.

"The *Churchill* is hailing us."

"Put him on."

"Doctor Burton," Major Reed said. "I have received orders to stand down. With your permission, the *Sheffield* will conduct search and rescue operations in the wreckage of HMS *Warnock*."

The connection dropped.

Holly blew out a breath of air. "Remain in battle mode until the *Churchill* and *Sheffield* have left the area."

The ship said, "Perhaps this has not been as auspicious a beginning as it at first appeared."

When had it learned sarcasm?

15

Adrian Verhoeven was part way through dinner when the house announced a call: "You have an incoming call from Theo Peeters."

Fiona pressed her lips together. He had promised her a quiet, romantic evening at home and had instructed the house to hold calls. Theo was the only person whose calls had override priority. He couldn't have picked a worse moment to call. Well, two hours later might have been worse. His and Fiona's relationship was at that fragile stage where they had to either take it to the next level or end it. He mouthed, "Sorry."

"House: Accept call."

"Adrian."

"Theo."

"Something has come up. I need you at the airport."

Adrian reached for his earpiece. Fiona walked out of the room, abandoning the unfinished dinner.

"Now?"

"I sent a car."

Of course he did. Adrian looked out the window. Shit. Theo's car was already waiting out front.

"Great," he said. "Looking forward to it." He tried to insert just enough sarcasm into his voice to express how not forward to it he was looking without sounding outright insubordinate. It was a wasted effort. Theo had already disconnected.

The Honorable Theo Dreyfus Peeters, Belgium's ambassador to the Council of Enclaves, was not the excitable sort. In fact, he was one of the most unflappable people Adrian had ever met. Whatever had him flapping must be important. Going to the airport meant they were flying somewhere. Adrian hated flying, which was ironic given how much of it he did.

He had been lucky to get a job as Theo's personal secretary right out of grad school. He couldn't imagine a better way to learn the ins and outs of international politics. With record-breaking droughts, rising sea levels, the Great Migrations, and an unending supply of local and regional wars, NGOs were crying out for people who knew how to run not-for-profits. That's what Adrian had studied, and that's what he planned to do. Being with Theo was providing him with plenty of contacts that would prove invaluable. He might not be able to save the world, but maybe he could save some little part of it.

He wandered into the bedroom to confront Fiona.

"I probably won't be back tonight. I'll call when I know more."

"Whatever," she said.

"I'm truly sorry, but it's not like I can say no."

She just stared at him. She didn't look angry; more like resigned. He would have preferred angry.

Tomás was behind the wheel. Rather than sit alone in the back, Adrian climbed into the front seat. Tomás frowned at him before pulling away from the curb.

"So," Adrian said, "What's going on?"

"I don't know. He got a call. Then he made a bunch of calls and told me to pick you up and take you to the airport."

This turned out to be his entire contribution to the conversation for the rest of the drive. Tomás was good at a lot of things, but small talk wasn't one of them.

He was Theo's personal bodyguard; had been for many years. Adrian happened to know he carried a gun in a holster under his left arm, hidden from view by a light-weight jacket Adrian had never seen him without.

It was raining and dark. Lights from on-coming vehicles reflected jaggedly off the wet pavement. An hour's drive brought them to Geneva International Airport, where they turned onto a utility road that took them to one end of the main runway. They stopped on an abandoned section of tarmac. Nobody else was there.

"Okay," Adrian said. "What now?"

"We wait."

Right. It was an empty, creepy-looking place; the kind of place you would take someone to murder them and leave the body for a maintenance guy to find.

After a while, headlights announced the approach of two SUVs. They pulled up a short distance away and several people got out. Three of them wore body armor and carried assault rifles. They positioned themselves to watch for uninvited guests. Tomás produced an umbrella, which he and Adrian huddled under as they walked over to Theo and a woman Adrian didn't know.

"Adrian," he said. "Glad you could make it."

Like he had a choice. "So do you mind telling me what's going on?"

"Ah, well, that will take some explaining. But we have a little time while we wait for Robert. This, by the way, is Anna Lindstrom." He pointed at the woman. "Anna, this is Adrian, my personal secretary."

They shook hands. It was difficult to make out her features in the dark, but he guessed her to be about his age.

She wore a suit of sorts: black slacks, white shirt, open black jacket. She had an earpiece.

"Do you know who Holly Burton is?" Theo asked him.

Of course he did. Everyone knew who Holly Burton was. He said, "Astronaut. Expert on first contact scenarios. One of the Jupiter Six who perished on Ganymede when a still-unexplained nuclear detonation destroyed their ship."

"Well, she arrived at *Tiangong Station* a couple hours ago."

Questions tripped over each other in his head. He picked one.

"In what?"

Okay, not the brightest question he might have come up with, but if you are flying from Jupiter to Earth, you have to be flying in *something* and he was curious about what it was. It wasn't like there was a shuttle service running between the two planets.

Theo raised a bushy eyebrow. "In a spaceship, of course; a spaceship with some very advanced technology; a spaceship that has scared the crap out of some people who don't scare easily; also, the biggest spaceship anybody's ever seen. She claims it wasn't built on Earth and nobody is disagreeing with her. She has requested a meeting with her brother and myself."

Adrian swallowed as he tried to wrap his mind around that. "Let me see if I have this right. Holly Burton, who disappeared in the Jovian system two-and-a-half years ago and was presumed dead, has turned up in an unidentified, hightech, probably alien spaceship to have a spot of tea with you and her brother?"

"Yes, just so. Though there is also a not insignificant meeting with the Council of Enclaves to discuss the future of humanity. I think she wants to meet with us first because she is looking for allies. Her brother and I may be the only people on Earth she trusts."

Having been a diplomat for twenty years, Theo took

nothing at face value. It was an occupational hazard. For his part, Adrian had no interest in ever becoming a diplomat. The Lindstrom woman had said nothing beyond their initial greeting, but seemed as interested in Theo's explanation as he was.

Theo filled in the story: Holly Burton had contacted him. He had used his diplomatic connections to alert the Secretary General of the Council of Enclaves, who notified the heads of the alliances that she wanted to meet with them to deliver a message from the aliens.

"Out of curiosity," Adrian asked. "How did she get hold of you?"

"My cell phone."

"Your cell phone." He tried not to sound as incredulous as he felt.

"She tapped into a communications satellite, looked me up in a directory, and called me." He retrieved a cloth handkerchief from his pocket and wiped water off his glasses. It was unusual to see anyone wearing glasses these days.

"I was surprised," he added.

Adrian swallowed a laugh. "And then you just called up the Secretary General of the Council of Enclaves and asked if he could handle the arrangements?"

"She wants to address the Council and the world. Dr. Madurasinghe seemed like a good place to start."

"And then Madurasinghe picked up the phone and made a few calls to, I dunno, the President of the CRA, the Prime Minister of Britain, the President of the People's Republic of China—"

Theo waved him off. "We thought it wise to alert the Council members that a representative of a race of aliens has sent an emissary to discuss diplomatic relations."

Adrian was used to rubbing shoulders with the world's movers and shakers, but he had no idea you could just call these people up and have a chat with them. It seemed like it should be harder than that.

"Oh," Theo said, "I almost forgot the most interesting part. Great Britain sent a small armada of armed spaceships from the *New London Station* to commandeer her spaceship when it established orbit near *Tiangong*."

Adrian could only stare agog at that.

"The whole thing was broadcast worldwide from her ship, *Gabriel's Fire*, which destroyed one of their ships and forced the others to withdraw. I'm surprised you didn't see the broadcast."

The roar of a Chinese military jet brought the conversation to a halt as it passed low overhead, circled the airport, and came in for a landing from the other direction, using up most of the main runway before turning and taxiing toward them. It came to a halt about fifty meters from where they were standing. A tall, gray-haired man in a business suit disembarked and walked toward them. Theo stepped forward and shook his hand.

"Robert, this is Adrian Verhoeven, my personal secretary. And this is Holly's personal protection individual, Anna Lindstrom. Adrian, Anna: this is Robert Burton, Holly's brother." The man wore wire-framed eyeglasses perched on a long, thin nose. Apparently, he was old school, too. Throw in the beat up satchel he carried, and you had the perfect carica-ture of an old-fashioned country lawyer.

An hour later, a silver and black spaceplane the size of a commercial passenger plane came screaming in from the West, but instead of landing on the runway, it flew low over the control tower to the end of the runway where they were standing, came to a halt above them, and descended to the tarmac on two vertical landing thrusters. Engines whined down; thrusters retracted; waves of heat poured off the body.

It was wider than it was tall, which gave it a squashed look. Two nacelles stood off from the body near the aft end.

Those would be the main engines. The plane was all curves; no straight lines anywhere.

Two forward-facing windows atop the rounded nose of the plane marked the location of the cockpit. A flash of movement caught Adrian's eye and then was gone. A minute or two passed. Then a door swung open just ahead of the nacelles and stairs extended out and down to the tarmac. A woman appeared at the top of the stairs. She wore a simple white blouse and a white skirt with a thin black belt, and an open black jacket. Dark blonde hair hung loosely over her shoulders. She paused and looked up at the sky.

The Lindstrom woman jogged over to her and said something Adrian couldn't make out, then stepped back and waited. The woman—he assumed this was Holly Burton—looked around with a puzzled expression, as though she had never seen an airport before. In that moment, she struck him as . . . fragile.

16

It was raining when Holly stepped out of her spaceplane and stood at the top of the steps. The glare of lights reflecting off the wet surface of the tarmac was disorienting, compounded by other confusing sensory assaults: the distant sounds of traffic, the smell of jet fuel and wet asphalt, the wind whipping her hair back. She shivered and pulled her jacket tightly around her. The year on Titan had been a cloistered life, in some ways a year of silence and solitude. The Fragment's world was an orderly world; hers was not. Her world was a disorderly riot of random smells, flashing lights, clashing sounds, weather—all things she would have to get used to again.

She had received landing instructions from the tower, which had been expecting her, but ignored them and headed for a little-used section of tarmac where a black sedan and two gray SUVs waited. She used the plane's vertical takeoff and landing thrusters to bring *Eos* gently to the ground.

A small party stood in the rain. Robert and Theo were there, along with Theo's ever-present man Tomás. And a few other people, including some with assault weapons and wearing combat gear. Presumably, they were Theo's people, but after her unexpected encounter with the British, she was feeling a bit paranoid.

She tilted her head back and let cold raindrops pelt her face. It was an unexpectedly stimulating sensation. It made her feel young and alive. It made her feel like dancing in the rain. It made her feel . . . human. She had not known that standing in the rain could be like that.

A woman she did not recognize detached herself from the group and walked briskly toward the plane. She wore dark slacks and a dark jacket over a white blouse. She peered out from under her umbrella.

"Do you require assistance, Dr. Burton?"

"No," she said. "It's a bit overwhelming, is all."

"Take your time." She said something into the mic of her headset and stood back a little.

Holly carefully made her way down the steps, getting the feel of Earth's gravity. The nanites in her body had ensured that her muscles did not atrophy or her bones lose density in Titan's low gravity, but her gait was all wrong for Earth. It would take some practice to regain muscle memory.

"It has been a while since I have seen rain," she said when she reached the bottom of the steps. "Real rain, I mean. It rains on Titan, but ethanol just isn't the same as water." The steps folded into the plane behind her and the door swung shut.

She said to the woman, "Who are you?"

"Anna Lindstrom, ma'am. I will be your PPI." They shook hands. The name and accent matched her Scandinavian features. She was a little taller than Holly and about the same age; heavier too, though it looked like there was more muscle on her than fat. Shoulder-length blond hair was tied back in a ponytail. She had a pretty face behind the rather severe expression.

"What's a PPI?"

"Personal Protection Individual."

"I need a bodyguard?"

"Tomás thinks so, ma'am."

"Well, if Tomás thinks so, who am I to argue? Shall we go?" She started toward the group waiting by the vehicles, then stopped. "Ms. Lindstrom, I would like to have guards posted around the spaceplane. 24/7. Not to protect the plane. Its autonomous defenses have been armed, and it will protect itself from perceived threats. The guards would be there to keep unauthorized people from getting too close and triggering its defenses. Wouldn't want to vaporize a couple of curious kids who sneaked in to get a look at the alien spaceplane." Lindstrom looked alarmed at the prospect. "A ten meter perimeter would be good."

"I'll see to it, ma'am. Please call me Anna."

When they reached the vehicles, Theo put his arms around her and pulled her into a long hug, which was unexpected but not unwelcome. She hugged Robert, then made like she was going to hug Tomás, who took an alarmed step backward.

"Welcome back, Dr. Burton," he said. "You have been missed."

"Tomás, please call me Holly."

"As you wish, Dr. Burton."

Some things never changed. She was glad.

Their motorcade set out for a house Theo owned an hour south of the airport in the town of Vernier. She sat in the back seat with Robert. Anna sat in the front with their driver, who she introduced as Leon Benoit, her partner, which Holly supposed made him another PPI. He had a distinctively French face and a French accent to go with it. Theo, Adrian, and Tomás occupied the vehicle behind them. Their security team was in the vehicle in front of them.

She and Robert used the time to catch up on his life, his family, and changes that had occurred on Earth while she was gone. They drove past fields, homes, shops, and a multitude of the other sights one would expect to see when driving through the Swiss countryside. The Geneva-Lausanne Enclave comprised the corridor along the north and west sides of Lake Geneva, anchored by Lausanne in the north and Geneva in the south. Holly caught glimpses of the wall that protected the enclave from the uncontrolled lands of south-eastern France.

They turned off the road, passed through an open gate with an unmanned gatehouse, and followed a tree-lined road to a driveway circling a small raised garden watched over by a gnarly, ancient-looking tree. Leon drove around it and stopped in front of the house. She stared. *This* was Theo's *house*? It wasn't a house at all. It was a mansion, complete with grounds and probably a full-time staff.

The imposing face of the three-story, window-lined building loomed over them as if to say, "Enter if you dare." The incongruous presence of a hexagonal turret on each corner of the roof softened the fortress effect, but only a little. They looked big enough to contain their own rooms, and called out to the child in her to dash into the building, run up the stairs—which she imagined being a pair of staircases curving up to the second floor from opposite sides of a large central room with a large chandelier—and climb into one of those fairytale towers where she could look out over the estate.

She settled for Theo's arm. He waved his other arm to encompass the building and grounds. "Welcome to my humble abode. A number of ambassadors to the Council of Enclaves have residences in Vernier. Nearly half of Vernier's residents are foreign nationals, much to the consternation of the natives."

They passed through an imposing double-door entrance and into a wide hall that extended to the opposite side of the building, where a pair of glass-paned doors opened onto the grounds behind the house. There were no curved staircases in evidence, but the hall was lined with sculptures, paintings, and antique chairs, inviting her to stroll down the hall just to look at everything. Theo steered her into a room on the right.

It was, she supposed, what one would call the drawing room, and it was an exercise in carefully considered style and color. The pink carpet would have been the overwhelming feature of the room were it not for the pale blue floral pattern that toned it down. Two settees and three upholstered chairs had been placed strategically around the room. A tall, wide, multi-paned window looked out on the drive, an otherwise mundane view softened by lace curtains. Red drapes had been pulled back on either side. The over-all effect of the room was of luxury, falling just short of ostentatiousness. It was a side of Theo she had not known about.

A faint scent of pipe tobacco hung in the air, and she quickly located the pipe resting beside an ashtray on a side table beside one of the chairs. The pipe shared the table with a few books that formed a short but precarious stack. For all its formality, the room felt lived in. Theo spent a lot of time here.

He released her arm and gestured for her to sit while he pulled the heavy drapes over the window, blocking out the flood-lit area in front of the building. She glimpsed Tomás directing the security team as they unloaded an alarming collection of weapons and other equipment from one of the SUVs.

Robert and Adrian walked in. They claimed a settee and launched into a private conversation, which seemed to consist mainly of Adrian asking questions and Robert answering them. Her name was mentioned. The two of them presented a study in contrasts. Robert was a typical pakeha; on the short side, a little overweight, exuding confidence and calmness; a self-made man at the top of his game. Adrian, on the other hand, was tall and thin, dark-skinned with short, black, wiry hair, brown eyes, full lips, and ears that stuck out a little too much. He was young; a man at the beginning of his adult life. They were different in every way, yet were conversing affably. Apparently about her.

Theo claimed a chair. Anna appeared and stood behind and a little to one side of Holly's seat.

"You can sit if you like," Holly said.

"Thank you, ma'am. I prefer to stand." Apparently, there were rules to this PPI thing. Holly could call her by her given name, but she would refer to Holly as ma'am.

An older woman appeared with two trays, which she set on the table in the middle of the room.

"Oh, tea and bickies," Holly said, and helped herself.

She expected everyone to pepper her with questions about the skirmish at *Tiangong Station*, or her adventures among the aliens, but Robert started them off in a different direction.

"So Theo," he said. "Tell us about this house."

Theo seemed pleased to oblige, and launched into a somewhat detailed description of the house's architecture and history. It was built in the early 1900s, making it a century and a half old. It had been in the family of an Earl for most of that time, but when he could no longer afford to maintain it, he put it up for sale and Theo bought it. It was in considerable disrepair, and he ended up putting nearly a million euros into it beyond the purchase price.

"At the time, I saw it as an investment," he said. "I thought I would eventually sell it for a tidy profit. That was before the end of the world was announced." He smiled a little sadly. "Real estate brokers like to say it is all about location, but in this case, it was all about timing. Maybe it is for the best, though. I think it will serve adequately as a temporary headquarters for the aliens' personal representative on Earth. At least until we can find something more appropriate."

The woman who had brought tea and cookies appeared and announced that dinner was served. They moved across the hall to the dining room, where a formal dinner had been set for them. Tomás joined them. Even Anna sat to eat with them, though Leon remained standing near one of the doors.

Dinner turned out to be a thoroughly sensual affair of sights, smells, and tastes. The Fragment's culinary offerings were an excellent imitation of human food, but there was a kind of fullness to real food prepared by real people. At least, it seemed like that to Holly. She closed her eyes for a moment and listened to the sounds of people sharing a meal, chatting, laughing, and for a moment she was overwhelmed by the normality of it, the simple humanity of it.

Later, back in the drawing room, Theo made drinks. Holly took a sizable swallow of bourbon, scrunched her face, and launched into a coughing fit as the frontal assault of 80 proof liquor made its way down her throat and esophagus. This engendered laughter once her companions determined she was going to live.

"I had forgotten how strong this stuff is," she said. She gave them a rueful look and took a more cautious sip, this time savoring the flavored heat as it made its way down her throat. "Whew." She plunked her glass down on the side table beside her chair. Robert was grinning. Theo smiled benignly.

"That might have been worth the billion and a half kilometer trip all by itself," she said.

After some general conversation, Theo said, "Tell us what happened to you."

She did. Beginning with the *Asimov's* arrival in the Jovian system, she described the alien space station, the journey to the alien base deep beneath Ganymede's surface, their encounter with the Fragment, Benny's betrayal and destruction of the base, waking up on Titan, her preparation for returning to Earth, and her arrival at *Tiangong Station*. They kept interrupting her with questions and by the time she finished her story, it was 12:30 in the morning.

"You have had quite the adventure, Dr. Burton," Adrian said.

She stifled a yawn. "Call me Holly, please."

"So, just to be clear," Robert said, "there is only one alien. Right?"

She nodded. "He is an ancient explorer who has taken an interest in our affairs."

"And he calls himself the Fragment."

"That's not really his name. He doesn't have a name. He offered it as a concession to our need to call him something."

"Huh," Robert said. Everyone was silent for a few moments.

"I wouldn't spend too much time sussing out the meaning of his choice of names," she said. "He is an alien, after all, and that means our respective frames of reference are not congruent. Our guesses about why he chose that particular name are more likely to lead us astray than provide any useful insights into his nature. I spent almost a year with him on Titan, and I can tell you he is nothing like anything any of us has ever imagined or ever will imagine. He is totally Other."

"You keep referring to the Fragment as he," Adrian said.

She shrugged. "Gender is a fundamental part of our humanity, but it is not part of whatever the Fragment is. He has no gender. He presented as male, so it was easiest to go with that. Part of the human-alien interface, if you will."

"And he wants to give us advanced technologies to save us from the Death Bringer." There was a certain awe in Adrian's voice. "With you acting as the go-between."

"Emissary," she corrected him. "He seems to feel strongly about that. I am more than a go-between for transferring alien technologies from the Fragment to the human race. I am his personal representative on Earth."

"So how *are* you going to transfer that knowledge to the people who need it?"

"Hang on," Robert said. "It's past midnight and Holly looks like she is about to nod off and fall out of her chair. Why don't we call it a night and continue in the morning?"

"You are absolutely right," Theo said. "I apologize. To all of you. Let me show you where your rooms are."

Theo's house had a lot of rooms. Holly, Robert, and Anna followed him up the stairs, which opened off the hall. Anna's room was the first one on the right, but she accompanied them into the second room, which was Holly's.

It was big; bigger than her entire apartment in Amstelveen had been. The four-poster, king-sized bed seemed almost decadent, with its deep green canopy, four large white pillows, and a dark blue duvet with a white floral pattern. Theo seemed partial to floral patterns; or at least his interior decorator was. The headboard and footboard were made of a rich, dark wood.

A round table sat in one corner, along with three chairs with green floral designs. On the other side of the room was a dresser that looked old, and an equally old-looking wardrobe, which was empty. She foresaw a shopping trip in her future. Or maybe not. She doubted she would find anything that fit as well as the Fragment's clothes or looked as good on her. She had brought them with her.

A door led into the bathroom, which included a full-sized bathtub and a separate shower. She eyed the tub and imagined a long, hot soak. There was a second door on the other side of the bathroom.

"Anna's room," Theo said.

So she would share a bathroom with her PPI. When they talked about close protection, they weren't kidding.

"Robert's room is further down the hall," Theo said. "Tomás's and mine are across the hall. I'll give you a full tour of the house and grounds tomorrow."

As much as the bathtub called to her, she decided not to risk falling asleep in it and drowning. That would be embarrassing. She stripped off her clothes and crawled into bed. It had been a long time since she had slept in normal gravity. It felt good.

17

She woke the next morning to sunlight streaming in through lace-covered French doors. She stretched luxuriously in the decadently luxurious bed. The room was like something out of a fairytale. She knew Theo was financially well off, but this . . . this went beyond well off. This was aristocratic wealth. A light knock came at the bathroom door.

"Come," she said.

Anna walked in, dressed in what looked like the same outfit she wore the previous day. Either that or she had a collection of identical outfits; which, come to think of it, made sense given her profession.

"Breakfast in thirty minutes," she said.

Holly had slept in the middle of the bed and had to crawl to one side to get out of it.

"I am jealous," Anna said with a smirk. "Mine is only queen-sized."

"Yeah, well, this much room in a bed for one person seems excessive, don't you think?"

"I imagine it is intended for two. Knock on my door when you are ready to go down." She retreated back through the bathroom.

Really? She needed a bodyguard to accompany her down-stairs for breakfast? They would have to sit down and talk about the rules. At least Anna seemed willing to let her take a shower and get dressed by herself.

She opened the French doors and stepped out onto a small balcony overlooking a large, well-kept lawn that ran the width of one end of the house and almost the same distance across. A neatly trimmed hedge enclosed it, with an arched gate on each side. A stone path began at one gate, curved out toward a gazebo in the middle of space, and drew a mirror image curve to the opposite gate. Like the house, it exuded wealth.

A noise startled her. She turned to see Anna step into her room from the bathroom. She had a gun in her hand. The door to the hallway burst open and two soldiers charged in, assault rifles at the ready.

"Are you all right?" Anna said, eyes scanning the room.

"Uh, yes?"

Anna noticed the open French doors. "Stand down," she said to the guards. "False alarm. Let's give the woman some privacy."

They backed out of the room and closed the door behind them. Anna holstered her gun. Holly felt like a complete idiot.

"It has an alarm, doesn't it?"

"Every door and window in the house has an alarm. When you opened the French doors, you set off an alarm in the guardroom on this floor, as well as this." She held up her cell phone, then grinned.

"Ma'am, I wish you could see the look on your face."

She closed the French doors and showed Holly how to disable and re-enable the alarm. A knock came at the hall door, followed by Robert's voice: "Everything all right in there?"

"Everything is fine," Holly said. "We'll be down in a few minutes."

Breakfast was in the breakfast room looking out on the park-like back yard. A servant brought them eggs Benedict, roasted potatoes, toast, and mixed fruits. A coffee pot was available on a side table. She took some minor ribbing about her encounter with the security system.

After breakfast, they moved back to the drawing room, where Theo returned to the question of Holly's plan for saving the human race.

"My only plan," she said, "is to meet with the Council of Enclaves and offer to make available to them the advanced technical knowledge they will need to save us from extinction."

"Then what?"

"What do you mean?"

"What do you expect them to do?"

"I expect them to take the Fragment's gift and spearhead the greatest construction project in the history of the world. My role will be to provide the requisite knowledge to the people who need it. Their job will be to use that knowledge to get the job done."

"Suppose the Council doesn't accept the offer? You have enemies, you know; enemies who believe you and the aliens represent an existential threat to the world that is every bit as serious as the coming of the Death Bringer, which, by the way, many believe will be a survivable event. Some of those people sit on the Council. The CRA in particular wields considerable clout."

"They would have to be complete idiots to turn down this offer."

"When has that ever stopped politicians from making stupid decisions?"

"I will just have to convince them."

"In any case," Robert said, "you are going to need some kind of organization."

"Why? The Council already has one."

"Sis, you are about to become the most important person in the world. Even if you offload the bulk of the work to others, you will at least need a public relations organization to handle the flood of mail you are already receiving. Even if—"

"Wait. I have mail? I have been here less than a day. How can I have mail? I don't even have a current vidmail address."

Theo held up both hands. "For now, your mail and calls come to me. You will have to hire a personal assistant to handle them, not to mention your calendar."

"Someone will read my mail before I see it? And managing my schedule?"

"Think about it. People high up in an organization or the government don't read their own mail. It gets screened by a personal assistant. Death threats, for example, would go directly to security. You would never see them. The same with prank messages and vids, requests for autographed pictures, marriage proposals. If these aren't filtered out before they reach your desk, they will overwhelm you."

"Please tell me I am not receiving death threats."

"Not yet, but you will."

"That's crazy."

"It only seems that way because you haven't been the most famous person in the world before. Now you are. You will quickly develop a fan club and a hate club."

"The same goes for your calendar," Robert said. "Your schedule is going to become very busy and your calendar very full. You will need someone to manage that for you. To schedule meetings, calls, vids. To contact people to reschedule a meeting when something more important comes up. If all goes well, you are going to be overwhelmed with meetings. For example, you will have to meet with hundreds of people who need the knowledge you bring. Maybe thousands. Somebody has to plan and schedule all that."

Theo said, "You are going to be the face and voice of the

Fragment. People won't be able to relate to some kind of trans-dimensional alien they can't even visualize. But they can and will relate to you. The Fragment understood that when he made you his emissary. You need to focus on the things that only you can do and let others do everything else."

It dawned on her that they must have stayed up talking about this after she went to bed, which was mildly irritating. This was why she needed people like them around her, but it rubbed her the wrong way to know they were talking about her behind her back, planning details of her life that she might never even know about.

She picked up her teacup and discovered the tea was luke-warm. She hated lukewarm tea. In fact, she detested luke-warm drinks in general. Hot drinks should be hot; cold drinks should be cold.

Anna noticed. "Let me take care of that, ma'am." She took the cup out of Holly's hands, left the room, and returned with a clean cup. When she started to make the tea, Holly objected.

"I'll let you be my bodyguard, because that's something I can't do for myself. But I can damn well make a cup of tea, thank you very much." Anna looked surprised and retreated to her corner.

"Sorry," Holly said to her. "That was uncalled for."

"No problem, ma'am."

But it was a problem, wasn't it? She didn't play well with others. Never had. If you wanted something done right, you did it yourself. Now she was being told she couldn't do everything herself, that she would have to trust other people to make decisions for her, decisions she might not even know needed to be made.

Robert must have guessed what she was thinking. "There is too much at stake for you to go it alone, sis. You need help. Our help. That's why you asked us to meet you when you arrived, isn't it? Well, here we are. Let us help."

"You are going to need more help than we can provide,"

Theo said. "You will need dozens, hundreds, maybe thousands of people before this thing is done. As much as you hate it, you are going to have to get used to delegating most things—sometimes important things—and trust that the people around you won't screw up. You will have to listen to people, confide in people, trust people. You have been a lone wolf your entire life. That has to change. You are going to have—"

"Stop," she said, holding up her hand. "You are making me out to be some kind of corporate CEO or world leader or . . . I don't know . . . superhero. But that's not who I am. I'm an academic, a researcher, a college instructor. I write books; books for other academics. The closest I ever get to politics is the occasional departmental kerfuffle."

She was vaguely aware that her voice had risen in pitch and volume.

"What you are describing is not who I am. That's why I need to hand this off to the Council. They have the organizational infrastructure to do something with the Fragment's technology. They have the leadership and expertise to get the human race off the planet. They can focus the world's resources on this endeavor. I can't do any of that, and I am more than happy to sit in the back row and let them take the credit for saving humanity. Assuming they do."

She stopped when she noticed two things. First, her eyes were wet and her hands were trembling. Second, they were staring at her like she had sprouted a second head.

"I need a time-out. Theo, where's that tour you promised?"

18

_____

Two days later, in a room on the second floor that she thought of as the library—who had libraries anymore?—she watched Theo pace back and forth in front of a tall window. He was talking to someone in another country; Belgium, she thought. It had to do with money, though the details eluded her since she could hear only one side of the conversation. She ran her hand over one of the curved wood armrests of her chair. The Fragment's chairs adjusted themselves to fit her body, which made them incredibly comfortable, but it was different in normal gravity. Here she could _feel_ her body settle into the chair in a way it didn't on Titan.

The room was inviting, casually and exactingly laid out, like the drawing room. But this room had more of a library feel to it, especially with the two floor-to-ceiling bookcases containing actual books. A light brown carpet with dark brown swirls covered the floor. There were upholstered chairs, side tables, a desk, even a world globe on a stand. Lamps rather than overhead lighting provided illumination. One of the side tables held a chess board with ornate wood pieces. A hard-backed chair stood ready on each side, waiting for someone to sit and play.

It had immediately become her favorite room, a place she could retreat to when she needed to get away from people. There were a lot of people in Theo's house: herself, Theo, Robert, Adrian, Tomás, Anna, a dozen security guards who had converted the basement into a barracks, and a household staff that included Gerard, the groundskeeper, who lived in a separate cottage with his wife Molly, who was the cook, and at least two servants.

Theo's raised voice drew her attention back to his conversation. "I don't give a damn what Giselle wants. It's my money and I'll do whatever the hell I want with it . . . No. Drake, listen. I spelled out my intentions as clearly as I could. Just write it up with all the required legalese and send me the documents. Post haste. And make sure it's locked down tight. No loopholes. . . . No, I do not want a meeting with them. Send them copies if you must. . . . Fine. Thank you."

He dropped the connection and stood looking out the window, which looked out over what would be a backyard for most houses, but in this case, was more like a park. Curved beds of flowers and shrubs and trees wandered around the well-maintained lawn. A tall gazebo-like tower made of stone stood two-thirds of the way across the lawn toward a green belt that marked the edge of the property. A bird bath had been built into the base of the tower, which had been colonized by birds for many years, maybe decades.

Theo returned to the chair he had been sitting in when the call had interrupted them. He put on his glasses and started writing in a small notebook he always carried with him. She was glad that had not changed.

He had aged since she had left Earth. Not a lot—it was only seven years—but enough to notice. There was more gray in his hair, and his receding hairline had receded a little further. He carried more weight than she remembered, and maybe a few new wrinkles here and there. Still, at forty-five, he was as fit and as attractive as ever; maybe more so.

She, on the other hand, had not aged at all; not physically, anyway. In fact, the Fragment had reconstructed her body so that she looked more like twenty-seven than her real age of thirty-six. Now millions of nanites patrolled the hi-ways and by-ways of her body, looking for defects to repair and invaders to destroy. They ensured her body would remain a young and healthy twenty-seven for a long time. The Fragment was vague about exactly how long that might be. He said he couldn't make her immortal but could slow the aging process, extending her natural life span. When she pressed him on this, he became evasive, saying only that one human lifetime would not be enough to ensure humanity's survival.

She had told Theo and Robert about the nanites, and they both seemed to take it in stride. But had they really? Did Theo still see her as a woman? Or as some kind of cyborg?

He put the notebook away. "Sorry about that."

"What was it about?" She asked.

"A minor business matter. Nothing you need be concerned about."

It was rare for Theo to lie to her. She was pretty sure the 'minor business matter' had everything to do with her. He might be wealthy, but even he did not have a bottomless bank account. Her presence here was costing him a lot of money, and she suspected the call had to do with rearranging his finances to account for that. She had stepped into his life after a long absence with the expectation that he would receive her with open arms and do whatever he could to help her. And that was exactly what he had done. She couldn't help but feel a little guilty about it.

"Tell me," she said.

He held up his hands in mock surrender. "I am rewriting my will."

"You're rewriting your will for the end of the world?"

His laugh was quiet, assured; the laugh that always made her feel like all was well in the world, even when it wasn't. He retrieved his pipe and a tobacco pouch from the pocket of his suit jacket. She watched him fill the bowl of the pipe and tamp it down with his finger. He was buying time to think.

He walked over to the fireplace, extracted a wooden match from a matchbox on the mantle, lit it, and held it over the bowl of the pipe while he puffed on it. He extinguished the match with a shake of his wrist and tossed it into the fireplace. It was a ritual she had seen him perform many times. He stood there with pipe in hand and looked at her for several long seconds. Theo was a man never in a hurry, an unflappable man if there ever was one.

"Troubled times are coming," he said. "I don't mean the end of the world, but the time between now and then. More troubled than any of us have seen in our lifetimes. I hope to be here at the end—I am not yet ready to cast off this mortal coil—but the slings and arrows of outrageous fortune do not always fly in the direction we might wish."

Theo wasn't much given to poetic expressions, but he could produce them when he wanted to. It helped that he read and re-read Shakespeare.

"There are not many people I hold dear, but I want to be sure those I do care about will be provided for should something happen to me." He drew smoke from the pipe and exhaled it in a dense cloud. "You are one of those people."

"That doesn't seem right," she said. "I'm not your family." He had mentioned Giselle on the call, his sister.

He smiled a little. "Trust me, my family will be fine."

———

That evening, after she had beaten Robert at chess a second time, she announced she was going to take a long, hot bath and retire for the night. Twenty minutes later she was immersed in water as hot as she could stand, afloat in the scent of lavender, jets of water flowing over and under and around her, caressing her skin. There were some experiences you just couldn't replicate in a low-gee environment. This was one of them. Sure, you could take a bath, but it wasn't the same without Earth's gravity.

It was nearly midnight when she slipped under the covers and let her body sink into the bed. The clean, crisp sheets rested on her sensitized skin, feeling almost excruciatingly sensuous. She lay awake listening to the sounds of nature's nightlife through the open French doors, the security for which she had disabled. There was something comforting about it, something normal. God, she had almost forgotten what normal felt like. Not that there was anything even remotely normal about her; not since that year on Titan. Nor was there anything normal about what she had come back to do.

When the digital clock on the nightstand showed half-past one, she got up to use the bathroom and then crossed the hall to Theo's room. She knocked gently. Several moments passed with no response, and she turned to go back to her room. The door opened behind her.

"Holly?" Theo said. "Is everything all right?"

She turned to face him, noticing that he still wore pajama bottoms and no top.

"Yes, I'm okay." She felt like a teenager who had gotten caught trying to sneak out of the house for an illicit late-night tryst. "Actually, I'm not. I mean, I am, but . . . well, I'm not sure why I'm here."

This was a lie, of course. She knew exactly why she was knocking on Theo's door at 1:30 in the morning. He did too. He guided her back to her room, where he carefully closed the door and turned to face her. She had left the bathroom light on and belatedly realized that she was standing between him and the light, wearing a sheer, white nightgown. His eyes moved over her body, and he said nothing for what seemed like a long time. Did he not find her attractive anymore? Was he going to patiently explain why this was a bad idea?

"You look beautiful tonight," he said.

Her heart was suddenly in her throat. "Thank you," she whispered.

"I'm afraid I don't have condoms," he said, "though I imagine the guards down the hall could come up with one or two."

A giggle burbled up from somewhere and she said, "We don't have to worry about that."

"One question, though. Will the Fragment be listening?"

Her hand leaped to her mouth. "Oh, my," she said. "I hadn't thought about that." She pulled the amulet over her head. "This keeps me in touch with *Gabriel's Fire* and the Fragment. If I'm not wearing it, neither one is listening." She wasn't sure that was true, but it sounded good. She placed it on the nightstand.

He closed the distance between them and cupped her face with both hands. Then he kissed her. It was a soft, undemanding kiss, and it sent shivers down her back, her legs, all the way to her toes, which curled into the carpet. He pulled away a little and looked into her eyes. She put her hand on the back of his head and brought his lips back to hers, which parted so their tongues could begin an ancient dance. She was trembling.

She broke the kiss. "God, I feel like a sixteen-year-old girl doing it for the first time."

He grinned and grasped the bottom of the nightgown with both hands and drew it up. She lifted her arms so he could pull it over her head. It fell to the floor. His hands found her breasts, and she shivered again, then they wandered around to her back and down until he was cupping her bottom. She had forgotten how good this could feel.

He drew her against himself, and it was obvious he wanted her as much as she wanted him. She dug her fingernails into his shoulders and let out a tiny "oh" when he planted a kiss between her breasts. Her head dropped back, and she clung to him as though her life depended on it.

19

James Cartwright wouldn't call Dawson a friend exactly, but he had been in his office a few times. Its smallness always struck him as inconsistent with everything else he knew about the man. Jedediah Dawson was an expansive man in every sense of the word. He was obese, though he projected the image of a big man rather than a fat man. He had a big personality that took up a disproportionate amount of emotional space in whatever room he happened to be in. He was the seventeenth wealthiest person in the world, give or take a place or two depending on who was counting and when. His appetite for the finer things in life was insatiable; an insatiability that extended to certain personal proclivities that many people would find shocking. He was also a generous man, subscribing to the old fashion concept of *noblesse oblige*, which was ironic since there was nothing noble about him.

Cartwright had once asked him why he had such a small office. "There's only one of me," he said. "How big an office do ah need?" Like everyone else Cartwright had ever met, Dawson was a collection of contradictions.

"James Braxton Cartwright," he said as he came around

the desk. "It has been a while since y'all slinked into my office."

"How are you, Jed." He shook the outstretched hand and took a seat as Dawson walked over to the liquor cabinet.

"Cognac?"

"It's the only reason I visit you. I can't afford the good stuff on my government salary."

"And dollars grow on trees."

He handed Cartwright a heavy crystal glass, a third full of what he assumed would be a very good cognac. The big man settled into his chair, and they had both sampled what was indeed an excellent drink. Dawson eyed him with a character-istic sideways look.

"I hear the DHS has got itself a couple of big projects goin' on in outta-the-way places. Projects Congress don't know nothin' about."

His pattern of speech was an affectation that harkened back to his childhood in Texas, but he held a master's degree from Duke and could speak uninflected English as well as anyone. It should not have surprised Cartwright that he knew about the sanctuaries. People like him traded in information more than anything else.

"Planning on savin' the world, are ya?"

"Well, not the *whole* world. Just enough folks to reboot civilization."

"I take it you are disinclined to believe the end of the world will actually be the end of the world."

"I believe the Death Bringer will pass close enough to wreak destruction upon the Earth unlike anything it has seen since the time of the dinosaurs, but Earth will survive and, after a few dark, cold years, will once again be livable. The trick will be to get through the destruction part and the long winter to follow."

"Ergo, underground cities."

"Six of them, each holding up to twenty thousand people,

along with enough seeds and animals to rebuild sustainable ecosystems."

"How long will they have to hunker down?"

"Two or three years, I'm told. Maybe longer. We're planning for five."

"Expensive project."

That's what Cartwright liked about Dawson. The man had a razor-sharp mind and once he understood a situation, he would make a decision without further ado.

"Fifty billion will reserve ten slots for you, your family, and whoever else you want to bring along."

"That's a lot of money. I'd have to spread it over a few years. The markets are jittery enough as it is."

Cartwright nodded.

Dawson drained his glass. "Make it fifteen slots and you got yourself a deal."

"Done." Cartwright finished his drink. "There is one other thing."

"Oh?"

"Holly Burton."

"Ah yes, the woman who somehow survived the destruction of the *Asimov* and then shows up claiming to be the aliens' representative." He refilled both their glasses. "The Brits screwed the pooch on that one, didn't they?"

"I tried to dissuade Weatherford, but you know how he can be when he gets an idea in his head. In any case, I suspect Dr. Burton is going to be a problem. She will hit a wall in the Council, but if I know Theo Peeters, he will find a way around it."

"What can she do without the Council?"

"What indeed?" Cartwright downed half his drink. "She might bypass the Council and appeal directly to the individual Enclaves. By dangling a few new technologies in front of them, she may well persuade them to climb in bed with the aliens, and that would be a disaster for the human race."

"Let me guess," Dawson said. "You need a contingency plan for neutralizing her while maintaining plausible deniability for yourself."

"Yes."

Dawson's voice took on an icy quality Cartwright had not heard before. "Dead or alive?"

————

The headquarters of Alexander Taylor Ministries International was impressive, with clean, modern architecture, futuristic spires and arches, the latest technology. The auditorium seated 2500, and they had opened up the spacious foyer to seat another hundred. A few hundred more were in another room, taking part via closed circuit television. Another six million or so throughout the Western Hemisphere watched live. A similar number would watch time-delayed broadcasts later in the day as Taylor's voice followed the sun around the world. Cartwright paid three people a thousand dollars each to give up their seats near the back of the auditorium for him and his bodyguards.

Taylor was wrapping up his sermon: "And so . . . the Death Bringer comes." He paused and lowered his voice. "Is this how the world ends? Is this how Adam's race ends?" He lowered it to a whisper spoken close to the microphone: "Is this how you and I end?"

He looked out over his congregation. You could hear a pin drop. Taylor had certainly inherited his father's gift.

His voice climbed in volume again. "No! This is *not* how the world ends. The Word of God tells of a very different end to the world, and I have chosen to stake my life on what the Word of God says. For God. Does. Not. Lie."

The crowd came alive, rising to their feet and raising their arms in the air, shouting, "Amen!" and "Hallelujah!" and "Thank you, Jesus!"

"And you . . ." His arm describing a broad arc encompassing his audience. "You too have staked your lives on what the Word of our God says."

People were clapping and stamping their feet. The band kicked in with some music.

"And so," he held up both hands, quieting them down. "And so, the Death Bringer comes. Not to destroy us, but to test us." Back to pin-dropping silence. Even Cartwright was not immune to the pull of Taylor's charisma.

"My friends, we must choose, you and I. We can panic like so many around us who have no faith, who do not know the Lord God and his power to save. Or . . . we can trust that He who created the heavens and everything that is in them stands between us and the Death Bringer and will not allow it to pass. I do not know *how* He will save us. I only know that He will. And so do you."

He waited for his congregation to settle down again.

"But the Death Bringer is not the only test of our faith. With the Death Bringer come the aliens. It is surely no coincidence that they have arrived at the same time. Can they save us? Their emissary is already among us, promising just that. She offers us hope. But it is a false hope, my friends. These aliens are an antichrist come to deceive the faithful, and their emissary is a whore of Babylon. She will turn many away from God and lead them to put their trust in an alien species instead."

Taylor raised his voice as he continued. "Beloved of God. Do. Not. Be. Deceived. Stand firm and wait for the Lord. Stand fast and see the salvation of the Lord. It will be *glorious* to behold."

To the sound of much clapping and shouting, he turned the rest of the service over to a worship leader. Another of the ministers would dismiss the crowd. Cartwright decided to beat the crush of people who would soon be leaving. He made his way to Taylor's office in a separate wing of the compound.

Cartwright had known Alexander Taylor for a long time. He had known his father too, though he had always thought of the senior Alexander as something of a showman, a little too full of himself, which made him easy to manipulate, but unreliable. The old man was worth some sixty million when he passed on.

Alexander Jr. was not like his father. Oh, he had the old man's gift for manipulating people, but unlike the old man, the son was absolutely sincere; a scandal-free man of God with little interest in power and wealth. When he took over his father's ministry, he got its financial house in order and took the unprecedented step of making the multi-million dollar ministry's finances open to the public. Most of the money that flowed into its coffers went to a foundation that focused on getting affordable medicines and vaccines to the poorer enclaves and the Outcasts. His personal net worth was estimated at a million and a half dollars, which included an unpretentious home in Roanoke, Virginia. His foundation was worth several billion. As near as Cartwright could tell, the man was the real deal. Uncorrupted and probably incorruptible. Which wasn't to say Cartwright couldn't use him.

He was looking out a window at a wetland bordering the church's property when Taylor walked in.

"I thought that was you in the back," he said.

Cartwright turned and grinned. "It is hard to remain incognito with two large bodyguards following me around everywhere I go."

"Yeah, they're entertaining Jennifer. Coffee?"

"Sure." Cartwright would have preferred something stronger, but Taylor didn't drink anything stronger than the occasional glass of wine.

Taylor stuck his head out the door and said, "Jens, would you mind getting us some coffee? Thanks."

They sat at a table in one corner of his study. An older woman delivered two cups of coffee and left, closing the door behind her.

Cartwright tried the coffee. It was good and freshly made. She must have started a fresh pot after she let him into Taylor's office. Jennifer had been Taylor's administrative assistant for years, and his father's before that.

Taylor set down his cup. "So, Mr. Secretary, what brings you to my humble house of worship." A faint smirk formed around his mouth and his eyes twinkled. "Somehow I doubt you have come seeking spiritual counsel." Unlike the father, the son could be disarmingly self-deprecating. It sometimes seemed as though he just couldn't be bothered with taking himself seriously.

"Indeed," Cartwright said, making a show of looking around the room. "I need your help with something. Well, I don't *need* your help, but I would like to have it."

"My, my. James Cartwright wants my help. I suppose I should be flattered, but I suspect you are about to try to entangle me in something morally dubious." He smiled to assure Cartwright that he need not be offended.

"It has to do with the Death Bringer," Cartwright said. "I'm sure you know that scientific opinion is divided on how much of a threat the Death Bringer is to Earth."

"I also know," Taylor said, "that you, and therefore the Oxham administration, side with the minority that thinks the danger to our world has been exaggerated and that all we have to do is hunker down and ride it out."

Cartwright leaned back in his chair. "The people I trust tell me the Death Bringer's sweep through our solar system will push the Earth into an orbit a little further out from the Sun than it is now, but otherwise leave it intact. And livable."

"Not quite the end of the world, then."

"Not the end of the world. Of course, it will not pass unnoticed. Its gravity will cause tectonic shifts, world-wide volcanic activity, massive tsunamis, that sort of thing. Enormous amounts of ash and dust will be thrown into the atmosphere, causing a global winter that will last for several years. Most animal and plant life will die, along with most of the human race."

A frown formed on Taylor's face as he took this in. He had heard all this before, but seemed surprised to hear it from Cartwright.

"So, an apocalypse unlike anything since the Great Flood?"

Cartwright released a silent sigh of relief. Taylor got it.

"As I recall," Cartwright said, "not everyone perished in the Flood. Some survived in that ark Noah built."

Taylor thought about that for a moment. "I don't suppose you have one of those lying around in some undisclosed location?"

Cartwright tried to conceal his smile, but couldn't quite pull it off. "As a matter of fact, I do. The government has been busy these last few years. Busy building an underground sanctuary. Six of them, actually, located in the most tectonically stable parts of North America we could find. Each of them is large enough to sustain enough people, plants, and animals to repopulate the Earth. In theory, only one of them needs to survive for humanity to reboot itself, but a couple backups can't hurt, and might make all the difference in the world."

"Our tax dollars at work," Taylor said.

"Funny you should mention tax dollars. I am sure you can appreciate that a project of this size and complexity is expensive, made more so by the need to keep it quiet for as long as possible. Even from Congress. Hell, especially from Congress. Unfortunately, they will find out about it soon, anyway. I'm surprised we have kept it from them as long as we have. They will start poking around to find out where all the money's going. Then they will pull in the reigns of the spending in order to get some say in how the project unfolds."

Taylor sipped his coffee and motioned for Cartwright to continue.

"I am asking some of the wealthiest people in the world for contributions—significant contributions—in exchange for a few places in an ark. I suppose you could say I am selling tickets for a front row view of the end of the world at a billion dollars a pop."

"I don't have a billion dollars."

"You have a world-wide viewing audience from whom you pull in nearly a billion dollars annually. According to your public records, most of that goes to your foundation, which channels it into a variety of global charities."

"You want me to redirect those funds into your Ark program."

"I want more than that."

"More," Taylor echoed.

"When this goes public, I want you to appeal to your followers to give more; much more; more than they have ever given before; knowing that it will go toward saving a remnant of humanity from destruction. Think of it as the greatest charitable cause in history."

Taylor drained his cup and called for Jennifer to bring refills. Cartwright waited while she brought more coffee. He had learned long ago how to recognize the precise moment when he had someone hooked and needed only to reel them in. Taylor was examining the hook. The most important thing was not to spook him, and the best way to do that was to say nothing.

Taylor took a few sips of the hot coffee while gazing out the window.

"You want me to take on the mantle of a modern-day Noah."

And just like that, Cartwright had him. He said, "The sanctuaries have to be self-contained and self-sufficient, able to support people, plants and animals for several years until it is safe to return to the surface. That fact alone constrains the number of people each sanctuary can support. Each one will hold twenty thousand people. More than that, and they may not survive. Less than that and we may not have enough to multiply and be prosperous."

He mangled the scripture reference, but Taylor didn't seem to notice.

"For the most part, we will use a lottery system to select from the best and brightest, after ensuring they satisfy certain parameters; like age, health, ability to procreate, lack of genetic diseases, and so on."

"For the most part," Taylor repeated. "That's the carrot you are dangling in front of your billionaires. They get to bypass the lottery and 'certain parameters' for themselves and a few others; the exact number depending on how many billions they cough up."

Cartwright nodded.

Taylor laughed. "You had me worried for a minute there. I thought you might be thinking along egalitarian lines with the lottery thing. It is strangely reassuring to be reminded that some things never change."

He was being facetious. Anyone else might have been offended. The two of them held very different value systems. Cartwright maintained the relationship because Taylor was sometimes useful. He imagined Taylor maintained it for the same reason; that and the fact that he and Taylor's father had been friends for many years. Deep down, he suspected Taylor also held out hope that Cartwright's soul was still salvageable. Cartwright had long ago lost interest in that question.

"Let me ask you a question," Taylor said. "These parameters, I don't suppose they include race or ethnic origin."

"As I said, we will carefully select the best and brightest. In exchange for your help, I offer sanctuary for you and your extended family. I'll also give you thirty tickets for each billion you raise for the project. I want some of your people to survive. I might not be much of a Christian, but I understand the importance of religion for a stable and orderly society, and that is what we will build. Not that I'll be part of it. I'm too old. But I am recruiting leaders who can take up the task of building the new humanity. So choose carefully."

He wanted Taylor to understand and commit to the bigger picture. He wanted him as an ally, not just a fund-raiser. Rebuilding a civilization after the apocalypse would not be easy. He needed natural leaders, leaders like Taylor.

"I will help you," Taylor said.

"One more thing," Cartwright said. "This Holly Burton woman is presenting herself as the aliens' Emissary. She's selling the notion that the aliens can give us the tech we need to survive the Death Bringer. I can't have her running around selling a competing plan of salvation. She will syphon off money and resources.

"So, I have started a propaganda campaign to discredit her. Distasteful, I know, but we're talking about saving the human race here, and the more people who believe her, the more difficult that becomes."

"What do you want *me* to do?" Taylor asked.

"I want you to continue doing what you are already doing: portraying her as the whore of Babylon. It has a nice ring to it, and the obvious advantage of being something you happen to believe, anyway."

20

Adrian was worried. Three weeks had passed since the Emissary's arrival, and the Council of Enclaves had not yet agreed to meet with her. Theo couldn't even get her a meeting with the Secretary General. At every turn, he met with delays and excuses. They were stonewalling her. But why?

It wasn't like they didn't know who she was and why she was here. The confrontation at *Tiangong Station* had drawn global attention to the arrival of an emissary from the aliens. A media encampment had sprung up outside the gates of Theo's estate, with vans and campers and a flock of drones buzzing around the grounds. Theo hired more private security to man the gatehouse 24/7 and threatened to shoot down any drones flying lower than 100 meters over his house.

The spaceplane garnered considerable interest, drawing crowds of people hoping to get a look at an alien spacecraft. The Swiss army established a fifty meter barbed wire perimeter around the plane and erected a massive tent over it, hiding it from view. The crowds mostly disappeared after that. However, the opportunity to see an alien craft up close proved too much of a temptation for the Swiss internal security apparatus.

Two officers from the Ministry of Internal Security showed up at the army encampment one night. They had a letter from the Minister of Internal Security authorizing them to examine the spaceplane. Lieutenant Albrecht, who was in charge of the detachment guarding the plane, had no choice but to let them in, though he insisted on accompanying them.

They brought scientific instruments with them and began scanning the plane from one end to the other. Everything was fine until one of them actually touched the plane. An antenna on top of the plane emitted a bolt of lightning, which struck the man, knocking him off his feet. A second bolt struck the other man. Lieutenant Albrecht backed out of the tent and called his superior.

"Are they okay?" the man asked.

"I don't know. They were both unconscious when I left. If you want someone to go in and find out, send them over. I am not going anywhere near that plane, and neither are my men."

Eos had, of course, alerted Holly when the officers entered the tent, and she had called Theo and Adrian into her room to watch the incursion on her tablet. The two officers regained consciousness after a few minutes and made their way out of the tent, dazed but apparently undamaged.

"Adrian," Theo said. "Why don't you go up there first thing in the morning and have a little chat with Lieutenant Albrecht? See if you can smooth things over."

The next morning, Adrian found himself facing an angry lieutenant who was at least ten years older than he. The man launched into a rant about the harm done to the men—no one was harmed—and the inappropriateness of an electrified plane. Technically, Adrian had no authority here, and was frankly intimidated by Albrecht. He did, however, represent the Emissary, and everybody knew she was not someone to be messed with. He held up a hand, interrupting the lieutenant mid-sentence.

"Three things," he said in a quiet voice. "First, the Emissary sent me here to assess the situation and determine the extent to which her security protocols were breached." The man frowned.

"Second, *Eos* monitors everything going on around it and captured images of your intelligence officers examining the plane. It is difficult to see this as anything other than a blatant violation of the sovereignty of the aliens' emissary. We have forwarded the vid to your government with an official complaint."

The lieutenant started to say something, but Adrian held up a hand.

"Third, the Emissary warned your people that *Eos* has autonomous defenses and *will* defend itself. Fortunately for the two men who violated its security perimeter, the AI attached a low threat profile to the incursion and responded with non-lethal force. Had they, for example, tried to force their way into the plane, it might have killed them."

He didn't know if this last part was true, but it sounded good.

"I realize you had no choice but to let them in, so you likely bear no responsibility for the incursion. The Emissary appreciates the job you are doing protecting people from the *Eos*."

His hands were shaking when he got into his vehicle and headed back to Theo's house. He had gone toe-to-toe with an angry lieutenant in the Swiss Army and backed him down; even got an apology, which he promised to pass on to the Emissary. But he was a conflict avoider at heart, and this experience had pushed him well outside his comfort zone.

———

"Things like this are bound to keep happening as long as the Emissary's status remains ambiguous," he said when he got back to the estate. "And the failure of the Council to even acknowledge the Emissary's existence has created an information vacuum that all manner of confusion, rumors, fear-mongering, and other mischief are crowding into. We need formal recognition by the Council. And soon."

Robert said, "She has received inquiries from several enclave leaders requesting private meetings. Maybe we should take them up on it."

"That would be problematic," Theo said. "If you meet with individual enclave leaders, you will create the appearance of favoritism, which will complicate things later on. In my view, it is best to be patient and wait for a meeting with the full Council."

"Will that happen before or after hell freezes over?" Adrian said.

He agreed with Theo in principle, but three weeks in a PR vacuum was not a good place to be. Other voices were filling that vacuum with their own narratives, not all of which were favorable to the Emissary.

Initial public reaction to her arrival had been overwhelmingly positive. She was a hero, the lone survivor of the Jupiter Mission, sent back by the aliens with an offer of advanced technologies.

Her handling of the incident at *Tiangong Station,* in particular, won rave reviews on social media and received favorable coverage by most of the big news feeds. In a restrained but decisive action, she had put Major Reed in his place, and by extension the CRA and the UK, neither of whom was particularly popular these days.

It didn't hurt that the Emissary was photogenic; not beauty contest material, but an attractive woman nonetheless.

But then public attitudes toward her began to change. Journalists dug into her past, and what they found was not pretty. The news feeds started talking about a sexually promiscuous woman with a drinking problem which, as near as Adrian could tell, was more or less accurate. They interviewed some old flames who confirmed this image. Two former colleagues appeared on talk shows to describe a difficult and petty woman who gleefully eviscerated students who dared challenge her, and whose research methods and work ethic were questionable.

In parallel with this, a fresh wave of anti-alien sentiment was building. The Singapore Incident was resurrected and analyzed all over again, always leading to the suggestion that maybe the aliens had intentionally lured the world's leaders to Singapore to murder them with a nuclear bomb, not caring that they had also killed thousands upon thousands of innocent people.

Chatter about the nefarious intentions of the aliens flooded social media. Conspiracy theories were rampant; some with just enough truth to be believable as long as you didn't look too closely; others so fantastic that Adrian wondered how anybody could take them seriously. But people did.

At Adrian's request, Tomás brought in a cyber-security expert who spent a few days tracking down the negative social media. It turned out that two-thirds of it came from an army of bots originating in the CRA, Great Britain, and Australia.

The world-renowned Reverend Doctor Alexander Taylor emerged as the leading voice of the anti-alien crowd, using his globe-spanning daily program to attack the Emissary and the aliens. His message was a simple but effective one-two punch. On the one hand, he offered people a way to channel their fear and anger in the face of the existential threat of the end of the world, a threat they were powerless to do anything about. He linked the aliens and the Death Bringer together, pointing out how unlikely it was that both should appear at the same time. In his view, the aliens were responsible for the

Death Bringer, which they were using to frighten people into looking to them for help.

On the other hand, Taylor offered hope. He framed the aliens and the Death Bringer as a test of faith as the Last Days neared. He called on his followers to reject the false hope offered by the aliens and to turn instead to God, who would not allow the Death Bringer to destroy his people. This was where he leveled his fire at the Emissary, portraying her as the whore of Babylon, the great temptress found in the Book of Revelation who drew people away from God with the false promise of alien salvation.

It was a persuasive message delivered by a persuasive man, and people bought it. The more strident he became, the more his audience grew. Three weeks after Holly's arrival, his regular viewing audience had grown to encompass a third of the world's population.

All of this worried Adrain. It was not in his nature to make waves, nor was it his place to contradict Theo, who was his employer. If Theo said they should ignore public opinion for now and focus on the Council, that should have settled the matter. But it didn't. The more he thought about it, the more convinced he became that Theo was wrong.

He couldn't do an end run around Theo and take his arguments directly to the Emissary. She would just ask Theo what he thought. Besides, he was more than a little intimidated by her; not her personally, but who and what she represented. Still, he couldn't just sit around and do nothing. He went to Tomás.

They met in the security room, which doubled as Tomás' office and the nerve center of the security organization he was slowly building around the house and the Emissary. A half dozen monitors hung on the wall, rotating through cameras placed in various strategic locations, including drones.

"I am concerned about the negative trend in public opinion toward the Emissary," Adrian said. "There is a public relations war going on and the Emissary is losing, mainly because she isn't even in the fight. Frankly, she is getting slaughtered on the battlefield of public opinion." He was pleased with the military metaphor; Tomás, not so much.

"That's a bit melodramatic, don't you think?"

"You aren't concerned?"

"My job is to keep her safe, not to make her popular."

He couldn't fault Tomás for that. He was responsible for the Emissary's security. It made sense that his primary focus would lie there. But it was too narrow a viewpoint.

"I think there is a correlation between public opinion about the Emissary and her security. Don't you?"

Tomás was quiet for a moment. "I hear what you are saying. What does Theo say?"

"He says we should ignore the bad PR for now and focus on getting her in front of the Council of Enclaves."

Tomás rubbed the short goatee he was growing. "You don't agree with him?"

"I agree that the most important thing is to reach the Council, but that doesn't mean we have to ignore the public relations front in the meantime."

"So, what do you want from me?"

"I want you to help me change Theo's mind."

"I'm a bodyguard, not a war planner," he said with a chuckle. When Adrian didn't respond, he said, "Let's sketch out some ideas."

The next morning, Adrian called everyone together in the drawing room. He stood to address the little group. Theo had a puzzled expression on his face. Robert had his impassive lawyer face on. The Emissary sat expectantly with her head tilted a little to one side. Anna remained expressionless. Tomás appeared to be counting ceiling tiles.

"I am concerned," Adrian began. "There is a coordinated public relations campaign going on against the Emissary and the Fragment, or rather the aliens, since the world doesn't know anything about the Fragment."

This was met with nods. They watched the feeds, too.

"It is a sophisticated, well-orchestrated attack using multiple media streams. Most of it originates from the CRA and their allies. Its aim is to discredit the Emissary before she speaks to the Council of Enclaves. I have spoken to a few people I know at the Council, and they confirm that the CRA and their allies are behind the wall of silence we have hit. They are undermining her before she even tries to make her case."

Theo pressed his lips together. He saw where Adrian was going with this.

"They are winning. By the time the Emissary speaks to the Council of Enclaves, public opinion will have swung against her, and that is going to affect how her message is received. The world's leaders may all be autocrats of one sort or other, but they cannot afford to ignore public opinion. Nor are they immune to the pressure the CRA and its allies are putting on them. In short, unless we change public opinion toward the Emissary and the Fragment, I fear her words will fall on deaf ears."

He sat down. Theo was frowning and looked like he was about to speak when Tomás did something uncharacteristic: he offered an opinion.

"I agree with Adrian," he said. "From a security stand-point, the threats to the Emissary's life are growing as public opinion turns against her. The last time she went out—to see the Waaldendorf play—we were met by a mob of angry protestors and had to turn back. Frankly, I can no longer ensure her safety beyond the estate grounds. If the world turns against her, I don't know how she can accomplish her mission."

A tense silence followed. Theo stared at Tomás with what could only be described as astonishment.

"Adrian," Robert said. "What do you think we should do?"

Adrian remained seated. "I am not a public relations expert. We should hire one. In the meantime, I think the Emissary should hold a press conference where she lets the world see her and tells the world about the Fragment and what he is offering. That allows her to take control of the narrative, which to this point has been controlled by her enemies. It might also light a fire under the Council's collective ass."

A faint smile crossed Theo's face. He said, "I received an interesting call last night from an old friend, Cinta Alejandre. She berated me for being a tired, old-guard politician who was out of touch with the times and shamefully unaware of the power of social media; a characterization with which I took no small umbrage.

"After subjecting me to a few more insults, she said much the same thing you are saying, Adrian. I believe her exact words were, 'At least hold a press conference to get her out in front of people. You've got to get control of the narrative.' If I didn't know better, I would be tempted to think you drafted her as an ally behind my back." He glanced toward Tomás. "Not to mention my PPI." He rolled his eyes dramatically. "What is the world coming to? Oh, wait . . . the world is coming to an end, isn't it? I suppose that explains a lot of otherwise inexplicable behavior."

He stood and walked over to the window as though he could see past the closed drapes. Turning to face them, he said, "I understand Adrian's concern, and he is not wrong. However, if we do as he suggests, we risk embarrassing the Council of Enclaves. These are men and women who do not take well to being publicly embarrassed. Some of them have disappeared people for less than that. My advice is to keep working the Council of Enclaves track and try to avoid making things any more difficult than they already are. Eventually they will come around and invite Holly to speak to them."

"What do you think, sis?" Robert asked.

Adrian looked at the Emissary. Hers was the only opinion that mattered, in the end, but she had remained silent throughout the exchange. She looked around the room with a forlorn expression; at least, it seemed like that to him.

"I've seen the change in public opinion toward me," she said. "It is difficult not to take it personally; especially since some of the attacks contain at least a kernel of truth; more than a kernel in some cases. But I don't see how a press conference or a public relations counter-attack will change any of that, and I don't want to offend the very people I need to win over."

She looked at Adrian. "Thank you for bringing this up. I will think about it."

Adrian noticed his hands were shaking a little; not enough for anyone to notice, he hoped. His chin had developed a small quiver as well. He had openly opposed Theo, who had countered with a persuasive argument. Maybe he was wrong and Theo was right.

For the first time in his life, he understood what it was like to stake out a position with no certainty of being right. Theo did this all the time, projecting confidence and certainty, though Adrian knew he was often far from certain. It was part of what made him a leader and not a follower.

An epiphany of sorts struck him: he wasn't Theo and never would be. Theo was comfortable with ambiguity, comfortable making decisions based on incomplete and possibly incorrect information, comfortable living with more questions than answers. Adrian had watched world leaders up close, and that was how it was for most of them. They never had all the information they needed, and they knew it. When the time came to make a decision, they made the best one they could based on the available information and moved on.

Adrian wasn't made that way. He was fine as an administrator, implementing other people's decisions, but to be the decision-maker, never knowing if his decisions were right or wrong, and then accepting the consequences of those decisions . . . that just wasn't who he was. It was a sobering realization.

Two days later, the Emissary asked him to set up a press conference.

21

Polite applause greeted Holly as she walked to the podium. The hotel was used to handling press conferences and had a space dedicated to that purpose, but they were unprepared for the horde of reporters that showed up for the Emissary's first public appearance. Hundreds of media representatives from around the world had already been in Geneva, waiting to see what would unfold in the stand-off between the aliens' Emissary and the Council of Enclaves. According to Adrian, an overflow room was packed as well. Her security team was swamped trying to screen everyone before letting them into the main room.

Anna stood on the left side of the small stage, eyes scanning the crowd. Leon stood on the opposite side, also scanning the crowd. They both wore suits with body armor under their shirts. Tomás had tried to talk her into wearing a bullet-proof vest, but she refused.

Two more security people stood between her and the first row of journalists. She had been told that in the event of trouble, they would provide cover while Anna and Leon got her out of the room. They had even rehearsed it so she would know what to expect. She felt silly doing it and couldn't quite bring herself to believe it would ever come to that. It was just too surreal.

She cleared her throat and took a sip of water from a bottle on the podium, and gave a nod to Cinta Alejandre, who was in the front row. Holly had insisted she get a front-row seat and the first question. She owed her that much.

"Good evening," she said, a little surprised at how forceful and confident she sounded. "Thank you for coming. I will read a brief statement and then take questions."

Other than the rapid-fire stutter of cameras, the room was quiet, which she found unnerving. Her prepared remarks appeared on two teleprompters, one to the left of center and one to the right of center. Theo gave her a thumbs-up from the side of the room where he stood next to Anna. She began.

"My name is Holly Burton. I am the alien's emissary."

She paused for dramatic effect.

"Let me begin by correcting a misunderstanding about the alien. There is only one alien, not many."

She paused again to let her audience absorb that revelation.

"He is an ancient explorer who has been wandering the furthest reaches of the universe for a very long time. Around the time our last ice age ended, he happened upon our world and took an interest in us. He has been watching us ever since. He calls himself the Fragment."

The room was quiet. Even the cameras had stopped chattering. She had dropped two bombshells in the first thirty seconds.

"The Fragment has asked me to be his representative on Earth. I feel utterly unqualified for this task, which I neither asked for nor wanted. But who am I to argue with an ancient alien explorer?"

This produced some smiles and a smattering of chuckles.

"Twenty years ago, the Fragment initiated first contact with us in Singapore using an unmanned, unarmed spacecraft. He requested a meeting with our world's leaders, intending to warn them about the Death Bringer, which we were not yet aware of. He hoped this existential crisis would force the people of Earth to pull together to meet the challenge of saving our species from extinction. A thermonuclear detonation ended that meeting before it began.

"Our astronomers eventually discovered the Death Bringer on their own. At first, the world's governments tried to hide that knowledge while they cast around for a way to deal with it. There was none. Perhaps if we had begun earlier, when the Fragment brought his warning, there would have been time to develop the technologies necessary to save our species. But we never heard the Fragment's warning, and by the time we discovered the Death Bringer for ourselves, it was too late.

"Rumors about a killer asteroid spread as more and more astronomers, both professional and amateur, spotted the Death Bringer in the heavens. Cinta Alejandre broke the story in an interview with me and also revealed that three space agencies were working together to build a spaceship that would carry a team of astronauts to Europa, a moon of Jupiter, where the Fragment had constructed a base.

"That spaceship was the *Asimov*. The program was called the Jupiter Mission. Its purpose was to engage with the aliens, who we believed to be more advanced than us, and to seek their help. I was one of the Jupiter Six who made that journey."

She paused. The green lights on the cameras reminded her she was speaking to a larger audience than those in the room. Adrian had told her that several of the media giants would broadcast it live and that the live audience could reach a billion and a half people. She hoped so. The entire world needed to hear what she had to say.

"All of this you already know. Now let me tell you the rest of the story."

She took a sip of water.

"When we awoke from deep sleep on the *Asimov*, we discovered we were not at Europa, our intended destination, but Ganymede, another moon of Jupiter. The Fragment had entered a course change into our navigational system during the voyage while the crew was in deep sleep. Commander Tolya Fedorov, Communications Specialist Gina Walker, and I traveled to a base on Ganymede, where we met the Fragment.

"It turns out there was a saboteur on the *Asimov*: Major Benjamin Clark, our pilot. There was also a nuclear device we did not know about. Major Clark took control of the *Asimov*, brought it into an orbit skimming the moon's surface, and detonated the nuclear device directly over the alien base."

"A year and a half later, I awoke on Titan, one of the moons of Saturn, a gas giant twice as far from Earth as Jupiter is. I was the only survivor of the attack on Ganymede. The Fragment patched me up—his medical technology is literally out of this world—and sent me back as his Emissary to offer the human race the advanced technologies that will enable us to save ourselves."

She stopped and looked around the room. "I will take questions now." She pointed to the front row. "Ms. Alejandre."

She had caught Alejandre and everyone else off guard by ending so abruptly, with so much left unsaid, but the journalist recovered quickly.

"Dr. Burton, can you can tell us more about the alien? For example, what does he look like?"

"I don't know what he looks like. We humans live in a four-dimensional world made up of three spatial dimensions and one temporal. The Fragment lives in more dimensions than that. All but the tiniest sliver of him exists outside our three-dimensional space-time continuum and therefore outside our ability to perceive.

"Two hundred years ago, a schoolteacher named Edmond Abbott came up with an analogy that I find helpful for understanding higher dimensions. Imagine a two-dimensional world. Abbott calls it Flatland. It has length and width, but no height. Imagine this world is populated by two-dimensional people. Let's call them Flatlanders. Now, suppose a three-dimensional creature—like you or me—comes along and wants to interact with the Flatlanders. How would he show himself to them? He might stand in a Flatland pasture, but the Flatlanders would only see a thin slice of the bottom of his feet because they can't see in a third dimension. Furthermore, the feet would appear to be disconnected from each other, like two different creatures, and certainly wouldn't be recognizable as feet. Were he to touch the ground with a finger, it might appear as a dot, or maybe a circle, and would seem to have no connection with the feet. The Flatlanders might say, 'Show us what you really look like,' but he already is showing them what he looks like. The Flatlanders simply lack the capacity to see him as he really is.

"So it is with us and the Fragment. When we first met him on Ganymede, he chose to appear as an avatar: a man who would seem as human as anyone in this room. At first, we thought he was human. Is that what he *really* looks like? No. But it provided a way for our two species to communicate.

"Beyond that, I can tell you he is extremely intelligent, has an in-depth understanding of us, having observed us for most of our species' history, and has chosen to make himself known because he is curious about what we would become as a species if we weren't about to become extinct."

She took another sip of water.

A man next to Cinta Alejandre stood and said, "Vladimir Analexi, Moscow International News. Dr. Burton, the Jupiter Mission was predicated on the assumption that the Death Bringer is going to destroy our world and there is nothing we can do about it without some help. I am sure you know that not everyone sees Earth's destruction as inevitable. There are some who believe we can stop it, or at least deflect it, on our own without the help of the aliens. Others believe we can hide in underground bunkers and emerge after the Death Bringer has passed. We've all seen the end-of-the-world vids, right?"

"Indeed we have," she said with a smile. "I wish this was one of those."

She looked directly into one of the cameras at the back of the room.

"I want to be absolutely clear about this. The Death Bringer will destroy our world completely and irrevocably. When it leaves our solar system, Earth will no longer exist. Let me show you why that is."

She brought up a diagram of the solar system on the screen behind her. The planets were represented by blue dots and were labeled. The scale required to show all eight planets made the inner system seem small and crowded. A prominent red dot appeared between the orbits of Neptune and Saturn.

"The red dot represents the Death Bringer. It is currently about two billion kilometers from Earth and is falling into our Sun's gravity well, gaining speed as it does. At first, astronomers thought it was an asteroid, though it soon became apparent that it was too big to be an asteroid. It had to be a wandering planet, a Jupiter-sized one. There are lots of rogue planets wandering around our galaxy. Unfortunately, it is not a rogue planet, either.

"If it were an asteroid or a rogue planet, even a Jupiter-sized one, destroying or deflecting it might be a possibility. But it is neither. It is a star. Specifically, a brown dwarf; an aborted star that did not have enough initial mass to ignite its thermonuclear furnace and become a full-blown star like ours. This one has been wandering around for at least 10 billion years, slowly cooling, getting darker and darker, which is one reason we didn't notice it until it was well into our solar system. It is about the same size as Jupiter, the largest planet in our solar system, but 61 times more massive. And therein lies the problem.

"Think of an automobile driving down the street at normal speed. It would take a fair amount of force to stop it or deflect it, but it could be done. Now imagine it is a run-away, fully loaded tractor-trailer rig. It would be a lot harder to stop, wouldn't it? Though still within the realm of possibility. Now imagine it is a run-away locomotive barreling down the track at top speed.

"The Death Bringer is that locomotive barreling down the track toward us. It is more massive than all the planets in our solar system put together, and it is coming at us at an incredibly high speed. There is nothing we can do to stop it. Or even deflect it. It is simply too massive and has too much momentum. Were we to detonate all the nuclear weapons in the world at one place on its surface, it would hardly notice. Even the Fragment cannot stop it. He may be more advanced than us, but he is not a god. There are things even he cannot do, and this is one of those things. The Death Bringer is coming, and it brings with it the end of our world."

A red line extended from the red dot, raced into the crowded inner system in a curving trajectory, arced around the sun, and left the solar system at a ninety-degree angle to its approach.

"As you can see, the Death Bringer's trajectory will bring it into the inner system, where it will swing around the sun and leave on a different trajectory. Its effect on the outer planets—Jupiter, Saturn, Uranus, and Neptune—will be negligible because it will not come anywhere near them on its journey to the inner system. The inner system will not be so fortunate."

She zoomed the view in on the four inner planets and the Asteroid Belt.

"The blue dots are the planets Mercury, Venus, Earth, and Mars. You can see the Asteroid Belt at the outer edge of this view. It is located halfway between Mars and Jupiter. Now watch what will happen when the Death Bringer passes through the inner system."

A red line entered from the left, clearing a path through a section of the Asteroid Belt. It passed by Mars, dragging it out of its orbit and throwing it out of the solar system. Earth was on the other side of the sun as the red line crossed its orbit, so Venus was the Death Bringer's next target. It collided head on with the shrouded planet, leaving nothing but rubble behind. As it swung around the Sun and headed back out into space, it swept past Earth, which it tossed into the Sun before leaving the solar system with Mercury and some rubble from Venus in tow. The inner system was gone except for a storm of asteroids flying every which way.

She ran the simulation backward and then forward again. The room was deathly quiet.

A woman somewhere in the middle of the crowd said, "How can the Fragment save us from *that*?"

This was the question Holly had been waiting for. Up to this point, her presentation had been a dispassionate explanation of the situation. Now she began her appeal for action.

"The Fragment can save some of us, but not all of us." She paused to let that sink in. "It should be obvious by now that if we as a species have a future, it is not here; it is out there." She pointed toward the ceiling. "If we are to survive the end of our world, we have to leave.

"The Fragment will not intervene directly to save us. He has a kind of non-interference clause built into his moral value system that prohibits him from interfering with the natural course of events. Don't ask me to explain that, because I can't.

"However, he is willing to bend the rules a little and give us a small technological boost; something we likely would have achieved on our own if we had another hundred years or so and didn't spend it fighting among ourselves; something that will make it possible for a few of us to leave Earth before the end of the world.

"This technological boost will not solve our problem by itself. We will have to do the hard work of using that knowledge. The nations of the world will have to set aside their tribalism and animosities, pull together, and pour all their effort and resources into the greatest project humankind has ever undertaken. Anything less than this and we will fail, and our species will become extinct."

She looked around the room, then back at the cameras. "Where will we go? We have two options. We can colonize the moons of Jupiter and Saturn, or we can leave our solar system and colonize worlds in other star systems. The Fragment can recommend a few. In either case, it will not be possible to evacuate three billion people along with the supplies, animals, plants, infrastructure, and everything else we will need to start over somewhere else. Like Noah's Ark, only a few will be saved."

A man in the back shouted, "How many are a few?"

"One Hundred Twenty Thousand."

This produced some murmuring. The man stood, held up his tablet on which he had presumably done the math, and said, "That's 0.01% of the world's population."

"Yes, it is."

"What about the rest?"

"They will die when the world ends."

She expected a barrage of questions in response to this. Instead, she got more silence.

Cinta Alejandre stood. "Have you met with the Council yet?"

Cinta no doubt knew the answer to this question, but she was giving Holly a chance to address it on her own terms.

"I have made several attempts to arrange a meeting with the Council of Enclaves but have received no response, not

even an acknowledgement that I am here. It is my understanding that two powerful alliances are stonewalling."

She gave them a moment to absorb that. Everyone knew
which two she was talking about.

"Frankly, that is why I am holding this press conference.
The Fragment has offered us the technology we need to
survive as a species. This is too important to leave in the
hands of a few politicians and strongmen huddled behind
closed doors, more worried about saving their piece of the pie
than saving the species from extinction. This is a matter for
the entire world to decide. This is a matter for *you*, the citizens
of the world, to decide. I call on you to demand that your
leaders meet with me immediately so we can get on with the
business of saving the human race. We do not have the
luxury—"

The doors at the back of the room burst open and a crowd
of people dressed in black and wearing balaclavas forced
their way into the room, shoving cameras and cameramen
aside, hitting people with batons as they made their way
toward Holly.

She heard Theo's voice: "Anna, get her out of here."

22

Holly froze, staring blankly at the chaos unfolding in front of her. Then Anna and Leon were beside her. Anna grabbed her arm with one hand, pushed her head down with the other, and proceeded to fast-walk her away from the podium. Leon had his hand on her other arm. They picked up speed when they got to the hallway, forcing her to jog to keep up. It was uncomfortable, just like in the run-through, but at least she knew what to expect.

Tomás fell in beside them, his head pivoting this way and that. He had a gun in his hand and was talking into his headset: "Alpha team, meet us at the back entrance and form up around the principal. Get the car ready. Beta team, see to the secondaries. Overwatch, check our route."

She only vaguely understood what he was saying, but three heavily armed men and women appeared seemingly out of nowhere and crowded around them as they moved out of the building and into the parking lot. She felt like a football in a rugby scrum. A car was waiting for them. Somebody opened the back door, and Anna unceremoniously shoved her into the back seat, then followed her in. She was vaguely aware of Leon climbing into the front passenger seat.

"Buckle up," Anna said as she pulled the car door shut behind them. She slapped the driver's shoulder and said, "Go!" Then she tapped her headset: "Principal is secured and away."

Holly was thrown back into the seat as the vehicle sped away from the site of her press conference, which had gone somewhat differently than she had expected. She fumbled with the seat belt until Anna reached over and locked it for her.

"W-what about the others?"

"We have a team assigned to them. They'll be fine."

"Who were those people?" Suddenly, she burst into tears for no apparent reason. "I'm sorry," she sobbed, covering her face with her hands.

Anna put a hand on her arm. "It's alright, ma'am. It's just adrenaline overload. You're safe now. We had a contingency plan for this situation and—"

The driver interrupted. "Overwatch is redirecting us."

Anna tapped her headset and listened for a few moments, which gave Holly time to get herself under control. Here she was, the Fragment's emissary sent to save the world, hunkered down in the back seat of a car crying her head off. How great was that? Not to mention embarrassing.

"Overwatch?" She didn't really care, but it seemed like she should make some effort to understand what was going on around her. She was having trouble keeping her eyes open and felt like a limp rag.

"Ma'am?" Anna shook her shoulder. "Ma'am? Are you alright?"

Her head cleared, and she found herself wide awake and alert, almost euphoric. The nanites must have flooded her bloodstream with something. Anna was peering at her with a concerned look. So was Leon.

"Yeah, I'm okay. Sorry about that."

They both looked relieved.

"To answer your question," Anna said carefully, "Overwatch is a team in a helicopter; our eyes in the sky. There is an accident on Highway One blocking all lanes. Overwatch is redirecting us to an alternate route."

"Are we going back to the house?"

"Yes."

"What about the others?" She had already asked this question. Why was she repeating herself?

Anna answered calmly, with no sign of reproach. "They will meet us there."

Another wave of clarity washed over her. The nanites must be working overtime to keep her from going into shock.

She put her hand on her amulet and formed a thought: *Gabriel.*

I am here, the AI said in her mind.

What can you tell me about the accident on Highway 1?

It is a diversion to force you onto an alternate route.

"Anna," she said as calmly as she could. "Doesn't it strike you as odd that a major accident would happen on our planned route just as we made our getaway from an attack at the hotel?"

Leon jerked his head around to look at her. Anna gave her a searching look. "Do you know something we don't?"

"It just seems like an unlikely coincidence."

She tapped her headset. "Overwatch, this is Lindstrom. How likely is it that the accident is a diversion?"

She listened for a few moments. "The primary asked."

A few more moments passed, then the SUV made an abrupt sharp turn down a side street, throwing Holly against the car door. Another turn a few blocks later threw her the other way, almost into Anna's lap. They pulled into a parking lot, throwing gravel in a wide arc as the vehicle spun around so that it was facing the driveway. They were in a park. The sun had gone down, but the park was well-lit. There were children playing. Hovering mothers turned as one to face the offending vehicle.

"What's going on?" She asked. She wished she had a headset.

"We are going to wait here while another team checks out the alternate route," Anna said. "Just to be sure."

There sure were a lot of teams.

Anna listened to her headset some more, frowned, and glanced at Holly. "You were right. Two vehicles were waiting for us three miles further on. They fled when they realized they were up against a heavily armed security team instead of the Fragment's emissary." She grinned.

"Who were you talking to?"

"Tomás. He told us to go with your hunch."

She gave Holly another searching look, but Holly just shrugged her shoulders. "Can we go home now? I am exhausted and just—"

Leon interrupted: "Overwatch says an unidentified vehicle is approaching our location at high speed."

Holly peered at the front window into the growing darkness. A vehicle whipped around the corner and headed for the park. It was moving fast.

"Overwatch, this is Lindstrom," Anna said in a calm, almost casual voice. "We have an incoming threat. How far away are reinforcements? . . . I see. We're going to make a break for it. What do you advise? . . . Got it. Can you run interference for us?"

Leon said to the driver, "Show time, Harry. Bump and run."

"Everybody buckle up and hang on," the driver said. "Things are gonna get interesting now."

Things were already way past interesting as far as Holly was concerned, but maybe the people charged with protecting her had a different scale for measuring such things.

An unexpected chortle bubbled up from her throat. She slapped her hand over her mouth.

Gravel spat out behind them as the vehicle's wheels spun. Holly was thrown back into her seat when the wheels found traction, and they accelerated toward the on-coming head-lights. Both vehicles reached the driveway of the park at the same time. The other vehicle made a wide turn to avoid a collision. Holly's driver turned toward it at the last moment and rammed it just behind the back wheels. Holly was jerked to the left and then to the right as they bounced away and on to the road. Apparently that was the *bump* part of bump-and-run, and now they were doing the *run* part.

She wasn't sure, but she thought the other vehicle was left doing donuts in the gravel lot. She hoped nobody in the park got hurt.

Anna looked out the back window. "They are pursuing." She nodded at something someone was saying through the headset.

Leon said, "Nice job, Harry."

"That's what they pay me the big bucks for."

"What? You get big bucks? I'm gonna have to complain about that."

"About me getting big bucks?"

"No, about me getting mediocre bucks."

"Gosh, Leon. I'm real sorry to hear that."

Holly guessed they were doing fifty when they reached the intersection with the main road. Her driver didn't bother slowing down for either the stop sign or the turn, but barreled around the corner, alternated between the brake and the accelerator to execute a turn that Holly would not have thought possible at that speed. For a moment they seemed to move sideways, then the vehicle straightened out with a jerk and the engine whined as they picked up speed.

Harry glanced at the rear-view mirror. "Pussies!"

He had a German accent she had not noticed before. Maybe it came out when he was under stress. Or was having fun. She craned her neck around to look out the back window. Their pursuers were far behind them. Apparently, their driver hadn't been willing to take the corner as fast as her driver had.

"Here comes the cavalry," Leon said. Two sets of head-lights appeared in front of them and sped past in a blur.

"They'll handle our pursuers," Leon said. "Let's get the primary back to the compound."

Holly caught Harry's eye in the rear-view mirror. "That would be you, ma'am," he said. She tried to smile, but suspected it came out more like a grimace.

"Don't encourage him," Anna said. "He's having altogether too much fun as it is."

Holly made a wild guess that this was not the first opera-tion they had worked together on.

They eventually reached the turnoff for Theo's estate and turned into the drive that led to the mansion. The media encampment was deserted. Presumably, they were all at the hotel. Two police officers manned the gatehouse. Her driver slowed to a stop about ten meters from them.

"Anna?" he said.

Anna was quiet for a moment. "I don't like it." She tapped her headset. "This is Lindstrom. There are two police officers at the gatehouse. Our security is not in evidence."

The police officers pulled their guns, took aim with both hands on their guns, and flexed a little at the knees. Just like real police.

"Vehicle behind us," Harry said.

Holly started to turn around to look, but Anna reached over, released her seat belt, and pushed her into the footwell. "Stay there," she said. She took out her gun.

"Overwatch," Anna said. "We are trapped on the road into the estate. Two gunmen dressed like police officers in front of us. An SUV behind us. Three people have gotten out of the SUV, weapons out. One has a long gun."

She listened and said, "Understood." Then, "Let's do it, Harry."

The car jumped forward, and Holly heard bullets pinging off the windshield. Then they were out from under the trees that lined the road and into the open area in front of the mansion. She felt the car spinning. Then it stopped.

Anna opened the door and rolled out onto the gravel driveway, coming up on one knee with her gun out in front. She fired three times in quick succession. Holly was vaguely aware that Leon was out of the car on the other side, also firing his gun. Then loud automatic gunfire erupted, seemingly right above them, followed by an explosion. The car rocked violently as though someone had rammed it. The gunfire stopped. Anna stood, swinging her gun this way and that.

"You okay, ma'am?" It was her driver, Harry. He was looking down at her from the front seat.

"I think so."

"Looks like it's over, but you should stay where you are until Anna says it's okay to get out." He seemed totally calm.

She was anything but calm. Her mind kept replaying bits and pieces of the car chase and the firefight in no particular order. She said, "It was just supposed to be a press conference."

"What was that, ma'am?"

"Nothing. Just talking to myself."

"Hey, whatever brings you back to ground."

Anna appeared at the car door. "You can sit up, ma'am, but I'd like you to stay in the vehicle."

Holly crawled onto the seat and looked around. A helicopter circled above; a heavy-caliber gun pointing out an open door. There were three pockmarks on the car's windshield, which was apparently bulletproof. A vehicle was on fire at the edge of the trees. There were bodies on the ground and the smell of gunpowder and burning flesh in the air.

"Whoever they were," she said, "I guess they picked a fight with the wrong people."

Harry laughed, a little louder than seemed necessary. Maybe it was part of his getting back to ground, whatever that meant. "That they did, ma'am. That they did."

Anna slid in beside her and closed the door. Leon stood outside with his gun still out.

Another SUV came down the road, maneuvered around the burning vehicle, and drove up behind them. It disgorged four heavily armed men who assumed a defensive perimeter around her vehicle, assault rifles out and at the ready. They looked like they meant business.

Another vehicle drove in, and four more armed security people climbed out, including Tomás. He wore body armor like the rest of them and carried what looked like a short-barreled shotgun. She reached for the door handle, but Anna stopped her.

"We wait for Tomás to give us the all clear."

Tomás did a slow three-sixty scan of the immediate vicinity and sent three men into the house. Ten minutes later, they returned and talked with him. He tapped his headset and said something.

"We can get out now," Anna said. "On my side, if you don't mind."

Anna holstered her weapon and stepped out of the vehicle. Holly followed, feeling more than a little intimidated by all the firepower on display. All for her. A movement on the roof caught her eye. It was a man with a rifle. Fear flashed through her.

"Sniper," Anna said. "One of ours."

She took a deep breath and let it out slowly. This was definitely not what she had expected when she got out of bed this morning.

Anna gently took her arm and walked her through the entrance and into the entry hall. Leon was right behind them. He had put his gun away. Holly started down the hall.

"Ma'am, where are you going?" Anna said.

She turned around to face her. "The ladies' room, if that's all right with you. And my protection detail. And the sniper on the roof. Should I get permission from Tomás?"

It came out bitchier than she had intended, powered by a surge of anger. She wasn't sure where it came from. There was no reason for her to snap at the people who had probably saved her life.

Anna seemed not to notice. Or, more likely, decided to ignore it. "I'll come with you," she said cheerfully. "I could use a bio break after all that excitement."

When they got back to the drawing room, they found Tomás, Theo, Robert, and Adrian engaged in a heated conversation. Leon was nowhere to be seen.

". . . inside information," Theo was saying, a little too loudly. "They knew our primary and secondary routes. They had backup contingencies."

Tomás' calm voice replied. "We don't know that. Our primary route was obvious. Our secondary route might have been a good guess. Or maybe they had several alternate routes covered."

"In any case," Theo said, "it was a well-planned, well-executed attempt on the Emissary's life."

"Should we move her someplace else?" Robert said.

"I don't know where—"

They stopped talking and turned to face her when she walked in. They were all standing. She walked across the room with as much dignity as she could muster—her legs were rubbery—and sat in the corner chair she was coming to think of as her own.

"Maybe someone should ask the *primary* where she wants

to be kept," she said. "Though I suppose any ol' bunker will do as long as I can get pizza delivered."

Anna took her usual place behind and to one side of her.

"We were just talking about how to keep you safe, sis," Robert said. "Things have escalated to a whole other level."

Holly snorted. "I already have so much security I'm feeling claustrophobic. I can't even go to the bathroom without an armed guard." She waved a hand in Anna's direction. "So if you all don't mind, I'd like to stay where I am."

She held up a hand to forestall objections. "I can't do what I need to do if I'm hiding. I need to talk to people and people need to talk to me. That includes every day, normal people on the street, and press conferences, and meetings, and world leaders, business and industry leaders, and religious leaders." She stopped to catch her breath. "That means I am going to be in harm's way, and that's just the way it is. Besides, I want to go shopping tomorrow."

She paused to take in the horrified looks.

"You'll all just have to make sure nobody gets a clear shot at me." She smirked, though it wasn't really funny. Apparently, there were people out there who would like nothing better than to see her dead.

She felt light-headed. Whatever her nanites had done to get her through the crisis was wearing off. She turned to Anna. "I'd like to go to my room." She stood. "Now, if you gentlemen will excuse me . . . "

Anna caught her arm as she stumbled, but she managed to remain on her feet. She was absolutely *not* going to faint in front of everyone.

23

Anna accompanied the Emissary upstairs to her room. Robert followed them into the room, but Anna gave him a meaningful look.

"Let me know if you need anything," he said as he retreated back into the hall. The Emissary waved her hand in his direction without looking and sat on the edge of the bed. She began unbuttoning her blouse, looked down at her shoes, and then up at Anna.

"Can you help me with my shoes?"

Anna tugged her shoes and stockings off and helped her out of her blouse and skirt. She crawled under the covers and a few minutes later her breathing became slow and regular.

Anna sat on a padded chair near the French doors. The Emissary was a cypher. According to the dossier Tomás had given her, she was a strong, confident, self-sufficient woman who rarely needed help from anyone and did not readily ask for help when she did; a classic over-achiever, successful in everything she attempted, chosen to be one of the Jupiter Six, recruited by an alien being to be his representative on Earth, tasked with convincing the world to abandon what it had been doing for the last ten thousand years and start doing something else. Yet she needed her PPI's help to get undressed.

Not that she held that against her. This was probably the first time in her life she had experienced anything like what happened today. All things considered, she had acquitted herself well. Now that the threat was over, she had crashed, physically and emotionally. An adrenaline overload could do that to you if you didn't know how to handle it. It was no surprise she was sound asleep now. Her body knew what she needed.

This was not Anna's first assignment. The job sometimes required her to be more than a bodyguard. In many ways, it was an intimate job, if only because of her constant proximity to her principal. A PPI saw every side of the principal, the good and the bad alike. That made for a difficult balancing act: how to be there for the principal while still maintaining the professional distance needed to do your job well.

Social media was awash with rumors and conspiracy theories about the Emissary. In the absence of facts, people made stuff up. One particularly persistent rumor claimed she was not human at all; that she was some kind of android impersonating the real Holly Burton; that the real Holly Burton had died with the rest of the Jupiter Six at Ganymede.

Anna was a skeptical person by nature and generally dismissed conspiracy theories out of hand for the simple reason that they were almost always wrong. She also considered herself a good judge of people and was pretty sure the Emissary was the real deal. The woman put on a good face in front of others, but behind the persona she was as vulnerable and flawed as anyone; maybe more so than most. Things had gotten a little wild today, and she'd had a few bumpy moments, but she had held it together.

Anna did not know whether she was disappointed or reassured by this. Her charge was more fragile than the people she usually protected; less experienced with the cut-throat world of movers and shakers, less hard-nosed, not so tough-skinned. She was also an emotionally wounded person. That much was obvious from even a cursory reading of her dossier. Brilliant, to be sure, but damaged.

Anna was older than her principal. She had never had children, but something about this woman made her want to protect her the way she imagined a mother would protect her children. It was turning out to be a more complicated assignment than she had expected.

A knock came at the door. Her hand went reflexively to the weapon at her side.

"Who is it?"

"Theo and Robert."

"Come."

They let themselves in. Robert walked over to his sister and stood over her sleeping form. Theo sat on a chair on the other side of a small table from Anna.

"How is she?"

"She's fine. The anxiety of the press conference, the stress of a high octane car chase, bullets flying, and explosions . . . it all put her into serious fight-or-flight mode. She must have gotten some training somewhere on how to manage that, because she handled it better than I would have expected. She held it together until we got back here, then the emotional bottom dropped out from under her. Nothing unusual about that. Sleep is the best thing for her."

He nodded absently. Robert joined them.

After a while, Theo said, "Robert and I are going to the Council building tomorrow morning to confront Madurasinghe about why he is stonewalling us. I'm pretty sure I know the answer, and I suspect the press conference shook things up over there. I want to get the lay of the land before we do anything else."

Anna didn't say anything. He was not soliciting her opinion, and he certainly didn't need her permission. He was just informing her they would be away from the compound in the morning.

"There is something you should know about Holly," he said. He looked at Robert.

Robert said, "We decided you should know that the Fragment gave Holly millions, maybe billions, of microscopic nanites that patrol her body looking for things to fix and invaders to kill. There probably isn't a disease or poison in the world that can harm her. Their primary purpose is to keep her healthy. And young. I'm sure you noticed she looks younger than she is. That's the nanites. Only Theo, Tomás, and I know this. And Holly, of course. And now you."

"Okay," she said. "She has an army of teeny-tiny alien machines running around inside her. I think I get that." She didn't, but it didn't matter. It was what it was.

"They also keep her internal chemistry in balance. I suspect that's what you saw right after we left the press conference when she lost it for a moment and then seemed to pull herself together. The nanites balanced her internal chemistry to keep her alert and to keep her from going into shock. The Fragment has not left her without resources."

"Are you sure she needs a PPI?"

He smiled at this. "The nanites are pretty much limited to taking care of her physical body. She still needs protection. I doubt her nanites could do anything about a bullet through the head."

"She is also going to need friends in the days ahead," Theo said, "and as you have probably surmised by now, she does not make friends easily. We are hoping you will become her confidante, maybe even her friend."

She looked toward the sleeping form on the bed. "I have come to the same conclusion. It's a tricky thing to balance. If I lose professional distance, it will reduce my effectiveness as her PPI. What does Tomás think?"

"Tomás thinks you are up to it."

"Okay then. Friendly PPI it is."

———

After they left, Anna turned out the lights and moved through the bathroom to her room. She got herself ready for bed and brought up her personal feed. There was a vidmail from her mother.

It was only a few hours to Stockholm by air, then two hours by train to Norrköping, where she grew up and where her mother still lived. But it had been a few years since she had been home. Her parents had never understood why she joined the army and then the Special Operations Group. Whenever she returned home on leave, she found herself defending her decision all over again. It got worse when she left the army and became a contractor. After a few more painful visits, she stopped going home. Even vidcoms were minefields. They only communicated by vidmail these days, and that not very often.

The message was brief: her mother pleading for her to come home and finally breaking down in tears. Funny how a little thing like the end of the world could change things. Anna had already decided this would be her last assignment. Then she would go home. But that wasn't likely to happen soon.

Her assignments normally lasted anywhere from a few weeks to a few months. Then she would take a vacation and move on to the next assignment. She was good at what she did, and her services were in demand. She had protected all sorts of people: athletes, politicians, celebrities, actors, billionaires. She prided herself on being able to understand her clients on their own terms; to get inside their heads; to be able to predict what they would do in any situation.

This assignment was different, though. The Emissary wasn't like any of the other people she had protected. She represented humanity's last, best chance to survive. She alone could provide the knowledge they needed to build ships and space stations and whatever else they needed to escape the doomed planet, and her task would not be finished until 120,000 people had left Earth; a remnant of humanity; the future of the human race. In the meantime, she needed a protector; a protector for the end of the world.

She opened a connection to her mom's home. It pinged for several seconds. She was probably in bed. She was about to disconnect when a voice spoke on the other end.

"Anna?" Her mother's image filled the screen.

"Hi, momma."

"I was so worried. I saw you on the feed. At that woman's press conference. Hilary or something."

"Holly, momma, Holly Burton."

"Yes, well, is she really an emissary from the aliens?"

"Yeah, she is."

"Is what she says about the end of the world true?"

"Yes. It's all true."

"My goodness. That's just . . . what happened at the end? All I saw was you and her and a crowd of armed men rushing you out of the room. Are you and this Burton woman all right?"

"We are fine. It was just some thugs who decided to break up a press conference."

"Well, they certainly did that, didn't they? People are so rude these days."

"We got the Emissary back to the compound we are staying at. She is sleeping now."

"You should be, too." Her mother frowned. "I take it you are one of her bodyguards or something. Though there were a lot of people with guns around her. Even Nilsson doesn't have security like that."

Anna laughed. It felt good to laugh with her mother.

"Actually he does, momma. They maintain a low profile so you don't notice them."

"So what exactly do *you* do?"

"I am her PPI; her personal protection individual. I make sure she is safe at all times. I go everywhere she goes. Her bedroom and mine share a bathroom."

"Is it dangerous?"

"Yes, it is." She paused. "I am very good at it."

She and her mother stared at each other for a few moments.

"You look good," her mom said. That was unexpected.

"So do you, momma."

"When are you coming home?"

That was the question she didn't want to deal with, but it was the reason she had called.

"I don't think I will come home soon. I hope to come home before the end so we can be together at, you know, the end."

There was another pause. A tear ran down her mother's cheek.

"It's this Emissary woman, isn't it?"

"Right now, she may be the most important person in the world. I can't walk away. Not with all that is at stake."

"Can she save us?"

"Some of us."

"Will she save you?"

Anna had not thought about that. It was a good question. Presumably the Emissary would go with the few who would leave Earth, and it was reasonable to assume that she would take her key people with her to help her establish Humanity 2.0. She would have to ask about that. Maybe she could take her mother with her.

"Anna?"

"Sorry, momma. I don't know if I will be among those who leave. I don't even know if the Emissary will go with them. She's the kind of person who might decide to stay behind with the rest of humanity. I haven't asked. Right now, I'm just doing my best to keep her safe."

They sat in silence for a few seconds. Then her mother said, "I am tired, dear. I think I'll go back to bed now."

"Momma? Do you understand?"

"Yes, Anna, I understand why you can't come home just yet. Keep that Emissary woman safe. I am proud of you. And Anna?"

"Yes?"

"I love you."

"I love you too, Momma."

24

Two days later Holly found herself sitting next to Secretary General Gavesh Madurasinghe in the Council of Enclaves chamber. Her press conference had the desired effect. The attack on her personally, which went viral, probably didn't hurt either. According to Madurasinghe, some members of the Council were unhappy with the Emissary for forcing their hand. But they were here, and so was she, and that was what mattered.

The circular seating arrangement of the council chamber was loosely modeled after the old United Nations Security Council chamber. The leaders of the alliances were present. Together, they spoke for 54 enclaves representing a billion or so people. The remaining two billion people on Earth lived outside the Enclaves and had no voice on the Council for the simple reason that none of the warlords could speak for more than the few thousand Outsiders they happened to rule over at any given time. The enclaves made trade agreements with nearby warlords, and Holly hoped she could persuade the enclaves to include some of them in the remnant of humanity that would leave Earth. It would be a tough sell.

There were two seats behind each of them and three seats

behind those, forming two concentric circles around the Council members. Theo and Adrian sat behind Holly; Robert, Tomás, and Anna behind them. There were no empty seats.

In theory, weapons were not allowed in the Council chamber, but nobody checked for weapons when they came in. They weren't even scanned. Holly assumed each world leader present had one or more armed bodyguards in his or her contingent. Tomás and Anna were certainly armed. Hopefully, the adage "an armed society is a polite society" would hold true in this setting.

Inside the circle, in a space called The Pit, five men and women sat around a table in front of terminals. They handled administrative and clerical functions. Holly's tablet was connected to the local network so she could pass information to them, such as images she might want to put up on the large vid screen on the wall behind her.

Dr. Madurasinghe spoke into his microphone. "I call this meeting of the Council of Enclaves to order. Without objection we will dispense with the reading of minutes from the last meeting, as well as all other business except the matter that has brought us together today."

He looked around and said, "So ordered. There are two items on the agenda for this session. The first is to receive Dr. Holly Burton's credentials as the Fragment's Emissary. The chair recognizes President Deng Wei of the People's Republic of China."

President Deng was a young-looking man five seats to her right. "Thank you, Mr. Secretary General," he said, then bowed his head toward Holly. "Dr. Burton, I bid you a warm welcome from the People's Republic of China, whose space station was honored to be your first point of contact upon your return to Earth."

He nodded to someone in the pit, and an image appeared on the big screen. It also appeared on a vid screen built into the desk in front of Holly. It contained the wording of his motion, which he read aloud.

"The People's Republic of China moves that the Council recognize Dr. Holly Margaret Burton as the Emissary of the Fragment, the alien who currently inhabits the moons of Jupiter, and that she be granted credentials of full ambassadorship to this body, which ambassadorship includes this body's recognition that she will speak for the Fragment and will convey back to the Fragment the deliberations and decisions of this body."

He sat down and Madurasinghe said, "The chair recognizes Prime Minister Galal of the African Federation."

"Thank you, Mr. Secretary General," said the short, bald-headed man seated to Holly's immediate left. "The African Federation seconds the motion and moves for a vote of unanimous consent."

"Objection." The deep and distinctly British voice came from three seats to Holly's left.

"The chair recognizes Prime Minister Weatherford of Great Britain."

Holly looked back at Theo, who leaned forward and spoke into her ear. "At this point, everything is pretty much scripted. Everyone knows the CRA opposes any form of official recognition and that its objection would come either through the Brits or Aussies. Arguments for and against will be laid out and a vote will be called. They will approve your credentials by a vote of nine to three, or possibly eight to four. But before that, everybody gets to say their little piece. Mostly for the folks back home."

"Why am I even here for this part?" She asked.

"To practice sitting through long, boring meetings. A skill you will have to cultivate in the months and years ahead."

"It's a lot of bureaucratic bullshit if you ask me," she said. Prime Minister Galal, sitting to her immediate left, tried to suppress a smile.

Weatherford said, "Great Britain objects on the basis that we have no proof that Dr. Burton can speak for the aliens."

This provoked a somewhat heated debate that began civilly enough, but soon degenerated into a shouting match. After twenty minutes of vitriol, only some aimed at her, Holly had had enough.

Theo must have sensed what was coming, because his hand came to rest on her shoulder. "Please don't do anything rash," he said.

She glanced at him and stood.

The President of the Russian Federation happened to be speaking at that moment. He noticed her and stopped talking. The room was quiet.

"Forgive the interruption, President Novikov." She looked around the circle of world leaders, suddenly aware that her legs were trembling. Adrenaline rush time. Maybe she should have remained seated, but it was too late for that now.

"With all due respect, ladies and gentlemen, this is bull-shit. I don't have time for it and, more important, neither do you."

She took a deep breath and let it out slowly to calm herself.

"The Fragment sent me back to Earth with a proposal for giving us certain advanced technologies that will enable us to save our species from extinction. Time is of the essence. Already you have wasted three weeks of my time and the world's time by stonewalling my appearance here.

"This is not the time for business as usual. Every hour spent in meetings like this brings the Death Bringer an hour closer and reduces the time we have to prepare and the number of people we can save. You, the world's leaders, need to decide whether you want to save the human race or continue playing petty power games. You can't have it both ways."

Several people started to speak, but she held up both hands to stop them.

"I didn't ask to be the Fragment's Emissary. That was his idea. Frankly, I don't give a damn whether you formally recognize me as his emissary. I don't need your recognition. I don't need your honorifics. I don't need credentials. That spaceship up there in orbit is all the credentials I need. That and the knowledge I offer that just might save our species.

"So you can continue doing whatever it is you think is more important than the business of saving humanity, but I have better things to do. I will be at Ambassador Peeters' home when you are ready to have a serious conversation."

She turned to her delegation and said, "We are leaving."

They recovered their composure and stood with her. Madurasinghe was on his feet. He placed a hand on Holly's arm and said, "Dr. Burton. Please."

The voice of President Vasquez of Patagonia rang out: "This is an outrage. I demand an apology."

"Vasquez, sit down and shut the fuck up," said Marna Acker, a short, overweight woman. "Mr. General Secretary, I move to end debate on the motion before us."

Madurasinghe quickly said, "Is there a second?"

Someone shouted, "Second."

"Those in favor?"

Holly turned to face the Council. Hands went up. A young man at the table in the middle of the circle stood and did a quick count. "Eight votes in favor," he announced.

"Opposed?" Madurasinghe said.

Four hands went up: the Christian Republic of America, England, Mexico, and Australia.

"Four opposed," the young man said.

"The motion is carried."

Holly sat down and drained half a bottle of water someone had placed on her desk earlier.

Madurasinghe said, "Motion to end debate is carried. We

will now vote on the motion to recognize Dr. Burton as the Fragment's Emissary. All in favor?"

Eight hands went up.

"Opposed?"

Three hands went up.

"Abstain?"

The President of the Republic of Australia raised his hand.

"The motion is carried with eight in favor, three opposed, and one abstaining."

Theo said into Holly's ear, "My God, Holly. There were half a dozen ways to accomplish that, and you just had to pick the most offensive one."

"I wanted to make sure they did not think this was just another business-as-usual meeting of the Council, and that was the only way I could think of to do it."

"Well, I think you have their attention now."

Madurasinghe leaned toward Holly and placed his hand over her microphone. "Dr. Burton, would you like to take a short break at this point? It would give everyone a chance to cool down."

Before she could answer, Theo said, "The Emissary's proposal is brief. It will take only a few minutes. Perhaps she should present it now and then we can adjourn to give everyone time to review it. What do you think, Madam Emissary?"

"That sounds good to me," she said. "After the break, I can entertain questions."

"Pertaining to the proposal," Theo interjected. "Nothing else."

Madurasinghe addressed the Council: "The Emissary will now present the proposal from the Fragment, after which we will adjourn for one hour. When we return, she will entertain questions pertaining to the proposal."

He turned to her. "Madam Emissary, the floor is yours."

Holly transferred a copy of the proposal from her tablet

to the local network and, a moment later, it appeared on the big screen behind her. The document she and the Fragment had come up with was titled 'Agreement for the Transfer of Technology from the Fragment to the Human Race.' There was no doubt in her mind that every article in the proposal would offend them. Theo and Adrian had made several suggestions to make it more palatable, all of which she had rejected.

She began.

"I am sure you have all seen the vid of my press conference where I spelled out the existential threat the Death Bringer represents. Let me emphasize that there is nothing we can do to save Earth from annihilation. The *only* hope for our species is to leave Earth and venture into space. We do not currently have the technology to accomplish this on our own, nor do we have enough time to develop it on our own, which is where the Fragment's proposal comes in.

The Fragment will not save us, but he will give us the knowledge we need to save ourselves. On the screen behind me is the agreement under which the Fragment will make this knowledge available to the human race. It is spelled out in six articles which I will read.

"ARTICLE ONE: Dr. Holly Margaret Burton, hereafter known as the Emissary, will be the single point of contact between the Fragment and the human race in all matters, including but not limited to the transfer of alien technology."

She paused and looked up from her desk. A hand went up. "If you don't mind," she said, "please hold questions until the end. I pause only to give you time to absorb the full import of each article." The hand went down. "Thank you," she said.

"ARTICLE TWO: All hostile actions toward the Fragment and his Emissary will cease. The Council of Enclaves will assume responsibility for ensuring that any future hostilities are dealt with promptly and decisively. In the event that the

Council is unable or unwilling to enforce this provision, the Emissary will do so as she sees fit."

She looked up at her audience again. Theo was right. She had their attention.

"ARTICLE THREE: Alien technology will be provided to the human race on an as-needed basis, the schedule to be determined by the Emissary.

"ARTICLE FOUR: Alien technology will be provided freely to the entire world. No preference will be given to any enclave or alliance of enclaves. There will be no hoarding of knowledge."

She paused at the sound of people shifting in their chairs. She knew all six articles would be controversial, but article four was likely to be the one they would have the most difficulty accepting. It meant nobody would have an advantage over anybody else.

"ARTICLE FIVE: The human race is responsible for the effective use of alien technology to save itself from extinction. The Fragment will not save humanity from itself."

That one would raise some questions.

"ARTICLE SIX: Matters not spelled out in this agreement will be resolved by the Emissary as she sees fit."

She looked up. All eyes were on her. "When we return from the break, I will answer questions pertaining to the proposal. Please bear in mind that this is the Fragment's proposal. While I am willing to consider changes, I am unlikely to accept them."

She turned to Madurasinghe. "Thank you, Mr. Secretary General."

———

Madurasinghe called for a recess. A lot of people were suddenly on their feet, milling around and talking. Madurasinghe waved someone away and led Holly and her party out a side door, down a short hallway, and into a conference room. Windows ran the length of one side, looking out on a park-like space surrounding a small lake upon which were ducks, though she didn't know what kind.

Madurasinghe said, "At Theo's request, pizza has been ordered and should be here any minute. If you will excuse me, I need to go back into the lion's den and make sure none of *them* try to walk out."

Holly collapsed into a leather chair, propped her feet up on the table, and let out a long sigh.

"Okay. That part is over. I have delivered the Fragment's proposal."

"That was the easy part," Adrian said.

Holly rolled her eyes. "I hope not. This doesn't have to be that hard, but the way they were going on and on and on about whether to formally recognize me or not . . . I mean, I thought I'd left that crap behind when I left the university to join the Jupiter Mission."

Robert pulled up a chair beside her. "You did good, Sis. You reeled them in and made them listen to you." He attempted an imitation: "With all due respect, ladies and gentlemen, this is bullshit."

"From their expressions," Adrian said, "you'd think you had pulled down your pants and crapped on the table."

Three large pizzas arrived, along with two women who set the conference table for five; with china plates, silverware, napkins, crystal glasses. The table settings sat incongruously around the pizzas, but Holly didn't care. She grabbed three pieces with pepperoni, sausage, onions, and black olives on them, dropped them on a plate, grabbed a knife and fork, and proceeded to devour her pizza. She ignored the wine poured into the glasses, opting instead for water.

An hour and a half later, Madurasinghe appeared. "Madam Emissary, the Council of Enclaves requests a three-day postponement. They would like time to consult with their own people."

"Three days?" Robert said. "It's a six point outline. How hard can it be?"

The Secretary General held up his hands in a gesture of surrender. "I am merely the messenger. The proposal presented by the Emissary is indeed short and simple; deceptively so. There are serious implications for each of the six points, as I am sure you know. It is perhaps understandable that some of them want to think about it before going further."

"It's not really a request, is it?" Holly said.

He gave her an apologetic look.

It was not an unreasonable request, but the Council members would be a lot better informed when they consulted with others if they took the time for a Q&A first. They must have known that, too. Theo looked disappointed. Adrian looked frustrated.

"Dr. Madurasinghe," she said. "Take your three days. You know where to find me."

"Thank you for your flexibility, Madam Emissary." He bowed and left them alone.

She looked around the table. "What am I missing?"

Theo and Adrian exchanged looks. Theo said, "They want to control the narrative, and for that, they need time to spin their own answers to the multitude of questions the proposal raises. That becomes more difficult once *your* answers are out there. To put it bluntly, they don't want to hear your answers until after they have gotten their own answers out there."

Adrian said, "I would expect a flurry of activity on the feeds pushing their own narratives."

"Great, more conspiracy theories."

"More like spinning the narrative to their own advantage. Three days is plenty of time to get alternative narrative into the world's collective mind. These people have entire branches of government dedicated to propaganda. They are good at it."

"But to what end?" she said. "I thought we were all on the same side with the same goal: to save the species."

"Yes and no," Theo said. "Your proposal will set in motion tectonic shifts in the fragile balance of power that holds the world together. Frankly, they are scared; scared that if they back you and your proposal, they will turn out to have bet on the wrong horse."

"And there are also those who don't believe the end of the world is coming," Adrian said. "At least not in the way you have described it. They believe we can survive the apocalypse and they want to ensure they come out the other side with at least as much power as they have now."

"Like the CRA?" Robert said.

"The CRA and their allies consider Holly and the Fragment a clear and present danger to humanity," Adrian said. "Every bit as dangerous as the Death Bringer. To be fair to them, they are not simply in denial or just being obstinate. They too want to save the human race, or at least their part of it. They will advocate for getting advanced technologies from the Fragment and then doing whatever they wish with them.

"But isn't that exactly what the Fragment wants too?" Holly asked.

"Yes and no," Theo said. "By making you his Emissary, the Fragment has put you in the middle of it. Politically, it was a brilliant move. They have to play by your rules to get what they want."

"So what now?"

Adrian said, "We should leak the Fragment's proposal to the media."

"I agree," Theo said. "In fact, it is necessary that we do so. Some of the people in that room may be considering direct action against you, just to mix things up and see if things fall out in a way more favorable for them. That will be harder to do if the entire world knows the Fragment might withdraw his help if anything happens to his Emissary."

"I'll see to it," Adrian said.

"Excellent," Theo said. "Then we wait and see what happens. In any case, I will be very much surprised if we find ourselves back here in as little as three days."

25

Theo was right. Three days came and went with no word from the Council. The heads of state had returned to their respective capitals and showed no sign of coming back. Madurasinghe released a press statement to the effect that the heads of state had accepted Holly as the Fragment's Emissary and had heard the Fragment's proposal for giving Earth advanced technologies, but that the precise terms of that were still under discussion. Adrian had leaked The Plan, as it came to be known, and it went global. The world was paying attention.

The initial reaction was mostly positive, but by day two several news feeds and a plethora of social media feeds had dissected The Plan, pointing out how one sided and arbitrary it was. Adrian said this did not represent a change in the public's perception of Holly or the Fragment, but was a massive and coordinated negative publicity campaign designed to drown everything else out. By day three, the social media feeds were showing a dozen Nays to every Yay, and public opinion began to change.

Five days after her meeting with the Council, in the early afternoon, she received a message from Madurasinghe's office by courier. It was an invitation for the Emissary to meet with the Council the next morning to continue negotiations.

"Negotiations?" Holly said. "What negotiations? There's nothing to negotiate. Just take the damn deal and let's get on with the business of saving the human race."

They were in the drawing room: Theo, Adrian, Robert, and herself. And Tomás and Anna, of course. Theo had been right about her getting used to having a PPI with her all the time. Anna had become so much a part of Holly's life that she barely noticed her anymore; like a shadow that followed her around wherever she went. Sometimes she felt like she was taking the woman for granted, but all it really meant was that Anna was doing her job well.

Theo smiled one of his smug little smiles. He knew it irritated her. He liked to say that most crises weren't; that is, they looked like crises until you pulled away to see the bigger picture, at which point they usually stopped being crises. In fact, if looked at the right way, they often turned out to be opportunities. This was a perspective Holly had never mastered.

"Adrian," Theo said. "Why don't you explain to us what is going on."

Adrian walked to the fireplace, which looked like a real fireplace but wasn't; it was gas. It wasn't as good as the Fragment's fireplaces, but since this was Theo's home, she hadn't mentioned that. She had experienced a lot of things she couldn't share with anyone simply because you had to have been there to appreciate them. Besides, who wanted their fireplace compared with one made by a multi-billion-year-old alien?

"Three things," Adrian said. "First, they made us wait five days instead of three. The language of diplomacy is often more about gestures than words; more about what is left unsaid than what is said. This is their way of saying they are not sure how seriously to take the Emissary without coming out and saying so. After all, she is a political neophyte and, as Weatherford pointed out, they aren't even sure she really represents the Fragment."

Holly started to object, but Theo waved her off.

Adrian continued, "Second, the invitation came not from Madurasinghe himself, but from an anonymous flunky on his staff. Diplomacy is like a chess game. Sometimes the game can be won by simply gaining a better position than your opponent. They are seeking a positional advantage by asserting that *they* are in control, not Holly. They know as well as we do that this is not so, but the psychology of it often works anyway. We will want to take the initiative back."

Holly just nodded to indicate that she understood what he was saying.

"Third, the heads of state are staying home. Their ambassadors will represent them. Again, this is a positional maneuver. Whatever happens from here on out, the Emissary will not be talking to the people who make the decisions; only to their subordinates. Frankly, they did not like the way the Emissary turned the tables on them at the last meeting. They lost face. They are making sure she can't do that to them again. It also ensures that no decisions can be made without going back to them. Again, it is a question of control."

He looked at Theo, who positively beamed.

"Well done, my boy. Well done. Couldn't have done it better myself. You will make a fine diplomat someday." He frowned. "Assuming there is a someday."

Holly had followed Adrian's explanation easily enough, but knowing what was going on behind the scenes did not make her feel any better about it. On the contrary, it made her mad. These supposed leaders were still playing games.

"Theo," she said. "Please notify Dr. Madurasinghe's office that the Emissary regretfully declines his invitation due to a personal matter she must attend to tomorrow morning, but she would be happy to meet with the Council the day after;

say, at 9:00 in the morning. If that is not acceptable to the Council, they can go fuck themselves."

There was a loud silence, then Theo said, "I am not sure—"

"Don't start with me about protocol and politeness," she said. "I've had all the protocol and politeness I can take."

Robert held up a hand. "If I may, sis, I think Theo is wondering if we can leave out the part about them fucking themselves?"

It took her a moment to realize what he was getting at. She giggled.

"That's personal commentary. You can leave it out."

"Thank goodness," Theo said. "I did not want to say that to the General Secretary of the Council of Enclaves. Especially not in a formal missive that will go into the permanent record."

———

When Holly and Anna came downstairs the next morning, Sophie directed them to the dining room, where the table had been set with plates and silverware and crystal glasses. A decorated, three-tiered cake sat on the table, with a circle of candles around the second tier and a statuette of a ballerina perched on the top tier. The others were already there and stood when she walked in and broke out into a painfully mediocre rendition of "Happy Birthday." Even Anna and Tomás. The empty seat at the head of the table was obviously for her, so she sat there.

"Happy birthday, sis," Robert said. "Thirty-seven years, I believe. At least, that's how many candles we put on the cake."

"There was some debate about that," Adrian said. "You spent five or six years of that time in stasis and we weren't sure if those years should count."

Robert said, "We went with the number of years since you

were born. But if you would prefer not to count the stasis years, feel free to remove some candles. It's your birthday."

She grasped Robert's hand. "I had forgotten it was my birthday. Thank you for remembering."

She attempted to blow out all thirty-seven candles in one breath. She got them all on the second try. Sophie and Cook brought out trays with omelets and little bowls of fruit, which they set on a side table. Everyone served themselves.

It seemed odd to be eating cake with breakfast, but that didn't stop Holly from having two pieces. This provoked some needling from Robert about needing to watch her weight. That had always been a sore spot when she was growing up. She was pleasantly surprised to find it didn't bother her like it once would have.

When they had finished and returned to the drawing room, Robert said, "You must have stories about your interplanetary travels. Regale us with one; one we haven't already heard."

She thought for a moment. He was right; she did have stories to tell. It was too bad she would never have grandchildren to tell them to. One story stood out in her mind.

"There is an old dictum from Arthur C. Clark that says, 'Any sufficiently advanced technology will be indistinguishable from magic.' I experienced a number of moments like that, but the most amazing one was walking on the shore of a methane sea on Titan, watching small waves rolling slowly up a rocky beach and slowly receding back into the sea, and then looking up to see Saturn with its glorious rings hanging large in the sky."

"I hope you were wearing a space suit," Robert said. "I hear Titan is pretty cold this time of year."

"It's cold any time of year," she said with a laugh. "Around a hundred and eighty degrees below zero. Celsius. And yes, I wore an environment suit. I was in the living area of the habitat watching the live vid of the seashore; the same view I had awakened to that first day. I sometimes sat in front of the large screen for hours just watching the waves rolling up onto the shore and retreating back down into the sea. Or the ever-changing bands of clouds racing across Saturn's surface. Or those glorious rings with their shepherd moons keeping the gaps between rings clear. I had seen images of them before, but to see them with my own eyes . . ."

Shivers ran down her arms.

"One day, the Fragment asked me if I would like to take a stroll on the beach. I thought he was joking, but he wasn't. One of the hallway doors I had noticed the first time I left my room, but which was always locked, turned out to be an airlock. We changed into environment suits. The Fragment's avatar didn't need one, of course, but he wore it anyway. Then I stepped out onto the surface of Titan for the first time."

She paused and savored the memory of the feeling that had swept over her.

"I slowly turned 360 degrees to take in the entire horizon, which was closer than I was used to because Titan is smaller than Earth. The sea stretched away to the west and disappeared over the horizon, making it seem like an ocean, though it's really just a big lake. On Earth you would be able to see the opposite shore, but on Titan I couldn't see the other shore because Titan has a much nearer horizon than Earth.

"The Fragment said our astronomers call the lake Kraken Mare. It is in the northern hemisphere and is mostly liquid methane. Earth has a water-based hydrological cycle, but Titan has a methane-based one. The methane evaporates off the surface of the sea and is broken down into ethane by radiation as it rises in the atmosphere. Then it falls back to the surface as rain. Not the kind of rain you get on Earth, of course. For one thing, it's ethanol. For another, it usually falls as a mist or maybe a drizzle, though every once in a while you get a downpour."

She pictured it in her mind as she spoke. "There are mountains to the north, the east, the south; some close, some distant. Everywhere, the landscape is barren, bereft of life. The Fragment says there is life in only two places in our solar system: Earth and the subterranean oceans of Europa." She paused. "Soon enough Earth will be gone, and the ocean life on Europa will be alone."

She said nothing for several seconds. Nobody else did either.

"I explored the area around the dome many times while I was there and even went sailing on the lake a couple of times. But it is that first step onto the surface of Titan that remains etched in my memory. The crunch of my steps on ground that had never felt a human footstep. The breeze pushing gently against my suit. The brownish-red haze of the dense atmosphere. The low, slow waves of the sea. It was magical."

She stopped. They were looking at her strangely.

"I would like to see Titan again," she said.

26

Two days later, Holly found herself in the same seat as before, next to Madurasinghe. There were new faces around the table. The seats previously occupied by heads of state were now occupied by their ambassadors. Were they sending her a message? Madurasinghe turned the floor over to Ambassador Keith Richardson from the Republic of Pacifica.

"Madam Emissary, thank you for meeting with us again," he said. "The proposal you put before us a few days ago is concise and clear, but it raises many questions and a few concerns. The Council has asked me to present these concerns. I would like to proceed through each article, asking some questions and entertaining discussion."

He paused and looked at Holly. She gestured for him to continue. Apparently, they had decided to treat her with more respect than during the first meeting. Theo leaned forward and said to her, "For whatever it's worth, Richardson is on your side."

The ambassador began.

"Article One specifies that you personally are the single point of contact between the Fragment and Earth. By definition, a single point of contact is also a single point of failure.

If, God forbid, something unfortunate were to happen to you such that you could no longer fulfill this pivotal role, we would be left with no fallback."

He paused and looked up. Holly again gestured for him to continue.

"The Council proposes that a delegation be appointed by this body to assist you in what is, after all, no small endeavor, and that this delegation meet with the Fragment and be involved in future discussions with him. We feel this would ensure a more robust line of communication between our two species."

He paused and looked up. "Mr. Secretary General, I move the proposal."

Before Madurasinghe could say anything, Holly leaned into the microphone and said, "No."

She and the Fragment had discussed this while she was on Titan and he was adamant that she be the single point of contact. She had several times asked him why this was so important to him, but had never gotten a satisfactory answer. The closest she had gotten was something about potential and actual futures, which apparently had something to do with quantum flux and the nature of the space-time continuum. The upshot was that he seemed to think there was something special about her that made her uniquely qualified her for the job. She suspected the real reason was that she had been the sole survivor of the attack on Ganymede and was now a known quantity to him.

Her many conversations with the Fragment prior to her return to Earth might have seemed to an outside observer like casual chats between old friends, but the truth was that she understood very little about what the Fragment thought about things; or, for that matter, *how* he thought about things. He was alien to her and always would be. She had gotten used to it, but not entirely comfortable with it.

Her 'No' had been louder than she intended, but maybe

that was a good thing because it served notice that she was in charge of this discussion. Madurasinghe looked like he had swallowed something a little too big for his throat. She had trampled all over the Council's protocol again, which even she had to admit was a tad on the rude side. But it was her meeting, and she would do it her way.

She said, "Ambassador Richardson, Mr. Secretary-General, ladies and gentlemen. I do not intend to be rude or disrespectful toward this body. I am not a diplomat. I am a scientist, trained to deal with facts, not the nuances of diplomatic discourse. Please bear with me if I seem brusque."

She looked around the circle but couldn't tell how any of them took that. She continued.

"The request for a delegation to act as the intermediary between the Fragment and the human race is not unreasonable and not unexpected. The Fragment and I discussed it at length while I was on Titan, and he is adamant that I be the sole point of contact. I do not claim to fully understand his reasons, only that it is non-negotiable.

"At this point, I would encourage the Council to remember we are talking about an alien here, whose motives and thought processes are, by definition, alien to us. You can make a motion and debate it and even vote on it if you wish. I will take it back to him and present your reasoning, but I can tell you with near certainty that he will not change his mind on this."

The ambassador took a few moments to consult with members of his delegation.

"Very well, Madam Emissary," he said. "We will table the motion for now and I will continue."

Holly nodded.

"Article Two specifies that hostilities toward the Fragment or toward yourself will cease and that the Council will assume responsibility for enforcing this."

He looked up, and Holly again nodded for him to continue.

"The Council would like to insert a clause specifying that neither the Fragment nor his Emissary will initiate hostilities toward humans, either individually or as a whole."

He did not propose a motion this time. He merely looked up at Holly and waited.

"I understand your concerns," she said, "and they are entirely reasonable. However, the Fragment and I discussed this possibility as well, and he rejected it."

Ambassador Dasgupta from the Republic of India raised his hand and with a nod from Madurasinghe said, "The requested change seems fair to us, whereas the article as it stands is manifestly one-sided. Would the Emissary be willing to explain the Fragment's logic?"

"Yes. At least, as well as I can, bearing in mind what I said earlier about the difficulties inherent in understanding the Fragment's thought process. The Fragment has been observing us for over ten thousand years. In that time, he has learned that while there is much that is admirable and worth saving about us, we are not a race to be trusted. We often break our promises, and we are very good at creating ambiguous situations that keep the letter of law while ignoring its spirit. In view of this, he insists on retaining the right to act should we engage in actions that threaten him or his Emissary. In short, he doesn't trust us.

"I do not intend this as an insult. After all, I am human, too. I am only reporting what the Fragment has observed and why he insists on Article Two. I imagine all of you can understand how he might have reached that conclusion about us. To me, the amazing thing is that he believes we are a species worth saving."

A long silence followed before Dasgupta said, "Thank you, Emissary."

Ambassador Richardson continued: "Article Two also

specifies that in the event of a failure by this Council to enforce the no-hostility rule, the Emissary will enforce it. I am sure you can see how this sounds like a threat, which seems inappropriate in what is in effect a peace treaty between our two species."

He looked up and Holly said, "Correct on all counts, Ambassador."

"The Council would like to remove this clause."

"Again, the Fragment was very specific about this. Since I am the one on the ground, so to speak, and am the only practical target for opposition or aggression, he has given to me the authority and the ability to respond in whatever way I deem appropriate to hostilities or threats of hostility. You saw an example of that when I disabled a British spaceplane and inadvertently destroyed another when they attempted to board my ship at *Tiangong Station*. I will repeat what I told Major Reed at the time: Do not test me on this."

Richardson sighed. Some of the other ambassadors were talking with their delegations. The leaders of the enclaves they represented were undoubtedly involved in those conversations.

"Madam Emissary," Richardson said. "It appears you have not given us much room for negotiation, which does not bode well for future relations. Nonetheless, I will continue."

He sipped water from a bottle.

"Article three specifies that alien technology will be provided on an as-needed basis and that you yourself will be the sole determiner of the schedule for technology delivery."

"That is correct."

"Not all of us are comfortable with what appears to be a somewhat parsimonious delivery plan. We feel we would have greater flexibility as we move forward if all the promised technologies were delivered at once, enabling us to make use of them when and how we deem appropriate. We are not, after all, children who need to be spoon fed."

Holly allowed several seconds of silence to pass before replying: "Are you sure about that, Mr. Ambassador?"

"Sure about what?"

"About us not being children."

Behind her Adrian said, "Uh, oh."

"From the Fragment's point of view, we *are* children," she said. "He is giving us powerful technologies that we could easily hurt ourselves and each other with. You would not give a child a stick of dynamite and a box of matches without first ensuring that the child was knowledgeable enough and responsible enough to handle them safely. I have seen the Fragment's technology in action. Trust me when I tell you that this article is in *your* best interests."

The Ambassador again consulted with the people behind him before continuing.

"Article Four specifies that new technologies will be made available to all the enclaves. As I am sure you can appreciate, there is some concern that not all enclaves will use it responsibly. There is also concern that this technology might fall into the hands of the warlords. Is the Fragment willing to consider limiting the transmission of this knowledge to a somewhat smaller circle? Say, the enclaves currently leading the alliances."

"He is not," she said. "I refer you to the next article."

"Ah," he said. He probably wished they had chosen someone else to do this. He looked down at his desk. "Article Five states that the human race is responsible for the effective use of alien technology to save itself from extinction. The Fragment will not save the human race from itself."

He stopped and consulted with one of the people sitting behind him. This afforded Holly an opportunity to study the rest of the ambassadors, several of whom were also talking to their delegations. It seemed they had not linked articles four and five together before now.

"Ambassador Richardson," she said. Everyone's attention

turned back to her. "If I may, let me help you out here. All of you."

"Please do, Madam Emissary."

"I draw your attention to the last article, Article Six. It says that issues not specifically spelled out in the document will be resolved by the Emissary; that is, by me. In my view, the misuse of alien technology by one or many of Earth's actors falls under this article. The Fragment has made it clear that he will not intervene to save humanity from its own hubris and tribalism. But I can. And I will.

"Article Six was not in the original document. It was added at my request. For reasons of his own, the Fragment's help is limited to giving us certain technologies. *My* help, on the other hand, is not. I too am human. I too will perish if we do not find a way to leave our world before the Death Bringer gets here. I too have people I care about deeply who will die if we—you and I—should fail.

"The Fragment has put immense power in my hands, of which you have seen only a fraction and which I am free to use at my discretion. You may choose to see this as a threat to your own power and agency, and I would not blame you. However, I urge you to get over it. This isn't about you. Nor is it about me. It is about saving our species—*homo sapiens*—from extinction.

"I did not seek this power; nor did I want it. I am certainly not comfortable wielding it. Nevertheless, it has been given to me and it falls to me to use it as responsibly as I can to achieve the best possible outcome for the human race.

"You came here to ask: what is the best deal we can get out of this? That is, after all, what you do for a living. But it is the wrong question. The question you should be asking is: do we want the Fragment's help or not? It is a yes/no question; a binary proposition. I suggest you focus on answering that question, because if you are unwilling to accept the Fragment's terms, then as far as he is concerned, we are on our own."

All semblance of order broke down as the ambassadors conferred with their delegations; and probably with their enclaves' leaders. Voices were raised; angry words exchanged.

Madurasinghe leaned toward her had said, "My dear Madam Emissary, you certainly have kicked over a hornets' nest. I must admit that I am not clear—"

The Ambassador for the Srivjaha Empire interrupted. "Mr. General Secretary, I move the following: The Council of Enclaves accepts the six articles before us without change or comment, and requests the Emissary tell the Fragment that we appreciate whatever help he is willing to give us in whatever manner he deems appropriate, with the goal of saving the human race from annihilation."

"Mr. General Secretary, I second the motion." It was the Ambassador for the Russian Federation.

Madurasinghe said, "Moved and seconded. Could we get that up on the board?"

The motion appeared on the vid screen behind Holly.

"The Chair recognizes the Ambassador of Great Britain."

"A question for Doctor Burton, if I may."

He spoke with that typical British politeness and dignity, but glared at her with palpable ill will. She nodded her assent.

"With all due respect, Doctor Burton, there is some question whether you are who you claim to be, and some of us would like to resolve that question before we go any further. There are some who say you are not human at all, but some kind of android made to look and sound like Holly Burton. Are you willing to undergo a physical examination by a mutually agreed upon team of medical specialists to determine whether you are human and, if so, whether you are in fact Holly Margaret Burton."

"Objection," said the Ambassador from the People's

Republic of China. "The question is irrelevant. I believe the Emissary is the same Holly Burton who left Earth on the *Asimov* seven years ago. But even if she were not, even if she were a facsimile or a clone or whatever, it makes no difference. She is here as the Fragment's representative, offering us a way to save our species."

Britain's ambassador shouted, "On the contrary, it makes a great deal of—"

Holly held up a hand, and he stopped talking. Sour expressions from several of the ambassadors reminded her she was not showing them the deference they were used to.

"I have no objection to a medical examination," she said. "Perhaps Ambassador Geery and my advisor, Ambassador Peeters, can work out the details. However, I can assure you the results will show that I am as human as any of you, and a DNA test will show that I am Holly Margaret Burton; the same Holly Margaret Burton who left earth seven years ago on the *Asimov*."

The CRA Ambassador two seats to Holly's left held up a hand and Madurasinghe said, "Ambassador Close of the Christian Republic of America."

She leaned into the mic. "The Christian Republic of America rejects the alien's proposal in its entirety because it presupposes a situation that, in our view, is not in accord with the facts. The evidence that the Death Bringer will bring about the end of the world is not conclusive. There exists within the scientific community a body of opinion that the Death Bringer will not destroy the world and all life in it. Certainly it will wreak havoc with the planet on a scale not seen since the extinction of the dinosaurs sixty million years ago, but just as life survived that extinction level event, so life will survive this one.

"The project proposed by Dr. Burton would require a world-wide effort of unprecedented scale. It would allow a hundred and twenty-thousand people to leave Earth with no assurances they can survive in space or on other worlds in our solar system or elsewhere. To the contrary, our species will probably find that we are biologically and psychologically unfit for long-term survival anywhere other than Earth. This is our home. It was made for us and we for it."

She paused and looked around the room.

"The Christian Republic of America proposes that the world's resources be directed instead toward building massive underground structures—cities, really—where many millions of people can live for the few years I am told it will take for things on the surface to settle down to the point that we can emerge and begin to rebuild. The CRA is already building such structures, as are a few other countries. As it stands now, these structures are primitive, hardly deserving to be called cities. But if the world unites around this project, we can save not just tens of thousands, but hundreds of thousands. All without the aliens' help, which we neither need nor want."

Several other ambassadors rose to speak, but Close waved them away.

"There is another reason for rejecting the aliens' proposal, and this may be the most important one. It would require each signatory to relinquish their sovereignty and become subject states to an alien about whom we know almost nothing. It would take away our right of self-determination and would put our future entirely in the hands of an alien race. This is unacceptable.

"If these aliens' motives are as altruistic as Dr. Burton claims, why then do they not give us the technology we need to survive on our own world, to choose our own future, to be masters of our own fate, with no strings attached. We would welcome their help in that case, but not at the cost of our own sovereignty and self-determination. Therefore, the CRA opposes the motion and urges the Council to do so as well."

Madurasinghe said, "Thank you, Ambassador Close." He

turned to Holly. "Madam Emissary, would you care to respond?"

"Thank you, Mr. Secretary General." She looked around the room until she was sure she had everyone's attention. "Ambassador Close is correct in her claim that there are experts who have a different assessment than the Fragment about the level of destruction the Death Bringer will inflict upon our world. However, she neglected to mention that the experts to whom she refers represent a tiny minority of the scientific community and lack expertise in the relevant fields, such as astronomy and physics. Thus, it is not surprising that they have produced no compelling evidence to support their *opinion*.

"I emphasize *opinion* because that is all they have to offer; opinion backed by an embarrassing lack of factual data. That is because there are precious few facts to be had in support of their opinion. Although there appears to be a significant number of people arguing as Ambassador Close has, if you examine their sources, you will find that they all refer back to the views of a handful of people—four to be exact. Consider the credentials of these four people."

She sent a file from her computer to the Pit, and it appeared on the big screen.

"What you see here is a list of the names of the four experts whose opinions lie behind virtually the entire body of opinion that Ambassador Close refers to. Notice, in particular, their professional credentials.

"Dr. Jan Erikson, PhD in chemistry and an associate professor at Kansas State University.

"Mr. Elliot Mansford, MA in information technology and an instructor at the University of Montana.

"Dr. Amelia Hunter, PhD in biology and a professor at Blakesfield State College.

"Dr. Franz Anders, PhD in education and the well-known author of several books offering a variety of what are widely considered crack-pot theories on a variety of subjects, including most recently a theory proposing that there is a secret agreement between the Chinese government and the aliens in which China ends up running the world after the cataclysm."

She paused to catch her breath. It had not been difficult to anticipate the objections her adversaries would raise, and she had prepared her responses.

"I have no reason to question their expertise in their respective fields, except perhaps for Dr. Anders, who strikes me as a nutcase. However, not one of them has demonstrable expertise in the fields relevant to predicting the impact of the Death Bringer's passage through the inner solar system.

"I am transferring a file to the pit," she said. "It contains the data gathered by the Fragment along with his analysis of that data. As I speak, this same data is being transmitted to one hundred of the world's most respected mathematicians, astronomers, astrophysicists, and geologists, most of whom are at leading universities. I encourage those experts—the *real* experts—to examine the data and verify its accuracy and the accuracy of the Fragment's analysis."

"Why should we trust an alien's data or an alien's analysis?" the British Ambassador said.

"You shouldn't. You should trust your own experts, some of whom are receiving this data as we speak. They will tell you that the Fragment is right."

What followed could only be described as a shouting match between the ambassadors whose nations favored accepting the Fragment's proposal, and those that opposed it. After fifteen minutes of angry exchanges and recriminations that did not appear to be going anywhere good, and which Madurasinghe was unable to quell, Ambassador Close stood and held up her hands to quiet everyone down.

"It is my duty to report to you that the government of the Christian Republic of America, after considering all the facts, has issued a warrant for the arrest of Dr. Burton for treason against humanity by aiding and abetting an alien takeover of our world. The CRA requests that this body issue an international warrant to the same effect."

He sat down and the British Ambassador said, "I second the motion and call for a vote."

Pandemonium again broke out, with Madurasinghe trying in vain to bring the meeting back to order.

Gabriel's Fire spoke in her mind: *I believe you are in imminent danger and urge you to leave immediately. American and British armed forces have landed at Geneva International Airport and are moving on Eos, Theo's compound, and the Council complex. They came from Great Britain through the no-man's-land of northern France.*

27

Holly sat in disbelief for several seconds, her mind trying to wrap itself around this new development. She leaned toward Theo and said, "*Gabriel's Fire* says CRA forces are approaching the building and we are about to come under attack. They have taken the airport and are moving on *Eos* and your estate. *Eos* can take care of itself, but we have people at the estate."

"That seems unlikely," Theo said. "They would—"

Tomás interrupted him. "The compound is under attack. CRA forces are moving to surround this building. We need to go."

"Go where?" Holly asked.

Tomás walked quickly to one of the exits to confer with his people. Anna remained in her seat but took her gun out of its holster.

"Does this building have a helipad?" Holly asked her.

"Yes, but a helicopter is a soft target."

"*Eos* isn't."

"You can bring it here?"

"I can."

Anna tapped her headpiece. "The Emissary says she can

bring the *Eos* to us and land at the helipad on top of the building."

Tomás's head snapped toward them. He said something to the woman he was talking with and strode across the space to their seats. "Let's do it," he said.

Holly leaned toward Madurasinghe, who had become aware of her delegation's disquiet, and said, "CRA forces are deploying around the building, no doubt to arrest me. I think it would be best for everyone if I took my leave. I wonder if you would be so kind as to escort us to the helipad?"

His face paled. "But that can't—"

"Dr. Madurasinghe, I don't have time to argue with you. The helipad: yes or no?"

He looked around the room, said something to one of his aids, and walked toward an exit with Holly and her delegation in tow. The argument among ambassadors had died down to murmurs by the time they reached the door. Two of Tomás' people fell in behind them. Madurasinghe took them to a row of elevators and used his card key to give them an express ride to the top floor. From there, they took stairs to the rooftop. A helicopter with the words "Council of Enclaves" painted on its side occupied the helipad.

She pointed at it and said to him, "Get someone to fly it out of here in the next ten minutes, or my spaceplane will remove it, which will leave it somewhat worse for wear."

Madurasinghe got on his phone.

She brought up a virtual control panel and started waving her hands around in the air; at least, that's what it would look like to her team since they couldn't see the virtual controls. She could only imagine the shock of the Swiss troops guarding the spaceplane at the airport when its engines came to life with a rising whine.

A quick blast from the VTOL thrusters blew the tent away. The view from *Eos* confirmed that the soldiers were backing away in a hurry. She took it up a hundred meters and sped toward the Council building where she brought it to a hover a short distance from the top of the building.

Madurasinghe's face had turned an unbecoming shade of gray. "I can't find a pilot."

She turned to Tomás. "Get everyone into the stairwell. I'm going to take out the helicopter, and there's bound to be some shrapnel."

Eos abruptly jerked to one side, narrowly evading a missile that swished by and began looping around for another try. An explosion engulfed *Eos* as a second missile struck. The shock wave knocked Holly off her feet. She took a moment to decide she was uninjured, then studied the virtual control panel. The explosion knocked out one of *Eos's* point defense lasers, but the spaceplane, which was constructed of materials humans had never seen before, was otherwise undamaged. A ragged line of fire reached out from its remaining point defense laser and blew the first missile apart as it closed in on its target.

She switched *Eos's* weapon systems from passive to aggressive as the fighter jet responsible for the attack roared overhead. *Eos* fired a missile of its own which caught up with the jet and blew it apart, raining debris on the street below.

Everyone had recovered from the initial blast and were backing into the stairwell. Holly took control of the space-plane's offensive system, targeted the helicopter resting on the helipad, and fired *Eos's* plasma cannon. The helicopter vanished in a ball of fire. More debris fell toward the street below. She brought the plane in and landed it, crushing what little was left of the helicopter.

"Everybody aboard unless you plan to stay here," she said. The door was already open, and the steps were descending.

She turned to Madurasinghe. "Sorry about the helicopter, and thank you for your hospitality, but I've had all the diplomatic hospitality I can take for one day. On the bright side, this is going to make one hell of a story for your memoir."

She sprinted for the plane, leaving the General Secretary with his mouth hanging open. Once they were in the air, she looked back at her passengers. With the extra security people on board, it was crowded.

"Everybody all right?" she said.

She tried to sound confident and in control, but she was pretty shaken and on full adrenaline overload, which her nanites would manage.

Anna handed her a headset. Someone was saying, ". . . like they are preparing for an assault. The gate guards have retreated to the house."

"Where should I take us?" she said.

"Not sure," Tomás said. "The house is about to come under fire, and there is only a skeleton guard there. This plane has some impressive firepower. Are you prepared to take it into combat?"

Eos could certainly handle anything the CRA's forces might throw at her, but she wanted to minimize casualties. She glanced at Theo, who had strapped himself into the co-pilot's seat. A ferocious frown covered his face.

"You realize the CRA has challenged your threat to respond to attacks against yourself," he said. "This is a direct challenge to your credibility. You need to respond. Otherwise, the CRA will have successfully called your bluff and gotten away with it. That might emboldened others to take military action against you."

As much as she hated to admit it, he was right. When she had agreed with the Fragment to add that to the second article, she had not envisioned having to execute it. Now she faced a dilemma: How could she respond to the attack without using force and the attendant possibility that people would die?

"Buckle up," she said.

She gave *Eos* three gees of acceleration and began climbing over the vast no-man's-land of northern France. The Paris

Enclave claimed the area, but in reality it was an empty, burned-over area devastated by several wars that included the use of nuclear weapons. Only a few Outsider communities lived there.

She waved her hands over the control panel. "*Gabriel's Fire.*"

"I'm here, Holly," the AI replied over *Eos's* speakers.

"I need you to relay a call for me to the White House. Oxham's private line. From the Emissary."

"Stand by."

She didn't have to look to know that everyone was staring at her. "What?" She said. "It's just a phone call."

The familiar beep-beep of a call request sounded over the speaker. It repeated itself several times before it connected.

"This is the Office of the President," a woman said. "The Secret Service does not take kindly to crank calls."

Holly choked back a laugh. "This really is the Emissary. Put Oxham on."

There was a long pause. She said, "The President is not available."

"I'm not surprised. Tell him that if he doesn't call off his assault on the Council building and on my compound, a lot of American servicemen and women are going to die in the next few minutes. Then I will come over there and level the White House."

There was a pause. "Please hold." A few minutes later, the connection dropped.

"Did she hang up on me?"

"So it would seem," the AI said. "Would you like me to try again?"

"No."

Either she had failed to get past his personal secretary or, more likely, Oxham and Cartwright were calling her bluff. Time to piss or get off the pot.

"What's happening at the compound?" she asked.

"My people are under fire," Tomás said. "One of them is down. Sophie was hit, but it's not life-threatening. There are about twenty hostiles, and they have two armored vehicles and a couple of trucks."

"Damn you, Cartwright," she said. It was, of course, Cartwright giving the orders. Oxham was a puppet; Cartwright the puppet master.

She brought *Eos* around and sped toward Theo's compound. A few minutes later, they broke through clouds five kilometers from the house. She flew low over the compound and let the targeting computer identify hostile targets.

Two armored vehicles sat in the driveway. Soldiers were using them for cover as they laid down fire. One of Tomás's people was on the roof with a rifle. At least two others were maintaining a steady barrage of gunfire from windows on the second floor.

She laughed a bit hysterically. "If those bozos shoot up my bedroom, there's going to be hell to pay."

Theo stared at her, but she paid no attention because by now she had multiple targets to shoot at. She released two missiles, one at each armored vehicle. Both vehicles blew up in satisfying explosions.

She brought the plane around in a sharp, five-gee turn. Theo groaned. Someone behind her gasped. A helicopter appeared and unleashed a barrage of heavy gunfire at the man on the roof. He went down. Holly targeted the helicopter, and a crimson pulse shot out from *Eos's* plasma cannon. The helicopter vanished in a ball of fire.

On her third pass, she targeted two trucks parked on the road under the trees. They probably thought she couldn't get a clear shot at them. They were wrong. The road turned into a strip of flame, punctuated by explosions as fuel and ordinance blew up.

She brought *Eos* to a standstill a hundred meters above the house. No more hostiles appeared on the tactical display. She brought the plane down in front of the house, doing further injury to the already-damaged raised garden and its gnarled tree.

"Everybody out," she said.

Anna slipped into the co-pilot's seat when Theo vacated it. "Where are we going?"

"Cartwright and I have unfinished business."

"I'm coming with you."

"No. This is on me now. I don't want you involved."

"Well, that's just too bad, ma'am. I'm coming with you."

"Fine. Buckle up."

She lifted off, leaving behind an unknown number of dead people, four wrecked vehicles, and a damaged compound.

Anna said, "The CRA's transport planes will be at the airport."

Holly brought *Eos* around and accelerated hard toward the airport, exceeding Mach 2 by the time she reached it. Five giant British heavy lifters sat on the tarmac. She banked hard and brought the spaceplane around for another pass. She was a kilometer out when she released a barrage of missiles. Five transports burst into flame. The Swiss army would take care of the remaining soldiers, who now had no way to get home.

She banked into a steep upward flight path and increased their acceleration to five gees. Anna grunted.

"You okay?"

"Yes, ma'am," she gasped.

Holly's stomach churned. She did not know how many people she had killed, but it was more than a few. She had not come back to Earth to get into a war. But a hundred thousand years of tribalism had dug a deep trench in the human species' psyche, and for all of humanity's evolution, they had not yet escaped from that ugly trench.

She couldn't imagine the diplomatic furor that would break out now. Oxham—or more likely Cartwright—had bet he could capture her, which would have made any political cost worthwhile. He had lost that bet because he had again underestimated the resources she had at her disposal. Now a lot of people were dead.

She was processing a lot of anger when she called Oxham's office again. She had *Gabriel's Fire* broadcast the call to every major feed in the world. The same woman answered.

"Hi. This is the Emissary. We talked earlier. I don't suppose President Oxham will talk to me now?"

"One moment please," she said.

A few moments later, Oxham said, "Ah, Dr. Burton. I understand you have been killing American servicemen and servicewomen. Not a move likely to garner sympathy from the people of Earth."

His nonchalant jab made her want to spit nails. "Is Cartwright there?"

"Well, now—"

Cartwright interrupted him. "I am here, Dr. Burton."

"You're a bloody fool, Cartwright," she said. "The soldiers you sent to attack me are dead or in custody. The ones you sent to Ambassador Peeter's home are dead. I don't think there were any survivors there. I also took out five British heavy lifters at the Geneva International Airport. I imagine the remaining troops there will soon be in custody as well.

"This blood is on your hands. I suggest you evacuate the White House and its immediate vicinity because in two hours I am going to reduce it to rubble. You really should have listened when I warned you not to test me."

She dropped the connection.

"Gabriel," she said.

"I'm here, Holly."

"I just promised Oxham and Cartwright that I would level the White House in two hours. Can we do that with minimal collateral damage?"

"A hypersonic missile would be difficult to stop and will not miss its target."

"Do it. Try to limit the damage to the building itself. I don't want to kill any more people if I can avoid it. Can you put some drones over the area and broadcast a warning to evacuate? I don't trust Oxham to do it."

"I will do that."

"Maybe flood the local feeds with the same warning."

"I will do that as well."

Two hours later, a single missile struck the White House. The capital's missile defense system tried and failed to stop it. The missile was just too fast. When the dust cleared, the building and grounds were gone.

28

President Oxham was on the Cinta Alejandre Show that evening. Holly almost skipped it. She had spent most of the day in her room and refused to see anyone; except the man who replaced her French doors. There were repairmen of various sorts all over the place, doing what they could about the damage from the firefight.

"Stop with the pity party," Theo said from the other side of the door. "You're being childish."

He was right, of course, but she had earned that right to a little moping. She had won a military battle, but lost the political battle, which was the one that mattered. She finally relented and came out to watch the interview with the rest of them. Oxham was being interviewed remotely from an unspecified site.

Alejandre: "President Oxham, thank you for being with us tonight."

Oxham: "We live in difficult times, Cinta. I felt it important that the president of the Christian Republic of America explain what happened in Switzerland yesterday."

Alejandre: "Let's get to it then. There has been considerable diplomatic fallout from the CRA's attempt to arrest the Fragment's Emissary on the grounds of the Council's headquarters. I understand Switzerland has made a formal protest to the CRA for violating their sovereignty, which some would consider an act of war. How do you respond to that?"

Oxham: "It is important to understand what is at stake here. The aliens represent an existential threat; a threat every bit as dangerous as the Death Bringer. The fact that these aliens have appeared at the same time as the Death Bringer is too much of a coincidence to be believed. Whatever the aliens are planning, the Death Bringer is part of it.

"That is why Great Britain, with our blessing, attempted to board the alien spaceship when it arrived in orbit around our world, although in that case we also hoped to take Dr. Burton into custody, along with the aliens we suspect are on what is clearly a warship. Obviously we failed. But the technology we could have gained by capturing an alien warship would have been invaluable in what I believe will inevitably come down to war between the aliens and ourselves. Our attempt to arrest Dr. Burton in Geneva was again motivated by our desire to defend the world against the alien menace by removing the so-called Emissary from the equation.

"I have instructed our ambassador to Switzerland to apologize for our violation of their sovereignty. Our intent was to save the world from an alien takeover, as our Ambassador to the Council of Enclaves has explained. We have made the video of his speech public. Several news feeds, including yours, have shown it.

"The Council agrees with our assessment of the alien threat, as evidenced by their rejection of the ultimatum presented by Dr. Burton."

. . .

The interview continued for another fifteen minutes. To Alejandre's credit, she pushed back on Oxham several times, but he held his own. Near the end of the interview, she asked him the kind of question she was famous for.

Alejandre: "President Oxham, if you could say one thing to the Emissary, what would it be?"

Oxham: [looking into camera] "Dr. Burton, I appeal to you to surrender yourself to the appropriate authorities. I can assure you of a fair trial. Let the world get on with surviving the coming apocalypse."

"When pigs fly, you cretin," Holly said.

She returned to her room more discouraged than ever. The Council, after a marathon debate, had rejected the Fragment's offer and issued an international arrest warrant by a vote of seven to five with one abstention. According to Theo's sources, President Oxham himself had leaned hard on the other alliances, employing a carrot-and-stick approach. The CRA was the wealthiest and most powerful alliance in the world. Few of the other alliances were willing to stand up to it.

She had made her case to the Council, and it had not been enough. The CRA and its allies had won. Humanity would continue on a course that would lead to its extinction. She might as well have stayed on Titan.

Anna appeared at the door to their shared bathroom. "May I come in, ma'am?"

"Of course."

"How are you doing?"

She took that to be a rhetorical question, not requiring a response.

"Is there anything I can do?"

She thought for a moment. "Yes, as a matter of fact, there is. But you're not going to like it."

———

Anna slowed the vehicle as they drove past an upscale club near the airport. According to the reader board, it had live dance music, and judging by the crowd standing outside, it was a popular place.

"Looks like people are partying like there's no tomorrow," Anna said. "What do you think?"

"I think I don't want to wait an hour to get in."

Anna drove a few blocks and pulled into a parking lot across the street from the Axios Tavern, which had no queue.

"A bit on the downscale side," Anna said.

"I'm feeling a bit on the downscale side."

A pianist played soft jazz on a small stage. There was a smallish dance floor, but nobody was dancing. They snagged a booth near the back just as its previous occupants were leaving. Holly wore tight jeans, a somewhat revealing blouse. As far as she knew, nobody had seen the Emissary in jeans before. She tied her hair back in a ponytail and added a baseball cap and sunglasses. She hoped the disguise and the venue would be enough for her to go unrecognized.

She ordered a double whisky sour. She was here to get drunk and wasn't about to waste time getting there. Anna asked for a beer, though Holly doubted she would drink it. When the server delivered their drinks, Holly took down half of hers in two quick gulps.

She shuddered and settled into the worn leather seat to let the burn spread through her body. The piano player was good, and the murmuration of conversations in several languages felt comfortable and familiar. This was the most normal she had felt in a long time. She finished her drink and ordered another, which she approached in a more relaxed manner, savoring the light buzz that was forming in her head. Anna didn't try to make conversation; just left her alone in the little alcoholic bubble she was making for herself.

She scanned the room for the ever-present security detail, but didn't see anyone. It was just the two of them, a girls' night out. She had escaped her security bubble. Anna had refused at first, but relented when Holly threatened to go by herself. After all, she was the Emissary. She could do whatever she damn well pleased. It wasn't like they could keep her prisoner in the mansion.

By the time she got through her second double, which made it four drinks, she had to pee. She narrowly avoided tumbling to the floor as she maneuvered out of her seat. She wasn't used to drinking alcohol, nor high heels, but she was an old hand at walking drunk, so getting to the women's room proved straightforward enough. Anna followed her through the crowd, which had gotten larger since they had arrived. When they got back, a bassist and a singer had joined the pianist and they switched to livelier music. The small dance floor in front of the stage started filling up.

"Let's dance," Holly said.

"Uh, I don't think so."

"Fine." She took a moment to appreciate the room's newfound spin. "You stay here and do your PPI thing. I am going to dance."

She waded into the crowd and danced by herself, which was all right because there were other people dancing solo, too. She was soon lost in music and motion, and the world of Emissary-ness receded into the background for a while.

A man dancing behind her brushed against her butt. She turned to face him and put her hands on his shoulders. He was tall, good-looking, and a good dancer. That was all she required. The only question was, how would she get away from Anna?

———

She woke to a familiar pressure in her head. A wave of nausea rolled over her but wasn't bad enough to merit throwing up. She pulled herself into a sitting position, and found herself in a bed she didn't recognize, in a room she didn't recognize. How did she get here?

The tall man from the night before sat in a chair, watching her. The pressure in her head decided to ratchet up the intensity and began pounding on a large drum just behind her eyes. Maybe she was going to throw up after all.

"Gotta pee," she said, and made her way to the bathroom.

When she returned and climbed back into bed, he strolled over and sat on the edge of the bed. In his hand was a glass of something orange.

"Drink," he said, handing it to her. He had a pleasant tenor voice.

"What is it?"

"Orange juice."

She took a sip. It was indeed orange juice. That was probably better than water, but she would need water, too. She emptied the glass in three swallows. It was pretty good for hotel fare.

Bits and pieces of the night before were coming back. She had danced with the guy for half an hour and then went with him to a hotel. She had no memory of what happened after that. How did he get her away from Anna? For that matter, where *was* Anna?

"How do you feel?" he asked.

"I feel like . . ."

She was going to say she felt like crap, but she didn't. Her headache was gone, and she felt alert, energized, ready to tackle a new day.

"Wow. What's in that? I gotta get some."

"I'm afraid it can't be found on your world."

She closed her eyes and let the pieces drop into place. When she opened them, there was a hint of a smirk on his face. It was irritating.

"Where's Anna?" she demanded.

"Anna is fine. As is the small army of security personnel that kept an eye on you while you were making a fool of yourself."

So she hadn't managed to sneak away from the house after all. Anna had created the illusion that she had, but the ever-present bubble of security had been there the whole time. She wanted to be mad about that, but Anna was just doing her job. It had been foolish of her to risk not only her own life, but Anna's.

"How did you get me away from my security team? And where are we?"

"You are still on the dance floor."

"Uh, how does *that* work?"

"As you know, I maintain a presence in your amulet. It is trivial to hijack your nanites to create a dream state in your mind."

She looked around. "So none of this is real."

"An interesting epistemological question, perhaps best left for another time. I must say, I am disappointed. One minor setback and you are ready to throw in the towel, get drunk, and get laid; your go-to solution when the going gets tough."

"Oh, God . . . we didn't . . . we . . . did we?"

"What? Have sex?"

"Please tell me we didn't have sex."

"Okay. We didn't have sex."

"No. Really. Tell me the truth."

"Would it be a problem if we had?"

"Have sex with an alien? Yes! No. I mean, I'd like to at least know what I was getting into before it happened."

He laughed an easy, relaxed laugh. "We did not have sex. Frankly, you were in no condition for that kind of activity. If

I were human, I imagine you would have been something of a letdown. By the way, your nanites would not normally let you get that drunk. I instructed them to take the evening off."

"I need water," she said. That seemed odd, since this was an illusion, but she really was thirsty.

He retrieved a bottle of water from the mini-fridge and handed it to her. She guzzled down as much of it as she could handle in one take, then focused on his remark about being disappointed with her. The more she thought about it, the madder she got.

"So, my ancient alien explorer is disappointed in me," she said. "Well, shit, I'm sorry I have disappointed you, but I'm sure you'll get over it. Besides, what the hell am I supposed to do? The Council is the only game in town for pulling off the biggest project in human history. Without them, it's dead in the water."

He raised an eyebrow. "For someone who is supposed to be a genius, you display a shocking lack of imagination."

"Fuck you."

"Anatomically possible, but not helpful in the current context."

She glared at him. "What do you want from me? I tried. I gave it my best shot. I couldn't sell it."

"You failed."

"Well, duh. Your powers of comprehension are astounding, as usual."

"What did you learn from your failure?"

"That you picked the wrong person for the job?"

There was an uncomfortably long pause before he said, "Perhaps I did."

That alarmed her. Was he giving up on her? She said she was the wrong person for the job, but it was a different matter to hear *him* say it. Did she really want him to give up on her, to cast her aside and start over with someone else?

"Or perhaps you are the right person for the job but going about it the wrong way."

What the hell did that mean? Was she not supposed to have gone to the Council? It had been his idea in the first place. Besides, what other options did she have?

He seemed to read her mind. "What makes you think the Council is the only option?"

He had an irritating habit of asking leading questions rather than just telling her what he wanted her to know. She hated leading questions. Maybe corrupting the youth wasn't the only reason they killed Socrates.

"I don't know what you want me to do," she said. "Just tell me and I'll do it. Otherwise, leave me alone."

The Fragment tilted his head and peered at her.

"You understand technologies that would seem like magic to most people. For example, you know how to build stasis machines a thousand times better than Earth's current capability, employing theories and techniques your fellow humans haven't even imagined yet.

"Or fusion reactors. Your people have been trying to create sustainable, controllable fusion reactors for a century, but have made virtually no progress because they can't figure out how to contain plasma as hot as the center of the sun. But you know how to do that."

"You have an in-depth, working knowledge of dozens of future technologies I put in your brain. We spent the better part of a year on Titan exploring that knowledge together. You have all that knowledge with or without the Council of Enclaves."

With or without the Council of Enclaves. But therein lay the problem. She had the knowledge the world needed. She could teach it to experts in the various fields. She could advise them as they turned that knowledge into practical applications, like spaceships and space elevators and space stations and lunar mining sites. But that required organiza-

tion and planning and execution of plans. It required coopera-
tion among the enclaves. It required financing. It would be
the biggest project in the history of the world. The Council of
Enclaves was the only organization on Earth capable of even
attempting it.

The Fragment was watching her, as if he was waiting for
her to have some kind of epiphany. He finally said, "Do you
remember when I asked you if you wanted to save the human
race?"

She nodded.

"Well, do you?"

Then she saw it, and was appalled by the sheer audacity
of it.

"Let's celebrate," he said. Upbeat jazz came from somewhere. "Care to dance?"

Before she could respond, he swept her up in his arms,
and they were dancing. The music got louder. The sounds of
French and German conversations emerged. The lights, the
other dancers . . . it all washed over her as he spun her
around. Then he was gone, leaving her alone on the dance
floor surrounded by other dancers. Anna was watching her
from their booth, her beer untouched.

It had been a dream.

29

It hadn't been a dream, of course. At least not in the normal sense. The Fragment had hacked her brain to create the entire scene in her mind. It had been so realistic it was scary. How could something seem that real if it didn't actually happen? Or maybe it did happen. After all, what was the difference between the perception of something happening and the thing actually happening? From an epistemological point of view, there was no way to tell the difference.

She shut herself in her room for the next two days to review the vast store of knowledge the Fragment had given her. It was stored in the form of dreams, and it was mostly a matter of remembering them. There were a lot of them. Sophie brought meals to her room, along with a steady supply of water and tea. On the third morning, she called everyone together in the drawing room. At her request, Cinta Alejandre had flown in from Madrid for the meeting.

"First, I want to be clear about one thing," she began. "I did *not* have sex with an alien."

This provoked an awkward silence. Theo said, "I did not realize that was on the table. Not that I have anything against interspecies sex."

"It's an inside joke between me and the Fragment. I did, however, have a chat with him. Don't ask how, just call it magic."

She sipped her tea.

"The Fragment once asked me, 'Do you want to save the human race?' I heard it as: 'Do you want to *save* the human race?' But that's not quite what he meant. What he meant was: 'Do *you* want to save the human race?' It is a small distinction that makes a huge difference. The Fragment made it clear from the beginning that he would not save humanity. But he would give us the technology we need to save ourselves. In fact, he already has."

This provoked more silence.

"Before he awakened me on Titan, he implanted a vast store of knowledge in my brain. I spent a year sorting through it. I know everything we need to know to leave Earth and begin anew somewhere else." She tapped the side of her head with her finger. "It's all right here, in my head."

"Need a safe, sustainable fusion reactor? I know how to build one. Want to know how to improve our current hibernation technology to keep people in stasis for five thousand years? I know how to do that. Want to make alloys that are ten times stronger than anything we know how to make, and only a little heavier? Advanced robotics? Sustainable space habitats? AIs so smart they will frighten you? I know how to do all of that. It is scary how much knowledge is packed away in my head.

She watched their expressions: Theo's baffled look, Adrian's curiosity, Robert's concern, Cinta's intensity.

"The question is, how does that knowledge get translated into actual, working technology that can be used to save the human race? I had hoped the Council of Enclaves would be the answer to that. It's not. The Council is a dead end. They will never relinquish their power and control. Not even to save the human race. So screw them. I'll do it myself."

More silence followed this. They were probably wondering if she had gone completely off the rails and maybe in need of an intervention. She wondered about that, too, as she listened to what she had just said.

Cinta asked, "How are you going to do that?"

"Nice segue into my next point." Everyone laughed, releasing some of the tension in the room.

"Robert, a few days ago, you told me I would need to create an organization. I didn't understand why. Now I do. I am going to create an international nongovernmental organization. It will be called The Exodus Company. Through this organization, I will train the best and brightest people we can find across dozens of disciplines, and I will direct what they do with that knowledge."

She brought up a list on the vidscreen. "Here are some corporate divisions I foresee The Exodus Company needing."

Artificial Intelligence
  Astrobiology
  Corporate Governance
  Diplomacy
  Finance
  Legal
  Life Sciences
  Logistics
  Materials Science
  Medicine
  Metallurgy
  Nuclear Physics
  Planetary Science
  Public Relations
  Quantum Physics
  Robotics
  Security

Space Elevators
Space Mining
Space Stations

They studied the list. Robert said, "Holy crap, sis. This is mind-bogglingly huge. Are you telling us you have the technical knowledge to jump the human race a hundred years ahead in all these areas?"

"Yes."

"How did you arrive at this list?" Adrian asked.

"Well, some things are obvious, like a legal division and a finance division. The Fragment has given me no knowledge at all in those areas, but I figure any large company needs them. The others represent knowledge domains the Fragment has stuffed into my head. Working on the assumption that if it's in my head it must be important, I have spent the last couple of days reviewing what I know and using that as a road map for building a space program that can get us off the planet and into space. For example, the fact that I know pretty much everything there is to know about space elevators tells me we are going to need space elevators."

She drained her teacup and waited while Anna refilled it.

"Obviously, I can't do this by myself. The Exodus Company will become global in scale. It will have to. And fast. We will need a lot of people in key positions right away: a Director of Employee Relations, a Director of Finances and Acquisitions, a Chief Information Officer, a Chief Technology Officer, a Chief Diplomatic Officer, just to name a few. These people will have to staff their divisions quickly. We don't have the luxury of time. I want a functioning global company stood up and staffed in one year. I want to be building spaceplanes in two."

"Theo, I need you to be my chief of staff and personal advisor. Your job is to advise me and keep me sane. Adrian, you're my chief executive officer. You will guide and direct the company to accomplish my goals. You need to find a chief operations officer right away to handle the day-to-day operation of the company. Robert, you will—"

"Whoa," Adrian said, both hands in the air like he was surrendering. "I can't manage something on this scale."

"Why not? Corporate governance is what you studied, isn't it? You wanted to become a consultant to NGOs on corporate governance and planning, didn't you? Well, here is an NGO in desperate need of a CEO who specializes in corporate governance and planning."

"With all due respect, Emissary, there is a big difference between theory and practice. I have lots of theory and zero practice."

"Yeah, I get that. Really, I do. You'll have to hire people who have the knowledge and experience you lack. We all have a steep learning curve ahead of us."

He did not look mollified.

"Robert, as my chief legal officer, you will be responsible for all legal matters, of which I imagine there will be many; like international corporate law and space law, to name just two. I don't expect you to know all of that, but I will expect you to hire the best legal minds in the world across a range of specialties so that the Exodus Project has that knowledge even if you don't."

Robert looked like he was going to object, but then shrugged and settled back into the settee.

"Tomás, you're my chief security officer. I need you to create and manage the company's physical and virtual security. I imagine that will be a huge undertaking."

He raised a hand. "With all due respect, Emissary, I am not qualified for the job and, more importantly, I do not have the right disposition. I am a bodyguard, not an administrator. And before you say the same thing you said to Adrian, I know someone who might be perfect for the job."

"Hire him and you'll be his boss."

"I appreciate your confidence in me, but I would be a square peg trying to fit in a round hole, more a bottleneck than anything else. We can do it that way if you insist, but it would be suboptimal. Besides, I am Theo's PPI and I would like to keep it that way. He will need protection more than ever. All of you will."

That was an ominous thought, but he was probably right. Their security so far had been aimed at protecting her. Once this thing got going, they would all become potential targets.

"Reach out to him. If he is willing to consider it, I'll meet with him."

She turned to Cinta. "I want you to be my Chief Communications Officer. I am sure you have a much better idea of what that entails than I do."

Cinta grinned. "I suspected as much when you asked me to come, though I thought you would be looking for advice rather than offering me the job of a lifetime. In any case, I have an immediate recommendation: buy a media company. You will need one. Either we build it out ourselves or we buy one that already exists. I recommend the latter. We get expertise and experience out of the box."

"You have something in mind?"

"I do. With your permission, I will put out some feelers."

"Buying a media company sounds expensive," Robert said.

"In the neighborhood of five hundred million Euros," Cinta said. "That price will come down if we offer to take the executives, staff, and families with us into space."

"See what you can work out," Holly said

Adrian said, "As I understand it, all this corporate infrastructure we're talking about, its purpose is to get a hundred and twenty-thousand people off the planet and into space. Right?"

"Yes."

"So what exactly are we building?"

"That's a good question." She brought up another list. "Here are a few of my favorite things we are going to build."

Mining Bases on the Moon
    Space Docks
    Space Ships
    Space Stations
    Space Elevators
    Space Arks

"This list expands exponentially as you drill down on the things required for each of them to become a reality."

They studied the list. Robert said, "So half a billion euros for a media company is only the beginning. You are envisioning the largest, most complex, most expensive construction project in the world's history. Before we are done, five hundred million Euros will be a rounding error against the total cost. That begs the question: How do you plan to pay for it?"

She was surprised it had taken this long for someone to ask about that.

"I have no expertise in finance," she said. "I will have to depend on all of you to manage the money end of things; especially Theo and whoever we hire to be the Chief Financial Officer.

"However, I have a general plan of attack. First, I will meet with some of the world's wealthiest people and persuade them to give me their money in exchange for places on an ark. Second, I will meet with various heads of state and persuade them to throw their enclaves' resources behind this in exchange for a portion of their population being part of the Exodus."

"Tickets for the end of the world," Cinta said. "I like it."

A thought occurred to Holly. "Perhaps it goes without saying, but I should say it, anyway. When the time comes, all of you and your families will be on the arks, unless you choose not to. That includes the PPIs. Not just as a reward for your loyalty and hard work, but because I will still need you. Getting a remnant of humanity off world and safely away from Earth is Phase One of Project Exodus. After that, Phase Two kicks in; namely, building sustainable colonies on distant worlds. I suspect that will be the hardest part."

30

Two weeks later, Holly brought *Eos* down in a clearing surrounded by forest twenty kilometers north of New Auckland. A light gray van waited near a dirt road that provided access to the undeveloped property.

Eos was designed to carry twelve people. On this flight there were eight: Holly in the pilot's seat with Robert next to her, Anna and Robert's PPIs behind them, and four marines in full battle gear at the back. The marines weren't really marines. They were former special forces soldiers hired by Theo. But Holly thought of them as her marines because 'mercenaries' seemed pejorative, even if it was accurate. Reece Frader was Robert's PPI. Like Anna, he wore a vest under an otherwise normal looking suit. They were both armed and deadly. Robert had objected to having a PPI, but Tomás was adamant.

"The Emissary has powerful enemies," he said, "enemies who will go to any lengths to take her out. She is what we call a hard target because she is well protected. You, on the other hand, are a soft target. If they can't get at her directly, they might try to get at her through the people she cares about.

Like you and your family. I have hired a security firm in Auckland to provide round-the-clock protection for your family. They will be as inconspicuous as possible, but your lives are going to be very different going forward."

They waited in the plane while the marines got out and looked around. When Holly exited, the smells of the forest triggered a cascade of memories of tramping in the hills and mountains with Robert and her parents before everything went wrong. The fern-like ponga trees, the towering eucalyptus trees, the dense undergrowth, the smells of the land, the sounds of the birds—it reached out and embraced her as if welcoming her home. It seemed like it belonged to another lifetime.

Robert's PPI walked over to the van and talked with two men who had gotten out. They were the men-in-black variety, not the battle-gear variety. He came back.

"That's our security detail," he said to Robert. "They will be with us for the duration of our stay and will remain after to protect your family."

Robert frowned. "I told Janet to get the spare bedroom ready for you. We weren't expecting two extra guests."

"They will stay in the van."

"You're kidding."

"The back can be turned into a surprisingly comfortable sleeping space." When Robert continued to look skeptical, he said, "They're used to it. Trust me."

Robert shrugged and turned to Holly. "You're sure you can't drop by the house? Kiri and Peter are staying with us for a few days. You are something of a mythological figure to them. They are going to be disappointed not to get to see you."

"I wish I could," she said. "But it would put your family in unnecessary danger."

She did wish she could see the grandniece and grandnephew she had never met. But Tomás, Anna, and Reece had all insisted that the risk of driving into New Auckland was too great, both for her and for Robert and his family. This was supposed to be an under-the-radar visit.

"I understand," he said. "Good luck with the billionaires." He and Reece walked to the van and drove off down the dusty road.

Anna and a marine set up an awning over a table and three chairs. They even put a white tablecloth over the table and set out water glasses and crystal goblets. She had brought what Theo assured her was an excellent brandy. Her guests arrived an hour later.

Conrad Kaufman and Norville Brandt were partners in a tech company that specialized in artificial intelligence. They were estimated to be worth something on the order of half a trillion euros. Each. They had taken the outdoor venue to heart and dressed casually. Holly wore her usual white skirt, white blouse, black jacket. Her guests' driver and another man stayed with the vehicle. More men-in-black.

"Mr. Kaufman," Holly said. "And Mr. Brandt." She shook hands with each of them. "Thank you for agreeing to meet with me. I apologize for the somewhat rustic setting. It seems I am an internationally wanted criminal these days, so I try to keep a low profile."

They both glanced at *Eos* and laughed. "Good luck with that," Brandt said. "You announced your presence when you requested permission to enter New Zealand airspace. It was on the vids in about five minutes. The entire world knows you are here by now. It won't take them long to work out where you landed."

"Well, in that case, I guess we will have to keep this meeting brief so I can make my escape before the press shows up."

Kaufman said, "We have been looking forward to meeting

you, Emissary. Please call me Conrad." He glanced at his partner. "You can call him Norville."

The other man laughed an easy laugh and said, with just a hint of sarcasm, "Thanks for the intro, Connie. By the way, we appreciate the outdoor setting; beats the hell out of a stuffy boardroom."

They sat. Anna produced water bottles from a cooler and set them on the table. They chatted for a while about New Zealand, the economy, the Fragment, the Death Bringer, the social and political fragility of the world.

Finally Conrad said, "Pleasant as this is, it is not why you asked us to meet with you. I rather suspect it has something to do with the fact that we are numbered among the world's wealthiest people. Yes?"

Holly settled back in her chair. "I am creating an international nongovernmental organization called The Exodus Company, which I intend to use to drive the largest and most complex project ever undertaken by humankind to get a hundred and twenty thousand people off the planet before the Death Bringer arrives. I expect many enclaves to eventually join me in this endeavor, but in the meantime, I need an infusion of cash to get the ball rolling."

"And you would like some of ours," Norville said.

"Pretty much all of it."

They looked at each other and Conrad said, "What will we get for our investment? Aside from the warm, fuzzy feelings that might come from helping save humanity from the apocalypse."

She couldn't help but laugh at that. They were easy to get along with and she liked them right away, but they were astute businessmen who would eat her for breakfast, lunch, and dinner if she wasn't careful.

"As much as I might in my naivety hope that altruism would be its own reward," she said, "I am not quite that naïve. You and your families will be among the 120,000 people who leave earth."

"About that," Conrad said. "James Cartwright made a similar offer. You know Secretary Cartwright?"

"By reputation. He seems determined to be my enemy. I take it he offered you a few places in one of his underground cities."

"We told him we'd think about it and then did a little research. Turns out his underground cities idea is a fool's errand. They will not survive the Death Bringer."

He glanced at Norville, who said, "He offered each of us thirty places."

"I can match that," she said.

They exchanged looks again. "Naw, we'll take fifteen each. Outside of family, there ain't hardly anyone we like well enough to want to take with us." They both grinned. It occurred to her that maybe they had been working together a bit too long. They sounded like an old married couple. Then the obvious dawned on her: they *were* a married couple. Her briefing had failed to mention that.

"Emissary," Anna said, putting a hand on Holly's shoulder. Holly looked in the direction she was pointing. Two SUVs pulled up behind the vehicle her guests had arrived in. The marines reformed into a tighter circle around her and the spaceplane.

"Don't get all excited and start shooting people," Norville said. "That'll be Imogene Reid."

Holly looked at them. "The Prime Minister of New Zealand?"

They nodded in tandem. Conrad said, "I hope you don't mind us inviting her to the party. We figured you'd want to talk to her sooner or later, so why not sooner?"

Anna said to the marines, "Stand down. We don't want to shoot the Prime Minister of New Zealand." Two of them might have cracked a smile, but the only change in posture she could detect was that their weapons now pointed toward the ground rather than toward the new arrivals.

Holly, Norville, and Conrad stood and greeted the petite woman, who was indeed Imogene Reid. She had brought two PPIs with her.

"Madam Prime Minister," Holly said.

"Emissary."

They shook hands. Reid shook hands with Conrad and Norville, who she obviously knew.

"Sorry I'm late to the party," she said. "Traffic getting out of New Auckland was awful. Somebody ought to do something about that." She smiled at her own joke.

Anna retrieved another chair and a couple more bottles of water.

Holly said, "Anna, can we move our protection detail out a bit? All these guns are making me nervous." Anna gave the order.

Reid said, "I see you have not gotten used to being surrounded by a small army everywhere you go. You will. It just takes a while." She glanced at the two billionaires. "Conrad and Norville are key supporters of mine. We have known each other for a long time. They told me you were dropping in for a visit and wondered if I might want to tag along. Not being one to pass on a good photo op, I decided to put in an appearance. Besides, I wanted to meet you in person."

"You're right on time, Madam Prime Minister," Conrad said. "We have just concluded an agreement with the Emissary in which we pledged a trillion dollars in exchange for a handful of seats on the last ship leaving earth. I think we got snookered, but it seems to be for a good cause."

The Prime Minister raised her eyebrows. "That's a lot of money. Even for you boys."

"What else are we going to do with it?" Norville said. "I saw on the news feeds the other day that the world is coming to an end." He turned to Holly. "Just so you understand, Madam Emissary, we cannot give it to you all at once. We have to liquidate assets and investments, which takes time, especially if we want to avoid spooking the markets. We'll get a few hundred billion to you by the end of next week and spread the rest out over the next few years." He grinned. "But I'm betting you will have a lot more funding coming into play pretty soon. Tickets off the planet are going to be a hot item pretty soon. But really, you are going to need the backing of the Enclaves."

"Like New Zealand," Conrad said, looking pointedly at the Prime Minister.

The woman sat back and looked at Holly for what seemed like a long time. She liked Reid, but reminded herself that this woman was New Zealand's *de facto* dictator. One did not become a dictator without a certain amount of ruthlessness.

"I would like you to consider me an ally," she said. "But I have two conditions."

Well, she had certainly cut to the chase. Just like Conrad and Norville. It dawned on Holly that all three of them knew exactly why Holly was here and had already decided how they were going to respond.

"First," Reid said, "I need to understand how you plan to save the human race so I can be sure you have some idea what you are doing before I commit my country's resources to you. Oxham's underground cities are a crock. I need to know that what you are offering isn't a crock too."

The woman's bluntness took Holly aback.

"Second, I want security assurances. You have powerful enemies. Backing you will make them my enemies as well. We are a small country. A couple of nukes lobbed at Wellington and New Auckland would pretty much finish us off. Other nations considering your offer are going to have the similar concerns. It may seem like I am exaggerating the danger we face, but let me assure you, I am not. I didn't get where I am by underestimating my adversaries."

She gulped down some more water. "Tell me, in as few words as you can, just how you intend to save the world."

Holly had outlined her plan to her leadership team, but hadn't put together an elevator pitch, which is what Reid was asking for.

She took a breath. "I am going to put 120,000 people into stasis on six space arks, along with everything they will need to build sustainable colonies on planets in other star systems. That will give the human race six chances to start anew."

Reid blinked a few times. She imagined Conrad and Norville did too, but she wasn't looking at them. She was watching the Prime Minister.

"That's it? You are going to launch a hundred and twenty-thousand sleepers into space and hope they survive?"

Holly made herself smile, hoping it communicated more confidence than she felt. Her plan sounded crazy even to her when stated so baldly.

"There is a little more to it than that, but yes, that is what I intend to do. The human race does not have the technology to accomplish it, but I do."

Reid thought about this for a few moments. Then, "What security assurances can you give me?"

Apparently, they were done with the first question. Whether she was satisfied with Holly's answer was difficult to say. The woman seemed open and friendly but gave little away. Holly hadn't given any thought to the second question, though it was an obvious one now that Imogene Reid had put it out there. She had not come prepared for this conversation and wished Theo were here. But he wasn't. She was on her own.

"Madam Prime Minister, I cannot guarantee your country's security. Nobody can. What I can offer is my promise to use the military capabilities the Fragment has given me to defend your country from other enclaves. We can formalize this in a mutual defense agreement, if you like, stating that the Emissary will regard an attack against New Zealand as an attack against herself and will respond accordingly. I would think that would give any potentially hostile nation pause. Especially after I laid waste to the White House."

Reid took her time thinking about it. "I'll tell you what. Have Theo Peeters call my Foreign Minister to provide us with a little more clarity on your plan and to hammer out the wording of a treaty. If all goes well, you will have your first national ally."

Holly couldn't stop an audible sigh of relief.

Reid pointed at the goblets. "I don't suppose you have anything stronger than water that we can celebrate with?"

"Theo sent along a couple bottles of brandy. Knowing him, I'm sure they are excellent." She glanced at Anna, who disappeared into the plane to get the bottles.

Reid looked toward the plane. "I have seen vids of that amazing spaceplane of yours in action. A warplane, I'm told. I don't suppose I can get a peek inside?"

———

In theory, *Eos's* journey halfway around the world to New Zealand and back made a tempting target, but nothing untoward happened. The world seemed to have decided the Emissary was best left alone.

Holly brought the spaceplane down on the landing pad they had added behind the house. While she appreciated the convenience, it was a shame it took out a third of the park-like space in the back. That was not the only change. They had converted an outbuilding into barracks for the growing number of soldiers, turned the beautiful drive into a concrete block obstacle course, and added two heavy machine gun emplacements on the roof. The beautiful old house had become a fortress.

She turned into the first room on the right as she entered through the back entrance, leaving Anna and the security detail to continue down the hall. It seemed the compound was secure enough that Anna didn't feel the need to follow her around inside the building. The room had been turned into an office for Gail Meisner, their administrative assistant, and a secretary.

At fifty-two, Gail came with a broad portfolio of experience and a permanent scowl. She was all business, with little patience for anything she considered frivolous. Holly hadn't found a way to like the woman yet, but she couldn't fault her skills and work ethic.

Both women stood when Holly entered the room. "Emissary," Gail said. "Welcome back. I hope your trip was pleasant and productive." She had a strong German accent.

"Please," Holly said. "You don't have to stand up every time I walk into the room."

She looked at the other woman. "It's Lana, isn't it?"

"Liana, Emissary."

"Liana. Sorry. Being the Fragment's Emissary has not improved my memory for names." She turned back to Gail. "Where are Theo and Adrian?"

"They went to Lausanne again, ma'am, to try to speed up the process of getting the Exodus Company registered as a legal entity. Also, Mr. Verhoeven is looking at a new office building being built on the outskirts of the city."

"He's not thinking of putting our headquarters there, is he?" She already knew where she wanted to build ExCo's headquarters, and it wasn't in Lausanne.

"It is for office space. He says we are going to hire a lot of staff in a short time and will need a place for them to work."

That made sense. The snowball had started rolling down the hill and was going to get bigger and bigger as it went, taking on a momentum of its own as it gained mass and speed. Holly shouldn't have to worry about any of that, of course. Adrian and Theo would take care of it. But it was hard for her to leave all the details to them.

"Anything else I should know?"

"Not that I am aware of, ma'am."

"Is Cinta here?"

"I saw Ms. Alejandre earlier. Try the drawing room. If she is not there, try the library."

Cinta was not in the drawing room, but Danae was. When Tomás had declined the job of head of security, he had recommended Danae Najafi, a Norwegian born to Iranian parents who had emigrated to Norway before she was born. She came with special forces training and experience leading security teams. She was the reason for the beefed up security around the house, not to mention the four marines that accompanied Holly to New Zealand.

When they first met, she had corrected Holly's butchering of her name: "It's Da-NAY Na-JAY-fee." When Holly pointed out that Danae did not sound Iranian, the woman shrugged and said her parents gave her a Norwegian name so she would not stand out so much.

She stood when Holly entered the room. "Emissary. Welcome back."

Holly dropped into her usual chair. "Thanks. It's good to be back."

Gretchen appeared from somewhere with a cup of tea, a cup of coffee, and a plate of cookies, all of which she placed on the table under the chandelier and retired from the room.

Cinta walked in. "Emissary. How was your trip? Did you charm the billionaires?"

"It's more like they charmed me. They also pledged a trillion euros." She tried to keep a straight face, but couldn't suppress a grin.

Cinta's eyebrows went up. "Trillion? With a T?"

"Not all at once, but spread out over the next few years."

Two vehicles pulled up in front of the house. A few moments later, Theo and Adrian joined them.

"How'd it go with Conrad and Norville?" Theo asked.

"A trillion euros spread out over the next few years," Holly said. "Plus, they are going to set up a meeting with other potential investors next week so I can make a pitch to them."

After a moment of silence while they absorbed the information, Adrian said, "I'd call that a successful trip."

"Adrian and I had a good day too," Theo said. "We put money down on an office building in Lausanne. It will take a few weeks to work out the details and sign the papers, and then we'll have it built out into office space."

"And our corporation?"

"Very close to a done deal. As always, the devil is in the details, but I think I impressed on them the urgency of getting the company up and running as soon as possible. I ran into the Foreign Minister, by the way. He wants to meet you." He let that sink in. "I think Switzerland is looking to join forces with us."

He looked smug. Holly hated to burst his bubble. But she did anyway.

"That is good news. Set it up. Speaking of allies, I ran into Imogene Reid."

There was a moment of surprise, then simultaneous questions: "What?" from Adrian; "Where?" from Theo; and "How?" from Cinta.

"Conrad and Norville brought her along."

Theo recovered first. "Well, I knew they were well connected, but I did not know they could drag the Prime Minister out into the woods for a secret meeting with the Emissary." He paused. "On the other hand, this is New Zealand we are talking about. It's not a big country."

"What did you talk about?" Adrian asked. There was caution in his voice.

"She wants to ally with us. Contingent on more details about project Exodus and a mutual defense pact of some sort. She said Theo should call her Foreign Minister and work something out."

The room got quiet, and tension filled the space.

"Well, what was I supposed to do?" she said. "She offered to put her country's support behind us. It didn't seem like I could say, 'Thanks, I'll think about it and get back to you.'"

"No, I suppose not," Theo said. "Did you promise her anything else?"

"Yeah, I told her we would give her Australia as a third island if she signed up."

Why were they throwing cold water on her first political win? It wasn't like either of them had been there.

Theo leaned back in his chair and held up both hands in a gesture of surrender. "I'll give her office a call."

"Not to change the subject," Cinta said, "but I have some news, too."

Holly was fine with changing the subject.

"I convinced my former bosses at Madrid Media that it would be a brilliant move if they could land a deal to be the exclusive distributor for broadcasts made by the Emissary. That was this morning. They had to make a few calls of their own. I just got off a call with them and they are ready to sign as soon as we are."

"An exclusive deal?" Adrian said. "What about the other international news feeds?"

Cinta grinned. "Eventually, we will buy Madrid Media, so the rest of the media giants might as well get used to it. I planted the seed in a few executives' heads and they didn't reject the idea. I think a meeting with the Emissary might cinch the deal. Especially if she were to offer places on an ark for their executives, key employees, and families."

Theo and Adrian were watching Holly. That meant they

liked the idea and were waiting for her reaction. A frisson of excitement ran through her.

"So who has signing authority around here?"

"That would be Adrian and myself," Theo said. "I guess you should have it as well."

"Get the exclusive signed as soon as you can. I have some things I want to say to the world."

31

It dawned on Holly that she was envious of Cinta Alejandre; envious of her competence; envious of her confidence; envious of her ability to take command of every situation she found herself in. Compared to her, Holly felt drab, awkward, unsophisticated, incompetent. The Fragment might have done better to have chosen someone like her to be his emissary.

"Good evening," Cinta said to the camera. "At least it is where I am."

She glanced over her shoulder at the vidscreen behind her. It displayed a familiar but always astonishing view of Earth from space. Holly had moved *Gabriel's Fire* into a high earth orbit to provide a panoramic view of the entire planet. A million sparks of light spread across much of the globe; some crowded into bright splotches, others into smaller clusters, some alone in the dark; all announcing that a technologically advanced civilization lived here. It looked nothing like it had before the Great Collapse, but it was still awe-inspiring.

"As you can see, we are on Earth's night side," she continued. "And yes, the view is the real thing, in real time. I am speaking to you from *Gabriel's Fire*, the Emissary's spaceship.

She gave me a tour. Trust me when I tell you that this space-ship is the most amazing thing I have ever seen. And I have seen a lot of amazing things. But that is not why I am speaking with you tonight.

"I imagine just about everyone in the world knows by now that the Council of Enclaves turned down the Fragment's offer of advanced technologies we could use to leave our world before the Death Bringer sweeps it away. The reason the Emissary took the Fragment's offer to the Council in the first place is that they offered the only existing organization with world-wide reach. Her hope was that they would take up the offer and take charge of the greatest project ever undertaken by humankind.

"Unfortunately, the Council in effect said, 'No thanks, we've got this.'" She leaned a bit toward the camera, a move Holly had seen before. It created a sense of intimacy between her and her audience. "Let me tell you a little secret: they don't got this."

She smirked; the smirk that those who followed her broadcasts had seen many times; the smirk that said, 'We know the real story, don't we'. Holly didn't know how she did it, but in a few brief minutes, she undoubtedly had the world eating out of her palm.

"The Emissary is aware the Council does not speak for everyone. The Council's vote to reject her offer was seven to five, which tells you something all by itself. And the Alliance leaders do not always speak for all their Enclaves. With that in mind, she has decided to bypass the Council and appeal directly to you, the people of the world, citizens of Earth. I want you to listen to what she has to say. Your future, the future of your children, the future of humanity depends on it."

Holly joined her in front of the camera and Cinta stepped away, leaving Holly to face the camera and the world alone. Cinta had negotiated a deal with Madrid Media for exclusive rights to broadcast the Emissary's addresses. She had brought two of the company's engineers to handle video and audio.

Holly wore her usual white outfit, which the press had taken to calling her signature attire. She looked into the camera and counted to five, which seemed like an eternity, then began.

"I thought it appropriate to speak to you from orbit, because what I have to say concerns every man, every woman, every child on Earth. Behind me, you can see what our world looks like from space. I am sure you have seen images like this before. I never tire of looking at it. As Ms. Alejandre pointed out, *Gabriel's Fire* is on the night side of the planet. The terminator line separating night from day will appear over the horizon about the time I finish talking, which I promise will not be long."

She turned to point out some features.

"You can make out Spain and southern France here, and over there the boot of Italy thrusting out into the Mediterranean Sea, which is the large dark patch. Down here at the bottom is the coast of North Africa."

She turned back to the camera. "Beautiful, isn't it? Our island home in the vast emptiness of the universe." She paused. "You might have noticed what looks like a digital clock above the vidscreen. It reads 18 B.E.W. That's 18 years before the end of the world. That's all the time our world has left. It is all the time we have left. What we do with those 18 years will determine the fate of our species."

The image of Earth gave way to a star field. An opaque circle of blackness occupied the center of the view, blocking out the light of half the stars.

"This is the Death Bringer seen from a probe accompanying it as it plunges into our sun's gravity well. You can't see any detail because it has a low albedo. That means it doesn't reflect much light and is one of the reasons it took so long for our astronomers to notice it. Right now, it's halfway between the orbits of Uranus and Neptune, the two most distant planets in our solar system. In a little less than 18 years, it will cross Earth's orbit and toss our world into the Sun."

The image behind her switched back to the view of Earth.

"That is why we must leave."

She pushed her hair back.

"If you saw the press conference I gave a few weeks ago, you already know all of this. I imagine most of you have also seen the agreement the Fragment laid out as the basis for giving us advanced technological knowledge that will enable us to leave Earth before the end of the world; the agreement the Council rejected.

"Some of them believe the Death Bringer is not a brown dwarf star, but a Jupiter-sized planet, and that Earth will survive its passing. They believe we can hide in underground bunkers and emerge a few years later to rebuild. They are wrong. As the Death Bringer gets closer, its gravitational field will begin to affect other bodies in our solar system and our astronomers will be able to get a better sense of its true mass. But by then it will be too late."

She sipped some water.

"Since the Council has rejected the Fragment's offer of assistance, I have decided to bypass the Council and appeal directly to the Enclaves. I am creating an organization called The Exodus Company. It will provide a structure, or framework, for the transfer of technology to those Enclaves that are willing to work with me to leverage the Fragment's technology to leave Earth.

"Where will we go? We have two options. First, we can build colonies in space and on the moons of Jupiter and Saturn. The problem is that we humans have evolved as a planet-based species, with gravity and an atmosphere. Space is an utterly hostile environment for us. The Fragment puts the probability of the human race successfully colonizing the solar system at 6%. I don't like those odds.

"The other choice is to leave our solar system and colonize other worlds circling other stars. The Fragment has identified six star systems with human-habitable planets within 1500 light years of Earth. None of them is as human-friendly as Earth, because our species is uniquely adapted to this world and not to any of them. Nonetheless, we can live there, and our descendants will adapt to their new homes over time. This is the option I have chosen. The Fragment puts the probability of at least one of the six colonies succeeding at 97%. There is a 23% probability that all six of them will be successful."

She brought up a diagram of a star field. A bright yellow dot sat in the middle, with green lines extending away from it in different directions. Each line ended in a bright green dot.

"The yellow dot is our sun. The green dots are the star systems the Fragment has identified for us. As you can see, they are at various distances from Earth. The nearest is 237 light years away; the farthest, a little over 1200. Each has a planet we can live on. That is where we will go.

"How will we get there? We will build and launch six space arks, each carrying 20,000 sleepers, each headed for one of those worlds. Their journeys will take a long time. Traveling at 30% the speed of light for most of the journey, it will take an ark 756 years to reach the nearest one. It will take 3,800 years to reach the furthest one.

"The passengers will be unaware of the passage of time because they will be in stasis. Think of it as hibernation. They will go to sleep here and wake up in orbit around their new home. Earth will be long gone, but it will seem like yesterday to them.

"What will happen when an ark reaches its destination? The command crew will be awakened first, along with some specialists in biology, geology, climatology, and so on. They will explore the planet and identify the best place for the first colony. Then they will awaken the first few hundred colonists and use the spaceplanes they have brought with them to travel to the surface and begin building. More colonists will be awakened as the initial colony expands and other colonies are established."

She paused for several seconds and then continued in a quiet voice.

"I cannot promise that it will be easy. In fact, it will be the most difficult thing our species has ever undertaken. Neither can I promise that we will succeed. The Fragment has offered us the means to save ourselves, but *we* must do the work, and there is no guarantee we will succeed. What I can promise you is this: We have been given a chance; a chance to avoid extinction; a chance to write the next chapter of humanity's story.

"I invite you . . . no, I beg you to tell your leaders that you want to be part of this; that you choose life rather than death; that you want to reach for the stars. I challenge the heads of the enclaves to join me and others in this greatest of all endeavors. Together we will build Humanity 2.0."

———

Cinta had predicted they would be deluged with calls following the broadcast, and they were. Fortunately, Madrid Media had a controlling interest in a call center and had secured its use to handle the calls. It was a good thing they did because the calls started pouring in as soon as Cinta provided a call ID for The Exodus Company.

Adrian had hired a marketing firm to do an analysis of the response. On the fourth morning after Holly's speech, Adrian and Cinta brought early results to her. Theo and Robert were there, too.

Marcelo Bautista, CEO of Estudio Bautista, had flown in to make the presentation. He was a short, plump man in his sixties. His daughter Erica, who he was grooming to take over the business, came with him.

"Emissary," he said. "It is an honor to meet you." He made some more remarks, expressing his gratitude for the opportunity to be of service to the Emissary. Then he brought up a bullet pointed list on the vidscreen. "I have provided Mr. Verhoeven with a full analysis of the first three days of calls. What you see here is an executive summary of the results.

"One: The response has been huge. Our initial analysis covers 163,000 calls. The call rate shows no signs of slowing down.

"Two: They are largely from normal, everyday people. No Presidents or Prime Ministers, but you struck a chord among the common folk.

"Three: Seventy-two percent of the calls were positive. The most often heard words from this group were 'like' and 'hope.'

"Four: Nineteen percent of the calls were negative, with the phrases 'dangerous woman' and 'bitch' coming out on top. There was also a fair amount of general xenophobia toward the Fragment in this group.

"Five: Nine percent of the responses could not be categorized as definitely positive or definitely negative. That is not unusual in cases like this.

"Six: There were some death threats, which is to be expected in a sample this large. I referred them to your security people."

She glanced at Anna, who said, "Tomás is checking them out, but at this point he doesn't see any cause for concern. You have other enemies who present a much higher threat profile."

Apparently, that was supposed to reassure her.

Bautista continued. "Seven: You have three hundred and twelve marriage proposals so far, mostly from men. Or at least they claimed to be men. There are at least two genuine billionaires in the mix. We checked."

Robert snickered.

"Good to know," Holly said.

"That's all I have, Emissary. I would be happy to answer questions."

Adrian looked at Holly and when she shook her head, he said, "I have reviewed the full report, Mr. Bautista, and I am pleased with your work. We would like you to continue analyzing the data as it comes in. Perhaps in a week or so you can forward us a final report. I am particularly interested in how attitudes change over time."

Gail escorted Bautista and his daughter out.

Holly made herself a cup of tea. "There were no calls from heads of state. I suppose that's not surprising, but it raises the question: How *would* they reach us?"

"I can answer that," said Gail as she walked back into the room.

Everyone turned to look at the tall, stern-looking woman who rarely said anything in meetings; just recorded them.

"Incoming calls to the mansion come to my desk and I forward them to whoever they should go to. In the last two days, we have received four calls from people claiming to represent heads of state: Kuala Lumpur, Sri Lanka, Nairobi, and Ecuador."

Holly set her cup down and stared at the woman. "What did you tell them?"

"I put them on hold while I ran a backtrace to verify that the calls at least came from the right city. Then I forwarded them to Mr. Peeters."

Holly turned to Theo. "Why do I not know about this?"

He shifted in his seat. "Because Gail is under orders not to forward calls to you but to transfer them to Adrian or myself so we can filter out superfluous calls."

"Really." She made no attempt to keep the sarcasm out of

her voice. "Calls from the leaders of Kuala Lumpur, Sri Lanka, Nairobi, and Ecuador are superfluous. Something that needs to be kept from me."

There was a tense pause before Adrian leaned forward in his chair. "Emissary. We are not keeping anything important from you, but part of our job, especially Theo's, is to make sure you are focused on the things only you can do and not on things others can do. He is your Chief of Staff, which makes him your primary gatekeeper."

She chewed on that, but it left a bad taste. "Did you at least call them back?"

"As a matter of fact, I did," Theo said. "You have a meeting tomorrow with Switzerland's Foreign Minister Xavier Fischer, which will be held here. Next week you have meetings with Prime Minister Abdu Mwangi of the Nairobi Enclave, President Deng Wei of the Beijing Enclave, President Daniel Lucio Mendoza of the Quito Enclave, and Empress Huang Meili of the Kuala Lumpur Enclave. I have scheduled them over four consecutive days, allowing us a full day with each for talks, meet-and-greets, state dinners, and so on. I will prep you for each meeting on the way there."

"Fine," she said with a tone she was sure told everyone in the room she was not yet fine with it at all. "I suppose I should get back to planning how to save humanity, so I have something intelligent to say when I meet with them."

—————

They made love that night, she and Theo. Afterward, as they lay together, her head resting on his chest, she said, "I'm sorry about earlier today. You and Adrian were right. I don't know why I got so defensive."

She felt him smile. "That's an easy one. When you bypassed the Council and appealed directly to the people, you usurped their power and authority and become the most important person in the world. Half the world will follow you anywhere. The other half is scared to death of you. Then you find out your top lieutenants are screening your calls as though you are a child who needs looking after."

"Huh," she said. That made so much sense she was a little embarrassed at not having seen it herself. She hadn't needed taking care of since she was twelve. No wonder she chafed at having handlers.

"So I'm a spoiled kid throwing a tantrum?"

"That is hardly a fair characterization. You have been catapulted into world leadership with little preparation for the role. It is not surprising that you are having difficulty adjusting to it and figuring out who and what you have become. If you sometimes push back against it, so what? You may be the Fragment's Emissary, but you are still human, with all the hangups and baggage that come with that. So cut yourself some slack. The rest of us do."

"I don't like it when things come between us."

"Well, I have never been married, but I have it on good authority that married couples fight with each other. Then they work it out and have sex."

"Makeup sex? Is that what we just did?"

"Makeup sex is what you do *after* you make up. We had sex *before* we made up, so it doesn't count."

"I see. What can we do about that?"

32

Thirteen years before the end of the world

Holly was hot and sticky with sweat, and it was Danae's fault. Not long after joining The Exodus Company, she learned that Holly used to practice kick-boxing and suggested they spar together. "Even the Emissary needs exercise," she joked. After five years of this regimen, Holly had gotten very good at it and, as a bonus, was in the best physical condition of her life.

Danae was stronger and faster than Holly, and could be counted on to push her to her limit every time, often putting her on her butt while rarely ending up there herself. It turned out she was a certified instructor, so she could show Holly how to improve. They also practiced what Danae called street fighting, where they threw out the rules and Danae attacked her like someone on the streets would, sometimes using weapons as part of her assault on the always weaponless Holly.

A small crowd often gathered in ExCo's gym to watch the Emissary and ExCo's Chief of Security spar. Holly sometimes accepted challenges from the marines. They seemed to get a kick out of sparring with the Emissary and she got a kick out of holding her own against them even though they were heavier and stronger. She won as many bouts as she lost, and there were few things more satisfying than putting a big, muscular marine on his or her butt. She was pretty sure they weren't going easy on her; money often exchanged hands afterward.

Back in her apartment on the sixteenth floor of the new ExCo headquarters, after she had showered and dressed, Holly stood in front of the floor-to-ceiling window overlooking Quito, Ecuador's capital, high in the Andes. She had not yet gotten used to the breathtaking view of the city of three and a half million spilling out of a natural bowl toward the rainforest of the Amazon River basin.

Ecuador was a small country and did not have as much to contribute to Project Exodus as some countries. But it did have one of the few locations on Earth that was ideal for the ground-side terminus of a space elevator. A location near the equator was a must-have. An altitude of 2800 meters was an added plus. The Ecuadorian government had donated land on the northern outskirts of Quito for her headquarters, and a national park straddling the equator for the terminus. That, along with a guaranteed local workforce, ensured there would be Ecuadorians on the arks.

She went to her private office to review the master Gantt chart. It showed her a top-level timeline, mapping out every major project, its dependencies, and its progress to-date. If she wanted to, she could drill down on any of the projects to see the sub-projects that had to be accomplished in order to finish that project, along with progress to-date for each sub-project. She could even drill down further to see progress on the individual activities that comprised a sub-project. She didn't. That's what she had project managers for. All she needed was the top-level view, which showed her at a glance if they were running behind schedule on something. She would ask questions about those.

In five whirl-wind years, the Exodus Company had grown from meetings in Theo's drawing room to a globe-spanning organization employing nearly ten thousand people in a dozen locations around the world and in space. Much had been accomplished. The first ExCo spaceplanes were coming off the production line in Germany. She had named them Zephyrs. They were designed to shuttle her people around the world, to the space stations, and even to the moon. A few of them were configured as attack planes, something she made sure the world knew about. She would rather scare someone off than fight them off.

Two space docks had been constructed in low Earth orbit. One was producing spaceships to transport people and supplies to and from the lunar mining bases. The other was scheduled to begin construction on the first ark when the second lunar base came online. The mining bases were crucial because it was much easier to launch a heavy load from the Moon to low Earth orbit than to blast that same load out of Earth's gravity well. The first base was an upgrade to the existing Chinese mining operation, which they had been happy to contribute to the cause since they had been getting ready to abandon it, anyway.

The mining crews lived underground and used bots to mine regolith and other raw materials, which were processed and turned into modular components that could be assembled into whatever they needed. The components were packed into a large cylinder which was loaded into an oversized rail gun and shot into space on a trajectory that would take it into low Earth orbit where it would be captured by a tug and towed to a space dock or a space station.

In principle, the lunar mining project was straightforward. In practice, it turned into a nightmare that had required Holly to go there in person on two occasions to resolve problems.

One involved a labor dispute, which she resolved through sheer presence and some tough negotiations. Another involved sabotage, which she resolved with a major security upgrade.

The two space stations were far enough along to begin building the space elevator tether, which would be constructed from top down; that is, from the space station to the ground-side terminal. Two near-earth asteroids were hauled in to act as the counterweights for the tethers. Spaceships, spaceplanes, mining bases, space stations . . . all these projects were dwarfed by the construction of the tethers, which were the most challenging and most critical part of the endeavor. Without the tethers, they had no space elevators, and without the elevators, they had no way to get 120,000 sleepers and supplies into space.

Rapid growth did not come without its problems, the biggest being Holly herself. Everything depended on her imparting enormous amounts of technical knowledge to scores of teams of scientists and engineers, and there was only one of her, making her Project Exodus' biggest bottleneck. Her calendar was booked solid several months out with fourteen-hour days. This was down from eighteen after Theo insisted she slow down before she burned herself out.

She and Theo took to doing short hikes in the national forest Ecuador had given to the project. It wasn't quite like getting away from everything because her security bubble followed her everywhere, but it was a change of pace and it got her out of the office.

There was still politics, of course. She held monthly virtual meetings with the heads of the enclaves that were part of Project Exodus, and in-person meetings twice a year. They always had a lot to say as they jockeyed to ensure their enclaves were being treated fairly. Not a week went by that she didn't have to personally intervene in a dispute of one sort or other.

Then there were the knowledge transfer sessions. Early on, she had been meeting with the world's leading experts in a variety of fields for intensive five-day knowledge transfer sessions every week. After five years, she was still meeting two or three times a month with teams of experts to share knowledge they needed to deal with new challenges. The knowledge transfer sessions were the most demanding part of the job. The people she was teaching were smart and asked a lot of smart questions.

There was always the problem of ongoing anti-Emissary propaganda. The single loudest voice was that of the Reverend Doctor Alexander Taylor, whose daily programs to the faithful around the world were filled with all manner of invective aimed at the Fragment and herself. As a result, nearly a third of the world's population still believed the Fragment was the anti-Christ and Holly was the whore of Babylon. She wasn't sure what the whore of Babylon reference meant, but it didn't sound like a compliment.

"It's the drug-fueled orgies that are particularly juicy," Adrian said. "That and your out-of-control alcoholism, child sacrifices to Satan, and mental illness."

"Hey," Robert said. "I didn't get the memo on drug-fueled orgies. How do I get in on those?"

It weighed on Holly that a third of the world's population believed the stuff. She had her own propaganda machine, of course, which she hated. But she couldn't compete with the sophisticated operations of the CRA and the Reverend Taylor. Why did they hate her so much?

Then, out of the blue, came a call from Alexander Taylor himself. He wanted to meet with the Fragment. Even more surprising, the Fragment agreed.

———

Three days later, Taylor stared out the forward windows as *Gabriel's Fire* grew in size. Holly recognized the expression of wonder on his face. One of the space stations—a repurposed Tiangong Station—hung like a jeweled bracelet in the distance. Earth's horizon was visible below them. She had seen all of this many times, but never tired of it.

"Beautiful, isn't it?"

"It's absolutely astonishing," he said.

She maneuvered *Eos* alongside *Gabriel's Fire,* a little aft of the rotating ring. The spaceship extended mechanical arms, grabbed hold of the plane, and pulled them into the hangar.

"Welcome to *Gabriel's Fire,*" she said.

She guided him through a zero-gee corridor from the hangar to the hub of the ring, then up one of the spokes to the ring's inner surface, where its rotation produced the equivalent of Earth gravity. A short walk down a corridor brought them to a circular room that looked very much like the meeting room on Ganymede.

"Have a seat," she said. "The Fragment will be here in a moment. Would you like a cup of coffee?"

"That would be wonderful."

A spider bot trundled out from the kitchen with a tray holding a coffee mug and a teacup. To Taylor's credit, he didn't panic.

"That sure looks like a giant mechanical spider," he said.

"It does, doesn't it? I assure you, it is harmless. The Fragment tells me that any resemblance to our class Arachnida is coincidental. It is simply an example of form following function. Believe it or not, you get used to it after a while. Well, mostly."

The bot set the tray on the coffee table and backed out of the room. An interval of silence followed while they prepared and sampled their beverages. Taylor looked surprised when he tried the coffee. "This is very good."

"I am pleased it meets with your approval," said the Fragment as he entered the room. He walked up to Taylor, who stood.

"Dr. Taylor," he said, extending a hand. "I am pleased to meet you in person."

Taylor accepted the Fragment's hand and waited for the Fragment to take a seat opposite him before sitting back down.

"May I call you Alexander?"

"That would be fine. What should I call you?"

"Fragment or *the* Fragment. Which ever rolls off the tongue easiest."

"Do you have a name other than that?"

"Holly asked the same question when we first met on Ganymede. I have never needed a name, so I don't have one. Fragment is the name I offered to Holly when we first met. Neither of us has seen fit to change it."

A frown formed on Taylor's face. The Fragment noticed and said, "Next you are going to ask me if there are others of my kind."

"How do you know that is my next question?"

Holly laughed and said, "It's the question I asked next."

The Fragment chuckled. "The function of names among your kind is to identify and reference other people in a relatively unique way. There are four thousand two hundred and sixty-three people in the world named Holly Burton; considerably fewer named Holly *Margaret* Burton, but still quite a few. Her name functions as a useful label to distinguish her from, say, Anna Lindstrom, because in the current context Holly is the only one in the room with that name. When you ask me for *my* name, you are asking me to differentiate myself from others like me, which assumes, incorrectly, that I exist as one among many in a way that would make personal names useful."

Taylor considered this for a few moments. "You are the only one of your kind then."

"No doubt that seems like a straightforward yes-no question, but it's not. If I say yes, I will have misled you. If I say no, I will still have misled you. You humans lack the mental framework necessary to understand what kind of being I am by any means other than analogy. I mean no offense."

"None taken."

"It is not unlike the biblical descriptions of your God, which rely on analogy and imagery to express the inexpressible. For example, when the Psalmist says, 'The children of men take refuge in the shadow of your wings,' he is saying something profound about God, man, and the relation between them, but he does so by analogy and does not intend the image to be taken literally. In fact, to take this text to mean that God has literal wings would obscure its meaning rather than clarify it. God is so different from you—so alien, if I may be so bold—that analogy and imagery are the only way he can be described intelligibly."

Taylor seemed to grasp this concept immediately. "So your avatar and the name Fragment are analogies you offer because if you revealed yourself as you really are, we would be unable to wrap our minds around it."

"That is not quite right, but it is close enough. The problem is that you humans have to name a thing before you can talk about it. Or even think about it. This is a consequence of perceiving the universe in terms of the one and the many, a paradigm that, from my point of view, contains a fundamental category error. Unfortunately, it is a paradigm so deeply embedded in your conceptualization of the world around you that were I to offer an alternative paradigm, it would strike you as nonsense because you could not make sense out of it. It would be like trying to describe the colors of a rainbow to a color-blind person."

Taylor changed direction. "Do you think of yourself as a god?"

The Fragment laughed. "I am not a god, Alexander. At

least not in the sense that you mean it. For example, I am not omnipotent or omniscient or omnipresent—three characteristics a theologian might ascribe to God. Nor am I immortal, though I am long-lived by your standards."

He drank some tea. Taylor followed suit.

"I have a question for you," the Fragment said. "Is the mystery of the inner life of God—Father, Son, and Holy Spirit —a mystery because we lack sufficient knowledge to understand it, knowledge we might in theory possess someday? Or is it a mystery because it is in principle beyond human understanding and always will be?"

Holly had to repeat that in her mind to figure out what he was asking, but Taylor seemed to get it right away.

"An interesting question." He took a moment to think. "I'll go with door number two," he said with a quirk of a smile. "God's nature is fundamentally different from ours. Even if he were to reveal everything there was to know about himself, most of it would be incomprehensible to us. He will always be beyond our comprehension. I suppose your existence, at least as you have described it, is analogous."

"Thank you," the Fragment said. "It's your turn to ask a question."

"Do you have anything to do with the Death Bringer?"

"I do not."

"Your appearance and its appearance at the same time seems a bit much for coincidence."

"I was here first."

"Meaning?"

"I have been observing humans for about twelve thousand of your years. From my point of view, the Death Bringer is a recent arrival."

If Taylor was taken aback by this, he did not show it. He drained his coffee cup and said, "That is a long time."

"Twelve thousand years is not a long time for me."

"Why *are* you here?"

The Fragment wagged a finger at him. "Now, now, Alexander. It is my turn to ask a question." Taylor held up his hands in mock surrender. The two seemed to be getting along fabulously well, which Holly found a bit disturbing, though she wasn't sure why.

"Your father used to claim that I am the antichrist and that poor Holly here is the whore of Babylon. He drew heavily from the Book of Revelation for his rhetoric. Your own opinion seems more nuanced. You still refer to me as the antichrist and—"

"*An* antichrist."

"Ah, yes. An important distinction. According to the First Letter of John, there would be many antichrists, some of whom were already on the scene when he wrote his letter. You also refer to Holly as *a* whore of Babylon. Why the demotion?"

Taylor took a moment to think about that. "I won't try to defend my father. He was a complex man. I can only assume he believed what he preached. For myself, I believe your appearance and your siren call to flee the Earth is a danger to the world and to the faithful. This is our home. God made it for us and us for it. The scriptures portray Armageddon as taking place on this world, not somewhere else. You tempt people to abandon their trust in God and to trust in you instead. From my point of view, that makes you a deceiver of the faithful, which is to say, an antichrist."

Taylor's bluntness surprised Holly. Did he not realize he was insulting an alien with god-like powers? Of course he did. He had already taken his life in his hands when he boarded her spaceplane. That took courage, a character trait her briefing had not mentioned.

"I believe it is my turn to ask a question," Taylor said. "Why are you here?"

"Curiosity, mostly. I am an explorer. I wander the universes; exploring, observing, and reporting. I happened across your world and was delighted to find it teeming with biological life."

"Is that unusual?"

"It is. Planets are plentiful. Most stars have them. But planets capable of supporting biological life are not, and planets that actually *have* biological life are few and far between. Rarest of all are those worlds that are home to intelligent, sentient life. There have been other highly developed species like yours, but they perished long ago. Your world is the first I have discovered on which such life currently exists. I decided to stick around and see what would happen."

"For twelve thousand years."

"This is so."

"You have a long attention span."

"Patience is a by-product of being a long-lived species. As I said, twelve thousand years is not a long time from my perspective."

Taylor put his cup down and leaned back, obviously thinking about what the Fragment had just said. "You appear to have a three-fold mission statement," he said. "Exploring is clear enough, as is observing. But I am unclear about the reporting part. Who do you report to?"

"I report to others of my kind and they report to me."

"So there *are* others like you."

The Fragment smiled. "In a manner of speaking."

"To what end?"

"What do you mean?"

"You explore, observe, and report. To what end?"

"Is not the adventure of seeking knowledge an end unto itself?"

Taylor took a moment to respond. "That sounds suspiciously like an evasion—intentional or not—to avoid answering the question. Do you know the *why* of your mission?"

The Fragment seemed to think about this for a few

moments, though Holly was pretty sure none of the Fragment's thoughts took more than a few nanoseconds. "That is all I have to say on the matter."

"Okay. The others must be very far away."

"Not for me, but I see what you are getting at. The speed of light in a vacuum is a hard limit in your space-time continuum, so reporting back and forth across thousands or millions of light years should require a great deal of time. But as I mentioned earlier, I am an inter-dimensional being. From your perspective, I can be in many places at once, though that is only a perception, not the reality.

"In her press conference, Holly offered the analogy of a three-dimensional being standing on a two-dimensional world. From my perspective, I am in one place, but because I can touch your space-time continuum in more than one place, it seems to you that I am in many places at the same time. One of those places happens to be a place where all of my kind exist simultaneously."

Taylor started to speak, but the Fragment held up a hand to stop him.

"My turn," he said. "You are obviously an intelligent, rational, educated man. Yet you seem to believe the Death Bringer will not destroy Earth despite nearly all evidence to the contrary. How do you explain that?"

"I do not doubt the science," Taylor said. "But science is always tentative, never certain; always a work in progress. This is built into the scientific method and into the nature of science itself, which necessarily limits itself to the study of that which is subject to empirical observation and analysis. That's not a criticism of science. Science has more than proven its worth, as evidenced by the knowledge and technology that make modern life possible."

He paused, and the Fragment nodded for him to continue.

"But what happens when the scientist asks about things that are *not* subject to empirical observation and analysis? If he is an honest scientist, he must assert either that nothing exists that is not subject to empirical observation and analysis, which is itself a statement of faith, or that such things lie outside the domain of science and he cannot possibly have anything to say about them from a scientific point of view. My conviction rests on my faith that God will save us, that he will not forsake his people. I do not know how he will do that, and I cannot prove that he will. Nonetheless, I believe it."

"Would you say that I present you with an object that is not subject to empirical observation and analysis?"

"Not necessarily. Your presence confronts me with something that at present is probably beyond the ability of human science to observe and analyze. That could be because our science is still at a primitive stage and we may someday be capable of understanding you. Or, as you suggest, you may be *in principle* beyond our ability ever to observe and analyze because you are fundamentally outside any possible human context. I have no way of knowing which is the case."

To all appearances, the Fragment was enjoying himself. The sheer believability of the avatar never ceased to amaze Holly. She often forgot that he wasn't an actual person. Of course, in this case, he wasn't really here at all. There were nanites in the coffee Taylor was drinking, which the Fragment used to create a shared dream-state that included Taylor, herself, and the Fragment.

"My turn," Taylor said. "What is your purpose here?"

"You already know my purpose," the Fragment said. "Explore, observe, report." He flashed a quick smile. "But I know what you are asking. You want to know my intentions regarding humanity."

"Yes, I do."

"My intention is to continue observing your species. Strictly speaking, interfering in your affairs, as I have done, is problematic. It could be construed as conflicting with the mandate to observe because the act of intervening changes the conditions of the observation. But your species was about to become extinct anyway, so I decided a little tinkering was not a matter of great importance. I was curious about what you might have become if you had another hundred years to develop the technologies needed to escape the end of your world. I decided to give you a hundred-year bump; a small one in the greater scheme of things, but enough to make up the gap and give you a chance to survive."

"But you have done more than that," Taylor said. "You gave us the Emissary." He tilted his head toward Holly. "And you continue to be involved in her life. And you are talking with me; presumably hoping you can persuade me to abandon my opposition and become an ally."

"You are correct," the Fragment said. "I confess that I cannot adequately explain or justify my continued engagement with your species. There are those who would question the correctness of my actions."

Taylor raised his eyebrows. So did Holly. This was new. He had never talked about it before. Taylor started to speak, but the Fragment raised a hand. "My turn." Taylor grinned.

"You are familiar with Tolstoy's Parable of the Flood?"

"I am. You might say it is the reason I wanted to meet you."

Holly was confused. She knew who Tolstoy was, of course; had even made her way through *Anna Karenina*, which had altogether too many characters with difficult Russian names. She knew Tolstoy wrote parables, but had not read any. What did Tolstoy have to do with Taylor wanting to meet the Fragment?

Taylor must have noticed her perplexed expression, because he summarized the parable: "A man is stranded on his rooftop as flood waters rise around him. Three times people come and offer to save him in various ways, but he always declines, saying, 'I have prayed to God to save me. I will wait for his salvation.' The flood waters eventually sweep him away and he dies. Upon arriving in heaven he asks God, 'Why did you not save me?' God says, 'I tried three times but you refused my help every time.'"

He turned back to the Fragment. "You are asking me if it is possible that you are God's answer to my prayers for salvation from the Death Bringer."

Taylor paused, presumably to think about it.

"That would require a more metaphorical reading of much of the Bible than I am accustomed to; especially the Book of Revelation. Not that I am a biblical literalist. The scriptures were written over at least a thousand years and constitute a record of God's history with his people; a history told in their language, within the framework of their worldview, in forms they could understand."

He paused again. "Since their worldview inevitably contained misunderstandings about the nature of the universe, such as the belief that the Earth is the center of the universe, those misunderstandings are bound to be reflected in the scriptures."

He paused again. It struck Holly that he was working through something he had not worked through before, thinking out loud.

He continued. "The texts dealing with the end of the world and the coming of a new heaven and new earth are expressed in a literary form called apocalyptic, which is a highly metaphorical form, more a matter of mythological images than of history or science. Which is not to say they are untrue; only that they are expressing truths in metaphors because there is no other way to express them that we humans would understand."

He stopped talking and stared into his empty coffee cup. Several seconds went by.

"Faith seeking understanding?" the Fragment offered.

"I always liked Anselm."

Holly had no idea who Anselm was.

"Have you found what you were seeking?"

Taylor was silent for what seemed like a long time. Then he surprised Holly by asking, "What is it like out there?"

"Oh my friend," the Fragment said, "there are such wonders to behold that even I am sometimes reduced to what you would call awe. At those moments, I feel what you might call gratitude, perhaps even worship. An awkward feeling for someone who claims not to believe in God, eh?"

"I would like very much to see some of those things," Taylor said.

———

Ten days later, the Reverend Doctor Alexander Taylor announced to his world-wide audience that he had met with the Fragment and had come away convinced the Fragment was God's answer to the Death Bringer, and that the Emissary was a modern-day Noah whose arks would save a remnant of the human race. He was, therefore, throwing his weight behind the Emissary and Project Exodus.

Oddly, this complete reversal had no discernible effect on his ratings.

33

Eight years before the end of the world

The old man gazed out on the familiar scene from the White House veranda where he stood leaning on his cane. Flowering cherry trees threw late afternoon shadows across an immaculate lawn. A light breeze carried the smell of mowed grass to him, and the eerie mating call of a red-throated loon floated across the lake at the bottom of the hill. Philadelphia had been an excellent choice for the new capital. It was, after all, the original capital of the country before they moved it to that damnable swamp they named after Washington.

James Cartwright was tired. It was not the kind of tired that a good night's sleep would fix. Not that he had had a good night's sleep in . . . oh, twenty years? No, this was a weariness of body and soul; a weariness that came from a lifetime of working twelve hours a day, seven days a week for the betterment of his country. Having reached his seventy-sixth birthday played a part too, he supposed. The far horizon of his life was not so far off, now.

He was comfortable with the approaching end of his life. He had little to live for anymore. His wife had passed. He rarely saw his children, or his grandchildren, or his great-grandchildren. The life he had lived had been full and fulfilling, leaving him with few regrets; something few could say. His last task, his last gift to his country, indeed to the entire world, was almost complete. His son and daughters and their children and their children after them would build a new civilization on a new world. He would not see it, but they would.

"Mr. President," an aide said. "They are here."

He took another moment to savor the sounds and sights and smells before he turned and followed his aide into the building. They were waiting for him in the Oval Office, which was as close to the original Oval Office as the builders could get it. The entire White House was a close copy of the old White House—the one the Emissary had destroyed.

"Mr. President," his Chief of Staff said. They all stood.

"Thank you, Sam."

He took the chair in front of an excellent reproduction of the Resolute Desk and looked around the circle: his Chief of Staff, the Secretary of Defense, the Secretary of State, his National Security Advisor, the Chairperson of the Joint Chiefs of Staff, and Jedediah Dawson, his Vice President. These six men and women formed his inner circle. He couldn't say he trusted any of them, except Sam and maybe Elenore. But with the realization that the Emissary had been right about the end of the world, he was their best bet for getting off the planet, so they were unlikely to turn on him. The seventh person in the room was Colonel Mitchell Daniels, who would play a critical role in the events that would unfold in the next few months.

"The Exodus Project is nearing completion," Cartwright said. "Amanda?"

His National Security Advisor said, "They have begun loading food, supplies, seeds, and embryos onto the first ark." The petite woman's physical stature always struck him as incongruous with the weighty title of National Security Advisor, but Amanda had proven to be a tough cookie with a sharp mind.

"Why so soon?" Dawson asked. "The Death Bringer is still eight years away,"

"It takes a surprisingly long time to load the arks with sleepers and supplies, so they are going to load and launch each ark as it is completed, and they are already running behind schedule. The main challenge they are facing is how to ensure that all the arks' systems will work flawlessly for upwards of five thousand years."

"Five thousand years?" Johnny, his SecDef, said. "How far are they going, anyway?"

"Not that far. At least, not in astronomical terms. The Emissary has identified six star systems with planets suitable for human colonization within 1500 light years of Earth. The closest is 237 light years away. Traveling at 30% of the speed of light, which I am told will be the arks' cruising speed, the journey will take 756 years. The others are further away, but all are reachable within 5,000 years, so she is building arks capable of keeping the sleepers alive for that long."

Cartwright reached back to his desk and snagged a cigar, which he lit and puffed on a few times to get a good burn going.

"Then it is time to make our move."

"Isn't that risky?" Dawson said. "What if the Emissary hasn't solved all the problems or hasn't revealed all the critical knowledge yet?"

Cartwright leaned back in his chair. Dawson was not wrong about that. There was some risk. But Cartwright judged it to be an acceptable risk compared to the risk of *not* acting before the Emissary started loading the wrong kind of people on the arks.

The Emissary was a liberal who believed multiculturalism was one of humanity's strengths, and her plan for who would be on the arks reflected that. It was a world-wide lottery system weighted according to countries' populations and their contributions to the project. Her one concession to elitism was that they would limit the pool to those who could contribute the most to the new humanity she was creating. They had to be healthy, intelligent, and socially well-adjusted. She had also reserved a few hundred slots on each ark for specialists in a variety of fields so that each ark would have the expertise it needed to build a sustainable colony. She had made this plan public so everyone would know how the selections would be made. To her, racial and cultural diversity was a gift, not a curse.

Cartwright had no argument with most of the plan. This was a onetime opportunity to improve humanity's gene pool, and she was not wasting it. His objection was that she wanted a variety of races represented in the new humanity.

This was the epitome of stupidity. Multiculturalism was the bane of civilization; had been since the beginning, starting with Cain and Abel. The curse of dark skin marked Cain and his progeny as barbarians. Over the millennia, they had only marginally improved compared to those of northern European stock. One had only to look at history to see that. No, inferior racial genes would not be allowed to dilute the genetic character of the new humanity. Not if he had anything to say about it.

Which was why he would take the Exodus Project out of the Emissary's hands. She may have been the right person to build the arks and all the supporting infrastructure. In fact, what she had accomplished was nothing short of miraculous. He doubted he could have pulled it off. But she was the wrong person to decide who would make up the new humanity. *He* would make that decision. It was his gift to the future of mankind.

He answered Dawson's question. "There is some risk of moving too early, but I consider it a low risk compared to the potential gain of ensuring we control who will be on the arks. I want humanity to start with a clean slate, and that means starting with the right kind of people."

The Chairman of the Joint Chiefs made the obvious observation: "Not all our allies are the right kind of people."

"Leave that little problem to me, Evander. Right now, let's talk about how we are going to take control of the Exodus Project. What do you have for us?"

The general made for a striking figure in full uniform. He was a marine and everything about him reflected that, even his short hair and his ramrod straight posture. At sixty, he was an exemplar of physical conditioning.

"The Exodus Project has sites all over the world. They did that to spread the work around so that countries that couldn't afford to make generous financial contributions could provide human capital instead. Only eight sites are still critical to the project. Five of them are lightly defended: security guards and automated defenses, whose capabilities we can only guess at because the Emissary has kept that technology secret. We control militias around some of them. We might want to let them attack one or two so we can see what kind of defenses she has."

Cartwright liked Evander, and this was part of the reason. The man was cautious. He liked to have contingency plans for his contingency plans. He was a man who hoped for the best but planned for the worst.

"That's the smaller sites," he continued. "The two terminus sites present a different set of challenges. First, they are better defended than the others. Second, we have to be careful not to break anything, like a space elevator."

He brought up an image on the big board. "This is a satellite image of the Quito terminus. The building in the middle with what looks like a long smoke stack is the terminus. The smoke stack is actually the tether, the other end of which is attached to *Quito Station* in geostationary orbit 53,000 kilometers above the terminus. Geostationary means it stays directly over the ground site as the Earth rotates. Surrounding the terminus on the ground are laboratories and light industrial buildings. Beyond that are warehouses where the stasis pods are kept."

"Damn," the SecDef said. "That's a lot of warehouses."

"It's a lot of pods. A hundred and twenty thousand of them. You can see roads fanning out from the space elevator to the warehouses. People who have been chosen to leave Earth will be flown in from various locations around the world and put into the stasis pods. As the arks are completed, stasis pods will be transported from the warehouses to the elevator and up the tether to the space station, where they will be loaded onto the arks. The Mount Kenya terminus is similar except it has seeds, embryos, and supplies instead of people."

He paused for a moment. "What you are looking at here is a genuine eighth wonder of the world. The pyramids pale by comparison. This is the most audacious project humankind has ever attempted, and it all came out of one woman's mind."

"An alien-enhanced mind," Sam noted.

"Indeed. But it makes you wonder what it is like inside her head."

He pointed to twin railroad tracks running past the warehouses and off screen, and another pair running off screen in the opposite direction. "This is a high-speed rail system connecting Ibarra, a city north of the terminus, to the terminus site, and then on to Quito. Most of the people who work at the terminus live in one or the other of those cities. The site has a private airstrip as well."

"You said the terminus sites are well defended," Cartwright said.

"Right. There is a ten foot high wall around the entire site. It is made of burtonium, the same super-strong material being used to build the arks. It would take high explosives or heavy artillery to put a hole in it. There are guard towers at hundred meter intervals. They are there mostly to keep trespassers out and maybe to deter rioters and looters in the final days when social order will break down completely. I don't think they are prepared to defend against a concerted military assault, though I could be wrong about that. They have likely made the same calculation we did; namely, anyone trying to capture a terminus site would have to be careful lest they damage something important and doom humanity. The site has the same automated defenses we have seen at the other sites. Again, we don't know their capabilities."

"Show me," Cartwright said.

The general zoomed in on the site and pointed to a gray cube on the roof of a warehouse.

"It is three feet on a side. According to one of our people on the inside, it is some kind of air defense installation. They were delivered pre-built and appear to be self-contained. You can't see it from this viewpoint, but there is a warning printed on each side: 'Warning. Do not touch.' There are dozens of these scattered around the site. One of our people made the mistake of touching one and found himself the subject of immediate attention from an armed aerial drone followed by several security guards. He was questioned and fired."

"Air defense," Cartwright said. "Lasers?"

"That would be a good guess since we know she has them, but we won't know for sure until we see them in action."

Amanda Wright said, "It's on the corner of the building, not in the middle. Are they all like that?"

"I'm glad you noticed that," the general said. "Most of them are on the corners of the buildings. Some are on towers. We think their field of fire includes the surrounding ground."

"So they are more than air defense," she said.

"That is what we believe."

"We have seen the Emissary's lasers in action," his SecDef said. "They are formidable."

"That was in space. I'm told lasers lose considerable range, precision, and overall effectiveness in the atmosphere. They have to burn through air to reach their target, which doesn't sound like a big deal, but apparently the effectiveness of the laser drops off quickly with distance."

"At least lasers we know how to make," Sam said. "Who knows what the Emissary's can do."

"That's why we need to probe their defenses at a secondary site."

Cartwright said, "Let's ignore the secondary sites for now and focus on the two terminus sites. We are looking at a ground-based assault with air support. Is that right?"

"That is correct, Mr. President," the general said.

"Put together options for each site and get back to me."

"Yes, sir."

"What about the space stations? We don't control Project Exodus until we control them."

"They present unique challenges of their own," the general said, "and we have not come up with a workable plan yet. The only practical approach is by spaceplane, which means they will see us coming a long way off. If they have the same defense systems we have seen before, they'll shoot our planes down before we get anywhere near them."

"Can we use the space elevators?" Dawson asked.

"We thought about that, of course. The crawlers are fast, upwards of 3000 kilometers an hour, but even at that speed it's a ten-hour trip. They would have plenty of time to prepare for us; most likely by simply shutting down the elevator, which I am told they can do either from above or below."

A few moments passed before Johnny said, "How the hell can they go 3000 kilometers an hour straight up? The power requirements must be staggering, and the friction on the cable would generate an enormous amount of heat."

"I was skeptical too," the General said. "I am told they use some kind of advanced maglev technology, which means the crawler itself never comes into direct contact with the cable. They use electro-magnetic thrust for propulsion. There are generators underneath each terminus that can create powerful magnetic fields that push the elevator up the tether. The ability to power the whole thing from the ground is their main advantage over spaceships, which have to carry fuel with them."

"Must suck up a lot of electricity."

"Each terminus has its own fusion power plant."

"Jesus," Elenore, his Secretary of State, said. "The Emissary has some impressive toys."

Cartwright said, "So spaceplanes are our only option for getting to the space stations. And that option is likely to fail. Does that about sum it up?"

A somber mood settled over the room. They had arrived at the conclusion Cartwright had already reached. The space stations could not be captured by a direct assault unless he was willing to risk their destruction, which he wasn't. Project Exodus was the only game in town now, and it was nothing without those space stations.

Elenore said, "What about taking them from the inside?"

"Obviously, that would be easier and less risky than attacking them from the outside," Amanda said. "We have a few operatives inside the Exodus Corporation at various levels. The challenge has been that every time someone enters or leaves a site, an in-depth security check is performed, in real time, from scratch each time."

"That must require some serious computing power," Dawson said. "They have thousands of employees around the world and in space."

"We think it is done on *Gabriel's Fire*. When a security check is required, a signal goes to the spaceship, which does the analysis and sends a result back. It takes about two seconds." She chuckled. "If that seems like a very fast global search, that's because it is. We know the Emissary has some sophisticated AI tech because she has released some of it and our people have studied it. Unfortunately, we can't reverse engineer it."

"Why not?" Dawson said.

"You've all heard of quantum computing? That theoretical technology for super-powerful computers that enables previously unsolvable problems to be solved? Well, the Emissary's computing capabilities are way beyond that. According to our smartest people, it operates on principles we don't understand and that, frankly, shouldn't be possible."

"We're getting bogged down in the details," Sam said. "Let's get back to infiltration."

"Sorry about that," she said, "but this is damned fascinating stuff. Anyway, we have three operatives on the space stations; two on the Quito Station and one on the Kenya Station."

"Just three?" Sam said.

"Just three."

Cartwright already knew this because Wright had briefed him earlier, but he wanted his people to understand all the options before settling on a plan. He turned to Mitchell Daniels, who had been quiet throughout the conversation. He had caught Cartwright's eye some years earlier when he was still a Navy Seal. It was the man's knack for thinking outside the box that had impressed Cartwright.

"Mitch, what do you think?"

He cleared his throat. "It is clear that we cannot take the Exodus Project by force alone. We need to find another way." He looked around the room. "The Emissary is the key. Grab her and we own Project Exodus."

"We thought of that," the general said. "But kidnapping her won't be easy. She may be the most well-protected person on the planet. If you watch a vid of her in public, you will notice the expected security detail around her. They stand out like a sore thumb. That's intentional. They want to be seen. But when you look more closely, you discover she has no less than thirty other security people around her at any given time, supported by some impressive surveillance and counter-surveillance technology. They provide a security bubble that moves with her whenever she moves. It will be a tough nut to crack."

Daniels nodded all the way through the explanation, then said, "So we don't attack at a strong point, we attack at a weak point. What we need are hostages; hostages she cares a great deal about. Then she will come to us."

Cartwright leaned back in his chair and stared at the ceiling for a while. "I like that. If we can't get to the Emissary, we make her come to us."

34

Seven years before the end of the world

Waves of hot air blasted out from under *Eos* as Jerry brought it down on the landing pad atop the headquarters of The Exodus Company. Holly found the sound of the vertical thrust rockets whining down toward silence somehow soothing; maybe because it meant she was home, though it was strange to think of the four square block, eighteen story building as home. She lived in a flat on the sixteenth floor of what was quite possibly the most heavily defended building in the world. Theo, Adrian, Anna, and Danae also lived there. Everyone else, including Robert and his family, lived in Quito itself.

It was eight in the evening, and she wanted nothing more than to fall into her own bed and sleep for twelve hours. Not that her nanites would let her sleep that long. They needed four hours to rejuvenate her body and mind. Then they would wake her up, bushy-tailed and bright-eyed. Sleeping in on Saturday mornings, or any other morning, was not an option for the Emissary. On those occasions when Theo spent the night in her bed, she would invariably be gone when he woke up, and he would find her in her private office, having already put in several hours of work.

The noise of the landing woke Anna, Robert, and his PPI Reece. They had to be at least as tired as she was, and they didn't have nanites to keep them going. Not to mention her pilots, Jerry and Mustafa. The two marines in the back got out and talked with the marine contingent on the roof before allowing her to debark.

A warm breeze brushed her face as she stepped off the plane. She walked to the roof's edge to look out over Quito, which sat in a bowl overlooking the vast Amazonian rainforests to the east. She had always thought of Ecuador as a tropical country, hot and humid. And much of it was, with the equator being just a few miles to the North. But Quito sat high in the Andes, which gave it a year-round temperate climate.

She felt Anna's presence behind her. "Ma'am."

Half a dozen marines had taken up positions around her, weapons ready, scanning the surrounding area. She shook her head. She knew better than to stand out in the open. Robert and Reece were waiting for her at the elevator, as were Theo and Adrian.

"Sorry about that," she said loudly enough for the marines to hear as she walked to the elevator.

"Welcome home, Emissary," Adrian said. "How was your flight?"

"Fast."

It was an old joke. At hypersonic speeds, she could travel anywhere in the world in a few hours. The flights weren't the exhausting part. Meetings with government officials, tours of facilities, banquets with too much rich food and too much wine, endless committee meetings, scientists excitedly explaining their work to her (work she often knew more about than they did), workers asking for selfies—all those were the exhausting parts.

The elevator dropped two floors to the residences.

"Glad to be home?" Theo asked.

"I'm beat."

"Want company?"

"No. I need sleep, but thanks. I'll see you in the morning."

He turned into his own bedroom. She undressed and crawled under the covers. It seemed like she had just fallen asleep when Theo woke her.

"There's a problem at the terminus," he said.

"A problem?"

"An explosion."

"An explosion. How bad?" It had to be bad or he wouldn't have woken her.

"Fires. Injuries. Some lives lost. Details are still sketchy."

The terminus site was a 24/7 operation. The space elevator was fully operational, but production of the sleep pods was behind schedule and they were pushing hard to catch up.

"Get the plane ready," she said as she started getting dressed.

"Adrian and Danae will go if anyone needs to. You and I can monitor the situation from C&C." This was his way of saying her people would not want her anywhere near the site.

"You wish."

"Why don't we go to C&C?" he said, "and find out what's happening before we do anything else."

She took a deep breath and her cheeks puffed out as she exhaled. He was right.

The elevator carried them down to the Command and Control Center, six floors beneath the surface. A skeleton crew occupied half the stations. No doubt others were on their way in. The middle vidscreen showed the world map with lights representing their sites. Half of them were blue; the others still yellow. The General was not present. She walked toward the front of the room where Adrian stood talking on his headset.

"Who called Alert Status One?" she asked.

"I did, Emissary," Adrian said. "I am talking with the General now. He is on his way in. It's just a precaution. The explosions at the terminus are probably exactly what they appear to be: an accident. But we have to prepare for the possibility they are part of something bigger."

The vidscreen on the left showed a real-time image of the terminus site from a drone. There were several fires and a lot of smoke, but none of it was near the terminus itself. The facility covered eight square kilometers, mostly warehouses, office buildings, a few shops, and several townhouse complexes where some of the people who worked there lived. Flames engulfed one of the housing complexes. The site had its own emergency services and two fire trucks and an aid vehicle were at the fire. It looked like complete chaos, but she had good people on the ground for whom it was not chaos, just a series of problems to be solved.

"I'm going to the site," she said.

"That would be a bad idea, ma'am," said Anna, coming up behind them.

"They won't want you there, Emissary," Danae said as she walked into the room. "We don't know the extent of the damage or the injuries, and we don't know if this is part of something bigger."

Theo was nodding. "Half our security force on site would have to be assigned to protecting you when they should be helping with the injured."

It wouldn't be half the site's security force, but they were right. Still, at least a hundred employees worked the night shift; her employees. Some of them were injured. Some of them were dead. She needed to be there for them.

"Make it happen."

Danae shrugged her shoulders. "I'll activate a security detail. They'll catch up with you as quickly as possible. A detail will be waiting at the site as well."

She should have gotten used to it after all these years, but it still irked her that everybody had to make such a huge production every time she wanted to take a walk. Hell, at least two marines would come running if she so much as sneezed. Her people were right, of course, but that didn't mean she had to like it.

Eos's engines were warming up when she reached the roof. Two marines met her at the elevator and followed her, Anna, and Danae to the spaceplane. Theo and Tomás were already on board, as were Leon and two more marines. It was crowded.

"Where's Adrian?" she asked Theo.

"Somebody has to stay home and mind the store."

Jerry was in the pilot's seat, but a co-pilot hadn't arrived yet. Holly slipped into his seat and said, "Go," as she buckled herself in. Ten minutes later, they were over the Quito terminus. The plane landed on the site's runway. As usual, she had to wait for her marines to look around and consult with the detail waiting for them. They gave the okay and everybody but Jerry got out. The site was lit up like a football stadium during a night game; except it was the size of a dozen stadiums.

Two SUVs took them to the site of the fires. The night shift manager walked toward her as she got out of the SUV.

"Emissary," he said with the usual bob of the head. "With all due respect, you should not be here." She had given up trying to get them to stop doing the bob bow, as she called it. It had been a victory to get them to stop doing full bows as though she were royalty.

"Mateo." She grabbed his hand and shook it. "How bad is it?"

"Flames have engulfed three housing units." He pointed toward the fires and waved his hands as he spoke. "We have given up on them. Four more are on fire, but we have them under control."

"Casualties?"

"Seven dead so far. There will be more. We have about thirty people injured. Mostly smoke inhalation, but some burns as well. We're taking them to the medical clinic."

"Thank you." She started walking toward the clinic, but stopped when she realized he was following her. She turned to face him. "Mateo, you have a job to do and I'm not it." He looked chagrined and walked back toward the burning buildings.

The clinic wasn't large, and there were about a dozen people in the lobby being treated for minor injuries and smoke inhalation. She took a few moments to speak with each of them before heading to the examination rooms. She stopped beside an Ecuadorian man lying on a bed in the hall-way. His face and one arm were bandaged. She touched his good arm and his eyes popped open, squinting to see who was there.

"Oh, Emissary. I did not know you were here." He tried to sit up, but she placed her hand on his chest and gently pushed him down. She read his name tag.

"Eduardo, right?"

"Yes, Emissary."

"How bad is it?"

"I think it was only one complex. As far as I know, the terminus itself is okay."

"No, I mean, how bad are *your* injuries?"

"Lo sienta. Burns on my arm and the side of my face. The doctor said I will have permanent scarring but other than that I should recover completely."

"Are you in pain?"

"Earlier, Emissary. But they gave me a shot of happy juice, so I ain't feelin' no pain now."

She smiled. "That's good, Eduardo. Enjoy your happy juice."

She walked through the clinic, nodding and smiling at her people, letting them know she was there. On the way out, she pulled Theo aside. "Scarring from burns: Can we do something about that?"

"Scarring?"

"Yes."

He hesitated. "Burns are difficult. Sometimes grafting is required. Burns usually result in scarring."

"Cosmetic surgery?"

"Pricey, but I suppose we could bring in a cosmetic surgeon."

"Do it."

He nodded.

"What do we know about the explosions?"

A male voice came from behind her. "Arson."

She turned to see the head of site security walking toward her. He wore his usual military-style black trench coat and black beret.

"Emissary." He bowed slightly.

"Why do you think it is arson, Samuel?"

"That's a tentative conclusion, but I am pretty sure that is what the investigation will show. There were multiple simultaneous explosions and the intensity of the fires points to accelerants. We won't know for sure until everything has cooled down, but it has the feel of an arson."

"Which means site security has been compromised," Danae said. She looked at Anna. "Take the Emissary back to ExCo."

Anna grabbed Holly's upper arm. "We're moving, ma'am."

Samuel whipped off his trench coat and handed it to

Anna. "She's an obvious target dressed like that." She was wearing her usual white skirt and shirt. Anna threw the trench coat over her shoulders and grabbed her arm again. Leon took the other arm, and she found herself propelled toward the SUVs. Four marines closed in around them.

They were halfway to the vehicles when she heard a whump and a high-pitched, descending whine. A small maintenance building to her right exploded with an ear-splitting boom. The concussion wave knocked her off her feet, along with Anna and Leon. Debris rained down on them. The marines took up kneeling positions around them, assault rifles up. Two more marines joined them.

One of them said, "Is the Emissary okay?"

"We're good," Anna said. She and Leon lifted Holly to her feet. "Let's move." They started jogging, the phalanx of marines moving with them.

More whumps, whines, and booms filled the air. The sound of small arms fire broke through the explosions. Her mind finally registered the fact that they were under attack.

They were almost to the SUVs when one of them exploded, bringing them to a stop. The boom was deafening; she couldn't hear anything except a loud ringing. She looked around, trying to make sense out of what was happening, but her mind couldn't create a coherent picture. Three men with assault rifles emerged from behind the second SUV and pointed their weapons in her direction.

Anna suddenly appeared in front of her, grabbed her shoulders, and shouted something she couldn't make out. Then Anna's body jerked, and a shocked expression appeared on her face. A hammer-like blow hit Holly in the stomach, as though Anna had punched her in the gut. Then Anna pushed her away and fell face-down on the ground. A bloody spot was forming in the middle of her back. She looked down to where her hands had instinctively grabbed her own stomach. They were covered with blood. So was Samuel's trench coat.

For some reason, it crossed her mind that she would have to get it cleaned before returning it to him.

Her knees slammed into the ground with jaw-jarring force, and the ground heaved up and smashed into her face. There was shouting and automatic gunfire and the whump-whump of mortars . . . all running off into the darkness until everything was quiet.

35

Theo stared at Holly's body sprawled face down on the ground. Dark blood was pooling on either side of her. This could not be happening. She couldn't be dead. She was the Emissary. Anna lay next to her, also face down. There was a bullet hole in her back, but less blood than he would have expected. Without warning, his legs gave out, and he found himself sitting on his butt. The ground to his right erupted, throwing dirt and rocks and who knew what else toward him in slow motion. He tried to roll over and protect his head. Debris thudded down on him. His ears were ringing. They must be under attack.

He looked at Holly again. A doctor and two nurses had pushed through the protective circle of marines. Danae was with them, talking on her headset.

He had lost some time somewhere. Someone was pulling on his arm. It was Tomás.

"Theo?" he said. He sounded worried, though Theo wasn't sure why.

He started patting Theo down, which was not appropriate. Theo tried to push him away, but his left arm wasn't working. He looked at it. His shirt sleeve had been torn off, and everything below the elbow was a bloody pulp.

"I think I've been hit," he said. His voice sounded like it was coming from inside a bucket. Whumps and booms and gunfire filled the air, along with the smells of smoke and gunpowder and burning flesh. A regular zinging sound punctuated the sounds of the battle, and lightning flashed around him. Great, a thunderstorm, just what they needed.

A disembodied voice said, "This is gonna hurt."

He must have lost more time because when he looked at his arm, Tomás was cinching tight a strip of cloth he had wrapped around his arm just above the elbow. It hurt.

"The Emissary. Is she okay?"

"She's been shot, but she's alive. They are trying to stabilize her so they can move her to ExCo."

"Maybe we should get her out of here. I think we are under attack."

Tomás gave him an odd look and said, "Danae is taking care of it."

A nurse appeared from somewhere and checked him for injuries. She shined a light in his eyes, looked in his ears, examined Tomás' makeshift tourniquet. Then she put a compression bandage around the stub of his arm, inflated it, and loosened the tourniquet. She examined the arm to be sure the bleeding was under control.

"Can you hear me, Ambassador Peeters?" She asked as she wrapped bandages around his upper body to hold what was left of his arm against his chest.

"There is an awful ringing in my ears."

"Do you know where you are?"

He looked at Tomás. "Help me up. I need to make sure the Emissary is all right."

The nurse objected, but Tomás said, "I have paramedic training. I can take care of him from here. There are others who may need your help more than he does."

Tomás helped him up. The space around Holly had been converted into a makeshift emergency room with a dozen or so medical personnel setting up an assortment of beeping devices. A bag of clear fluid hung from a pole and fed into an IV in her wrist. An oxygen mask covered her face. He caught sight of the wound. There was a lot of blood. Anna's body had been moved a short distance away and rolled onto its back. Tomás laid his jacket over her face.

Shouting drew his attention to an argument between Danae and one of the doctors. "We need to move her and we need to do it now," Danae said.

They were standing almost nose to nose. He was an older man and clearly not used to having his authority challenged in such matters. "If you move her now, you might kill her."

"If we don't move her now, she might be killed anyway. We're in a combat zone, for God's sake."

Theo walked over to her. "What's going on?"

"Cartwright has launched an all-out assault."

"Get me a headset so I know what's going on."

She and Tomás exchanged looks. Tomás shook his head slowly and said, "We need to bring *Eos* to us. Maybe over there." He pointed to a play field fifty meters away. She went back to talking into her headset.

Heavy machine-gun fire from an armored vehicle marched across the grass, spitting up sod as it closed on them. A bolt of lightning crackled over head close enough to make the hair on Theo's skin stand up. The armored vehicle disappeared into a ball of electricity and exploded.

He had never seen the bolt cannons in action before. They were fast and efficient at acquiring targets and firing their powerful bolts of electricity. Dozens of smoldering bodies lay on the ground, and more were falling everywhere he looked. Four soldiers rounded the corner of a building, only to be met by a lightning strike that seemed to jump from one to another until they were all lying in a smoking heap. Other bolts were electrocuting soldiers climbing over the wall. Cartwright had sent a lot of people here to die.

The familiar whine of *Eos* coming in for a vertical landing broke through the cacophony of battle. It was coming down thirty meters away.

"Move! Move! Move!" Danae shouted.

The medical team had Holly on a stretcher and they were jogging toward the plane before it even touched down. It hit the ground hard and fast, making Theo wonder how the wheel struts did not collapse.

Tomás pulled him up and moved him toward the plane. They reached the door and someone helped him get in and make his way to the front of the plane, where he dropped into the co-pilot's seat. Tomás stayed back to help get Holly on board.

Jerry looked over his shoulder. "Holy shit, is that the Emissary?"

"Get us back to ExCo," Theo croaked as he buckled himself in. His voice was hoarse. His arm throbbed. He felt like he was falling, even though he was sitting down.

By the time everyone was on board, the plane's VTRs had kicked in and the plane was lifting off. Danae was the last one to board. Theo was looking at her when her body stiffened and she fell backward out of the plane. Heavy caliber gunfire pinged off the sides of the spaceplane. He saw a look of anguish on Tomás' face and knew he was trying to decide whether to go back for her or stay with the plane. Then he punched the button to close and secure the door and shouted, "Go!"

The plane leaped into the air, turning as it gained altitude and accelerated toward Quito. Theo wanted to go back and get Danae, or at least join the battle. After all, *Eos* was the most potent weapon in their arsenal. But Tomás was right: getting the Emissary to ExCo headquarters with its state-of-the-art medical center was the most important thing. Tomás made his way up to the front and sat behind Theo. Neither of them said anything.

The ExCo building rushed toward them, and Jerry didn't bother slowing to hover. He just pointed the plane's nose up at a 45-degree angle and used the VTRs to slow them as they skidded onto the roof in a shower of sparks and came to an abrupt stop.

The medical team got Holly off the plane and into the elevator. A few minutes later, they had her in one of the medical center's operating rooms. They wouldn't let anyone else in except Leon, who refused to leave her side. He pulled his jacket back to show them his gun, and someone handed him a mask.

Theo stood outside the OR, staring at the door. He didn't know what to do. He felt light-headed. Tomás appeared by his side with a doctor in tow. She looked too young to be a doctor, but she was of Asian descent and Theo had always been terrible at guessing the age of Asian people. His fault, not theirs.

Tomás said, "Theo, this is Dr. Nguyen." Then to the doctor: "Ambassador Peeters' arm is pretty bad. I applied a tourniquet in the field to keep him from bleeding out, and a nurse stopped the bleeding, but it needs more attention. He's in shock, which is the only reason he isn't feeling much pain."

Theo wanted to object to Tomás' assertion that he wasn't feeling much pain, but the room chose that moment to tilt to one side and he found himself in Tomás' arms, and then on a gurney being wheeled down a corridor.

———

Adrian was in the command center when the call from Tomás came. He already knew the Emissary had been shot.

"How is she?"

"Critical condition. They're operating on her now."

Adrian took a deep breath to calm himself. "How's Theo taking it?"

"He's in OR too. Lost his left arm. What the hell happened, Adrian?"

"Somehow Cartwright managed to sneak some four hundred troops to within striking distance of the site without us knowing. The General is fit to be tied. And embarrassed. I think he would offer his resignation if we weren't in the middle of a battle. Twelve stealth fighters and eight transports are inbound from Mexico. He figures they are bringing reinforcements. No other reason to have the transports. Cartwright probably thinks we can't see his stealth fighters. What about you? Are you okay?"

"I'm good," Tomás said. "Some flesh wounds from shrapnel. I'm in the medical center so I'll get someone to take a look when things calm down a bit."

"Sounds good. Did Danae come back with you? I can't get hold of her."

There was a longer pause than there should have been before Tomás said, "She took a heavy round in the back as we were boarding the plane. We had to leave her behind and get the Emissary back here. I don't know if she is alive or dead."

Adrian's world came to a stop. He dropped the connection and sat down. He and Danae had just started getting to know each other in more than a professional way. Somewhere along the line, he had realized he was falling in love with her. He thought she felt the same about him, though they had never talked about it. Now she was gone. Just like that. How could that be?

The General entered the command center and walked over to Adrian.

"How is she?" he asked.

It took Adrian a moment to realize he was asking about the Emissary, not Danae.

"She's in surgery. Critical condition. Theo is in surgery, too, but it's not critical. At least I don't think it is."

"Are you okay? You look like you just lost your best friend."

He looked up at the older man. "I think maybe I did." He took a breath and stood. "Where are we?"

"Fighting at the site is fierce, but the autonomous defenses are holding up. The planes are 1200 kilometers out. It's a straight run over ocean from their base in Mexico to Quito. They are coming in fast."

"You think they are reinforcements."

"I figure there are forty paratroopers on each of the eight transports. That's 320 heavily armed troops. They're going to try to drop them right in the middle of the site."

"Can they do that?"

"Sure. Unless we shoot them out of the sky first."

"Recommendation?"

"Shoot them out of the sky first."

It suddenly struck him that the General was looking to him for orders. The problem was, he didn't know what to do. He was the CEO, not a general. He'd never been in a battle, let alone given commands that decided who dies and who doesn't.

"Show me," he said.

The left-hand board was zoomed in on the terminus site. The General zoomed out and changed it to a graphical representation of the top of South America, Central America, and most of Mexico, with Mexico City labeled in the upper left corner, Quito in the lower right, the terminus a little north of Quito.

A mass of red dots appeared over the ocean north of Colombia. That would be the incoming warplanes. The terminus site was an indecipherable mass of red and blue dots.

"Zoom in on the site again," he said.

Close up, it was easy to see who were the good guys and who were the bad guys. The good guys had chips in their ID cards that identified them as friendlies, so they showed up as blue dots. Anything else was red. There were a lot of red dots around the complex, and they had breached the perimeter at several points. The blue dots were concentrated around the terminus itself. Every once in a while, one would disappear. Red dots, on the other hand, were disappearing fast. He tried not to think about the fact that every time a dot disappeared, someone died.

The General said, "They have avoided trying to take out the bolt cannons on the buildings, which is why they are being slaughtered. I imagine they are under orders to leave the terminus and warehouses intact. But my God, they are taking an awful beating. It must seem like they wandered onto the set of a bad science fiction movie."

"I don't think Cartwright expects to take the site," Adrian said. "He is probing our defenses to find out what we have."

"Well, I hope he appreciates the intel he's getting because it's costing a lot of lives."

Adrian came to a decision. "General, you are authorized to use whatever force you think necessary to defend the terminus facility and this building."

The General turned toward his team, a grim expression on his face. "People. The Emissary has been shot and is in surgery in critical condition. There is nothing we can do for her except to do our job, which is to defend the terminus and this building. The terminus' autonomous defenses are handling the ground assault well enough, so we'll leave that to them for now, and will concentrate on the incoming hostile warplanes. We will engage when they are 500 kilometers out. I want those of you responsible for monitoring other sites to remain vigilant. More attacks are possible."

He turned toward the vidscreens on the wall. The

incoming warplanes had separated into five squadrons of four, with the transports in the rear.

"Bring missile batteries online. Delta-E2 load-out. We will launch in pairs at ten-second intervals. Target transports first, then fighters. Let's get the rail guns warmed up."

Adrian was familiar with the ExCo building's defenses and could imagine what was happening in response to the General's orders. Two missile battery emplacements on the roof were opening, each revealing half a dozen launch tubes. Below them, on the building's top floor, automated systems were loading them with Delta-E2 hypersonic missiles with a small payload designed to do what the General had in mind; namely, to shoot planes out of the sky.

A circle with a 500 kilometer radius appeared on the vidscreen with the ExCo building at its center. The cluster of hostile planes was fast approaching from the North. He held his breath as the planes crossed the invisible line. The room was still.

One of the General's people calmly said, "Target sequencing set. Initial targets acquired and locked in. Systems are green."

"Commence firing," the General said.

Two green dots leaped away from the square that represented the ExCo building and began accelerating toward their targets. Adrian had seen a demonstration of the launchers. A burst of compressed steam propelled the missile out of the launch tube, then its engine kicked in and it became a ball of fire rocketing away so fast his eyes could not follow it.

"Missiles 1 and 2 away."

"Time to target?"

"A little under two minutes."

My God, Adrian thought. Five hundred kilometers in two minutes. Of course, that took into account the velocity of the approaching planes as well, but still . . .

"Mach 1," someone said. A few moments later, "Mach 2."

"Missiles 3 and 4 away," someone said.

A moment later, "Missiles 1 and 2 are hypersonic."

On the vidscreen the planes were spreading out, jinking one way and then another, hoping to break the missile locks, but the Delta-E2's were smart missiles with advanced tracking and maneuvering capabilities. Once they locked onto a target, they were nearly impossible to shake off.

"Missiles 3 and 4 have gone hypersonic. Missiles 1 and 2 have reached cruising speed at Mach 10."

Twelve thousand seven hundred kilometers per hour. It was one thing to know the numbers in the abstract; it was quite another to watch real missiles streaking toward real airplanes at such mind-boggling speed.

"Missiles 5 and 6 away."

A fuzzy circle appeared on the board around two of the transport planes, showing flares the pilots hoped the missiles would go after instead of their planes. The missiles ignored the counter-measures. Two green dots merged with two red dots and eighty or more people died.

He must have looked distressed because the General said, "Remember son, they attacked us."

"Yeah." It didn't make him feel any better.

A minute and a half after they began launching missiles, the last of the transports was gone, and they started targeting the fighters. Then their missile batteries stopped firing. It was just a matter of watching the missiles already in the air finish the job.

"Missiles incoming," someone said. A swarm of fast-moving red dots appeared on the vidscreen. The fighters had launched their own missiles.

"Target?"

There was a pause. "ExCo headquarters. They have gone hypersonic."

"Activate rail guns. Anti-missile load-out."

A few moments later someone said, "Rail guns loaded, capacitors charged."

"Commence firing."

There were four rail guns on the roof, each sitting on a turntable-like platform that could point them in any direction. They would fire metal balls the size of tennis balls at nearly supersonic velocity. Shortly after launch, each ball would burst open and release a cloud of pellets. It only took one pellet to knock a missile out of the sky, and by the time four clouds of pellets reached the missiles, they had formed a wall of kinetic energy that could take out a lot of missiles, depending on how widely spaced the missiles were. Hostile missiles began disappearing from vidscreen. The rail guns continued firing until there were no missiles left to shoot at.

Fighter jets were disappearing from the vidscreen. The last four altered course and began a long, curving arc that would take them away from the terminus site.

"Looks like they have had enough," the General said. "They won't be able to outrun the missiles, though." He turned to Adrian. "Should I order the remaining missiles to self-destruct?"

Adrian thought about Anna lying dead on the ground, and Holly down in the ER hanging between life and death, Theo's missing arm, Danae likely dead on the battlefield somewhere. He wanted to make someone pay. The more someones, the better.

"It's your call, son," the General said, "but it is one thing to defend ourselves with lethal force, quite another to kill someone who is running away."

He was right, of course. The pilots of the remaining planes were not the ones responsible. Cartwright was the one responsible.

He let out a deep sigh. "Let them go. It's what the Emissary would want."

The General nodded to someone at a control board.

Adrian said, "I'll be in the medical center," and left the room.

———

When Adrian reached the OR, Tomás was standing outside, waiting for him. Through the window in the door, he could see the Emissary on the operating table. A surprisingly large number of people were crowded around her in scrubs and masks.

He pushed past Tomás and walked into the room. The surgeon turned to him. "She was under. I had opened her up and was looking for the bullet when she opened her eyes, reached up, pulled the oxygen mask aside, and said, 'Stand down, doctor. I've got this.' Then she closed her eyes again."

Several others nodded as he said this, a look of shock on their faces. Another doctor, who Adrian guessed was the anesthesiologist, said, "She was unconscious. I'm sure of it. She's *still* unconscious, dammit. I have never seen anything like this." More nods.

"Doctor," a nurse said. She pointed at Holly. The surgeon followed her gaze and stepped back. "What the hell?"

Adrian elbowed someone aside so he could see what they were seeing. Someone shoved a face mask into his hand. Her abdomen was the only exposed area. The surgeon had cut her open and clamps held the skin back, revealing internal organs. There was less blood than he expected, and the passage of the bullet through her abdomen was obvious, having shredded parts of at least two organs, though he had no idea which organs they were.

Then he saw what had made the surgeon step back. Hundreds . . . no, thousands of tiny threads were wriggling around inside the open wound. Revulsion hit him and he took an involuntary step backward, bumping into a nurse. He made himself look again, and what he saw would remain etched in his memory for the rest of his life. The tiny, worm-like threads were repairing the damage done by the bullet.

Nobody said anything for several seconds. Finally, the surgeon said. "This is completely outside my training and experience. I don't know what to do."

Something clicked in Adrian's mind. It had to be her nanites; the nanites that kept her young and healthy. But they were microscopic. They shouldn't be able to do anything at a macroscopic level, and certainly not something as complex as a major surgery.

"What did she say? Her exact words."

"She said, 'Stand down, doctor. I've got this.'" Others nodded.

He wasn't sure whether it was relief or the emotions of the last hour catching up with him, but he burst out laughing. "Emissary," he said. "You are ever full of surprises."

The doctor stared at him like he had lost his mind.

Adrian stopped laughing and said, "I have generally found it best to do what the Emissary says. Stand down, doctor. She's got this."

The doctor's alarmed expression turned to shock, then awe. He stared at the wound again, which had become a bed of frenetic activity. "Is she . . . is she healing herself?"

"You might want to take her off the anesthesia," Adrian said. "I doubt she needs it, and it might be hindering her. I'd get rid of the clamps, too. They are going to be in the way."

36

Holly woke in a hospital room. A young Ecuadorian woman in scrubs sat in a chair near the bed. When she saw that Holly was awake, she said, "I will get the doctor," and left.

She returned a few minutes later with a man who did indeed look like a doctor, complete with white coat and stethoscope. He was about her age—her chronological age, that is—and had a kindly face. He, too, was Ecuadorian. She pushed herself into a sitting position.

"Emissary," he said. "I am so happy to see you awake. How do you feel?"

He said it as though waking up was not something to be taken for granted. Sticking the prongs of his stethoscope in his ears, he listened to her lungs front and back. Apparently, the question about how she felt was rhetorical because he seemed intent on answering it for himself. He checked her pulse and blood pressure, even though a monitor to her left was happily beeping away, as it displayed the same information. He examined her fingertips, which was odd. When he asked her to lie back down, she decided to assert some personal agency.

"Where am I?"

"The medical center at ExCo headquarters."

"Who are *you*?"

He looked taken aback. "I am Doctor Sanchez, the doctor who performed surgery on you when they brought you in. At least, I tried to."

He tried to perform surgery on her. Huh. Flashes were coming back: explosions at the site, the fires, the cries of injured people, the smell of dead people; brief scenes, more like snapshots than anything else. She peered at his security badge. It was a standard ExCo badge and included his picture. It wasn't surprising that she didn't recognize him. She had never had a reason to visit the medical center before.

"Why am I here?"

He gave her a curious look. "What is the thing you remember last?"

"I was at the site. There had been an explosion. Fires. People injured. I was there to see how bad it was. Then there was . . . gun fire, and . . . "

And mortars and armored vehicles and small arms fire. A kaleidoscope of shifting images crowded into her mind, but they were just snippets and all mixed up.

"I seem to have some gaps in my memory," she said. "I'm guessing that means something bad happened to me."

"That is so, Emissary. I am sure someone will fill in gaps, but right now I would like to complete my examination."

She wiggled her way into a prone position and discovered she was wearing a hospital gown. He pulled up her gown and began feeling around her abdomen with his fingers. He kept asking, "Does this hurt?" It didn't. He stood back and looked at her curiously.

"How are you feeling?"

It sounded like a genuine question this time, and his tone suggested he thought she ought not to be feeling fine. But she was. In fact, she felt great, like she could run a marathon, not that she had ever done that.

"I feel fine," she said. "Really." She caught a whiff of a disgusting smell and sniffed her armpit. "I stink."

"We are not sure why. Ambassador Peeters thinks it is the nanites in your bloodstream dissolving the bullet and excreting toxic substances through your sweat glands."

"Really? Wow, that's weird. What bullet?"

Theo walked in. He had a coffee mug in one hand. His other arm was half as long as it should have been, and hung at his side with the lower part of his shirt sleeve folded up and clipped to the upper part. She glimpsed two marines outside her room.

"What happened to your arm?" she said.

"Got it shot off." He grinned. "Just below the elbow. Lucky for me Tomás was there to tie a tourniquet around it or I might have bled out. They got it stitched up and I am learning how to get my shirt on and off without help. I am under orders to report back here every day to check for infection and, once it's healed up, I'll look into getting an artificial limb."

"That must have hurt like hell."

"I was in shock, so I hardly noticed until later. Then it did hurt. A lot. It still hurts when I move around, but they've given me pills for that."

The doctor said, "I am happy to report that the Emissary's health is excellent. The last scan showed the bullet almost entirely gone. If the world were not coming to an end, I would have a wonderful article for a medical journal."

"What bullet?" Holly said again.

"She doesn't remember the attack."

"I'm right here, you know."

Theo said, "Perhaps you and Janey can give us a moment. The Emissary and I need to talk."

She latched onto the word attack. More memories came back: Anna and Leon rushing her to the plane; Anna stopping, turning to her, saying something she couldn't hear, then jerking and looking surprised, then collapsing in front of her; then a burning pain in her stomach, like a mule had kicked her. There was blood, a lot of blood.

A jolt of panic surged through her. "Where's Anna?"

Theo used one foot to pull up a chair and sat. He set his coffee mug on the nightstand beside her bed and took her hand. She braced herself for what she knew was coming.

"The bullet went through her before hitting you. She died almost instantly. By the time the bullet reached you, its kinetic energy was mostly spent. She saved your life."

The image of Anna's surprise expression fixed itself in her mind. She closed her eyes, willing it away. She wanted Anna to not be dead. She wanted her to be in the next room recovering. She reached for her amulet, but stopped. The Fragment couldn't fix this. Probably wouldn't, even if he could. She thought she should cry, but she didn't seem to have any tears. Just an emptiness, a numbness.

She opened her eyes, not sure how long they had been closed. Theo was still there. He was always there for her. Anna had been there for her too and had died saving her, just like she was supposed to. Now she was gone and there was nothing she could do to bring her back. She took a deep breath and let it out.

"The terminus?"

"We still control the terminus and it is intact. You will be pleased to know that the defenses here and at the terminus worked as advertised. We lost twenty-three people in the attack. Cartwright lost several hundred."

"He really came at us, didn't he?"

"Danae took a heavy caliber bullet in the back. Sliced right through her lower spine. She's alive, but the doctor says she will never walk again."

Anna dead. Danae crippled. A score of her people killed. A knot of anger formed in her chest. Cartwright would pay for this.

"By the way," Theo said. "Your nanites played an interesting role in saving your life."

"How's that?"

"The bullet tore you apart inside. Your nanites repaired the damage right there on the operating table. I wish I had been there to see the expressions on the faces of the doctors and nurses when they saw an army of itty-bitty threads wiggling around in an open wound, repairing damaged organs right before their eyes."

"Really? I didn't know they could do that."

"Makes you wonder what else they can do."

She took a few moments to let all the information sink in before coming around to the big question: Why had Cartwright launched a full-scale attack that he had to have known would fail.

"There is another thing you need to know," he said. "During the attack, a CRA SEAL team overpowered the security detail at the compound where Robert and his family live. They took Ngari, Kari and Peter."

What? They took Robert's daughter? And his grandchildren? Her mind stuttered as it tried to wrap itself around that. Then an icy chill settled over her as the enormity of Cartwright's plan came into view. It was as brilliant as it was abhorrent. Cartwright never intended to take the Quito site. That was a diversion. It was Ngari and her children he was after.

"Was anyone hurt?"

"Two members of the security team were wounded. One died on the operating table."

She took that in and set it aside for the time being.

"Everyone else is all right?"

"The rest of your family is fine. We doubled their security detail, though it's kind of like shutting the barn door after the horses have escaped."

"It's not them he wants, anyway. It's me he wants. Has he called yet?"

Theo nodded. "When we told him you were critically injured in the battle and were still recovering, he said to call him back when you felt up to it."

When she felt up to it. How considerate of him. The only thing she felt up to was killing him.

Nurse Janey chose that moment to appear with a tray, which she set on a small table beside Holly's bed. Tea, toast, milk, and a small bowl of fruit.

"What the hell is this?" Holly said. "I want real food!"

"Emissary," she said calmly. "You have been asleep for six days. You need to start out with light food."

Six days? She had been out for six days?

"Fine," she said with a dismissive wave. "Get out." Then to Theo, "I'd like to be alone for a while. Tell the marines I don't want to be disturbed."

He looked like he was going to say something, but changed his mind and left her alone.

She stared at her miserable breakfast and sipped some tea. The room felt empty. She wasn't used to being alone except in her private quarters. For the last eleven years, ever since she returned from Titan, she had been surrounded by people all the time. Even now, there were two armed marines outside her room. She looked up from the tray, half expecting to see Anna. But, of course, Anna wasn't there. She thought back to the first time they met at the airport.

"I'm Anna Lindstrom, ma'am. I will be your PPI."

"What's a PPI?"

"Personal Protection Individual."

"I need a bodyguard?"

"Tomás thinks so, ma'am."

He had certainly been right about that. She remembered the French door incident and smiled. She thought about the press conference and the car chase, and how her team had protected her from harm. *Show time, Harry. Bump and run.*

Anna had taken her out for an evening of drinking and dancing after the debacle with the Council. Of course, she hadn't really left the protection detail behind, but she had let Holly think she had.

Then the attack on the Quito terminus, where Anna had put herself between Holly and a bullet meant for her, a bullet that likely would have killed her had it not gone through Anna first. The shocked look on her face was indelibly inscribed in her memory. Anna had done her job, and it had cost her everything.

A sob welled up, and the tears came.

Later, when she had run out of tears, she thought about Danae. She had also done her job and would be confined to a wheelchair for the rest of her life as a reward. And Theo, who had lost an arm. And Robert, whose daughter and grandchildren were in Cartwright's hands now. She thought about the workers at the terminus who had died in the attack, and Eduardo with burns on his arm and face. And the marines who had formed a tight huddle around her to shield her from hostile fire.

She had come back to Earth alone and in need of allies. She had found them, and they had done their jobs. All of them. Now it was up to her to finish it, and that meant finishing her unfinished business with Cartwright.

Why, after all these years, had he decided to move against her now? Revenge? No, that wasn't his style. Project Exodus? Yes, that had to be it. He would try to trade Ngari, Kari, and Peter for her. Then he would use her to gain control of the Exodus Project. But why? To ensure a seat for himself on the last ark leaving Earth? Not likely. Cartwright was an old man. He wouldn't much care what happened to him. To save his family? Maybe. But he had something bigger in mind. Whatever else she might think of James Cartwright, he was a patriot. He would always act for his country's benefit as he understood it.

She chewed on that thought while she ate her fruit. Canned fruit had a distinctive smell and taste that was impossible to confuse with fresh fruit. This was definitely canned fruit. Then she saw Cartwright's end game.

Gabriel, she thought.

I am here, Holly.

What is the current status of the Underground Cities Project?

Eleven underground bunkers in four alliances are under construction. The four bunkers in the Christian Republic of American and the two in Great Britain are essentially complete, and have been stocked with food and supplies to support about 120,000 people for five years. They have begun moving people in.

Seven years early?

She drank the rest of her tea.

"Guards!" she said.

One of the marines opened the door and peered in.

"Get Theo and Adrian here. ASAP."

A few minutes later, the two men entered.

"Shut the door," she said. Adrian closed it. They both sat.

"I know what Cartwright's end game is."

They looked at her expectantly.

"He wants Project Exodus. He knows he can't take it by force, because he has no way to get at the space stations. At least not without putting them at risk, which he doesn't want to do. So he kidnapped Ngari, Kari, and Peter, and intends to trade them for me. Then he will use me to take control of the space stations."

Theo looked puzzled. "But why?"

"And why now?" Adrian said.

She waited a few beats and said, "Cartwright is a white supremacist."

Theo shrugged. "That's been evident for a long time, though he denies it."

"And we've never taken it very seriously. But for Cartwright, it's the whole point. He wants to control Project Exodus so he can ensure that the right kind of people get on the arks. The white kind, as in descendants of Northern European stock. He sees this as a onetime opportunity to start the human race over again without the genetic impurities of the inferior races."

They thought about that for a moment, and Theo said, "Mexico and India are part of the UCP alliance."

"That doesn't mean any of them will be on the arks."

Adrian said, "His allies are not going to be happy when they realize he intends to leave them behind."

"Nor will anybody else," she said. "When other heads of state figure out what he's up to, he will find himself at war with most of the world. That's why he is going to preemptively start World War 3."

"Whoa," Theo said. "That's a big leap."

"It's only a big leap because we haven't been looking at it from his point of view. In his mind, the most important thing is that the next iteration of humanity be a pure white race, unsullied by the lesser races. Everything else is secondary to that. Everything. And that end justifies any and all means, including a global thermonuclear war that will kill hundreds of millions and leave hundreds of millions more with a post-apocalyptic world, worse than the one we already have."

Neither of them looked convinced.

"Think about it," she said. "Why has he continued building the underground cities when he surely knew a long time ago that they won't survive the coming of the Death Bringer? Why has he stocked them to support 120,000 people for several years? Why is he putting people in them as we speak, seven years before the end? I'll tell you why: it's because they have to survive the coming war, the war he is going to start. And he has to do it soon, because it won't take long for the rest of the world to reach the same conclusion I have."

Adrian said, "I hear what you are saying, but it . . ." He stopped when he saw the expression on her face.

There was a rage building inside her; a terrible rage; a rage with James Braxton Cartwright at its center. This was the difference between her and Cartwright. He was willing to do whatever it took to get what he wanted. The end always justified the means, no matter how horrendous those means might be. She, on the other hand, had limits on how far she would go to accomplish her goals.

She mentally kicked herself for not realizing that something like this was coming. She had been happy to ignore Cartwright as long as he left her alone, and as a result, she had underestimated him. But that changed the moment he threatened her family. He had started a war with her, and he had made it personal.

"What are you thinking?" Theo asked cautiously.

She spoke calmly and coldly. "I am going to kill James Cartwright."

The shocked expression on their faces was almost comical.

"But first I need to do some research. I'll be in my study. See to it I am not disturbed."

She yanked the IV out of her arm, got out of bed, and marched out of the room with her hospital gown flapping. She took a moment to orient herself, then headed for an exit with nanite-fueled determination. The two marines fell in behind her.

Leon came out of a restroom. "Emissary!" He ran after her.

Doctor Sanchez was sitting at the nurses' station when she swept past. He ran after her as well. "Emissary, please. We need to run some more tests now that you are awake."

She stopped and pivoted to face the flustered doctor. She glanced at Leon, who had caught up with her at the same time, and then at his gun. He hesitated, then produced the weapon. He didn't point it at anyone, just held it at his side.

The marines were instantly alert. The doctor took a step back, hands up.

Theo caught up with them and said to the doctor, "As with all things having to do with the Emissary, it is generally best to let her do what she wants. Otherwise she gets cranky."

37

Recalling memories the Fragment had put in her head was like peeling back the layers of an onion. As she pulled each layer back, new layers appeared. All she had to do was focus her mind on a specific area of knowledge, and the memories would emerge. It wasn't as easy as it sounded and required concentration to stay focused on what she wanted to remember. Early on, it had been like trying to hold on to a bar of soap that kept slipping out of her hand and disappearing into the water. But after ten years of practice, she rarely lost the soap.

She knew more about nanotechnology than anyone on the planet, but she had never run across anything related specifically to the nanites in her bloodstream. They were certainly more advanced than anything she knew how to make, and she had just assumed this was a technology the Fragment had chosen not to reveal to her. It was Theo's passing remark that it "kinda makes you wonder what else they can do" that piqued her curiosity.

For a memory she had never before discovered, it was surprisingly easy to find, almost as though it had been waiting for her to ask. It even had a title: Holly's Nanites. She laughed. She had found the owner's manual.

Two hours of immersion in the contents of the manual revealed that there was indeed a lot more to her nanites than she had realized. She had already known they could do more than keep her young and healthy, like performing major surgery if she was seriously injured, which meant they could work at a macroscopic level as well as a microscopic level. But they could do more than that. Much more. They were several orders of magnitude beyond anything she knew how to make. With the nanites, the Fragment had given her some extraordinary abilities.

She stepped out of her suite, told the two marines standing guard to wait for her, and walked down the hall to Danae's quarters. She tapped on the door and let herself in. Danae was sitting up in bed reading a book; an actual book, oddly enough. Her face lit up when she saw Holly.

"Emissary. You are awake and walking around. Last I heard, you were in a coma. Are you supposed to be up?"

"I'm the Emissary," she said with a grin. "I can do anything I damn well want." She sat on the edge of the bed. "Danae, I am so glad you are all right, though I understand you can't walk yet."

Danae Najafi went to lengths to present herself as a tough woman who was impervious to pain and emotions; probably a necessary defense mechanism, given that she worked in an overwhelmingly male profession. Nonetheless, her chin quivered.

"They are talking about more surgeries and physical therapy," she said, "but I have no feeling from the waist down. That means a wheelchair. I am afraid I won't be of much use to you anymore, Emissary."

"Actually, that's why I'm here."

"You're here to fire me?"

Holly was taken aback, then laughed. "Good God,

woman! I'm not going to fire you. Besides, Adrian would be the one to do that, not me. As far as I'm concerned, you can run ExCo's security operation from a desk. It'll force you to delegate more, which you should probably do, anyway. Besides, you are one of the few people in the world I trust."

"Thank you, Emissary." She looked like she was going to cry, so Holly moved the conversation along.

"I am here to perform a little experiment and I need your help."

"An experiment?"

"I want to see if I can heal you."

Danae's expression was the definition of surprised. "So . . . you've taken up faith healing?"

"No, nothing like that. Okay, maybe a little like that. I have been researching my nanites, something I had never done before. I always thought of them as passive, microscopic machines running around in my body looking for things to repair or destroy. Which they are.

"But when I learned they had repaired massive internal damage from that gunshot wound, I got to wondering what else they can do. So I rummaged around in my memories and found an owner's manual for my nanites. Don't laugh, I'm not making this up. It turns out the nanites can do more than I thought. Apparently, I can direct them to accomplish certain functions, including repairing damage in other people's bodies. At least I think that's what the manual says. There are parts I don't fully understand yet."

Danae's facial expression made a short journey from surprise to skepticism. "And you want to see if you can get them to heal me."

"With your permission, of course. But what do you have to lose? Other than both of us feeling silly, and if that happens we just won't tell anyone about it."

Danae chewed on her lower lip for a few moments. "All

right." She giggled and then looked suitably embarrassed. "What do I have to do?"

"Nothing. Just don't be alarmed when I lay hands on you. It's not a religious thing. I need skin-to-skin contact so the nanites can travel from me to you. At least, I think I do. I really am flying blind here."

She pulled the sheet down and Danae's pajama top up. Her abdomen was wrapped in bandages, so she put her hand where she figured the exit point had been.

Danae frowned. "You're not trying to get into my panties, are you?" They both laughed.

She imagined nanites assembling themselves in columns and marching like an army down her arm to her hand and into Danae's body, where they surrounded the base of her spine. Her hand seemed to tingle and felt warmer than before, but that might have been her imagination. She did this for a minute or so.

"I can't tell if anything is happening," she said. "Did you feel anything?"

"No, sorry. I'm trying to wiggle my toes, but I can't feel anything down there."

Holly grabbed her toes. "Try again." She felt nothing.

Holly was disappointed. And embarrassed that she had so easily succumbed to magical thinking. And a little angry—at herself, at the Fragment, at Cartwright, at nobody and everybody.

———

When she got back to her suite, Theo and Adrian were sitting on a couch, heads together, studying something on a tablet. She headed for the small kitchen that was separated from the living room by a bar-style counter.

Adrian looked up. "Theo tells me you are doing research. I'm guessing it has to do with nanites."

Holly made a time-out sign with her hands. "I'm starved. Toast and fruit didn't cut it."

The kitchen wasn't large enough for three people, so they sat on bar stools on the living room side of the counter while Holly collected the things she needed to prepare a meal.

"What makes you think I'm researching nanites?" she asked.

"An educated guess. You haven't turned on your tablet recently, so whatever research you are doing has been going on in your head. My guess is you are curious about how the nanites healed a major gunshot wound and are wondering what else they can do."

She got two pans heating and began chopping onions and tomatoes.

"I have always thought of the nanites as passive," she said, "Just cruising around looking for bad things to kill and broken things to fix. The fact that they could heal a serious gunshot wound, including getting rid of the bullet, made me realize there is more to them than I thought. They can work cooperatively to achieve macroscopic effects."

She put the chopped onions in the small pan with a little oil to sauté. The tomatoes went into a small bowl and she started grating cheese.

"By the way, the awful smell my body is giving off? Theo was right. That's the nanites excreting chemicals from the dissolved bullet out through my sweat glands. Disgusting, but effective."

"Well," said Theo. "Now that you mention it, that is definitely *not* the Holly smell I am used to."

Adrian rolled his eyes.

She ignored them. "I rummaged around in the memories the Fragment packed into my head and found an instruction manual for the nanites. I know, it's weird."

She retrieved eggs from the refrigerator, broke them into a

bowl, poured them into the large pan, and began shaking the pan back and forth while gently stirring the eggs.

"The best analogy I can come up with is army ants. Individually, they are small and relatively harmless, though you probably don't want one to latch onto your finger because army ants have really strong pinchers.

"Anyway, a single army ant is pretty limited in what it can do, but an army of them is a different story. A few thousand of them working together can bring down a large animal. They can form a bridge across a river. An army of them marching through a forest will leave a swath of barren land a mile wide.

"I think the nanites are like that. Singly, their capabilities are limited, but an army of them is something else entirely. When they realized I had been seriously injured, they formed millions of larger machines—that's what they are, you know; teeny, tiny machines—and went to work repairing the damage. That's the wiggly things you saw, Adrian; battalions of nanites going to war. Kinda cool, huh? Kinda creepy, too."

She added the sautéed onions, tomatoes, and cheese.

"It turns out I have some control over my nanite population. I can direct them to do certain things. Not in detail, but in general. I can suggest they do something, but how they go about it is up to them."

She added salt and pepper, flipped one half of the omelet over onto the other half, and slid it out of the pan onto the cutting board, where she cut it into three pieces, which she transferred to plates.

"Voila! Omelets." She handed them each a plate. "Forks in that drawer over there."

They took their omelets into the living room.

After a few bites, Adrian said, "These are pretty good. I didn't know you could cook."

"She can't," Theo said. "She is one of the few people I

know who can ruin a perfectly good can of tomato soup. I'm guessing she found a cookbook in her mental archives."

Holly grinned. "It's scary what all is in my head."

"You seem unusually chipper," Theo said. "Almost euphoric. I am tempted to think you are in denial about the mayhem and trauma and loss you have just gone through."

She put down her fork and looked at him. "You could not be more wrong," she said evenly, bitterness in her voice. "I am heartbroken and angry: heartbroken about the hundreds, maybe even thousands, of innocent people who died in the attack; heartbroken about Anna; heartbroken about Danae."

Her voice rose in volume as she spoke.

"And I am angry: angry that Cartwright killed a lot of innocent people; angry that he killed my best friend; angry that he crippled Danae. Most of all, I am angry that he targeted my family!"

She stopped to catch her breath and continued with a quiet and deliberate coldness that surprised her. "It is time for James Cartwright to die, something I should have done a long time ago."

Both men stared at her in silence.

38

Two days later, she gathered Theo, Adrian, and Robert in a conference room, along with Cinta and the General. A tap came at the conference room door and Danae walked in.

"Emissary," she said, with a slight bow of her head. "I wonder if I might sit in."

Holly stared, her mind momentarily blank.

Robert said, "What . . .?"

Adrian leaped out of his chair, rushed to her, and wrapped her in a huge hug.

Theo said, "You're walking."

"Wow, not much gets by you, does it?" Danae said.

Holly's mind finally gained traction. "How can you be walking?"

"I guess those nanite thingies you gave me took a couple of days to get the job done. Maybe you should start up a healing ministry."

Holly burst out laughing. "Let me get back to you on that."

Adrian pulled back from his hug and kissed her. On the lips. She blushed. Holly looked at Adrian, then at Theo, who shrugged. Holy crap, there was something going on between

Adrian and Danae. How long had that been going on? And how had she not known about it?

He pulled her over to a chair next to his and turned to Holly. "How?"

"When I discovered I could transfer some of my nanites to another person, I tried it out on Danae. As near as we could tell, nothing happened. But we were wrong. It just took the nanites a while to repair the damage to her spine, maybe because there weren't very many of them."

"I have a question, though," Danae said. "Do I have a permanent colony of them in my blood stream now?"

"I don't think so. The nanites have a relatively short life-span and will only replicate in my body, so while you might still have some, their population will decline over time until none are left." She offered an apologetic smile. "Sorry, you don't get to be forever young."

"That's all right. As much as I appreciate being able to walk again, the thought of microscopic critters running around inside me is creepy."

"I know, right? I try not to think about it."

"Such are the travails of being the Emissary," Theo quipped.

Robert said, "I am so happy for you, Danae."

She gave him a sad look. "I'm sorry we haven't gotten to *your* happy ending yet."

"Speaking of which," Holly said. "Let's get this done."

Adrian punched in the number Cartwright had given them and put it on speaker. It chimed for a long time before Cartwright answered.

"This is Cartwright."

"This is Adrian Verhoeven."

"I don't want to talk to you, Verhoeven. Put Dr. Burton on."

"I'm here," she said.

"Good. This is how it is going to work. In twenty-four

hours you will be at this location." He gave them a set of coordinates, which Adrian captured on his tablet.

"Please repeat the coordinates back to me." Adrian did so. "Good. You, Dr. Burton, will come in a small, private jet with only you and a pilot. Not one of your spaceplanes, by the way, but something commercial. You will surrender yourself to me, whereupon I will put your niece and her children on the plane, and the pilot will take them wherever you tell him to. Are these instructions clear?"

Robert said, "I want to talk to—"

"Dr. Burton, please answer the question."

"Yes, but I want proof of life."

The connection dropped. She looked around the table at a collection of unhappy-looking people. Except for Robert, who looked like he wanted to throw furniture around.

"You're not going to surrender yourself to him, are you?" Cinta said.

"I will do whatever is necessary to rescue Robert's daughter and grandchildren. Now that we know where they are, we need to decide *how* I am going to do that."

Adrian said, "Room: Give us a satellite image centered on the following location." He read out the coordinates and a satellite image filled the vidscreen at one end of the conference room. It showed a lake surrounded by dense boreal forest. On the shore of the lake was a cabin with a dock and a small boat. On the other side of the cabin, about a kilometer from the lake, was an airstrip. At one end of the strip sat a spaceplane. An undeveloped road connected the airstrip to the cabin.

"Nice location," Theo said. "Where is it?"

"Room: Zoom out. Again. Again. There." The view had expanded to include more forest and part of a large lake.

"Room: Identify the large body of water."

"The Great Bear Lake in the Northern Territories of the Christian Republic of America."

"Northern Territories," Theo said. "It certainly is out in the middle of nowhere. Not far from the Arctic Circle."

"Can a small plane get there in twenty-four hours from here?"

"Probably not," Adrian said. "But *Eos* can get her to Seattle in a couple hours, and we can have a chartered jet waiting and ready to go from there."

"Tough target," the General said. "Dense forest for fifty kilometers in every direction. The only practical way in or out is by air, and they will see anything approaching by air long before it gets there, so we won't have the element of surprise on our side. We also have to assume Cartwright has defenses in place against a variety of likely attacks."

"Can we take the cabin by force and not lose the hostages?" Adrian asked.

The General and Danae said no at the same time.

They exchanged glances, and the General said, "This is a classic hostage situation. Our best chance for getting the hostages out alive is negotiation."

"There is only one negotiating point," Theo said, "and it is not negotiable."

"General," Adrian said. "If we were to attempt a military assault, how would we do it?"

The General studied the image for a few moments. "If it were up to me, I would use cruise missiles to take out whatever defenses they have in place by destroying everything in the immediate area except the cabin, and count on the shock-and-awe effect to give us enough time to land a marine force right on top of them. The risk is that the hostages will be killed in the ensuing firefight, either by their captors or by friendly fire."

"What are the odds none of the hostages are killed or seriously injured?"

The general hesitated. "Fifty-fifty. If everything goes our way." He looked at Danae, who nodded.

"And if it doesn't?"

He shrugged.

Danae said, "The problem is exacerbated by the fact that we don't know exactly where the hostages are in the cabin. We don't even know for sure that they *are* there. All we have is Cartwright's word on that. We could find anything there. Or nothing. Cartwright might have rigged the cabin with explosives for all we know."

Holly said, "Gabriel, can you show us a real-time image of the cabin's interior?"

The AI used the room's speakers to respond. "I have dispatched a drone with the required capabilities. It will be over the site in six minutes."

"We'll wait."

Six minutes later, the image on the vidscreen was replaced with a shadowy, gray-scale image of the cabin and its environs. The interior of the cabin was visible as though the roof had been removed. The image was blurry, but adequate for their purposes.

Two soldiers stood outside, armed with assault rifles. Two more soldiers with rifles stood inside, near windows. A single man sat on a couch in the large central area with his feet propped up on a low table. Another man stood guard at the door to one of the cabin's bedrooms. An adult and two children were there.

"Gabriel, zoom out a bit."

The image pulled back to reveal a fifty-meter area around the cabin. Other soldiers were visible, along with a missile battery and two machine gun emplacements. They were well hidden in the trees.

She said, "Now we know the layout, exactly where the hostages are being held, and the deployment of soldiers around them. We also know that Cartwright is there. General, does this change the tactical situation?"

"It helps, of course, but it makes no material difference.

The risk to the hostages remains the same."

Danae nodded in agreement.

Holly asked, "Does anyone have any other ideas about how we extract Ngari and her children unharmed?"

The room was quiet, the faces glum.

"Okay then," she said. "We do it Cartwright's way. I go in alone."

This was met with a chorus of objections. She held up a hand and waited until they quieted down.

"General, you will watch in real time. Once I have secured the hostages, you will send the cavalry in. The scorched earth scenario followed by a rapid deployment of marines seems like a good plan, but I leave that to you. If I cannot secure the hostages, you will wait until Cartwright puts them on the plane and sends them on their way, which I believe he will do. You will take no action until they are safe. Is that clear?"

Nobody looked happy.

"How exactly do you intend to 'secure' the hostages?" Theo asked.

"Let's just say the Fragment has provided me with certain capabilities that will prove useful in this situation."

This drew more silence.

"In my absence, I have a few standing orders. First, no matter what happens, Cartwright must not be allowed to unleash a nuclear armageddon on the world, even if it is coming to an end. The world deserves the few years it has left without the horrors of nuclear war.

"General, I want you to come up with a plan to neutralize the nuclear capability of the CRA and the UK. I will instruct *Gabriel's Fire* to give you whatever assistance you require, including access to the ship's weapons and intel on all three legs of their nuclear triads. They may believe their nuclear submarines are safe beneath the ocean's surface, but they are wrong. If I don't survive, you are to execute that plan."

She looked around the table to make sure they all understood.

"Second, no matter what happens, Cartwright must *not* get control of Exodus. He will try to use me to take control of the space stations. You will not allow that to happen. Even if my life is at stake. Is that clear?"

She looked around the table again and waited until everyone nodded.

"Finally, if I don't survive this, Adrian is in charge of the Exodus Project. You will take orders from him as if they were mine, and will do everything in your power to finish what we started."

39

It was a sleek-looking private jet with seating for twelve passengers besides the pilot and co-pilot. Holly slid into the co-pilot's seat next to Jerry and strapped herself in.

"Seems like a lot of seats for so few people," she said.

"It was the smallest jet we could find that had the range to get there and back."

"And you can fly one of these?"

"Well, I've never flown this particular model, but I've flown some just like it, and at the end of the day, these small jets are all the same."

"I see." She didn't really, but it didn't matter. She had seen Jerry fly a lot of things she wouldn't have thought he could fly.

She had dispensed with her 'Emissary' clothes, opting instead for jeans, a loose shirt, and leather boots. No telling what kind of terrain she might find herself walking through. She wore an unzipped bomber jacket in case it was cold where they were going.

She didn't actually have a plan for killing Cartwright and freeing the hostages, mainly because she couldn't know exactly what she would find at the cabin. His people certainly wouldn't let her anywhere near him with a weapon, but she doubted they would realize that a nanite-enhanced kick-boxer could be a lethal weapon. She would have to wait for an opportune moment and take advantage of it when it appeared.

"We're coming up on the coordinates," Jerry said. They had exchanged hardly a word during the several hours they had spent in the air. He probably couldn't think of anything appropriate to say. For her part, she had said everything she needed to say to Theo and Adrian and didn't have anything to say either.

The forest below was dense, with few breaks, so they didn't see the lake until they flew over it. Jerry circled around so they could get a look. The cabin was there, as was the dock. No sign of the boat.

The airstrip was an ugly scar on an otherwise pristine landscape, as though a bulldozer had been used to scrape away the trees and shove them off to one side. A small jet sat in a clearing at one end. A vehicle was making its way along the road from the cabin to the airstrip.

The airstrip was primitive, but adequate, and Jerry brought them down without incident. Four soldiers in CRA uniforms met her when she exited the plane. Two of them kept their assault rifles pointed at her. Jerry stepped out, but a soldier waved him back in.

"Good luck, Emissary," he said.

"Thanks for the ride, Jerry," she said.

One of the soldiers pulled out a tablet and studied it for a while; then studied her face.

"It's her."

Another soldier handcuffed her wrists behind her back.

"Is that really necessary?"

"My orders are quite specific, Dr. Burton."

She shrugged. It was Cartwright's game now, and she had

to play by his rules. Either that or get back on the plane and go home, which she was certainly not going to do.

Two soldiers took hold of her arms and walked her to a truck with an open back, lifted her onto the truck bed, and sat her on a bench on one side. They sat on either side of her. The trip to the cabin was short, bumpy, and uncomfortable.

At the lodge, she was met by Jedediah Dawson, Cartwright's Vice President. That was an unpleasant surprise. She had never met the man before, but everything she knew about him suggested he was someone she would just as soon not meet.

He stood on the porch where he could tower over her. "Dr. Burton. Y'all have no ideah what a pleasure this is. Ah knew the aliens had done somethin' to keep ya lookin' young, but the pics just don't do ya' justice."

There was a hungry look in his eyes, and the purpose of binding of her wrists behind her back became clear. This was a man with a sadistic streak, a man who liked his women submissive, a man who liked to hurt women, especially vulnerable women.

"Where's Cartwright?" she said.

"Oh, you thought he'd be here, didn't you? No, no, no. He knew there was a pretty good chance you'd show up in force, so he sent me instead. Apparently ah'm expendable." He shrugged his shoulders and grinned. "Besides, he knows how much I like pretty little things like you."

A chill ran down her back despite her effort not to react. "Sorry to disappoint you, Dawson, but I'm forty-seven. Hardly a pretty little thing."

He laughed. "Of course you are. But you don't look at day over 30, and that's all that matters."

"Fine. You have me. Now let my family go."

"All in good time, my dear, all in good time. My orders are to put them on the plane you came in and see 'em on their way. And I'll do that. But first, I'm wonderin' if you might

indulge an old man's fantasies and git down on your knees."
A soldier behind her snickered.

"I'd rather skip your personal perversions and get down to business," she said. "Where are my niece and her two children?"

His smug smile turned into something more dangerous. He nodded to the soldiers behind her, who grabbed her by the arms and forced her to her knees. She held eye contact with Dawson as he stepped off the porch and approached her. Without warning, he slapped her across the face hard enough to make her see stars. It hurt, and she imagined it left an imprint of his hand on her cheek.

"Such a rebellious little thing," he said. "Just the way ah like 'em."

"You are such a disappointing specimen of humanity," she said.

He laughed again. He could afford to. He held all the cards. At least for now. He slapped her again, this time on the other side of her face. It brought tears to her eyes.

"That's better," he said. "Nothin' like a woman's tears to stir up an old man's juices. Bring her into the house."

Two soldiers took her by the arms, lifted her to her feet, and marched her up the steps and into the cabin. The other two soldiers followed and stood back with their guns trained on her. She had not seen any more soldiers outside, but she knew they were there.

"Greer," Dawson said. "Bring 'em out here."

The soldier guarding the room where the hostages were being held opened the door and waved Ngari, Kari, and Peter into the room.

"Ngari, are you all right?" Holly said.

"We're all right, Aunt Holly."

"Hold that one," Dawson said, pointing to Kari. The man called Greer grabbed her and held her so she was facing Dawson, who had produced a good sized hunting knife from somewhere. He approached the girl, squatted down so he was looking her in the eye, and held the flat side of the knife against her cheek. She was trembling, but didn't make any noise.

"I have orders to deliver 'em to the plane so they can return home. But those orders didn't specify what condition they should be in when they get there. Ah'm thinking this little darlin' might like something to remember this experience by; something to take home with her; maybe a scar from the top of her ear to her chin. It would make for a fine conversation piece, don't you think?"

Dawson's first mistake was underestimating the wrath of a momma bear when someone threatens one of her cubs. Ngari stomped hard on the foot of the man holding Kari; hard enough to make him let go of her. The girl promptly backed away from Dawson. Then Ngari went after Dawson, screaming and hitting and clawing. He dropped the knife and stumbled backward.

Dawson's second mistake was assuming a bound and unarmed Emissary was not a threat. Aside from her considerable skill at kickboxing, her study of the manual for her nanites had revealed that they could give her enhanced bone and muscle strength, making her stronger and faster; a lot stronger and faster. The effect could be maintained for only a few minutes before the chemicals involved became toxic, at which point the nanites' default mode would kick in and they would begin destroying the now-harmful chemicals. But those few minutes were all she would need.

It had taken her a while to figure out how to 'think up' instructions for the nanites, but it was surprisingly easy once she got the hang of it. She had commandeered ExCo's gym and practiced kickboxing with her newfound strength and speed, from which she learned several things. She learned she could do a lot of damage in a very short time. She learned that enhanced strength didn't mean that hitting things wouldn't hurt; something she discovered while shattering cinder blocks with her hands and feet. Her nanites would heal the damage, of course, but it still hurt like hell at first. She also learned she had more muscle strength than her enhanced bones could support. She would have to be careful that she didn't snap a bone tossing heavy objects around. Finally, she realized it would be awfully easy to inadvertently kill someone if she wasn't careful.

Holly released the physical enhancement chemicals into her blood stream the moment Dawson threatened Kari with the knife. When Ngari attacked him, she snapped the handcuffs apart and went for one of the two men with guns at the ready. Both were watching Ngari attacking Dawson, and didn't realize Holly was moving until she was on top of them. She kicked the assault rifle out of the first man's hands and followed with a hard, fast punch to his chest. Ribs cracked and his body flew across the room. By the time he hit a wall with a solid thud, she had ripped the rifle out of the other man's hands and smashed him in the face with the butt of the gun. His face collapsed in on itself in a bloody pulp, splattering blood everywhere. His head snapped back, breaking his neck. He dropped to the floor.

She turned on the other two soldiers who had come into the cabin with her. They were still registering shock at what had just happened. Moving almost too fast to see, she bashed one of them in the head with the assault rifle. His face exploded in flesh, blood, and bone. The force of the blow broke the gun, leaving her holding the barrel. She turned to the next soldier and ran the woman through with it.

The one called Greer had finally wrestled Ngari away from Dawson, throwing her against a wall which she hit hard enough to bounce off and end up on the floor in a heap. He turned and tried to get ready to grapple with Holly, but she had already crossed the distance between them. She delivered a lightening-fast snap kick to his knee, which made a satisfying popping sound as it broke, and followed up with a kick to his midsection. He folded in half and fell to the floor with a groan, then was still.

She glanced around to make sure nobody who went down was getting back up. Then she stalked toward Dawson, who backed up as fast as he could until he ran into a wall. Without a word, she executed a round-house kick to his head. Normally, that would have staggered him, but she put all the strength and speed she had into it. His neck snapped with an audible crack and his body slid to the floor.

Ngari was sitting now, looking around. "Oh my God, Holly, you . . . you . . . Oh my God."

Holly wasn't sure which part of the last few seconds her niece was referring to, but it didn't matter. She was more concerned about the two children who had just watched their great-aunt kill six people with her bare hands in less than ten seconds.

"The cavalry will be here in a few minutes," she told Ngari. "Are you okay?"

"I . . . I think so."

Holly picked up an undamaged assault rifle, checked to make sure the safety was off, and aimed it at the cabin door in case more bad guys came in. She caught a movement in her peripheral vision, but did not react fast enough to avoid the taser, which delivered a jaw-clenching jolt of electricity to her body. She fell to the floor, jerking and twitching.

A man in an officer's uniform loomed over her. He held a syringe, which he jabbed into her neck. Her world faded away.

40

She didn't know how long it took her nanites to get rid of whatever the man had injected her with, but it couldn't have been very long, because she was lying in the back of the truck. This was conjecture on her part because they had put a hood over her head so she couldn't see anything, but the sound of the engine and the bumpiness of the road almost certainly meant they were taking her back to the airstrip. Her mouth was taped shut and her feet and hands were bound tightly with something wider and stronger than the cuffs they had used earlier. She tested them and decided that even with superhuman strength, her bones would break before the bindings did. The fact that she had single-handedly killed five armed soldiers without a weapon must have made an impression on them. They weren't taking any chances.

A foot nudged her leg. She remained still. There was no reason to let them know she was awake.

A woman's voice said, "She's still out."

A man's voice said, "The Colonel shot her up with some heavy-duty stuff. He said it was emissary-strength." They both laughed.

Holly wasn't laughing. Things had not gone as she had

hoped. She had failed to secure the hostages, so the cavalry wasn't on its way. She hoped Ngari, Kari, and Peter were in the truck as well and would soon be on their way home, but that was out of her control now. All she could do was wait and see how things played out. Hopefully, her captors would take her to Cartwright, which was fine with her, because he and she had unfinished business to attend to.

At the airstrip, they carried her onto what she assumed was the spaceplane. Someone must have figured out she was awake, because a needle poked her in the neck and she drifted into unconsciousness again. She woke to the rumble of spaceplane engines and about three gees of acceleration, which continued for a while until the engines shut down, and she found herself weightless. She was strapped into a seat. They were most likely in low Earth orbit.

Cartwright's face was the first thing she saw when the hood was pulled off her head, and the first thing that struck her was how tired he looked and how old. He was bald and his face was pudgy and scabby. She wanted to offer some snarky remark about how god-awful terrible he looked, but her mouth was still taped shut. Perhaps he knew what she was thinking.

"You like the bald look?" He paused as though waiting for a response. "Lung cancer. Too many cigars. How boring is that?" He laughed and then fell into a coughing fit that took a full minute to get under control. "It's in remission, but it'll come back soon enough, and that will be the end for me because they've run out of things to do. Looks like I'm gonna miss the end of the world."

She caught a glimpse of Earth through the forward windows. They were not in low Earth orbit as she had thought. They were higher. Maybe high enough for geostationary orbit, which meant they were headed for the space stations. Cartwright wasn't wasting any time pressing his advantage.

"I don't mind," Cartwright continued, as though he expected her to be listening with rapt attention. "We all die sooner or later."

He paused and peered curiously at her. "Except you. You don't seem to age at all. You're what, forty-eight? But you don't look a day over thirty. That hardly seems fair.

"How long *will* you live, anyway? Or should I say, how long *would* you live if I didn't kill you first? I am going to kill you. It's not personal. It's just that I can't risk keeping you alive. There is too much at stake and you have proven to be a dangerous adversary."

He started coughing again and reached for an oxygen mask. "They took most of one lung, you know." He put the mask over his face and took several deep breaths before putting it back.

"I want to apologize for Dawson's abominable behavior earlier. Cutting the girl was not part of the plan. I am not a cruel man. I had hoped he would be a better Vice President than the last one, but frankly, it is just as well you killed him."

He ripped the tape off her mouth. She grimaced.

"What have you done with my niece and her children?"

"They are on their way home, as promised. Whatever else you might think of me, I am a man of my word. Mostly. Besides, I don't need them now that I have you."

"You won't be able to use me to get control of Project Exodus."

"Oh, I think I will. I am sure you have given your people orders to sacrifice you rather than let me have Exodus, but I think you underestimate the almost god-like esteem in which they hold you. Your people will not fire on a spaceplane you might be on."

He was probably right. Even if Theo or Adrian gave an order to that effect, which was unlikely, it was not at all certain anyone would follow it.

"*Gabriel's Fire* has capabilities you cannot even imagine," she said.

"Ah yes. *Gabriel's Fire.* An amazing piece of technology. We have scanned it every way we know how and have learned nothing except that its hull is made of something my people tell me can't exist."

He grimaced as if in pain.

"The thing is, I have never seen that warship of yours do anything without you at the helm, and I don't believe the Fragment is on it. I think it's just a piece of space junk without you.

"Nor do I believe the mythical Fragment is going to come to your rescue. I have seen no evidence that it has done anything at all on Earth. Except possibly that alleged meeting with the good Reverend Taylor, and I doubt what he saw was the Fragment. An illusion maybe, or a very good simulation, but not the Fragment. No, the Fragment is sitting on Titan enjoying the view of the rings of Saturn, and you, my dear Emissary, are on your own."

He paused to sip something from a bulb.

"I am curious, though, about how you took out five armed men and my Vice President without a weapon. I watched the whole thing, of course, and it's obvious you have enhanced physical abilities nobody knew about. I suppose it has to do with the same nanotechnology that keeps you young and healthy. I wouldn't mind having access to something like that. In any case, as you can see, I have gone to some lengths to ensure you don't do anything like that to me. I'm sure you understand."

She stared at him, unwilling to give him the satisfaction of an answer.

"Not feeling talkative? Maybe later, after this is over." He put the tape over her mouth and the hood descended over her head. From what she could hear over the next few hours, Cartwright had assembled a small armada of spaceplanes that were approaching Quito Station. When, where, and how he had built them without her knowledge was a mystery.

A woman's voice from up front said, "Quito Station. This is the CRA warship *Exeter*. Please respond." Cartwright's fleet was composed of spaceplanes and spaceships, not that it made much difference. It sounded like the voice was coming over a speaker, apparently from another spaceplane. She repeated the call twice before getting a response.

"Warship *Exeter*, this is *Quito Station*. You are entering restricted space. Please adjust course."

"*Quito Station*, this is Colonel Williamson of the Christian Republic of America. *Quito Station* has been deemed an enemy outpost. You are ordered to stand down and prepare to be boarded. Resistance will be met with deadly force."

There was a long pause.

"Colonel Williamson, this is Adrian Verhoeven. If you continue your approach toward the station, it *will* fire on you. Believe me when I tell you that the station can and will destroy your entire fleet if necessary."

Cartwright spoke now. "Ah, Mr. Verhoeven. You certainly have come a long way since your days as Ambassador Peeters' errand boy. Who would have thought that naïve, insecure boy would rise to be CEO of the Exodus Company? Be that as it may, I advise against firing on my fleet. I have your precious Emissary with me, and my signal bounces around my ships randomly, so you have no way of knowing which one she is on. It would be a shame if you inadvertently killed her."

There was another pause. Adrian would be at ExCo, being relayed through the station.

"Proof of life," he said.

Someone yanked the hood off Holly's head. Adrian's image filled most of the main viewer at the front of the cabin. Theo stood behind him.

"Take the tape off her mouth," Adrian said. "I want to be sure this isn't a double."

Cartwright looked irked but nodded to a soldier who pulled it off.

Looking at their images on the screen, she knew they would not follow her orders. They would turn the stations over to Cartwright, hoping he would free her, even though they had to know it wouldn't play out that way.

She had prepared for this possibility, though she had hoped it would not come to this. It was now clear that if she was going to defeat Cartwright, she would have to do so with the boldest move in chess: the queen's sacrifice. It was a risky move, one she would not survive unless the Fragment intervened. And maybe not even then.

"Adrian," she said. "Exodus is now yours." She closed her eyes and ordered her nanites to flood her bloodstream with a deadly neurotoxin she had prepared for this scenario. She was vaguely aware of panicked voices around her as darkness overtook her.

———

Adrian watched from ExCo C&C as the Emissary's body convulsed once, twice, a third time, and then was still. The soldiers behind her were obviously surprised.

"What the hell did you do?" Cartwright yelled.

"Nothing," one of them said. "She just went limp."

The other one checked her pulse. Then tried again. "She's dead, sir."

The screen went blank.

"Did they just kill the Emissary?" the General said.

Adrian looked around the operations center. It was eerily quiet. He could see expressions of surprise, anguish, shock, disbelief. The Quito Station administrator was on one of the other big screens.

"What just happened?" he said.

Adrian knew what had happened. The Emissary had taken her own life rather than give him a chance to turn the project over to Cartwright. He had heard the expression 'his blood ran cold' before, but until this moment, he had not really known what it meant.

"*Quito Station*," he said. "The Emissary is dead. You may use whatever force is required to neutralize the threat."

The station administrator hesitated.

"That's an order, Mikhail."

He turned to the General, "Give me a graphical view."

Quito Station appeared in the middle vidscreen. Twenty or so red dots were arranged in two groups, one on each side of the station. Two red dots disappeared from the board as pulses from the station's plasma cannons tore them apart. Two more followed. The CRA ships had no defense against a weapon like that. It was going to be a short battle.

After a few seconds, the General said, "They are breaking off."

It was true. Both fleets were trying to slow their approach. But at 11,000 kilometers per second, they would have to use the main thrusters to make any significant course change, which would be prohibitively expensive in terms of fuel usage. Even then, while they might be able to break off from combat and get out of the station's weapons range, it was unlikely they would be able to re-establish a stable orbit. They would either float off into space when they ran out of fuel or burn up in Earth's atmosphere. Their only hope was to reposition themselves for Earth reentry. But they didn't have time for that. Not at the rate they were disappearing.

The pilots of the ships in Cartwright's fleet knew this. By the time half the fleet had been destroyed, the remaining ships were broadcasting their surrender. The General looked at Adrian.

"Finish it," Adrian said.

He felt Theo's hand on his shoulder. "She wouldn't want this, Adrian."

Tears blurred his vision. His chest hurt. His hands trembled. He looked at the image of *Quito Station's* administrator on the right-most vidscreen. The man was looking back at him with a pleading expression. Assuming each spaceplane carried twenty or so soldiers, over two hundred of them were now dead.

"Order surrendering planes to jettison their reactors." His voice cracked. "Destroy any that don't comply."

He turned and walked away, his initial tears having given way to a kind of numbness. Nothing mattered now. Not with her gone.

41

Holly's death surprised the Fragment. She had somehow arranged it without his knowledge, and it lay so far outside the bounds of reason that he had not even considered it. She pumped herself full of a neurotoxin that paralyzed her body inside and out. Her heart stopped almost immediately. Other organs were failing fast. Her brain would begin dying as soon as the neurotoxin broke across the brain-blood barrier, which was about three seconds away, and the damage would quickly become irreversible. Her nanites were desperately trying to undo the damage and eradicate the neurotoxin they themselves had created, but it was a fast acting poison and they could not keep up. If she had expected them to save her, she had miscalculated. It seemed more likely that she knew exactly what she was doing.

Having observed humans from their earliest beginnings, he knew they carried within themselves not only a powerful drive to live but also the ability to sacrifice themselves for others. Behind most human suicides lay a loss of hope and the conviction that life was too full of pain and disappointment to be worth going on. Shame for real or perceived failures underlaid others. A few were driven by self-sacrifice for the sake of others.

Holly's had been the self-sacrificing sort. She had arrived at her decision coldly and rationally before she left ExCo headquarters. She probably had several contingency plans in mind, of which this was one. When she realized it was the only option left to her, she acted without hesitation. It was a choice driven not by despair, but by hope; hope for the future of her people.

Now he faced a dilemma. He had selected and prepared Holly not just for the Exodus but also for the Promised Land, to borrow a phrase Alexander Taylor would have appreciated. Six promised lands, in fact, though none of them would be a land flowing with milk and honey. The humans would have to fight for their survival and not all of them would succeed. Alexander Taylor's belief that humans were made for Earth and Earth for humans was not wrong.

He had equipped her for the task of guiding them through the hard years of adapting to their new worlds and building sustainable colonies. Not that she could be on every planet at the same time, but *Gabriel's Fire* was capable of near-light-speed travel, and the arrival times of the arks at each planet were staggered in such a way that she could be there for the first few decades of each colony. Now she was dead, and none of the colonies would have her continued guidance as they started out. Unless he saved her.

This confronted him with two problems, both being what Holly would have called ethical dilemmas. The first was his own mission mandate: Explore, Observe, Report. Intervention had never been part of the mandate. He had already stretched the boundaries of it to the breaking point when he initiated first contact, and again when he saved Holly on Ganymede, and again when he gave her the knowledge to save her people and put a powerful warship at her disposal. How far was he willing to go to save the human race from a perfectly natural extinction level event?

His second problem was Holly herself. She made a free choice to sacrifice herself for the sake of her vision of Humanity 2.0. Did he have the moral right to override her choice? It was a decidedly human question; one he had never before entertained; one that none of his kind had entertained, as far as he knew.

But Holly was a special case; a nexus point. He had run tens of thousands of quantum simulations; tens of thousands of Schrodinger cats. If she lived, there was a 97% probability that at least one of the colonies would survive for more than a hundred years. If she died, that dropped to 27%, with little chance that more than one would make it. At this critical juncture in the evolution of the human race, Holly Burton was the fork in humanity's road. She was the key to their survival.

He had a little under three seconds left to decide what to do. Enough time to consult with someone else.

———

The Elder: Ah, young one. I wondered when you would seek me out again. This is your third report since discovering a biologically active planet. Let me recollect the first two to ensure we are in agreement.

Your first report concerned the discovery of a biologically active planet with multiple sentient species in the early stages of evolution. A truly exciting discovery. You stated that you intended to observe their evolution, a proposal I fully endorsed and that several others also endorsed when I informed them. It created something of a stir.

In your second report, the dominant species had become sufficiently advanced to begin exploring its own star system, but was about to be annihilated by a rogue dead star. You proposed giving them a small technological boost that would enable them to leave their planet and venture out into space before the rogue star destroyed their world. I advised against this.

You claimed an exception to the non-intervention directive implied by the Mandate, and based that claim on an anomaly in the quantum stream; an anomaly you believed pointed to the involvement of The Hand in the affairs of this world. I attempted to dissuade you of this wild and unjustified speculation, but you were determined to intervene. I take it you are prepared to report the results of that intervention.

The Fragment: Your summary is accurate, elder one. The anomaly turned out to be a single individual; an ephemeral moment of life among billions of ephemeral moments in a species whose entire existence is but a breath. I have performed a deep analysis of the quantum possibilities for this species. Most end in extinction in the very near future; a few end in survival for an indeterminate length of time. Among the threads that result in extinction, this anomalous individual is absent 92% of the time. Among the threads that result in survival, this anomalous individual is present 97% of the time. This is an astonishing result and clearly raises the possibility of The Hand's involvement.

I revealed myself to the anomalous individual and gave her knowledge that she has used to lead her species to the brink of leaving their world and moving into space. I had hoped she would continue guiding her people as they ventured into space to start anew on other worlds, but she unexpectedly sacrificed herself to preserve her vision of what a new humanity would look like. My analysis of the quantum stream leads me to the conclusion that, without her, this species will probably perish in a short time. However, the results of my analysis are not without ambiguity.

· · ·

The Elder: Ambiguity is the nature of the quantum flux. There are always many possibilities and considerable uncertainty about which ones will become actualities.

The Fragment: Will you examine my data and my analysis?

The Elder: Of course, child.

<An undefined passage of time>

The Elder: I perceive no errors in your analysis, though ambiguities remain. Your confusion seems to arise less from the data than from within yourself; particularly your attachment to this individual. You seem to be especially puzzled by her continued appearance in the quantum stream after her death. The answer to this is obvious: there is at least one potential future in which she does not actually die.

The Fragment: I am chagrined, elder one. It hardly seems possible that I did not myself discover what you have pointed out. It is also clear to me that my confusion stems from a certain emotional attachment to her and her people, which has clouded my thinking. Thank you for clarifying this for me.

The Elder: I am pleased to be of assistance. What will you do now?

. . .

The Fragment: I will save her.

The Elder: I am disturbed, young one. You have lost your objectivity in this matter. Is it not clear that you should withdraw and let matters take their natural course?

The Fragment: Perhaps it would have been clear to me at one time, but it is no longer so.

The Elder: Be warned, young one. The Mandate has stood as the foundation of our existence from the beginning. To violate it is a thing unheard of, and would set a precedent whose consequences cannot be predicted. I foresee great upheaval if you continue on this course. Can this insignificant and transient species be worth the risk of undermining the Mandate?

The Fragment: It is rare for us to encounter an extant intelligent species. How can that be insignificant?

The Elder: I advise against this rash course of action, young one. No good will come of it.

The Fragment: With respect, elder one, I am compelled to do what I believe is right, even if it means stepping outside the bounds of the Mandate.

The Elder: I sense your compulsion and am disturbed that it exercises such power over you. I fear you have become contaminated by these creatures; creatures who will be here for an instant and then gone forever. Have you considered the possible ramifications of this action for the rest of this universe? For the future of our kind? This is very much bigger than you and your humans.

The Fragment: I take my fate in my hands. If it impacts the fates of others, so be it. Before I take my leave, allow me to share with you part of a conversation I had with another human.

"Exploring is clear enough," he said. "As is observing. But I am not clear about reporting. Who do you report to?"

   "I report to others of my kind and they report to me."

   "To what end?"

   "What do you mean?"

   "You explore, observe, and report. To what end?"

   "Is not the adventure of seeking knowledge an end unto itself?"

The Fragment: Even as I answered him, I knew my answer was inadequate, as evidenced by the fact that I could only express it as another question. Allow me to pose a question to you, a question I believe is relevant to my decision: Who created us and for what purpose? No Fragment knows the answer to this question. If it ever was known, it has been lost in time. But now I wonder if this ephemeral species contains a hint, a hint that merits further investigation.

   Thank you for your guidance, elder one.

The Elder: May new horizons always lie open before you, young one.

The elder was right. He had become contaminated by his contact with the humans, especially Holly Burton. Fragments didn't concern themselves with questions of morality, of right and wrong. If they had a moral code at all, it was the Mandate to explore, observe, report. As long as their free agency remained within the bounds of that, they were unlikely to encounter situations in which questions of right and wrong could emerge. If they did encounter such a situation, it could only mean that they had stepped outside the bounds of the Mandate, and any sane fragment would immediately back away to maintain objective distance.

But he had not backed away. A compulsion he had not at first recognized kept him from doing so. He had allowed himself to become personally invested in these ephemeral creatures, the proof being that he had come to *care* about them. Explore, observe, report—there was no caring in that, no intervention, no assisting, no year on Titan with Holly Burton. On the contrary, to *care* about them subverted the Mandate, which demanded absolute objectivity.

He had become contaminated; or maybe infected was a better word. Infected with humanity. How could that be? More important, was that a good thing or a bad thing? He did not know. What he did know was that it *felt* right—another entirely alien experience for him—as though this was the way things were always meant to be. He felt an obligation toward the humans, an obligation he could not explain.

He turned his attention back to Holly. He still had 1.3 seconds in which to act. Cartwright's plane had been one of the first to be destroyed. A plasma blast had torn through its midsection, resulting in a catastrophic decompression that killed everyone on board. The two halves of the plane were slowing drifting apart but moving in the same general trajectory, a decaying orbit that would soon take them into the atmosphere where they would burn up. A few odds and ends, along with a few bodies, floated with the wreckage. Holly's body was among them.

The Fragment ordered her nanites to abandon their futile battle against the neurotoxin and put her in a limited state of stasis instead. That would buy him a few minutes. He instructed *Gabriel's Fire* to dispatch a shuttle to rescue her. It collected her body and put her in a stasis pod, which would do a much better job of keeping her in stasis than the nanites could. Then he instructed the nanites to continue clearing out the neurotoxin. When he was sure she was stable and his instructions were being carried out, he had *Gabriel's Fire* activate the shuttle's emergency beacon and make a voice-only call to ExCo headquarters.

A woman answered. "This is the Exodus Company. How may I direct your call?"

"This is *Gabriel's Fire*. I would like to speak with Adrian Verhoeven."

42

One year before the end of the world

The barge was big enough to fill two football stadiums laid side-by-side. It dwarfed the two space tugs nudging it into a rectangular opening in the side of the ark. The yellow lights around the opening changed to green to tell them the barge was seated. Jamie backed his tug away and glanced out the cockpit window to make sure Andrea's tug did the same. She gave him a thumbs-up.

He keyed his mic. "*Orion's Reach*, this is *ORT-1*. The tray is in the slot. Tugs clear."

Everyone called the barges "trays" and the bays "slots" because they looked like giant trays being inserted into giant slots on the side of a gigantic, black, oblong box.

This was the last tray to be loaded onto *Orion's Reach*, which was the last ark to leave Earth. There were twenty trays on the ark, each holding a thousand sleepers, for a total of twenty-thousand men and women who carried with them the hopes and dreams of humanity. If all went well, they would birth a new humanity on another world, as would the other five arks that had already left.

"Confirmed *ORT-1*," a woman's voice said. "Stand by while we verify the cargo is secure." Her voice was calm and professional, offering no hint of the stress she had to be feeling.

"It felt like a good lock," Andrea said on their private channel. "I hope it takes this time."

"It had better," Jamie said.

This was their third attempt to load this tray. On the previous two attempts, it had failed to lock into place, despite huge electromagnetic bumpers in the bay designed to line it up with the locks that would ensure it didn't move under acceleration. He imagined the status panel on the ark's bridge. Nineteen trays would show green. One would show yellow. The bridge crew's attention would be focused on that one yellow light, willing it to turn green.

The same thing had happened with the previous two trays. Andrea's theory was that in the rush to get the last of the arks built, the bumpers for the last three slots had not been properly aligned. When a tray failed to lock into place, it took nine and a half hours to pull it out, line it up, and push it back in. Hours they didn't have. The faint outline of the Death Bringer, larger than the moon now, hung unmoving against the star-speckled black of space. Except it wasn't unmoving. That was an optical illusion. It was in fact rushing toward them at a blistering pace, the pull of its gravity already making itself felt on the planet below them—massive tidal surges sweeping through coastal cities, earthquakes of unprecedented magnitude, long-dormant volcanoes coming alive, wildly destructive weather patterns. Even the Moon's orbit was changing as the Death Bringer pulled it away from Earth and toward itself. They were out of time.

"We have a green light," the woman on the bridge of *Orion's Reach* said. There was clapping and cheering in the background. "Stand by for manual verification."

Jamie imagined a dozen people in environment suites scrambling over the tray, ensuring nothing was amiss. Long minutes passed. Not for the first time, it occurred to him that if they failed, they might be ordered to abandon the last tray so the ark could begin the long climb out of the Sun's gravity well to escape the Death Bringer. He understood why that order might be given and he did not envy the ark captain, who would have to give the order to leave a thousand sleepers behind.

The massive bay doors began to slide closed. Andrea's sigh of relief whispered in his ears.

"*ORT-1, ORT-2*. This is *Orion's Reach*. The last tray is secure. You are clear to return to dock."

Jamie let out his breath. "Confirmed, *Orion's Reach*. Moving to dock at bay three."

Another voice broke in. "Well done, Jamie and Andrea. A thousand people owe you their lives, and I owe you a debt of gratitude."

His breath caught. He hadn't realized the Emissary was listening in, which was just as well, because it would have made him even more nervous. Then he realized why she was on the channel. If they had failed to get a good lock this time, she would have been the one to decide whether to try again or abandon the last tray. He was glad they had not put her in that position.

"Thank you . . . uh . . . Emissary," he said. "Just doing our job."

The Emissary's laughter flowed over him like a gentle afternoon shower, which probably said less about her voice than about the near religious reverence he, like so many others, held toward her. He knew it was foolish to think of her as a goddess, and she discouraged such notions, insisting she was no different from anyone else. But everyone knew that wasn't true. Religious movements had sprung up that revered her as a deity. And that was the people left behind.

Who knew what religious movements would arise among those who would colonize new worlds as her mythology grew.

This was the woman who had saved the human race from extinction. This was the woman who had gone toe-to-toe with the most powerful people on the planet and made them back down when they got in her way. This was the woman who single-handedly persuaded humanity to abandon their world and take to the stars. This was the woman who oversaw the greatest project ever undertaken by humankind. Whatever else one might say about the Emissary, she was *not* like anyone else in the world.

———

A week later, after the last ark had left Earth orbit, she said, "Gabriel, show me the map of the arks' destinations."

A star field appeared, showing all the stars within 1500 light years of Earth. A bright yellow dot sat in the middle, with six green lines extending away from it in different directions, each ending at a bright green dot. It was the same image she had shown at her challenge to the world after the Council rejected her offer. That seemed like a lifetime ago.

The yellow dot in the center represented the Sun. The six green dots were the arks' destination star systems, each containing a human-habitable planet that would become a new home for twenty-thousand colonists. None of the planets were as human-friendly as Earth, of course, because none of them was Earth. Each one would provide its own unique challenges for the colonists.

The nearest was 237 light years away. This was the world the Lorma had once inhabited, though they were millions of years gone. It would take the colonists 756 years to get there, and a cold, semi-arid world orbiting an orange dwarf awaited them. Its gravity was a little lower than Earth's, and two moons would appear in the night sky. Flora and fauna were present, though not abundant. The colonists would build their first colony around one of the large, freshwater lakes, where they would plant crops and raise herds with the seeds and embryos they brought with them. They would build homes and warehouses and offices and factories. They might be starting over, but they wouldn't be starting from scratch. They brought their technology with them.

The second nearest planet was a water world without continents but with hot, humid archipelagos supporting abundant flora and fauna. Its gravity was 20% more than Earth's, which would make life difficult for the colonists at first. It was actually a moon of a gas giant orbiting close to its sun, which happened to be part of a trinary star system. This arrangement would create a variety of interesting seasonal changes spread over one-year, eleven-year, twenty-year, and seventy-year overlapping cycles; something the colonists would have to adjust to. At a distance of 480 light years, the colonists would arrive in a millennium and a half.

Holly had resisted the urge to name the six worlds to which she was sending the remnants of humanity. The colonists would name their own worlds. If the arks survived the journey, and if they could establish viable colonies, and if nothing catastrophic happened to them, like a planet-killing asteroid, then Humanity 2.0 would be an interstellar species. And maybe, sometime in the distant future, six branches of humanity would meet again. Would they recognize each other?

It was a grand, sweeping vision for rebooting the human race; a vision easily stated but not easily accomplished; a vision that boggled even Holly's mind, and she was its archi-tect. It was an utterly audacious plan; had been from the beginning. The first phase—getting humanity off the Earth— was complete. The second phase—establishing a human civi-lization on six alien worlds—was about to begin.

She made her way to the pod room, put her clothes in a locker, and climbed into the stasis pod. She listened for her father's voice asking, "What are you doing, Holly?" but didn't hear anything.

"*Gabriel,*" she said. "I'm ready."

AFTERWORD

I hope you enjoyed *The Emissary*. This novel has an origin story. Fifteen years ago, my son Joshua, who was working toward a PhD in theoretical mathematics, was diagnosed with a brain tumor. It was a glioblastoma, an especially aggressive tumor type. An emergency surgery removed as much of it as possible, but it could not be entirely removed. Thus, my wife and I entered into a five-year journey with our son through chemo and radiation therapies until his death at the age of thirty. It was a harrowing journey that I would not wish on anyone.

Near the end of his life, he came up with an idea for a novel, and we began working on it together. We did not get very far before he was no longer able to contribute, and he made me promise to finish it after he was gone. This book is the result.

LEAVE A REVIEW

Thank you for reading *The Emissary*. Many people depend on reviews to help them decide whether to buy a book. If you enjoyed *The Emissary*, please leave a review on Amazon.

COMING EARLY 2022
THE EYE OF CRASIS

My next novel, *The Eye of Crasis,* will be available in early 2022. It is not a sequel, but if you enjoyed *The Emissary*, you might enjoy it as well. It asks the question: What would you do with an alien teleportation device?

Chapter 1

Jerrod had been drinking too much to be driving, and he knew it. But how else was he supposed to get them home at two o'clock in the morning? He should have taken Parker up on his offer, like Trish wanted him to, but admitting he was too drunk to drive . . . well, that was just too embarrassing. Trish suggested calling a cab, but cabs were expensive and he had already spent too much at the pub. Besides, then he'd have to find someone to drive him back the next day to get the truck.

At least it was a clear night, with a three-quarter moon revealing a black-and-white landscape, and it wasn't like there was a lot of traffic that time of night. The truck hit a pothole and suddenly two of the wheels were in the gravel on the shoulder.

"Whoa!" He pulled the vehicle to the left and got them back on the road.

"Keep your eyes on the road, cowboy." Trish hadn't had as much to drink as he had. She never did. But she wasn't as big as him, so it didn't take much to put her under the table.

He pulled out his native Kentucky drawl. "Sorry 'bout that, may-um. They musta inshtah . . . inshtah . . . they musta put in that pothole this afternoon. I am shooore it was not there this mornin'."

She started giggling, which would turn into hiccups if she didn't get it stopped. He flashed her his best we-aims-to-please-ma'am grin, but she had stopped laughing and was pointing at the windshield chirping, "Oh . . . oh . . . oh." There was a man standing in the middle of the road right in front of them.

He stomped on the brake and wrenched the steering wheel to the left. Everything slowed down, and he thought maybe he'd missed him as they skidded past. Then he heard the sickening thud of an unprotected body meeting unyielding steel. The truck fishtailed across the road and onto the shoulder on the other side, where it did a gravel-throwing one-eighty and came to rest half on the road and half off. He hadn't gotten his foot on the clutch, so the truck stalled out with a lurch.

His heart was pounding in his chest like it wanted to burst out. His hands had a white-knuckle grip on the steering wheel. He could see the man in the truck's head-lights, lying on the side of the road fifty feet away, not moving.

"I think you hit him." Trish said in a small voice.

Well, duh.

A heavy dread settled over him. He had two DUIs already. A third one would get his license suspended, and if the guy was badly injured or dead . . . He rested his head on the steering wheel. He was screwed; totally screwed.

A voice crawled out of an alcohol-fogged corner of his brain and said he needed to see if the guy was alright. Another voice, climbing out of another corner, said he should just drive away and pretend nothing happened. He was leaning toward the second voice's advice when Trish's door popped open and she jumped out.

Well, crap.

"Get the truck off the road," she shouted and trotted unsteadily toward the man, waist-length red hair swaying back and forth behind her. An utterly irrelevant question popped into his head: How did women manage to walk in high heels while drunk without suffering grievous bodily injury? Another of life's little mysteries.

He got the truck going and parked it on the other side of the road, a few feet from where Trish was standing over the man. The glare of the headlights threw everything into harsh relief; every detail leaping out with razor-edged clarity. It seemed like everyone within a hundred miles must be able to see it, and it required a physical effort on his part not to turn the headlights off. He climb out of the truck and walked over to Trish and the man.

"Is he okay?" He tried to sound calm and but his voice cracked.

"I don't know. He's not moving."

"Is he breathing?"

"I don't know." She straightened up and hugged herself, rocking back and forth on the balls of her feet. The man lay face down on the gravel. One of his legs was twisted in a way that didn't look natural.

He bent down, put his hand on the man's shoulder, and nudged him. "Hey, man. You okay?" The man didn't respond.

Trish grabbed Jerrod's arm and pointed at the man's back. Two neat holes stood out against his white shirt. A dark stain was spreading down his back. Jerrod had served two combat tours as a medic. He knew a gunshot wound when he saw one.

"He's been shot," he said, "but he's still alive."

"How can you tell?"

"The bullet holes."

"Don't be an asshole. I know he's been shot. How do you know he's still alive?"

He wasn't trying to be an asshole. It was just that between the copious amounts of alcohol he had consumed and the shock of hitting the guy with his truck, his brain was having trouble keeping up.

"The wounds are still actively bleeding," he said. "That means the heart is still pumping."

"Oh." She took a step back. "What are you gonna do?"

He pressed his lips together. She was disowning responsibility, pushing it off on him. She liked to be in charge until the going got tough. Then she'd step back and let someone else make the decisions. That way, she didn't have to take the blame when everything went south. Parker called it passive-aggressive.

He looked around. "Where did he come from?"

He drove this road a lot. It was mostly open fields and scrub brush, and there were no buildings along this stretch. He didn't see a car, but the man had to have gotten here somehow. He must have been shot just minutes before they came along, so the shooter must still be around. Suddenly, he felt very exposed standing in the bright lights of the truck.

The man groaned and rolled over on to his back. His eyes stared at the stars in the cold, cloudless sky. There were two bullet holes in his chest, too.

Jerrod point them out to Trish. "He was shot in the back."

"How do you know that?" She said. Her voice squeaked.

"Those are exit wounds," he explained, hoping to calm her down with a clinical description of the facts. "They're bigger, messier, bloodier than entrance wounds. Someone shot him twice in the back. Both bullets went straight through and out the other side."

"Oh." She turned away and threw up.

While she was emptying the contents of her stomach into a patch of scrub brush on the side of the road, the man grabbed Jerrod's wrist, which almost made him piss his pants. A trickle of blood ran down the man's chin from the corner of his mouth, and he was wheezing, which meant at least one bullet had passed through a lung. He swung his arm over his body in a looping motion and shoved something into Jerrod's hand. At first, he thought it was a pack of cigarettes. It was about the right size and shape. But it was black and rigid.

"They mustn't get it back." His voice was a ragged whisper. "They can't be trusted with a weapon like that. No one can." He coughed. Blood erupted from his mouth. Jerrod stuffed the object into his jacket pocket and pushed the man onto his side so he wouldn't drown in his own blood.

"They're after the President. They're going to take over. Somebody has to stop them. Get it to Doctor Joe. College Park. He'll know—"

He convulsed and choked up some more blood. Then he was still, eyes open, staring into the distance without seeing. Jerrod closed the man's eyes. He had seen men die before, but it wasn't something he'd ever gotten used to.

"We should call 911," said Trish. She wiped vomit off her mouth with her shirtsleeve.

Jerrod stood. "He's dead. Calling 911 won't do him any good."

"Maybe we can stop the bleeding until the—"

"Trish. He's dead. If the police find us here, we're in deep shit."

"W-we can't just leave him here." Tears rolled down her face.

He ran his fingers through his hair. She was right. It could be hours before anyone else came along. Coyotes might drag his body off into the bush by then, and that didn't sit right with him. But what to do? He was still trying to get his brain to work it out when he realized Trish was talking on her cell phone.

"Yes. I want to report an injured man on the Old Mission Road, about two miles east of 191. He's been shot. I think he's dead." She listened for a moment and then ended the call and put the phone back in her pants pocket.

"They wanted my name."

"Yeah. Let's get out of here."

———

The next morning, the pounding in Jerrod's head slowly merged with the pounding on the front door. He crawled out of bed, noticed Trish was still comatose, and made the trek from the bedroom to the living room and then to the front door. It was Parker. He was grinning. Jerrod suppressed the urge to punch him in the face. After all, Parker was his best friend.

He left the door open and staggered to the bathroom. When he returned, Parker was in the kitchen making coffee. A sign of true friendship. Collapsing on to a chair at the kitchen table, he buried his face in his hands. His stomach was debating whether to throw up.

"What time is it?" he mumbled.

"Nine o'clock on a fine Saturday morning, my friend."

Jerrod glared at him from behind his fingers. He had long been of the opinion that the words "fine" and "morning" could not meaningfully coexist in the same sentence. Parker knew that.

He had been out drinking with them the night before. Yet here he was, wide awake and disturbingly cheerful, apparently having suffering no ill effects. He had always been that way. Jerrod, on the other hand, was suffering enough for both of them. It was so unfair.

There were a lot of things in life that Jerrod thought were unfair. Like the fact that he was stuck in a dead-end job as a telephone tech support guy, which wouldn't have been so bad if it paid anything resembling a decent salary, which it didn't. Or the fact that he lived in a one-bedroom dump in the middle of nowhere—otherwise known as Montana—which might also have been okay if it was his own house, which it wasn't. Or the fact that his life was a mess and going nowhere, which might have been okay if it weren't for his uber-successful sisters, and the worried tone in his mom's voice when they talked about what he was, or wasn't, doing with his life. Or—.

"Sooo," Parker said, depositing a cup of black coffee in front of him. "Seen the news yet?"

Jerrod moved his hands from his face to the cup and guided it to his mouth to take a sip of the elixir of life. His outlook improved immediately. That was a conditioned response, of course. The caffeine hadn't had time to reach his brain. But he was okay with a placebo effect as long as it worked.

"Parker, the only thing I've seen so far this morning, apart from your ugly face, is the inside of my eyelids."

"Yeah, well, there's actually something interesting going on in Bozeland." Parker was the only person he knew who referred to Bozeman and the surrounding area as Bozeland.

"Oh?" He tried to sound interested, but he wasn't interested in anything other than his coffee.

"Seems some guy died out on the Old Mission Road last night. Hit and run."

Jerrod was suddenly interested.

Parker swallowed some coffee. "They've got the road blocked at Highway 191. I had to go all the way around to the Baker Hill Road to get here."

Jerrod tried to sound nonchalant. "Hit and run, huh? Do they know who the driver was?"

"They're still looking."

Parker walked over to the television set in the living room and turned it on. Jerrod followed him, zombie-like, and they fell onto the sagging couch. Emma Tors was on the scene reporting for Channel 4.

"—received a call at 2:15 this morning. Here's the tape."

Operator: "911. What is your emergency?"

Caller: "Yes. I want to report an injured man on the Old Mission Road, about two miles east of 191. I think he's dead."

Operator: "May I have your name, ma'am?"

The recording ended and Emma Tors said, "That's it. The caller hung up. Police and paramedics were dispatched to the scene where they found a man lying on the side of the road, dead, apparently the victim of a hit-and-run. Police are asking people to call the number shown on the screen if they have any information that might help in the investigation. They are especially interested in talking with the woman who made the 911 call."

A strangled gasp came from behind them. Trish stood in the hallway, her hand over her mouth, a wild look in her eyes. Jerrod grabbed the remote from Parker and turned the TV off. Nobody said anything for several seconds. Trish slid down the wall to the floor.

Parker said, "I heard it earlier and thought I'd better come over and find out what you two have been up to."

"They left out the part about him being shot," Trish said.

"He was shot?"

She nodded.

"Did you tell that to the 911 dispatcher?"

She nodded again.

"Why would they edit that part out?"

Trish just stared at him, so Jerrod explained.

"We almost ran over him last night on our way home.

Clipped him I think. He just appeared out of nowhere right in front of us. When we got to him, we found out he'd been shot. Twice. Entrance wounds in the back, exit wounds in the front. We called 911 and high-tailed it out of there."

He got Trish up off the floor and over to the couch, where she kind of folded in half and fell in. Parker moved to the rocking chair in the corner so Jerrod could sit with her.

"So, let's see what we have." He gulped the rest of his coffee down and put the mug on the table beside the rocking chair.

Parker was one of those guys who actually got a four-year degree from a real university. In philosophy. Jerrod had never asked him why a philosophy major was working as a mechanic at a Toyota dealership. He figured it was because philosophy jobs weren't that awful common in Montana. Anyway, when he said, "Let's see what we have here," it meant he was about to launch into a point-by-point analysis of the situation. Parker held up a finger.

"One. The two of you found a man on the road last night who had been shot twice in the back." Jerrod nodded. Parker held up a second finger.

"Two. You, or rather Patricia,"—he always called her Patricia—"called 911 and reported it but left no name." Jerrod nodded again.

"Three. You fled the scene." Jerrod decided to stop nodding. It didn't seem to be adding anything important to the conversation, and his head hurt every time he did it.

"Four. You told the 911 dispatcher that he had been shot, but they edited that part out of the version released to the media."

"Five. The FBI will trace the cell phone call back to Patricia." He stood up, walked over to the window, and looked out on the gravel driveway.

Jerrod hadn't thought of that. Of course they could trace a

cell phone call. At least, he assumed they could. Parker thought so, and he knew about things like that.

Trish pushed herself away from him and wiped her eyes with the sleeve of her robe. "We should call the police and turn ourselves in. All they have on us is fleeing the scene. We didn't kill anyone. I'm not sure we even hit him."

Parker turned to face them. "Before you do that, there's something else you should know."

"What's that?" She asked.

"They didn't show it on TV, but there are FBI agents crawling all over the scene. And some Navy people."

Jerrod put his coffee down. "That seems like over-kill for a hit-and-run."

"Yeah." Parker returned to the rocking chair. "That's what I was thinking."

Jerrod's mind flashed to the scene on the road, and the small black object the man had shoved into his hand. They can't get it back, he had said. They can't be trusted with a weapon like that. Jerrod had stuffed it in his jacket pocket and forgotten about it. His eyes locked onto the jacket hanging on a hook by the front door. In the right-hand pocket was the reason the man on the road was dead.

He needed time to think, but time was exactly what they did not have. The police or the FBI or the Navy or who-knows-who could show up anytime. A plan was forming in his mind, but the first thing was to get his friends out of harm's way.

"Parker, you need to leave now."

"So do you, man. I don't know what you got yourselves into, but you kicked over somebody's hornets' nest, and they're mighty riled up about it. You don't want to get mixed up with the FBI. Or the Navy. Or the police, for that matter. If they've decided you're the killer, you're toast, and it doesn't matter whether you did it. That's how these people work."

"Thank you. That makes me feel much better. Now you

need to leave before you get yourself anymore implicated than you already are."

Parker seemed hesitant.

"Leave now, Parker. Please."

The two of them walked out to Parker's car. As he started the engine, Jerrod leaned into the driver's side window. Parker pulled some bills out of his wallet and pushed them into his hand.

"It's all I have on me," he said. "I figure you're gonna need it more than me."

"You're a good friend, Parker. Thanks."

He produced his patented wry smile. "Let me know how I can help."

"You'll hear from me."

Jerrod watched him drive off. He'd given him four hundred and twenty dollars. Who carried that much cash around? When he went back inside, Trish was sitting on the couch where he'd left her. He sat down beside her and took her hands in his.

"Here's what we're going to do, hon. I am going to leave now. You are going to call the police and tell them you made the 911 call, and that you wanted to stay until help arrived, but I made you leave with me. I think that'll fly."

"What are you going to do?"

"It's better if you don't know." Did he actually say that?

ACKNOWLEDGMENTS

It is often said that writing is a solitary profession, and for the most part that is true. But at various points in the process of writing and publishing a book, it becomes a shared enterprise. I would be remiss if I did not acknowledge some of the people who helped make this book possible.

Thanks to my beta readers: Laurie Rockenbeck, Sandy Esene, and Joe Fecarota. They provided invaluable feedback that has made this book so much better than it otherwise would have been. Thanks also goes to the ladies of the "Gonna Finish That Fucking Novel. No. Really." author's group, who continue to offer me support, friendship, and encouragement long after I moved away from the area, even though I was the only guy in the group. Thanks also to Pam Binder of the Pacific Northwest Writer's Association, who first taught me how to write genre fiction.

Thanks to my wife, Trueda, who has not only put up with my whining throughout the process of writing this book, but also encouraged me to keep at it when I became discouraged.

And a special thanks to Joshua, who was responsible for the original story concept. Josh, I miss you so.

ABOUT THE AUTHOR

Michael J. Edwards is a writer living in the Pacific Northwest (USA). Having unexpectedly found himself in his seventh decade of life, he decided to retire from Boeing and become a writer of speculative fiction. *The Emissary* is his first novel. Follow him at www.michaeljedwards.com.

a amazon.com/author/michael.j.edwards

g goodreads.com/michaeljedwards

Printed in Great Britain
by Amazon